NATIONAL TREASURE

Peter Bleed

RKLOG Press
5878 S. Dry Creek Court
Littleton, CO 80121

Library of Congress Cataloging in Publication Data

Bleed, Peter
    National Treasure
    Fiction
        1. Fiction
        2. Japan – Fiction
        3. Anthropology – Fiction
        4. Japanese swords – Fiction

Library of Congress Catalog Card Number: 00-130486

ISBN: 0-9675798-1-3

RKLOG Press trade paperback printing, first edition.

Cover by Dika J. H. Eckersley

Printed in the U.S.A. by Eastwood Printing, Denver, Colorado

Other books in the
ANTIQUITY ALIVE Series
Published by RKLOG Press

Spirit Bird Journey, by Sarah Milledge Nelson
*A story of archaeology, adoption and
          Korea past and present*

Available from RKLOG Press
5878 S. Dry Creek Ct.
Littleton, CO 80121

Prologue | Ashiya Hidetaka
In which defeat creates a treasure.

Takasaka, Japan - 1340
Ashiya Hidetaka, loyal retainer of the Emperor Go-Tembo.
Bankyo, a rustic warrior and ex-priest who rode with Hidetaka for more than 12 years.
Yamada Dai, Fujii Sekitei, Kanda Tomokiji, Hidetaka's lieutenants.
Kujiro, Headman of Takasaka village.

Like boys rushing home from a victorious game, Hidetaka's band had spent the day hurrying along the wood-lined Sumitani valley. The group was noisy and boisterous and some of the younger soldiers had run and roughhoused until quite late in the afternoon. At the midday stop, Yoshiro, a pikeman on the right flank, had amused the entire party when he offered to share his rice ball with the severed head he had carried since morning on the blade of his *naginata*. The officers made no attempt to stop any of this because they knew the men were elated and relieved.

The day had started with a perfectly executed ambush of a forward element of the Natsushima army that had pursued Hidetaka and his men for the past twenty-three days. Only a tenth the size of Natsushima's force, Hidetaka's band had been able to stay well ahead of their pursuers and could have avoided even this morning's contact. The decision to hang back in ambush for the Natsushima vanguard had been a risk. It could have gone wrong, but it had not.

Hidetaka had selected a perfect spot and the country samurai from the Niida clan who formed the pursuing vanguard were still digesting their breakfast when the trap was sprung. The surprise had been complete and the attack flawless, so although the eighty-five Niida men should have been able to hold their own against Hidetaka's 106, they were all dead in thirty minutes.

The main Natsushima force would not find the bloody results of the fight until midday, but Hidetaka took no chances. As soon as the victory was complete, while his men were still full of spirit and disbelief, he hurried them on up the valley. Hidetaka stayed behind on the battlefield only long enough to leave a message scroll for Natsushima. On a piece of fine paper carried for just such an occasion, he wrote a Chinese epigram in his distinctive, well-trained script:

> **How are victories decided? Who charts our fate?**
> **Do the acts of men matter to the gods?**
> **Will the robins sing tomorrow?**

Ordering his aide to roll the message and hang it on the Niida standard, Hidetaka had mounted his horse and for a moment let himself believe his plan might be working.

"Do you think it's time to end this merry-making, Bankyo? Or should I let the men go on all night?"

"They're still full of pep, sir. I think they could go on with neither rest nor food," replied the big man.

"Indeed they could, but it's time," the leader said, looking around at the lay of the countryside. "The river sweeps across the valley just ahead and the road crosses to the other side. That village has the look of a place that can spare a few bowls of rice," he added, pointing to a small cluster of thatched buildings.

Gathering his officers, Hidetaka issued orders for the evening. Kanda Tomokiji was to lead the band across the bridge and prepare a bivouac. With ten men, Yamada Dai was assigned the task of burning the bridge as soon as the band was across. It was unlikely anyone was close behind them, but the river would form a barrier to pursuers Natsushima might have sent rushing up the valley. Young Fujii Sekitei was ordered to take three men mounted on the party's horses up the valley to reconnoiter the next day's route.

Finally, Hidetaka turned to the big man at his side, "Bankyo, convey my greetings to the headman of the village. Tell him he has the honor of hosting a band of patriots loyal to the Emperor Go-Tembo. Encourage him to demonstrate his patriotism by providing us with rice and pickles for our evening meal. Then bring him to me."

With that, Hidetaka addressed the group. "We will meet in council as soon as camp is set." The men departed to carry out their assigned tasks. Hidetaka stood alone for a moment before turning toward the river. Sitting on a large rock at the water's edge, his men saw him in quiet thought.

Kanda selected an outlying farmstead as the campsite. He assigned men to the necessary chores so when Hidetaka rejoined his officers, pickets had been set, a communal bath was prepared, and fires had been built to cook an evening meal. The leader also found Bankyo and a nervous peasant waiting for him.

"This is the village headman, Excellency," said Bankyo when his master arrived. "He claims to oversee a community well on its way to starvation, but after a short conversation and examination of my fine sword, he remembered a bit of grain and just a few vegetables in salt. These are hardly ample, but they'll make a meal."

"How very generous," Hidetaka smiled. "When our battle's won and His Majesty the Emperor Go-Tembo is reestablished in the capital, this generosity will be remembered." Turning to the headman, he asked, "What is this place?"

"Excellency, nothing in this entire district deserves any recognition," the peasant said kneeling, "but we call the collection of shacks you see 'Takasaka.'"

"What are you called?" continued Hidetaka.

Chuckling with discomfort, the peasant smiled. "Noble sir, I am Kujiro, son of Muhatsu." Hidetaka was amused by the peasant's rude dialect and the plain farmers' names he related.

"Tomorrow we will continue on our way," Hidetaka announced.

"Good," the peasant said with sincerity but no thought. Realizing the implication of his statement, he began to babble an explanation. Hidetaka simply laughed and silenced him by continuing. "Tell me about the route across the peaks of Tanigata by way of the Ohira Pass and on to the Plains of Takase."

"Excellency, we are rice farmers. We know nothing of other districts. The Ohira Pass is at the end of this valley, but I have never been there. I do not know the way." The peasant could say nothing else, but he feared his truthful answers would anger his questioner.

"How long does it take to cross the pass?" Hidetaka continued.

"Travelers have told me it takes two days, Excellency." The peasant was still kneeling. He no longer found Hidetaka terrifying, but he was eager to please and searched for something more to say. "In years past, traveling salesmen used this route, but we have not seen any of them for some time."

Hidetaka was silent as he thought about how the confusion and fighting of the recent years had reached even this isolated spot. If this simple rustic understood the suffering Hidetaka had seen, the wealth destroyed, the families ruined and the good men killed, he would not miss the visits of itinerant peddlers. Hidetaka looked down at the headman, "You may go, but stay close as I may have more questions." Relieved, the peasant crawled away from the armed men as quickly as he could and scampered off as soon as he was outside their circle.

Turning to his officers, Hidetaka continued. "Fujii will bring us better information when he returns from his trip up the valley, but we'll not wait for Natsushima. If we can move as fast tomorrow as we did today, we should cross over to the Takase Plain by the day after tomorrow. A few more days will see us to the domain of Noda Heihachi, who has stood with us since the beginning. A winter with Old Noda will have us ready to continue. I can already taste the sweet bean paste that's the Takase specialty."

The officers chuckled at this bit of levity because the future really did look clear and positive.

At just that moment a picket shouted, "Riders coming!" and a commotion arose on the far margin of the camp. The officers ran to get a clear view of the situation. They saw the men on picket duty run toward the road only to part again to let the riders pass. Fujii was in the lead, riding at full gallop. Two horses followed. One was riderless and, on the other, the rider was slumped in the saddle with an arrow in his side.

Fujii galloped to the center of camp and jumped to the ground, letting his horse run free. Seeing the officers, he ran toward Hidetaka in extreme agitation.

Kneeling in front of his commander, Fujii breathlessly made his report, "The way ahead is blocked by a huge force."

"Where are they?" asked Hidetaka.

"They were making camp as we came upon them about five miles ahead. We met only their forward pickets and did not see them arrayed, but their camp is a big one. I counted six brigade banners. It's a big force," Fujii added.

"What crests are on the banners?" demanded Hidetaka.

"Sire, I saw two crests. The center and left of the camp fly white banners with round wisteria crests," Fujii replied, slowly regaining his breath.

"It's Mitsunaga. He's come up from the coast, the rascal. I wouldn't have given him the credit for being able to move so fast. Natsushima must have sent a force to get him organized," said Hidetaka. He spoke crisply, but sounded relaxed and thoughtful. His manner set the others at ease. Continuing, he asked, "Are there Natsushima banners on the right?"

"There was a Natsushima standard, but I saw no banners," Fujii replied.

"Which banner flew on the right?" asked Hidetaka.

"The right flank and the pickets all carried the double diamond crest, sire," Fujii replied.

The group was stunned. Old Kanda, who had been through so much, reeled in disbelief. He reached out to steady himself on Yamada's arm. Hidetaka asked, "You're sure?" and Fujii replied, "Absolutely, Excellency."

"Noda's gone over," Hidetaka said quietly. Everyone had already drawn that conclusion from the information Fujii had presented, but the leader's steady tone and straightforward analysis made the disaster seem simple.

"We shouldn't be surprised. Its amazing that Noda could stay with us as long as he did. With Mitsunaga in the Takase, Natsushima must have been able to put unbearable pressure on him. Imagine how he must have agonized," the leader said.

A sergeant approached the officers. "Excellency, Gempei is dead. This is the arrow that killed him."

Fujii took the arrow and passed it to Hidetaka. All the officers saw that it bore the double diamond crest. Hidetaka turned to the sergeant, "Gempei was a good man. How did he die?"

"Well, sir, he needed no help and showed no agony," the sergeant replied.

Turning to the others, Hidetaka said, "Kanda, have the evening meal prepared and served. Yamada, get the pickets back at their posts. Bankyo, prepare my bed." Then to the entire group he said, "We will meet again after dinner to plan for tomorrow."

Hidetaka ate nothing but passed among the men as they had their dinner. He revealed nothing about his plans and said nothing about the next day, but his easy conversation and personal attention set them at ease. It was well past sunset when the officers met again.

"Tomorrow is the day we have awaited," Hidetaka began. "We can finally engage the full force of the cruel usurpers who drove our Emperor from his throne."

"Sire, we could live to fight another day were we to climb out of the valley," Yamada offered. "In the wooded hills, Natsushima could not find us."

"No, tomorrow is a day for fighting, not mountain climbing," Hidetaka said. The officers knew that climbing out of the valley would require abandoning their armor and their horses and, with Noda lost as an ally, there would be no haven. Clearly, the leader was making the right decision.

Still, Old Kanda explored another possibility. "Excellency, I long to meet the swamp slime Mitsunaga. I couldn't stand him even when he was a pimply-faced pup leading his daddy's minions at Uenodaira. Tomorrow I want a chance to do what I should have done twenty-five years ago."

The officers chuckled to hear this from the normally formal Kanda. He continued, "Excellency, it is important you carry on our cause. Let me lead the band tomorrow. You take Bankyo and a few others into the hills. If you get to the eastern districts you can rally our allies there and keep our cause alive." Yamada and Fujii voiced their agreement.

"As always, I appreciate your good advice Kanda, but we will spend tomorrow together. The justice of our cause will rally our allies and the purity of our action will destroy our enemies."

Having said that, Hidetaka laid out the strategy for the coming day. The band would wait for Mitsunaga's arrival at a narrow point just up the valley. The battle would take place there. Hidetaka honored Kanda's request to be allowed to make a direct challenge to Mitsunaga himself. When that was resolved, the band would engage the attacking force in three separate ranks. At the narrow point, a front of thirty men would be able to block the attacking force for some time. There would be no retreat. As one rank fell, the next would takes its place. Hidetaka would stay with the group until the third rank was engaged. Then he and Bankyo would return to the camp site to end his life. The strategy was clear and there were no questions.

"Very well. That leaves only a few details to attend to," Hidetaka said with finality. "Kanda, bed the men down and let them sleep this evening. We needn't worry about a night attack. Bankyo, go to the village and bring me both the headman and whoever it is that passes as the abbot of the village shrine. Yamada, I want to speak with the Pikeman Yoshiro. Send him to me."

As the others left, Hidetaka turned to Fujii. "What sword did Gempei carry?"

"His was a good blade by the swordsmith Yasunaga of Osafune in Bizen province," Fujii replied. "It's well-maintained and nearly a hundred years old."

"How big is it?" the leader continued.

"It's a full size tachi, two shaku and three sun at least. It always gave Gempei good service."

"Fine, have it brought to me. I'll carry it tomorrow."

Yoshiro was surprised to be called to the leader. He had never spoken to his master directly and had no idea why he was wanted. Hidetaka was kneeling on a small mat as he approached.

"Excellency, you sent for me," he said from some distance.

Hidetaka had been dozing, but he turned to his visitor with a smile. "Ah, Yoshiro, come closer and be seated."

Yoshiro did as he was ordered and Hidetaka continued. "Time and again you have entertained the band with your stories and your wit, Yoshiro."

"Master, I had no idea you had ever listened to my ramblings. My stories are no more than harmless time-fillers," the soldier replied.

"Oh, they're far more than that. Your stories inspire the men and keep alive the exploits of heroes."

Yoshiro was speechless.

"I want you to do the same for us tomorrow," said Hidetaka.

"Master, I will do whatever I can for our cause and for you."

"Our great battle will occur just up the valley. I will not let Natsushima write its history," Hidetaka said as Yoshiro listened. "Tomorrow morning as we join battle formation I will call you out.

In front of your fellows, I will order you to climb to the top of the hill opposite the battlefield. You must do as I order."

Yoshiro tried to protest, but Hidetaka would not let him.

"It is important that you survive the day. Leaving the band will take far more courage than staying, but you must remain alive to tell our story. Will you obey my order?"

Yoshiro was silent. Finally he spoke, "Master, I'm a pikeman. I killed twelve men in front of Kakuniyama and was wounded four times at Fukui. I would prefer to stay with the ranks."

"Your orders will be to observe the battle from the hills. If you will not obey, I will deal with your insubordination now," Hidetaka said harshly. "Will you do as you are told?"

"Yes, Excellency," Yoshiro replied.

"Very well. Return to your post," and Yoshiro was dismissed.

Hidetaka sat quietly until Bankyo arrived with the headman and the abbot. Hidetaka addressed them with a sharpness that Bankyo knew meant his master was growing tired.

"Headman, in coming this way we meant you no harm, but it appears that by making you famous, we will become a burden."

The headman began to say he did not understand, but Hidetaka ordered him to be silent and listen.

"Tomorrow morning, Bankyo will burn a couple of your barns and buildings." The headman gasped as Hidetaka continued. "You may select them and be sure that they are empty of all valuables. I suggest you select buildings that are easy to see since they will let you claim to have given us no voluntary aid. No one needs to know that you helped us in any way. I hope the burnings will protect your village from more grievous damage."

All of this happened so fast the headman was overwhelmed. Hidetaka did not wait for him to catch up. He turned to the abbot.

"You are the abbot of the local Shrine?" he asked.

"I am, noble sir," the abbot said.

"Whom does your shrine revere?" Hidetaka asked.

"Excellency, our shrine reveres the local *kami*, but we have an imperial charter and are dedicated to gods of the country," was the reply.

Hidetaka doubted the abbot understood the philosophical depth of his words, but they were exactly what he had hoped to hear. As an imperially chartered shrine, the local spiritual center was part of the national faith based on the divinity of the Emperor.

"Excellent," said Hidetaka crisply. "I am Ashiya Hidetaka, loyal retainer of the Emperor Go-Tembo who was dethroned by the forces of the Natsushima family. Bearing the burden of the *kami*, I have fought twelve years for the reestablishment of my liege Lord, the Emperor."

The abbot's eyes widened as he took all of this in.

Hidetaka continued, "In all my battles I have carried this blade." He placed his long sword on the mat at the abbot's feet. "It was made at the forge his Imperial Highness has established at Osone by the master swordsmith Munemasa. The Emperor himself took part in the forging. It has never been used for an unjust cause and has never failed me. Now I wish to dedicate it to your shrine." Hidetaka waited for a reply, but there was none. "Do you understand?"

"Noble sir, our treasury contains nothing like your sword, but I know how to receive gifts to the gods," the abbot said.

"Fine, see that it is preserved. Let no one know that you have accepted it for at least ten years. Do you understand?" The abbot assured the warrior that he did.

"My aide will bring the sword to the shrine as soon as I have written its history and a dedication." Hidetaka paused. "Are my orders clear?"

"They are, sir," replied the abbot.

1 | Eric Mallow

In which treasures are discovered but unclearly appreciated.

The Des Moines Gun Show - present day
Eric Mallow, dentist who collects fine firearms
Dawn Watanabe, Eric's girlfriend
Jim Sime, a gun dealer from Chicago, Illinois
Mrs. Viola James, a widow from Adel, Iowa
Lloyd Peterson, Mrs. James's next door neighbor

Eric Mallow leaned back from his patient's mouth and put his probe and inspection mirror on the instrument tray. "Well, Mrs. McReavey, everything looks fine. The X-rays show a weakening in the enamel on that back molar, but I don't think there's anything we need to do right now. We'll keep an eye on it. You're doing a fine job keeping your teeth clean. Keep up the good work and I'll see you again in six months."

"Thanks, doctor," Mrs. McReavey cooed and Eric gave her a reflex wink as he smiled his, "So long."

Dropping Mrs. McReavey's file on the receptionist's desk, he asked, "How we doin', Pam?"

"Just fine, doctor. Mr. Hamilton is already in X-ray and Cindy is starting to prep your 3:45," she replied.

"You two run this place so well you don't need me at all," grinned Eric. "I'm going to try to get a hold of Dawn before I start the 3:45. Well you dial her for me? I'll take it back at my desk."

By the time Eric got to his desk and picked up the phone, Dawn's number was ringing. "Thanks, Pam. I'm here now," he said and heard the receptionist click off just as the voice at the other end said, "This is Dawn Watanabe."

"Hi'ya," was Eric's opening line.

"You certainly sound chipper this afternoon."

"I am pretty chipper. How are you?" Eric continued buoyantly.

"Oh, I'm pretty glad its Friday," Dawn replied, trying to sound slightly less buoyant than Eric. "I don't suppose you're calling to say you don't need me to drive you out to the airport."

"Sorry, the trip's still on. Is there a problem?"

"No. I was just hoping that I could talk you out of going to the dumb gun show. Why don't you stay in town and we can go to a movie - or something?" Dawn let her voice trail off ever so slightly.

"I don't want to go to a movie," said Eric.

"Then we could 'or something,'" countered Dawn.

"Now, what would Grandmother Watanabe say if she heard you talking like that?" Eric asked playfully.

Dawn giggled softly and knew that Eric's mind was made up. "Oh, all right. What time shall I pick you up?"

"All my stuff's at the office and I'll be ready to go by a quarter to five. The flight's at 6:20 so we'll have to move right along," explained Eric. "Are we going to fit in the Miyata?" asked Dawn.

"No problem. I'm only taking small stuff. See'ya," said Eric as he hung up.

Eric finished the afternoon's appointments with forced attentiveness. He had been a dentist for nearly eight years so the technical work was largely automatic. Remaining conversational when he was distracted could be an effort and this afternoon he was distracted.

As a serious gun collector, Eric was looking forward to spending the coming weekend at the annual spring gun show in Des Moines, Iowa. It had been some time since Eric had been able to devote a whole weekend to his hobby, so even though the Des Moines show would be a relatively small gathering, he was looking forward with anticipation and hope he might find something to add to his collection.

When his 4:15 appointment asked Eric if he was looking forward to the weekend, he said he was, but he did not go into detail. Gun collecting is not an easy hobby to explain. Most people view guns as dangerous weapons and can't be convinced that they can be historically, technically, and aesthetically interesting. Friends who knew about Eric's collection assumed that it cost him a great deal of money. In fact, the collection more than paid for itself. Friends also found it remarkable that Eric was not a shooter. He did hunt occasionally and some years ago had become proficient with semi-automatic pistols, since they were one of his collecting interests, but he had given up regular target practice because it took a great deal of time and didn't really support his collecting interests.

The last patient of the day was finished up at 4:40, giving Eric just enough time to change clothes, check out with Pam and Cindy, and collect his things before Dawn arrived. All he would need for the weekend was contained in two aluminum Haliburton suitcases. After putting these in the backseat of Dawn's car, he tried to make himself an attentive suitor as they drove to the airport.

"How was your day?" Eric asked as Dawn pulled out of the parking lot. Dawn was an editor of children's books and she merrily told him of the problems she was having producing a book in which the central character was a bear who periodically removed his fur. "I mean honestly! What would I tell the illustrator?" she asked.

When she dropped Eric off at the gate, Dawn asked, "Okay, I'll pick you up at 7:30 Sunday, right?"

"That's it. I'll look forward to seeing you then. Maybe we can take in a movie," he paused, "or something."

"Guess again, Buster. You lost your chance," she replied playfully.

The Des Moines gun show is held twice a year in a large barn on the state fair grounds. With only four hundred tables, it is smaller than the major national gun shows, but draws dealers and collectors from across the Midwest. Furthermore, between the public opening at 9:00 a. m. Saturday and closing on Sunday afternoon, about four thousand locals pass through the show. Eric had always found that mix was sure to yield something interesting.

From the airport, Eric drove his rental car directly to the show. The general public is not admitted on Friday evening, but dealers who pay $45 each for their tables can arrive then to set up their displays and begin their dealing. This was the time Eric liked best.

The show manager -- a deputy sheriff who runs the event twice a year as a side job -- was sitting at the registration table inside the front door of the hall when Eric arrived.

"Hi, Herb. I don't think you've moved since I saw you last winter," said Eric putting his suitcases on the table.

"Ahh, bullshit. I've moved plenty since then. Running these goddamn things is wall-to-wall bullshit and I've just about had it," he replied. Regulars calculated that Herb made several thousand dollars at every show, but still, he complained about the hassles he endured.

"Mallow. Pistols. Two tables, right?" asked Herb, looking over his glasses.

"That's it," smiled Eric.

"Okay, I've moved you a little closer to the front this time," he said pointing to a floor plan of the table arrangement. "You're right here at the end of column two. That's damn good space and I won't change it so don't ask."

"Herb, be cool! That's a great location. Thanks a lot," Eric said as he started toward his tables.

Looking around, Eric saw only a few tables that were open for business so he decided to begin by setting up his own display. He had enough English flintlock pistols and artistically engraved guns to offer fine displays, but at this show his presentation would be on Mauser "broomhandle" pistols. Two weeks ago he had added a very special broomhandle to his collection and he was looking forward to showing it off.

First, Eric took a heavy green table cover from one of the suitcases and spread it on his tables, making sure it was smooth and that its embroidered legend, **"Mauser Self-Loading Pistols, 1896-1942"** was centered across the space. Eric then slid that suitcase away and opened the other, which contained the five pistols he had selected for the display. Each gun had a machined plastic stand to hold it upright and a laminated label describing it.

Eric favored Mauser pistols because they were among the first successful semi-automatic small arms. He liked the variations and interesting associations the pistols had acquired in their forty-five years of production, from before the turn of the century until the early years of World War II. Four of the guns Eric had selected for this display were excellent examples of rare variations of the Mauser design: a pistol and shoulder stock made in 1896--the first year of production, a Chinese copy of a Mauser made to shoot .45 caliber ammunition, a German military pistol that had been captured and reissued by the Bolshevik forces during the Russian Civil War, and, finally, a gun that had been made for the Turkish army before

World War I. These guns were primarily there to highlight Eric prized possession which he placed at the center of the display.

Its label indicated it was an early, officer's model Mauser and translated the German inscription engraved on the left side of the frame: **HOLD ME WITH HONOR! Kaiser Wilhelm II shot five rounds from me at the Spandau Arsenal, April 12, 1897. Hail the Power of Greater Germany!** In setting this gun out, Eric made sure the silver medallion on the fine silver cable that sealed the gun's action was clearly visible.

"What's that you got there, Ric?"

Eric turned to see Jim Sime, a high end gun dealer from Springfield, Illinois, standing at his side. "Its a broomhandle Mauser I picked up two weeks ago," Eric said.

Jim leaned toward the cased pistol and examined it closely. After a moment he said, "Holy shit! Where'd you find that?"

"Isn't it nice?" smiled Eric.

"Nice? It's fabulous." Turning toward Eric, Jim asked, "Is it real?"

"Absolutely!" Eric said confidently.

"I suppose you got it from the vet or something?"

"Damn near. I got it from the estate of the widow of a collector. He bought it in the '30s from Ted Dexter who'd offered it in one of his catalogs. I got a copy of the catalog and notarized correspondence from the US colonel who brought it back to the States in 1920. He was the American representative on the German disarmament commission and took it out of the Spandau Works. It's a hundred percent," Eric said.

"Wow. Amazing," Jim said, shaking his head. "It looks like that wire seals the action."

"Exactly," Eric said. "After Willie fired five rounds from the gun, the arsenal sealed the action with that silver cable. Nobody has shot it since. It's the six shot model, and the inscription says the Kaiser only fired five, so there must be one more round still in chamber. It's still loaded with the Kaiser's bullet! If you pulled the hammer back, it would be ready to go." Eric was obviously pleased to be able to describe the gun to someone who appreciated its rarity.

"Amazing," Jim said again. "What'd you have to give for it?"

"It wasn't cheap," said Eric with a coy smile.

"Well, then, let me ask you the other obvious question," said Jim. "What do you figure its worth?"

"I'm not planning to sell it so I haven't really thought about it," said Eric. "What do you think?"

"That's a tough one," Jim said shaking his head. "By itself, the gun is worth probably ten, maybe twelve grand, but the link to the Kaiser is very sexy. I'm sure there's a bunch of Krauts in Germany who'd really go for that Kaiser's bullet stuff." He paused in thought before saying, "I'd expect to get between 60 and 70 K for the gun."

"That last bullet is a temptation, though," Eric said. "Wouldn't it be neat to find out if it's still good after better nearly a hundred years?"

"Eric, whoever breaks that seal to find out if that bullet is still good better expect to take about ninety percent off the value of the piece. If it was mine, I'd let the next owner snap that cap."

Before continuing on his way, Jim asked, "What'd you bring to sell?" to which Eric replied, "Oh, nothing important."

"Well, bring whatever you got over to my table," Jim said. "I'm over against the front wall," he added pointing. Before going on his way he took one of Eric business cards and added, "I'm serious about the Kaiser's pistol, Ric. If you ever want to sell it, let me know."

Eric checked his display one more time. It met with his approval. He took satisfaction in knowing that any Mauser collector would be glad to own any of the guns he was presenting and that very few other collectors could offer a display of comparable rarity and worth. The fact that only a handful of people at the show would fully appreciate the display did not bother him, although it did remind him to get his "Do Not Touch" signs out of his domestic suitcase.

By the time his display was out, several other dealers had arrived and begun setting out their merchandise. Eric started out toward the section of the show he guessed Jim Sime had not yet visited. Several dealers were setting out either new guns or low quality shooters' supplies. There were also a depressing number of dealers selling camouflage clothing and survival gear. Seeing this, Eric wondered if it had been wise to bring top quality items to a blue collar show like Des Moines.

Stopping at a table being arranged by a fellow in a flannel shirt and jeans, Eric asked permission to look at a pistol holster. "Sure, go ahead," was his automatic response.

As he turned the holster over Eric asked, "What do you have on it?" to which the man replied with a shrug, "Seventy-five bucks."

Looking inside the flap, Eric said, "It's kind of neat. Do you suppose it's a military holster?"

"I really don't know nothin' about it," the man said with another shrug.

Holding the holster so the man could see, Eric rubbed his fingers across the light scuffs in its surface and asked, "You got the gun for it?"

"Nope," apologized the man. "I got it with a bunch of shit from an old guy over in Cedar Rapids. He didn't know nothin' about it and said he never had a gun to fit it."

"Boy, ain't that the way it always is?" Eric said as he put the holster back down on the table. "Can you do any better on it?"

The man shrugged his shoulders yet again and said, "Oh, I'd take a half for it."

Eric picked it up again, looked it over and said, "Yeah, what the heck. That's fair." He gave the man a crisp $50 bill and continued on through the show.

As he walked on, Eric had to suspect he could have paid less for the holster. The seller had certainly paid no more than a few dollars of it, but he hadn't done his homework. Eric was sure he could sell it for a profit. At other tables Eric looked at some Russian medals, an Indian basket, and a nicely engraved Smith and Wesson pocket pistol, but he bought nothing else until he found Jim's table. He was pleased to see that Jim had brought a nice assemblage of collectors' pistols. Eric was looking these over when Jim approached him and, pointing at the holster, asked, "What'd you bring me?"

"It's a Weimar period Luger holster," Eric said as he picked up one of Jim's best Lugers sliding it carefully in. Showing Jim that the fit was perfect, Eric said, "These are police acceptance codes, aren't they?"

Jim looked at the small marks. "Yeah, I think you're right. It sure ain't a World War I army holster and without Nazi stamps, I suppose it must be Weimar. Of course, it could be Norwegian or something."

"And that would be even better," countered Eric.

"What do you want for it, Ric?" Jim asked.

"It will look real nice with that Weimar reworked Luger you got, there, but I'm easy Jim. It's yours for a bill."

"I could use it. How about 60 bucks?" countered Jim.

"No. A bill's fair," said Eric without emotion.

"Okay," Jim said, getting a hundred dollar bill out of his nylon hip pack. In doing so, he was discrete, but didn't mind letting Eric see he was carrying a large wad of cash.

Taking the money, Eric asked, "Did you bring any broomhandles?"

"I got a couple of guns that came in from China last year," said Jim pointing to two pistols near the end of his three tables. "That one is a Chinese copy, but the condition leaves something to be desired."

Eric walked down to look at them. Mauser pistols had been popular with Chinese Warlord troops of the 1920s and 30s. They used both World War I surplus arms and copies made in their own arsenals. In recent years, thousands of these guns have been imported to the United States even though their long history of intensive use has left most of them in very rough condition. The Chinese copy Eric looked at had been crudely crafted by a machinist working with only rudimentary tools. It was heavily worn, but it was an interesting variation.

"I see what you mean," Eric said, putting the gun down. Returning to where Jim was standing he noticed that in addition to his pistols, Jim had a rack holding a couple of Japanese swords along a sign saying, "I Buy Japanese Swords, Matchlocks and Armor."

"When did you get interested in Japanese stuff, Jim?" asked Eric.

"I'm not interested in it. I just got a Jap customer who's a good buyer. He takes everything I get and pays damn good money. I don't find that much, but he taught me what to look for and pays enough to keep me looking," Jim said offhandedly. "You got any Jap stuff for sale?"

"Relax, Jim. I was just making conversation."

"The stuff is a little soft right now because of their economy, but basically those Jap dealers pay real good money for stuff they want," continued Jim.

"Yeah, good Japanese stuff is neat," Eric said conversationally, "but it always seems too complex to me."

"I suppose it is," Jim said straightening up some of his merchandise. "It helps if you can read all that chicken scratching-- which I can't do. But basically, it's pretty easy to pick out the good stuff. And, like I said, my Jap buyer pays real good."

"Well, good luck, Jim. I hope a fully armed samurai walks in for you." Eric smiled as he started away from the table. "I'm going to check out the rest of the show. Maybe we'll talk about your Chinese Mauser later on."

"Hey, I'll work with you, Ric. We can use it as part trade on your Kaiser's gun," Jim laughed.

The next morning, after a quick shower and breakfast at a MacDonald's, Eric got to the gun show by 7:30. Dealers who hadn't set up the night before would be arriving and Eric wanted to look over their merchandise before the general public got into the show at 9:00. At 8:30, as he was having his third cup of coffee, Eric made his first purchase of the day, a Nambu pistol with holster. Nambus were the standard Japanese army officer's sidearm during World War II. They were not one of Eric's interests, but he bought it because it was an early example in very good condition and cheap at $275.

Once the show opened to the public, Eric returned to his display to wait for interesting items to come by his table. Virtually everyone who passed Eric's table stopped to look at his pistols. Some examined them carefully and even took time to read the labels; about a dozen seemed to appreciate the rarity of the Kaiser's pistol. Three of the people who passed by before noon mentioned they had Mauser pistols. Eric asked them about the guns and encouraged them to bring them in for identification.

Later that afternoon, Eric was passing time by cleaning the Nambu pistol he had bought earlier, when he looked up to find a thin blond man looking intently at his display. Seeing Eric look up, the young man said, "These are really nice."

"Thank you," Eric said. The man appeared ready to talk but said nothing, so Eric continued. "It's nice to have people appreciate them. Do you collect Mausers?

"Ah, no," said the young man shaking his head. "I got a couple of working guns, shotguns and stuff, but I can't afford anything like this." As if searching for something more to say, he pointed at the Chinese Mauser in the display and said, "Was this one here actually made in China?"

Eric explained what it was and described the different kinds of Chinese Mausers. The young man listened intently. When Eric was finished, the man pointed to the Nambu pistol Eric had been cleaning. "You interested in Japanese guns, too?"

"They aren't one of my main interests, but I pick them up when I can," Eric said. "What do you know about Japanese guns?"

"Not very much, but the lady who lives next door to us has got a couple and I helped her clean them once," he replied.

"What kind are they?" Eric asked trying to sound nonchalant.

"I think she's got two just like that one and then there's a littler one and maybe some other stuff," the young man said. Eric held the Nambu out to him and he took it. The way he handled the gun convinced Eric that he didn't know much about the pistols.

"Where'd she get them?" Eric asked.

"Her husband brought them back after the war, but he died a couple of years ago."

"Would she be interested in selling them?"

"I suppose, but I never really asked her about it," the young man said uncertainly. "Her husband's dead and her boy was killed in Vietnam."

"Come back here and sit down," Eric said, extending his hand to the young man. "My name's Eric Mallow."

"Lloyd Peterson," said the young man and they shook hands.

With a little encouragement, Lloyd explained that he was from Adel, Iowa, a town about forty miles west of Des Moines, that he worked at a farm implement dealership, had a wife and two children, and had lived next to Mrs. James for the past four years.

"Lloyd, I'm a serious collector," Eric said, "and I pay top prices for quality pistols."

"Oh, those guns of Mrs. James' are real nice."

"I'd love to take a look at them," Eric said. "I won't take advantage of the woman," he continued. "I'll try to treat her fair and I pay a ten percent finder's fee. You'll get ten percent of whatever I pay for the guns."

"Gee, that'd be great." Lloyd's eyes lit up.

"Tell you what," Eric said, getting a couple of dollar bills out of his wallet, "why don't you get some quarters at the registration table and give Mrs. James a call? Tell her I'm here at the show and that I'd like to see her guns. If it's all right, see if we can drop by at, oh, say 8:00 tonight."

Lloyd agreed and returned in a short while. He had gotten hold of Mrs. James and she would be waiting for them at 8:00. "Ten percent, right?" he asked and Eric nodded.

Mrs. James welcomed Eric and Lloyd to the front room of her home. It was neatly furnished with 1950s furniture, but the shades were drawn and it was musty and close. Mrs. James was a heavy woman with blue-white hair. She lived alone, but Eric noticed two photographs on her mantel: one of a smiling WWII GI, the other one of the mass produced photos taken at the end of basic training, showing a solemn young soldier. Attached to it were medals Eric recognized as a Southeast Asia Service Medal and a Purple Heart.

When Lloyd saw the large cardboard box waiting on the coffee table he sat down on the couch, eager to see whatever it contained. Eric, however, began the evening by giving Mrs. James one of his cards. Taking it, she said, "Oh, you're a dentist."

"Yes ma'am, but on this trip I'm a gun collector," smiled Eric.

"Well, these are some guns my husband brought back after World War II," Mrs. James said pointing toward the box. "He had some other things when we got married, but he sold some of the swords to buy our first car. I don't know what's left, but they've always made me nervous."

Lloyd began to open the box, but Eric stopped him by asking Mrs. James a question. "Your husband was in the Army?"

"Yes, Lee went in 1942 and didn't get out until 1946," she said.

"He was in Japan?"

"That's right. He started in Cedar Falls, then they sent him several other places before going to the Philippines while they were still fighting. After the war was over, he was sent right to Japan."

Mrs. James was clearly proud as she related this history, but rather vague. "We didn't meet each other until after he got back, so I'm not too sure where all he was."

With that, she seemed ready to look in the box and Eric let the conversation lapse as she opened it. He was pleased to discover that it contained five Japanese pistols in holsters: a Type 10 Flare Gun, a Type 26 revolver, and a Nambu like the one he had bought at the show that morning. The best of the guns was a "Baby Nambu," an elegant 7mm semi-automatic pistol carried by high ranking Japanese officers. The two character inscription on the top of the frame meant it had been given to a one of the top graduates of the Imperial Army War College.

Eric looked closely at each gun and explained what he could about their history to Lloyd and Mrs. James. She listened politely but without great interest. At one point she added, "Lee was always real careful with this stuff. He would never let Ronny play with any of it."

After all the guns were out, Eric looked through the rest of the box to find a few American uniform pins and some post-war Japanese trinkets. As he was looking through the box, Mrs. James got up and took a long Japanese sword from behind one of the side chairs. Holding it gingerly, she brought it to the coffee table.

"He had this, too," she said grimacing. "Ronny really wanted to play with it, but it scared me so much that we always kept it in the attic."

Eric pulled the sword from the scabbard. The outside fittings were dusty, but the blade was flawless and had a bright polish. Over the years, Eric had also seen enough Japanese swords at gun shows to know this was not a wartime military sword. It was of good quality, but he was entirely sincere when he said, "Mrs. James, I really don't know very much about Japanese swords. Some of them are very valuable, but I've never studied them."

"Well, I don't know anything about it. Only that it I don't like it. Maybe Lee pulled it out of a body or something," she added with a shiver.

"These pistols are very nice, and I'd like to buy them, but I can't say much about the sword. I really don't want to cheat you," Eric said.

"Well, I don't want to keep it, so you just make me an offer for the whole works," she said firmly.

Eric arranged the pistols in a straight line on the coffee table and scratched the back of his head in concentration. "I can give you $300 apiece for these four guns. I think the little gun is worth eleven hundred," he said. "I really don't know what to say about the sword, though."

"Well, Lloyd said you'd treat me fair. So you just go ahead and tell what you'll pay." She leaned back in her chair and looked at him intently.

"I'll give you $3300 for the four guns and the sword," Eric said. "That figures the sword in at $1000, which I think is fair."

Turning to the young man, Mrs. James asked, "Lloyd, what do you think?"

"Those are the kinds of prices that I saw at the gun show, Viola," Lloyd said earnestly.

"Well, if you think that's fair, you can have them at that price."

Eric counted out $3300 in $100 bills. Mrs. James seemed intimidated by the stack of large bills and handled it carefully. "Well, I suppose the bank will be able to take these, won't they?" she said uncertainly.

Eric assured her that the bank would have no problem with the cash. He began to assemble his purchases in preparation for leaving when Mrs. James said, "Lee had another box of things. Would you like to see that?"

Eric sat back down and said, "Why sure, Mrs. James. I'd like to see whatever you have."

Mrs. James left the room and returned a few minutes later with another cardboard box. "I'm not sure what's in here. It was Lee's personal stuff." Her eyes misted over and she waited a moment before saying, "To tell the truth, it makes me feel kind of bad." Exhaling deeply after another pause, she continued. "After Ronny died in Vietnam, Lee never got any of this out and now there's no one who cares about it."

As if to change the subject, she turned to the box and began to examine its contents. There were more American military devices and a thick-covered photo album. As she looked through the album she said, "These are pictures of Lee in Japan." After looking at a couple of pages, she said, "I think he liked it over there."

Eric could see that most of the photos were snapshot of GI's, but there were also scenery pictures and some postcards pasted in. Several pictures had captions written below them. "Those are interesting," he said politely.

Back in the box, Mrs. James found a paper scroll of dancing geisha girls and another of Mt. Fuji with the inscription "Japan 1946." Finally, she found a finely made plain wooden box with writing on the lid. She gave this to Eric, saying, "I think this is a knife."

Eric opened the box to find that it contained a dagger in a plain wood mounting. Carefully opening it he found a simple brightly polished steel blade. When he put it back into the box, he noticed there was space for another dagger, but that it was empty.

"Mrs. James, I think this could be a very good piece. Some of these Japanese daggers are worth thousands of dollars."

"Oh, I think its just something Lee picked up," she said dismissively. "I've never felt good about it and I'd rather you take it, too," she said.

"I'm sorry Mrs. James, but I wouldn't know what to offer you. I just don't have any idea of what's a fair price."

"Well, this old stuff is doing me no good at all. You just tell me what you'll give for it." Mrs. James was using a firm tone but her voice had a desperate edge.

"Mrs. James, I just can't do that. I don't want to cheat you or myself. And to tell the truth, I don't have a very much more cash with me," Eric said.

This seemed to make sense to Mrs. James, but she looked both disappointed and unsettled, so Eric continued. "I'll tell you what we can do. I'll take the dagger for you and show it to some people I know who are interested in them. After I find out what it's worth, and after we both know what you've got, I'll try to sell it for you. Would that be all right?"

"I don't care. If you want to do that, it's fine with me. I'm just ready to get rid of it," she said with finality.

Eric wanted to be very sure that everyone knew where things stood so he said, "These pistols and this sword are mine. Right? I've already paid for them?"

"Yes, that's right," said Mrs. James holding up the stack of bills.

"And I'm going to take this dagger and try to find out what it's worth, but it is still yours. Right?" asked Eric.

"You just go ahead and take the whole box. Sell it all for me," Mrs. James said putting the albums and other things back in the box and pushing it toward him.

Eric took the time to write receipts for both the things he had bought and for the dagger and other things in the box. He signed one for Mrs. James and had her sign one for him. Then he had Lloyd sign both as a witness.

"Mrs. James, we've stayed a long time. Are you feeling all right?" Eric was genuinely concerned that the evening had been too much for her.

"Yes, I feel fine," she said looking around the room. "I'm just glad to get these old things out of here," she added.

Eric wanted to get back to his motel to look over his newly acquired guns so he declined Lloyd's invitation to have a cup of coffee. Instead, he took three $100 bills and three tens from his wallet.

"Here's your finder's fee."

Lloyd took the money and said, "Gee, thanks."

"I hope you're satisfied, because I'm real pleased with the pistols."

"Oh, yeah. This is great," Lloyd said. "I think you treated Mrs. James real well, too."

"Yeah. I think I did," Eric agreed. "Now you understand, that's just for the stuff I bought tonight." Eric gave Lloyd two of his cards. "I don't know what I'll do with the dagger, but put your address and phone number on the back of one of those. When I find out something about the stuff in the box, I'll give you a call. Okay?"

"Hey, that'll be great," Lloyd said, taking the cards.

Sunday mornings are always relaxed at gun shows because no one expects anything new to appear. The sword Eric had bought the night before did not fit into either of his suitcases, so he left it in the trunk of his car when he got to the show. The pistols fit in the box with the photo albums and he brought them in so he could finish cleaning them and have them available for conversation or trade. He was behind his table when Jim Sime walked over to see him.

"You got something new in that box, Ric?" asked Jim.

"I bought a couple of Japanese pistols last night," Eric said looking up.

"Show me what you got," Jim asked eagerly. Eric was happy to oblige. Jim swooned over each of the guns as Eric took them from the box. Discussion of the guns moved in the direction of values and then prices and within an hour a deal had been struck. Jim owned the five guns Eric had gotten from Mrs. James as well as the Nambu he had purchased earlier. Eric had Jim's Chinese broomhandle Mauser and $3700. Both were satisfied.

After the dealing was finished, Jim turned back to the box that had held the pistols and asked, "What else did you get?"

"There's some other stuff, but I haven't closed the deal on it," Eric explained as Jim picked up the photo album.

"This is kind of neat," Jim said thumbing through an album, "but unless they've got either good pictures of stuff like airplanes or really gory battlefield scenes, albums don't sell worth a shit."

Jim put the album aside and continued pawing through the box until he found the wooden box containing the dagger blade. "Was this part of the deal?" he asked as he began to open the box.

"No, that doesn't belong to me," Eric said trying to slow Jim's curiosity. It did no good. Jim got the dagger out and examined it closely.

"Ric, I like this a lot. What do you want for it?"

"I told you, Jim, it isn't mine," Eric said. "I'm suppose to find out about it and get back to the owner."

"What's to find out? It's a flashy Jap dagger. If the blade is less that a foot long it's called a *tanto*. This one looks real good. Is it signed?"

"You mean on the tang?" Eric asked. "I haven't had the handle off."

"Well, let's check," Jim said taking a small brass hammer from his pocket. He showed Eric a bamboo peg in the plain wood handle and used the hammer to tap it out. Then Jim held the dagger in his left hand and rapped his wrist several times with his clinched right fist. Nothing happened.

"The handle's real tight, but don't worry. They're made to come off," Jim explained. Eric had seen many other collectors go through this process so he let Jim proceed.

When repeated banging on his wrist did not loosen the blade, Jim tried another approach. He carefully tapped the blade end of the handle against the side of Eric's table. After a few taps, the blade began to give way and eventual slid entirely out of the handle. Jim looked closely at the blade tang and said, "Yeah, it's signed."

"What does it say?" Eric asked looking over Jim's shoulder.

"I don't know," Jim admitted, "but it looks pretty old."

"What do you mean?" asked Eric trying to get a sense of Jim's expertise.

"They been making these things for like a thousand years," Jim explained, trying to sound knowledgeable. "They always kept the blades polished, but the tang is left alone so it gets rusty. This one has old, black rust, which means it's at least a couple of hundred years old."

Eric took the dagger and looked at the inscription on the tang. In doing so, he touched the blade.

"Don't touch the blade, Ric. Condition is real important and if you let those fingerprints rust in, you'll ruin the polish."

Jim took the blade back and wiped it with the corner of the table cover. "Ric, I like this. I can make us both some money with it. What do you have to have for it?"

"Jim, I'm not kidding. It doesn't belong to me." Eric said earnestly. "I'm supposed to find out about it for the owner."

"What's to find out? Its a Jap dagger and I'll give you $800 for it," Jim countered.

"No, I can't let it go, for a while," Eric said trying to cool Jim's desire. "There's no hurry."

"What the hell? I'm here now. I'll make it an even thousand," Jim said.

"Jim, relax. The dagger is not going to sell today so just chill out. Okay?" Eric said firmly. He had considered telling Jim about the sword still in the car, but decided against it. He had not been impressed with the knowledge Jim was demonstrating and certainly didn't like Jim's greedy aggressiveness.

"Okay, but let me make a rubbing of the signature so I can do some research," Jim said. After getting a roll of pressure sensitive paper from his own table, Jim placed a piece of paper over the inscription on the blade tang. He rubbed the surface of the paper with the back of his comb, producing a clear copy of the Japanese characters cut into the steel. He measured the length of the blade and made a few notes on the rubbing.

As he was reassembling the dagger for Eric, Jim said, "Now, Ric, I'll get back to you about this, but promise me that you'll let me have firsts on this thing. Okay?"

"No deal. I can't promise anything because it isn't mine," Eric said with some exasperation. "Let's just leave the deal as simple as possible."

Jim seemed to understand that Eric had made his mind up so he backed off. "That's cool, Ric. Just let me have a chance. Okay?"

"Whatever, Jim," Eric said trying to end the discussion. "I'm already wishing that I'd just left the damn thing where I found it."

As the show was winding down Sunday afternoon, and Eric was considering how he was going to get the sword and photo albums home, Terry Carlson, came by his table.

"How was the show for you. Ric?" asked Terry.

"Real good, Terry. How'd you do?

"Not so bad. I got a nice Remington Zouve musket," Terry beamed.

"Are you driving back to Minneapolis?" Eric asked.

"Yeah. You want me to carry some stuff for you?" Terry offered.

"It would be great if you could, Terry," Eric said. "I bought some stuff last night that won't fit in my cases."

"Sure. No problem, Ric," Terry said pleasantly.

Eric gave Terry the box with the dagger and the albums and the keys to his rented car so that he could also pick up the sword. When Terry returned the key, they made an appointment to get together Tuesday evening so that Eric could retrieve the swords.

"Okay, then, Ric," said Terry as they shook hands. "I'll look forward to seeing you on Tuesday."

"Thanks, Terry, you're a real lifesaver."

2 | Lee James
In which a great defeat scatters a treasure.

Takasaka, Japan - January, 1946
Sgt. Lee James and **Sgt. Hervey Stimpson**, American soldiers
from the 308th Regimental Combat Engineers assigned temporary
duty to a Civilian Affairs unit
Sgt. Arlon Matsuda, Japanese Language Specialist also assigned
to the same Civilian Affairs unit

"Herv, it doesn't matter if Captain Breedmore ain't a combat
veteran," Lee James said from behind the wheel of the Army
weapons carrier he was driving. "It doesn't even matter if he acts
like a fairy. What matters is he's a captain and we got no choice but
to carry out his given orders."

"I know, but this shit he's got us doing just don't make sense,"
said Hervey Stimpson.

At just that moment the weapons carrier hit a deep pothole that
had been hidden by muddy water. The vehicle bounced deeply and
lurched to one side.

"Jesus, Lee! Do you *try* to hit those goddamn things? I make it
across the bloody beaches of the Pacific and now Iowa's answer to
the kamikaze is going to kill me on a dirt road in Japan," Arlon
Matsuda said from the back seat of the vehicle.

"Don't hand me that bloody beaches crap, Arlon," said Lee
pulling the truck back on a straight course. "The main action you
saw was helping that G2 Major work up a dictionary of dirty Jap
words." It was true. One of Sgt. Matsuda's assignments as a
Japanese language specialist had been helping an intelligence
officer compile a classified intelligence manual entitled **A Glossary
of Vulgar Japanese Vocabulary Used by Enlisted Personnel of
the Imperial Japanese Army**.

"When you gonna teach us some dirty words, Arlon? How do
you say 'pecker'?" Lee asked over his shoulder.

"'Pecker'! Lee, you been hanging around with Captain Breedmore too long," laughed Hervey. "Arlon, you can teach me how to say 'pussy.'"

"Talk's cheap, Herv. A couple of cans of Spam down on the Flat's will get you a lot more than vocabulary," Arlon countered.

Another series of potholes forced Lee to concentrate on driving and conversation lagged. When the way seemed clear, Hervey spoke again. "That's another thing. Have you noticed that Captain Breedmore never, and I mean *never*, goes down to the Flats?"

"So what?" asked Arlon, more to keep the conversation going than to defend their Captain.

"It means he don't like girls, that's what," replied Herv.

"Maybe it just means he ain't attracted to the same kinds of girls as the rest of the entire 42nd Division," said Lee.

"It ain't just that he don't go down to the Flats," Hervey continued seriously. "Look at all the queer stuff Breedmore does. All these pictures and pots he's got us picking up? Is that manly stuff? And it ain't like he's picking up a little bit of stuff for his mother and his aunts. He's got a ton of that stuff in his room in the BOQ? When I brought him that crate of stuff we got last week, it looked like a museum in there. I think he's queer for that stuff."

"Jesus, Herv!" said Lee. "Look at all the money other guys throw at booze and dames. Captain Breedmore goes for paintings and pots. At least he'll have something more than clap to bring home."

"Well, I think a normal guy would mix some poontang with his paintings and his pots," chuckled Herv.

"As far as I can tell, Captain Breedmore isn't 'buying' any of this stuff," Arlon added in a more serious tone.

"That's what I'm talking about," Herv said jumping in. "I think we could be in a lot of hot water over some of the shit he's got us doing. Disarming the country is one thing, but whose going to believe our authorization covers confiscating some of the stuff we pick up. Those eight suits of armor we got from that place last week? I suppose those would make all the difference in the next war."

"You don't think those ended up in the bay with the Nambu light machine guns?" asked Arlon knowing full well the armor had been among the materials delivered directly to Captain Breedmore's residence.

All three men chuckled, but Lee said, "I'm not worried. The Captain must know what he's doing and I'd sure as hell rather be doing this than blowing up pill boxes and defusing mines."

"What about those Japs he hangs around with? You got to admit there is something goofy about them."

Indeed, the sergeants did not know what to make of the three Japanese who often accompanied Captain Breedmore and the team on their forays. The oldest of the three wore a traditional kimono but always had a flowery fan and colorful accessories. The sergeants called him "Pinky" because he wore a large pearl ring on the little finger of his right hand. "Slick" was a younger man who got his name from his pompadour haircut. Slick took charge of inspecting the art objects the team often found itself confiscating.

The only one of the Japanese the sergeants knew by name was "Yoshi," a barrel-chested man who either stood around by himself or helped the team with materials they confiscated. Once or twice, the Japanese had met the team at spots in the country and on those occasions Yoshi drove a small old car. This in itself was amazing because there were virtually no private cars to be seen on the road and black market gas was precious beyond cigarettes, nylons, or whiskey.

Yoshi spoke no English and rarely talked with anyone but Slick. Perhaps because of Pinky's ring, the men noticed Yoshi had no little finger on his left hand. Once, while they were taking a break while cleaning out an old fireproof storehouse, Hervey asked about the missing digit. He pointed to Yoshi's hand and grinned as he made a scissoring motion with his fingers. Yoshi shook his head as he grinned back his pantomimed reply. He extended his missing finger on to the top of a box and, with an imaginary ax in his right hand, chopped it off. Having done this, Yoshi stopped grinning and looked unblinkingly into Hervey's eyes.

While working in a stuffy temple storehouse. Yoshi had taken off his suit coat and his shirt. When he pushed up the sleeves of his union suit and loosened its top buttons, the men could see that his whole body was covered with multi-colored tattoos.

"Do you know where we are, Arlon?" asked Lee, bringing the conversation back to a concrete reality.

"Pretty much," Arlon said checking a map that was open on his lap. "We're on the road the Captain marked and unless I'm all screwed up, the town is just up ahead. He said the shrine is on the hill on the far side of town."

"What's the name of this place again?" asked Hervey though he didn't really care.

"The town is Takasaka and the shrine is called the Omon Hachiman."

"How the hell could there be any war materials way the hell out here in the country?" Herv said. "If you ask me this is pure bullshit!"

"Clearly the Captain didn't ask you, Herv," Arlon said philosophically. "I got the order right here. It says, 'Proceed to the town of Takasaka and remove any and all weapons, arms, and war materials held in or near the precincts of the Omon Hachiman Shinto Shrine, including traditional arms that could be used by insurgent or irregular combatants motivated by strong nationalistic zeal.'" Arlon shook his head and said, "Sounds like some more armor."

"I wish you guys would stop worrying about this. The Captain signed the order," Lee said with finality. "Besides, these people don't need all the shit we've been picking up."

"That must be Takasaka," Arlon said as the vehicle rounded a bend in the road.

"We'll check in with the cops," Lee said. "It's getting late enough that we'll just have them put us up for the night. Then we can go on up to the church tomorrow morning and get on the road early enough to get back to the base by dinner.

"Sounds fine to me," said Arlon.

"Me too," agreed Hervey. "Maybe the chief of police can round up some company for the night."

"Herv, you got a one track mind," Lee said shaking his head.

The men always found police and other local authorities they encountered in their travels, especially in isolated communities, were very accommodating. Their official requests were carried out quickly and sleeping arrangements, meals, hot baths, and even girls were arranged for the team with no questions asked and no payment required.

As the weapons carrier entered Takasaka the men saw it was nothing more than a big village set near the base of tree-covered hills which formed one side of a rather narrow valley. It was still chilly, but the farmers had begun to prepare paddy fields on the valley bottom. Water had been let into some of the paddies and in others men were breaking up the soil with simple wood plows pulled by oxen. As the vehicle passed, work stopped and attention focused on the intruders.

Most of the buildings were thatched-roof houses. Along the dirt main street were a few unpainted frame buildings that appeared to be commercial establishments-- not much to write home about. They all had sliding front screens opening directly onto the road, but it was hard to know what they actually offered since most appeared empty. In another time, all of this might have been quaint, but on this overcast day, Takasaka was plain and dirty.

The sudden appearance of American soldiers caught the town off guard. As their vehicle passed by, virtually all of the residents stopped what they were doing to look up and assess the situation. Some children ran to get a better look and a few followed the truck. In other towns, children had learned that GIs in jeeps were usually friendly and disposed to hand out candy, but the children of Takasaka were not yet sure that Americans were not monsters. Certainly their parents communicated no positive feelings as they watched the strangers drive along their main street.

Lee had no trouble finding Town Hall. It was the only brick building in town. Without giving the matter conscious thought, he drove through the iron gate into the court yard of the building and parked only a few paces in front of the police box. As Lee was stepping down from the driver's seat, a short man in a blue uniform emerged from the building. He looked in surprise at the small truck and its passengers. Standing directly in front of Lee, the man bowed from the waist and, looking straight at the ground in front of Lee's feet, began speaking.

Lee looked over his shoulder to the far side of the vehicle and called, "Arlon!"

Arlon came around the truck to join Lee. The policemen stood and was visibly relieved to see in Arlon a familiar face. Turing toward Arlon he again bowed and began speaking. The chief made a formal introduction to the sergeants, but Arlon was not comfortable with the flowery language and formal usage so he did not try to follow the entire statement. He let the chief speak until he thought enough had been said. Then he spoke in Japanese.

"Thank you! We are soldiers of the United States Army. Please give me your name." Arlon spoke with a stern tone.

"I am Senior Constable Nakada Kujiro," the chief said with a short bow.

"Fine," Arlon continued. "This is First Sergeant James. That is Technical Sergeant Stimpson and I am Staff Sergeant Matsuda. We represent the 308th Regimental Combat Engineers now stationed in Camp Hata. Our commanding officer is Captain Lawrence Breedmore, who is a graduate of Yale University and the Army Officer's Training Program at Fort Balfour. We have been sent to the town of Takasaka on the expressed orders of the Supreme Commander of Allied Powers. Our mission is to search for and confiscate war materials. You are instructed to help us in our mission. Do you wish to see our order?"

"No, sergeant," was the reply. Arlon had used this routine several times and he never had to show the sheaf of mimeographed papers he carried just in case the locals had any questions.

"Excellent! Your support will be positively noted in our report." The chief smiled.

Standing erect, Arlon looked at his wristwatch and continued. "It is too late to begin our operations today. We will begin our work tomorrow. Obviously, the more help we receive from you and the people of this village, the sooner we will be on our way. Please arrange a billet for us for the night. We have rations, but will need to have them cooked."

All of this appeared to be hitting Chief Nakada very hard. He looked blankly at Arlon and the other men and regained enough composure only to say, "I see. Perhaps the sergeants would like to step into the Town Hall." The chief motioned the men to the front door.

As they entered the sergeants realized Takasaka Town Hall was a "shoes off" establishment. Immediately inside the door, on street level was a cement-floored vestibule where visitors could step out of their shoes. Neatly arranged rows of slippers waited on the raised floor of the building. Not surprisingly, the floors were spotlessly clean and mirror smooth.

"Ah shit! Here we go again," Hervey said. "These people and their goddamn floors."

"Whoever invented this custom sure didn't have to wear combat boots. What do you think, Arlon?" Lee asked. The team learned this was a critical point in dealing with local authorities. Sitting down to wrestle off their boots could break the rhythm and risk the loss of face. Likewise, if they wanted to intimidate their hosts, all they had to do was barge ahead, boots and all.

"The chief seems pretty easy to deal with, I don't think we need to push him," Arlon said.

"Well, piss on it. I don't want to take my boots off." Herv remained firm.

Still smiling, Chief Nakada again gestured his visitors in. He smiled and said, "Please."

Arlon pointed to the floor and said, "Our heavy boots."

The chief seemed to realize the men were considering walking on the floor. He said, "Ahh, so" as his mind raced for another response.

"How thoughtless of me. I most sincerely beg your pardon. Perhaps the Honorable sergeants would be more comfortable sitting on the chairs in the police box at the corner of this humble building."

"He wants us to sit down in the police box where they got a table and chair. Sounds good to me," Arlon reported to his friends.

"Yeah, but we can't let him feel too good about it. Ask him which room is his office," Lee said. Arlon asked and the chief pointed to a door about thirty feet down the hall from the vestibule.

"Herv, go make sure there ain't any war materials down there," Lee said, pointing the way with his thumb. Hervey, the only member of the team wearing a .45, stepped onto the floor of the Town Hall and walked to the designated room. He looked in and called back, "Don't see nothin'." As he returned to the vestibule, his boots sounded hard against the wood floor.

Inside the police box the men and the chief sat down at a small Western style table. A wood-fired stove warmed the room and one of the chief's men poured four cups of tea from a large pot that appeared to remain on the stove at all time. It was not real tea, but a wartime substitute made from parched barley. The chief apologized for this, but no one else spoke while it was being poured. Lee lit up a cigarette and offered one to the chief. He accepted with a bow. The other policeman produced an ashtray and the room was quite.

"With all respect to your commander, I must assure you that there are no war materials of any kind here in Takasaka," Chief Nakada began earnestly.

After Arlon had translated this, Lee asked through Arlon, "None at all?"

"No, Sergeant. None at all," the chief replied directly to Lee.

Without waiting for a translation and looking straight at the chief, Lee said, "Our orders indicate the presence of such materials." The chief had to wait for Arlon's translation.

"You must be misinformed, Sergeant. Takasaka is a small place of no importance. There has never been an army installation of any kind here. Never even a Reserve Hall. Our young men were inducted into military service in the district center at Furukawa. They served on many fronts, but those who have returned brought no arms with them."

The sergeants listened to Arlon's translation without reaction. In a flat voice, Arlon added, "I think he's probably telling the truth."

"He probably is, but tell him our mission is to locate old swords and other weapons that trouble makers could make use of."

As Arlon explained this the chief nodded in comprehension.

"I see," he said. "There may, indeed, be a few ancient weapons in this area, but I assure you, Sergeant, there are no troublemakers in Takasaka. How do you wish to proceed?"

After translating this Arlon made a suggestion. "Let's not go into detail now. It's getting late and if he knows what we're looking for, he could get the stuff out of the Shrine before we get there."

"Damn right," Hervey agreed. "Let's let him sleep on what he's got. Besides, I'm getting kind of hungry."

"Okay," Lee said, taking charge. "Tell him that we'll begin in the morning and that for now all he has to do is arrange a billet for us."

After Arlon's translation the chief seemed vexed. He had a very worried look and scratched the back of his head. To fill time, he had his assistant pour more tea.

"I am eager to help, but Takasaka is a poor community. We have no public accommodations except a travelers' inn of the third class. It is very rustic."

Arlon understood this, but did not translate it to the others. He was not going to get involved in the chief's dilemma.

"In the old days, samurai who came to this place spent the night at Budoji, our main Buddhist temple."

"Is the temple near here?" asked Arlon crisply and it was only then that Chief Nakada realized he had hit on a solution. Smiling broadly, he pointed down the road and said, "Budoji is just two blocks down the street. It is a modest building with no modern amenities, but if the honorable Sergeants would accept our hospitality, we could offer you accommodation at the temple."

"He wants us to stay at a Buddhist temple down the road."

"Is that the place we're supposed to get the weapons from?" asked Hervey.

"No. They're at a Shinto Shrine. He's talking about a Buddhist temple. You think it will work, Lee?" Arlon asked.

"It'll be bedrolls on straw mats, but it sounds okay. Twist him a little bit Arlon, and then take it."

Arlon turned to the chief. "Is this place secure?"

"Entirely, Sergeant," was the earnest reply. "The temple is surrounded by a grove of ancient pine tress. No one will bother you and you can park your vehicle in the rear yard."

"I assume there is someone who can cook our dinner," Arlon asked.

Hearing this the chief made a small gesture to his assistant who left the room quietly. "I am sure that the priest's housekeeper will be happy to prepare your meal. She is an excellent cook," he said.

The temple was unheated and drafty, but the men slept comfortably in the *futon* mats and heavy quilts that had been laid out for them. Lee woke first. He got up at 6:30 and decided to look around the temple grounds before breakfast. He tried to be quiet as he rolled out of his bed but Hervey woke as he was pulling on his pants.

"Lee, for Chris' sakes what are you doing? What the hell time is it anyway?" Hervey asked sleepily.

"Oh Herv, give it a rest," Lee responded irritably. He had been looking forward to a short bit of privacy.

Hervey climbed out of his bed and sat cross-legged on the floor beside his futon. He lit a cigarette and rubbed his chin. "You awake, Arlon?"

"Yeah, I am, and I was thinking about what a couple of charmers you guys are in the morning."

As soon as Arlon spoke, one of the screens at the side of the room slid open to reveal the cook kneeling with her forehead on the floor. She rose smiling and brought a tray with small bowls and a steaming pot of tea to where the men had slept. Her cheerful smile, bows, and friendly gestures did not sit well with the men's cotton-mouthed sleepiness. They took the tea she offered and each of them managed to smile and nod back to her.

After giving Arlon his cup, the old woman knelt beside the tray and watched the men. They in turn looked sleepily at one another and the old woman, uncertain what to do next.

Lee spoke first. "I wonder how long she was waiting out there."

Hervey turned to him in mild surprise. "You think she was waiting for us to get up?"

"Of course she was," said Lee. "We didn't hear her coming down the hall, but she slid the screen open as soon as she heard Arlon. I'd say they're keeping pretty close tabs on us." Taking another sip of tea he said, "Arlon, tell her the tea is very good." He smiled broadly and bowed to the old woman.

Arlon's translation made the old woman beam. During her response she alternately bowed and pointed back over her shoulder. Arlon's conversation with her ended when she covered her mouth with the back of her hand and giggled merrily.

"She says there's hot water back in the washroom and after we're done washing up and shaving, she'll serve us breakfast." Turning to Hervey, he added, "She's really impressed, Herv, that American soldiers have got hairy legs." The old woman giggled again when Hervey winked at her and said, "Tell her that ain't all we got."

As the men returned from the washroom, their day stood in a delicate balance. The cold gray weather was not to their taste and they would have preferred to be back in the familiar surroundings of their base. Still, they had slept well and were enjoying a day without direct supervision. Their assignment also seemed to be going smoothly. As luck would have it, though, breakfast started the day in a bad direction.

For dinner the old woman had simply heated the contents of the cans the men had given her, adding only a few simple seasonings and making a pleasant arrangement. The sergeants had been very satisfied since they had expected no more. The woman had no idea how to turn the canned food into a morning meal and decided, instead, to offer the sergeants a Japanese breakfast. The meal she prepared would have been lavish by local standards, but to the Americans it was a dismal failure.

Rice and soup did not match their expectations. The grilled fish and the salty pickles she gave them were too unfamiliar to be palatable and the portions were far too small to be satisfying. When Hervey noted that the sticky substance on one of the side dishes "looks like snot," all three of the men found it even harder to eat what they were being offered.

The clincher came when the old woman brought each man a fried egg. Eggs were a delicacy even in the base mess hall so that these could have been a real treat. Unfortunately, to assure that there would be no problem, the old woman had cooked the eggs the previous evening. When they arrived they were cold, tough, and covered with congealed cooking oil.

The men did not speak as they gathered their gear and prepared to get on with the day. Leaving the room they had slept in, they found their combat boots freshly polished and waiting for them at the bottom of the temple's front steps. Arlon and Lee sat down and began pulling their boots on, but Hervey lingered to stretch and light a cigarette. He was not comfortable with the silence and said, "Ain't this place the shits? I wonder if the sun ever shines here." His friends did not respond to this attempt at civility and Hervey wished he had said nothing.

As Hervey joined the others on the bottom step, Chief Nakada entered the courtyard in front of the temple. He was all smiles and walked confidently toward the sergeants. Two paces behind him was another uniformed policeman directing the efforts of a civilian who was pulling a rusty two-wheel cart. The civilian wore baggy pants, split-toed tennis shoes and had a white towel wrapped around his head. The cart was piled so full its wheels crunched as they moved through the gravel of the temple yard.

Lee, who had finished lacing his boots, rose and said, "Now what?"

The chief bowed to Lee, turned to Arlon, bowed again, and began speaking. Arlon rose from the bottom step and listened carefully to what the chief was saying.

Hervey looked intently at the chief until he realized he had no idea what was being said and glanced at the cart. He was the first to realize it was loaded with swords, spears, and other old weapons. These were covered but not hidden by a straw mat. Hervey quickly pulled on his boots and made a beeline for the cart.

"Jesus, guys! Look at this stuff."

Lee joined Herv at the cart. The uniformed policeman threw back the straw mat and with gestures invited Lee and Hervey to examine what it had covered.

Hervey greedily reached into the pile and pulled out a short sword. Removing it caused other swords to tumble toward the bottom of the mass. Hervey studied the piece he had selected and said, "Jesus, Lee, do you realize what this stuff would be worth back at the base? Samuels got a hundred bucks from one of those Air Corps guys for a sword that wasn't near as nice as this."

Lee picked up a sword with a black scabbard and a long handle that was wrapped with white silk cord. With the policeman's encouragement, he pulled the blade part way out of the scabbard. It was as bright as polished silver. Lee brought it toward his face for a closer look. He saw his own reflection on the flawless surface until a cloud of condensed breath formed in its place. He was about to touch the edge to test its sharpness when he heard Arlon speak. Reluctantly, he pushed the sword back into its case and turned toward the chief.

Arlon asked a couple of questions to which Chief Nakada replied, *"Hai, soo desu."* The second time Lee heard this he said, "What's going on, Arlon?"

"The chief says that these are all the old swords and weapons to be found here in town. He says he picked this stuff up to help us carry out our orders."

"What does he mean by that?" Lee asked, genuinely uncertain of what to make of the situation.

"Remember when we arrived yesterday? We told him we were here to get old weapons. Apparently, he thought we meant <u>all</u> the old weapons in town, so he and his boys got busy last night and rounded up this stuff while we were sleeping."

Lee cocked his head in disbelief. "You mean this is all the old weapons in town?"

"Yeah. I asked him twice and he says this is the whole works. He wants to know if his assistants can load it into the weapons carrier so that we can get on our way back to the base." Arlon grinned broadly as he explained this. "See anything you like, Herv?"

"You're damn right I do!" Hervey replied. "Jesus! Look at this!" He pulled a short matchlock rifle out of the cart. It had a strange pistol grip and a barrel that was only about two feet long but encrusted with gold and silver overlay in the pattern of a long dragon.

The chief said something to Arlon.

"He wants to know if we want to inspect the stuff, Lee."

"I don't see why we need to inspect it. We aren't even supposed to pick it up."

"But that don't mean we can't take it," interjected Herv who now truly wanted this trove and viewed at least a part of it as his.

"I don't know, Herv. Captain Breedmore only mentioned the stuff in the Shrine. He didn't say anything about the rest of the stuff in town."

"To hell with Captain Breedmore," Hervey said as he walked toward Arlon and the chief. "Why the hell shouldn't we get some of this stuff? We can just keep the extra and there's no way he'll ever find out."

Arlon thought the chief might find this conversation confusing so he said, "Let's work that out later, guys." Turning to the chief he continued in Japanese and a firmer tone. "No inspection will be necessary. Do you have a list of these war materials?"

The words 'war materials' sounded ominous to the chief. "No Sergeant, we had no time to make a complete list."

"Very well." continued Arlon. "We will accept them with a simple receipt. Please begin loading everything into the vehicle."

The chief spoke to the civilian who immediately pulled the cart to the back of the weapons carrier where he and chief's assistant began transferring the weapons. The chief took a short pencil and a sheet of paper from the pig skin pouch he carried on a shoulder strap.

"What's going on, Arlon?" asked Lee.

"We're taking the stuff home," Arlon said with more firmness than he usually demonstrated. "Herv's right. Why shouldn't we have some of this stuff? Besides, the chief wants us to take it. What are we supposed to do, tell him to bring it back?"

Lee was still uncomfortable. "Are we going to have to sign for it?"

"Just a simple receipt, Lee. If you don't want it, I'll sign for the stuff."

"Yeah, I will too," added Hervey.

By this time the load was in the back of the weapons carrier and the chief had finished his receipt. He handed it to Arlon who looked it over and said, "Very well. This seems to be in order." He took out his own fountain pen, signed the paper with a flourish and gave it back to the chief. Turning to Lee he said, "There. That wasn't so hard."

Are you sure the stuff the Captain wants from the Shrine is in the load?" asked Lee.

"It must be. I asked the chief twice and he said that this was the whole shootin' match. All the weapons in town."

"We better make sure," Lee said. He did not want to have to come back to this place and also wanted to end Arlon's display of independence. "Ask him specifically to identify the weapons from that shrine. What's it called?"

"Omon Hachiman Jinja," said Arlon. At these words, Chief Nakada looked up sharply.

"Yeah, that's it," said Lee. "Have him show us the weapons from the Omon Hachiman Jinja. Those are the one's we'll have to give to the Captain.

Turning to the chief, Arlon again assumed a firm tone. "Have your man identify those objects recovered form the Omon Hachiman Shrine. Our records indicate that an especially threatening body of weapons was stored at the Shrine by individuals who are under investigation for war crimes."

The chief blanched and Arlon said sharply, "Is there a problem?"

"We collected no weapons from the shrine," was all the chief could stammer. The news that someone in his community could be under investigation for war crimes had never crossed his mind.

"Are you aware of the weapons held at the shrine?" pushed Arlon.

"There are some swords among the Shrine's treasures," Chief Nakada said vaguely. "But they would be of no interest to war criminals."

"Perhaps we know more about your town than you realize," Arlon said and the chief blanched again.

Turning to Lee, Arlon said, "The chief says he didn't get the stuff from the Shrine. What do you want to do?"

"We could just tell the Captain that some of this shit was the stuff from the Shrine."

"Nah, bullshit! The stuff in the weapons carrier is ours," said Hervey, who had already begun to plan how he could use the weapons in sale and trade.

"Yeah and I'll bet the Captain has a list of the stuff he wants. I don't think he'd buy the story," Arlon added.

"You're right. We'll have to go get the stuff at the shrine. Tell the chief we'll drive him over there. As soon as we get those swords, we can get the hell out of here."

"The First Sergeant has decided that you can accompany us to the Shrine in our vehicle. After the Shrine has been disarmed and we can certify that this town is no longer a threat to peace, we will be on our way." Arlon set his jaw both to look firm and to avoid breaking into a grin. Like Hervey, he had begun to appreciate the windfall that had presented itself.

Getting to the Shrine was trying for both the men and Chief Nakada. Hervey drove and the chief had been placed in the front seat to give directions. He had ridden in other trucks and cars, but it was not a routine experience. He sat nervously on the edge of the seat and grasped the door handle so hard his knuckles turned white. Twice Hervey missed turns and had to back up to get back on course. All of this gave the chief a headache and the fact that he had no idea what would happen at the Shrine made him very nervous. He was not sure he was handling the situation correctly. He worried he was being too accommodating, but he did not know what else to do.

The previous evening, when he met with the leaders of the community and the heads of the major families, Chief Nakada had explained he was working to get rid of the foreign intruders. By then, everyone in town knew of their arrival and many people had heard of their mission. He had no trouble convincing his neighbors these men were uncouth and dangerous. When he explained his master stroke of entertaining the barbarians in the police box rather than the Town Hall, the men of the community had nodded with approval. Likewise, the decision to put them up at Budoji was universally seen as wise. "Where else could they stay?" the chief had asked and all of the community elders had to agree that the chief was, indeed, handling a bad situation magnificently.

No one had argued with the chief's recommendation that the old weapons of the community be surrendered and considered it a cheap price to pay to get these creatures on their way. A few minor samurai families had made their home in Takasaka, so there were some swords and spears to be found in the fireproof store houses of the wealthier families. These were of no special interest to anyone. The men who were trying to guide the community though the agonies of military defeat and economic collapse gave no thought to the useless hardware of a life now gone forever.

Heads of the households with weapons to give had welcomed the chief when he visited them the night before. Working by lantern light, the citizens of Takasaka had rummaged through their belongings and offered up whatever they had. At each stop, Chief Nakada had pointed out it was far better to do this task without the foreigners present. Everyone agreed. The idea of the foreigners actually entering the storehouses was unthinkable. The chief took almost everything that might be considered a weapon, although in a couple of houses he had let an object or two be retained by their owners. In those cases, he pointed out that if the Americans were overseeing the search, they would certainly take every weapon and more.

In the previous night's discussion, no one had ever mentioned the sword and dagger stored at the Omon Shrine. Like everyone else in Takasaka, Chief Nakada knew about them. They were brought out every year at the shrine festival. But no one thought of them as weapons. Some years ago a man from the government in Tokyo had come to Takasaka to inspect the blades. He had taken them back to Tokyo for registration and polish and kept them almost a year. When they were returned they came with papers that had been duly filed with the Board of Education, but no one gave the documents serious thought because everyone already knew the stories associated with the blades.

The chief had last seen the sword and dagger two years previously when the priest had taken them out to show the young men who were about to enter national service. The young men had listened with bowed heads as the priest had recited the history of the long sword. He talked of the sword's *kami* and with it in his hand had spoken of the National Entity, the warrior's spirit, and the beauty of a soldier's duty. It had been a moving occasion and had helped the young men go off to war.

As he recollected all of this, Chief Nakada decided this was why the Americans wanted to go to the Shrine. They had destroyed the Nation's military and now wanted to take away the spirit that had supported Japanese might. This realization brought the chief comfort. He decided that he was not mishandling the crisis that had befallen his town. The invaders were venal bloodsuckers, but they did not understand that the heart of the people was deeper than material symbols.

The annoying voice of the driver brought the chief back to immediate task and crystallized his hatred for these men.

"Where do we go from here, chief" Hervey asked leaning over the steering wheel.

When the chief made no reply, Arlon repeated the question in Japanese.

"The shrine is ahead through the *torii*," the chief replied pointing the way with a nod of his head.

"It's through that wooden arch up ahead," translated Arlon. "The chief seems kind of moody all of a sudden."

"To hell with the chief. Can we drive up there?" Lee was anxious to get on with the task before them.

"Sure," Hervey said. "The truck will fit through the arch with room to spare," and he roared ahead, skillfully guiding the weapons carrier through the ceremonial arch that marked the sacred confines of the shrine. He continued up the cobblestone lane and rolled to a stop in front of the main shrine building. The chief had never seen a motorized vehicle in the shrine grounds, and would have protested but Hervey had proceeded so quickly and confidently the chief could not appreciate the enormity of the sacrilege that was taking place.

After he stepped down from the vehicle, but before anything else could happen, Chief Nakada turned to Arlon and said, "This is a sacred area. You must move the truck." His face was set in an unblinking scowl.

"It looks like the chief's got a bee in his bonnet. He says we can't park the weapons carrier here. It's a sacred area. I think we ought to humor him."

"Yeah, what the hell. Herv, pull it down there the other side of that last stone lantern," said Lee pointing to the far end of the open area in front of the shrine. The chief was disconcerted by the quick and easy response to his demand. He was trying to decide what to do next when Arlon said, "Please take us to the man in charge here."

"The head priest is Yamaki-san. His residence is in the back." The chief led the men around the shrine building which was of simple design, plain unpainted walls and a thick thatched roof. There were a number of smaller shrines and other buildings around the mains building and the entire compound was surrounded by a stand of huge evergreens. As the sergeants rounded the rear corner of the shrine, they saw the priest's quarters next to a small cut stone storehouse. That would be where the swords are stored, Lee thought, as the chief stepped to the residence door and hailed the priest.

A thin man in a gray kimono appeared. He bowed deeply to the chief, but looked very surprised when he saw the Americans who were standing a few paces back. The chief returned the bow and began talking in low, hurried tones that Arlon could not understand. As he listened, the priest's face became very serious. He asked a few short questions and as he did the conversation became louder. When Arlon heard the priest say, "That cannot be!" he turned to Lee and said, "It looks like we better step in."

"Yeah, see what's going on," advised Lee.

Arlon stepped forward, "The First Sergeant wants to know if there is a problem." The priest looked up in surprise when he heard the Japanese. He began to speak, but the chief cut him off.

"Yamaki-san is extremely surprised that the America Army wishes to take the weapons owned by the shrine."

"They are not weapons," the priest corrected firmly. "They are treasures of the Japanese people."

Lee sensed the problem and said, "Explain our orders to them, Arlon."

"The First Sergeant has ordered me to say again that we are acting under the direct command of the Supreme Commander of Allied Powers in Tokyo. We have been specifically ordered to bring these war materials to our Captain. You must make the priest understand that if he does not help us with our mission, the United States Army will use whatever force necessary to remove these dangerous items."

As Arlon was saying this Hervey came walking around the corner of the shrine. The Japanese turned to see him and Arlon was pleased to note that he was wearing his .45. It hung low from his pistol belt as he walked nonchalantly toward where the others stood.

"If you do not help us, it will look very bad for your community," Arlon added.

The chief and the priest spoke to one another again. After the exchange, the chief turned to Arlon and said, "What will happen to the weapons?"

"They will be held by Military Authorities," Arlon responded. In fact, he had no idea what Captain Breedmore would do with them.

"Can we recover them at some time?" the priest asked. The chief looked uncomfortable with this persistence.

"That decision will have to be made by higher military authorities," Arlon responded. "Our orders are simply to take them into military custody."

"There was a long silence as the soldiers looked at the Japanese. In a low, tense tone, the chief said, "We have no choice. Give them the swords."

The priest said nothing and after a moment walked to the stone storehouse. The others followed. The priest opened the rusty old lock and pulled open the door. He stepped into the doorway and said to the chief and the soldiers, "You may not come in!"

The inside of the storehouse was unlit, but through the open door the men saw the priest walk to a low, iron-bound chest. Opening it, he removed a long silk bag and a plain wooden box. He brought these to the door and gave the two objects to Arlon, who asked, "Are these all of the weapons held by the shrine?"

"Yes. It is only these two that the Americans fear so much," replied the priest.

"He says this is it, Lee. What do you think?"

"I think we ought to get out of here. There couldn't be a hell of a lot more in there. Let's go."

Arlon was pleased with the decision. He turned to the chief. "The First Sergeant says that we will not need to search further. We will also report that you have been cooperative." Turning to his friends, he said, "That's it. Let's go."

"Wait!" said the priest. "I want a record of this."

Arlon tried to sound calm. "We have already signed a receipt for the chief. That constitutes a record for all of the materials we have collected."

"We must have a separate record for these objects," the priest persisted.

"That will not be necessary!" replied Arlon. "The chief has all of the information you will need."

Speaking to the chief, the priest said, "Give me a piece of paper." When he had it and a pencil, he said to Arlon, "What is your name?"

"What's going on?" asked Lee.

"He wants our names."

"Christ almighty, this is getting complicated," said Lee.

"Give him our name," said Hervey. "What's he going to do, sue us?"

"I am Staff Sergeant Arlon Matsuda," said Arlon. The priest repeated the words slowly as he wrote them down, "Matsuda Aaron." Arlon could see he used Japanese characters to write his family name but *kana* symbols to record the syllables of his first name.

"And him?" asked the priest pointing to Lee.

"That is First Sergeant James, Lee James."

Again the priest repeated the words he heard as he wrote them in the Japanese syllabary, "Jyaimuzu Rii."

"And that man?"

"He is Technical Sergeant Stimpson, Hervey Stimpson." Arlon knew the priest would have trouble with this one and he did.

"Say it again, please."

Arlon repeated Hervey's name and heard the priest say, "Sujimupuson Hahbi " a couple of times, marveling at the complexity of the foreign names.

"All right. It looks like we're done here," Lee said with more than a hint of relief. "Arlon, see if the chief wants a ride back to town."

When Arlon explained this to the chief, he said, "No! I will walk."

To Arlon's translation, Lee said, "If that's how he wants it, it's swell with me. Say good bye to'em, Arlon," and he and Hervey began walking to the weapons carrier.

Arlon turned to the two Japanese. "The First Sergeant has asked me to say once again that your cooperation will be positively noted. It will probably be unnecessary for us to return. Good-bye." Then Arlon turned and walked quickly to catch up with his friends.

As soon as the weapons carrier was through the gate of the Shrine the men broke into giddy conversation.

"Was that smooth?" asked Lee from the driver's seat. "I thought things were going to get a little messy when the priest got his shit in an uproar."

"I know what you mean, but they were so anxious to get rid of us they would have given us their daughters," laughed Arlon.

"Screw their daughters," said Hervey who was sitting in the backseat examining one of the swords the chief had given them.

"That's just what I would have done, Herv," said Arlon.

"I'm serious," said Hervey earnestly. "This stuff is damn good. It'll be a lot handier than just some poontang."

"Don't stab yourself, Herv. This road is pretty bumpy," cautioned Lee. To rein in Hervey's greed, he added, "How do you want to split the stuff up?"

The men spent the next hour discussing how the chief's weapons could be divided among the three of them. They agreed they would have to look the collection over when they got back to the base. Finding a private place to do this would be difficult, but Lee was sure they could get into the shed behind the motor pool for a couple of hours. Beyond that, they also agreed that they would not tell Captain Breedmore about the extra weapons. This was a windfall that belonged to the sergeants. The Captain would only get the sword and dagger from the Shrine.

Even this took a bit of discussion because Hervey looked into the wooden box the priest had given them. He found a dagger mounted in plain wooden mounts. Carefully nestled beside the blade were a scabbard and handle. These were wrapped in their own silk bag and held together by an exact wooden replica of the dagger blade. The fittings were covered in rich gold-flecked lacquer and the various metal parts were finely carved out of what appeared to be solid gold. Hervey suggested that one of the other daggers could be substituted for this one, but in the end they decided there was no safe way of keeping the Shrine's items from the Captain.

A couple of blocks outside the main gate of their base, Arlon saw a figure at the side of the road who appeared to be waving at them.

"Is that guy waving at us?" he asked pointing through the windshield.

"Yeah. He is. It's one of the Captain's Japs. Its Yoshi," Lee said as he pulled the a stop.

The man who was hailing them was indeed Yoshi and he was visibly relieved to see the sergeants. He hurried to the door on the driver's side of the truck and said to Lee in broken English, "You go Takasaka?"

"Yeah," replied Lee tentatively.

Again Yoshi asked, "You go?"

And again, Lee replied, "Yeah, we go Takasaka."

"You got swo'd from Omon Hachiman Jinja?" demanded Yoshi pointing his index finger right at Lee's face.

"Yeah. We got the swords. What's it to ya'?"

"Caputen Buriidomoru say you givu me swo'd," said Yoshi now pointing at his own chest.

"What?" Lee asked incredulously.

"Caputen Buriidomoru say," Yoshi repeated slowly in an attempt to make himself understandable, "you givu me swo'd. Un'erstand?"

Lee looked at Arlon and back to Yoshi. "Is that so? Well, Captain Breedmore didn't tell *me* to give you the swords." He put the weapons carrier in gear and began to pull away.

"Sutopu, Sutopu!" Yoshi cried, but Lee drove on. "I ain't taking my orders from a greasy Jap," he said disgustedly.

The men said nothing more until the were back in camp. They passed through the main gate with a simple wave to the sentries. When they pulled up to the motor pool, Sgt. Samuels hurried to where they were parked. "Where they hell have you guys been? We been looking all over for you."

"We had orders," Lee said. "Captain Breedmore had us out looking for military stores out in the country."

"You ain't heard, then?" asked Samuels.

"Heard what?"

"Breedmore was killed last night. There was a fire in his room in the Bachelor Officers' Quarters. It destroyed the place and burned him to a crisp."

3 | Odagiri Satoshi
In which a search for lost treasures is begun

Tokyo, present day
Odagiri Satoshi, Japanese businessman with many connections as well as interests in politics and religion
Tsuji Takeru, "Boss" - or Oyabun - of the Kawabayashi-gumi, one of Japan's leading underworld syndicates

Stepping from his chauffeured car, Odagiri Satoshi walked smartly through the glass doors of the Odagiri Building Number Seven and strode toward his office. No press photographers were waiting for him this morning, but Odagiri still made an effort to look confident and energetic. His personal secretary met him in the lobby of his primary office building and passed along some bits of news as they made their way to Odagiri's private office. Everyone they passed bowed and said, "Good morning, Mr. President." Odagiri returned these greetings with smiles and nods, but he moved along swiftly. Only after entering his office and closing the door did Odagiri let himself acknowledge the stress he felt this morning.

A traffic accident near a construction site in Roppongi had created a huge snarl of cars that had lengthened his commute by nearly an hour. He had tried to make use of the time by dictating a couple of personal notes into his miniature tape recorder. His laptop computer had let him polish a position paper he would be issuing later in the week, and he had made a couple of necessary calls, but still he hated to start a day behind schedule.

Alone in his office, Odagiri walked to a plain wooden altar that occupied one corner of the space. He was pleased to see that fresh flowers and a mound of five perfect apples had already been set out in front of it. He clapped his hands together then held them in front of his face as he lowered his head in meditation. Working to clear his mind of the trivial concerns that detained him, he focused his attention on the spiritual centers of his life. As the irritations of the morning fell away from his mind, he said, "Ji, kyo, koku," Japanese for, "self, community, nation." Having said these words, he paused, exhaled and clapped his hands again. As if a weight had been lifted from his shoulders, Odagiri felt ready for the tasks that awaited him.

The first major appointment of the morning was a welcome meeting for this year's "SCN Teaching Fellows." These were twenty-two American college students who would spend the next year teaching at the SCN English schools Odagiri operated in small and medium size town of central Japan. As he walked to the meeting, Odagiri recalled opening his first school in 1959. Thanks to his countrymen's enthusiasm for English, it had been a profitable success and grown into a chain of schools. Recruiting good instructors had been a consistent problem until Odagiri had hit on the idea of making the teaching positions awards. Now, honor students from a number of liberal arts colleges in the American Midwest competed for the opportunity to drill Odagiri's student for 36 hours a week. The fellows were given a place to live and small subsistence allowance. Additionally, a sum equivalent to $500 a month would be waiting for them when they returned to the United States. Many of them counted it the high point of their college years.

The SCN Schools were a minor part of Odagiri's business empire, but they were profitable and carried both tax and prestige advantages so Odagiri was happy to make time for the welcoming ceremony. Before entering the auditorium, Odagiri's secretary pinned a festive red and white pompom on his lapel and ushered in his translator who was needed because Odagiri himself spoke essentially no English.

In front of the docile students, Odagiri was a fatherly benefactor. He welcomed each one and briefly explained the philosophy behind his enterprises. Starting with his experiences as a fifteen year-old cadet in the Imperial Japanese Army Air Force, Odagiri described the demoralization and despair of the post-war years. He explained how his life and fortunes had changed when he discovered the Jikyo-koku faith in the early 1950's. Virtually the only English words he used in the presentation were his own well-studied translation of Jikyo-koku - "self, community, nation." He also gave the English abbreviation--"SCN"--that had become the common name of the sect. Some of the fellows were moved to smile at Odagiri's awkward pronunciation - "Essu, Shi, Ennu" - but most of the group found his statements sincere and interesting.

Odagiri did not try to explain the philosophical precepts of the Jikyo-koku faith since he was sure foreigners could not appreciate the subtle connections that bound individual Japanese to communities and their nation state. He was also not at all interested in explaining the complex web of relations that linked his many personal businesses to the Jikyo-koku faith or its political arm, the Jikyo-tai. Instead, he closed his comments by encouraging the fellows to use their time in Japan to learn about the country and the Japanese. He told them to protect their health and to make friends with common Japanese people, then he led them into a seminar where they could meet and get to know the managers of the schools. While the excitement was high, Odagiri said good-bye to the group which gave him a warm ovation before he returned to his office.

Odagiri next had to meet with twelve donors who had made substantial contributions to the Jikyo-koku building fund. Before joining them, Odagiri removed his pompom and hung a narrow brocade sash around his neck. As he entered the meeting room where they were seated around a large mahogany coffee table, Odagiri clapped his hands together softly and held them together in front of his chin. All of the donors rose to their feet and made a similar gesture. Several said, "Ahh Sensei, welcome." Odagiri warmly asked them to sit back down.

In a soft tone very different from the one he had used to address the American college students, Odagiri thanked the donors for their generosity. He assured them he understood their donations to be demonstration of their dedication and of the power and purity of the faith they shared. The donors beamed and nodded to acknowledge his thanks.

Odagiri turned to an architectural rendering of the new Shrine under construction at the Jikyo-koku Headquarters in Takasaka. The drawing showed a massive structure of reinforced concrete that mixed traditional Japanese elements with futuristic industrial design.

"This will be our world headquarters in two years. Isn't it wonderful?" Odagiri beamed. "The design is a sublime reflection of the Jikyo-koku faith," he said, bending forward slightly and placing his hand on the table. The group nodded their approval, and Odagiri continued.

"In the new building, as in our society, each level is linked to the others. The bottom supports the top, but the top does not smother the lower levels." The visitors listened with rapt attention.

"You know," Odagiri continued with a gentle sweep of his hands, "I like to say this building is just like Japanese society. It is totally unique and every part contributes to the whole. Nothing is wasted. And," he said with soft emphasis, "there is no elevator. The way to the top is hard work." He paused to let the words sink in, but no pause was needed. As members of the Jikyo-koku religion, the visitors had easily understood this example of the conservative political and economic values of their faith.

Odagiri continued. "Completion of the renewed and rededicated Ozaki Shrine at Takasaka will be the fulfillment of the dream of our founder, Takahashi Jinzaburo, who pointed a way out of the despair that bound us in the dark days after the Pacific War. We must practice his views of religion and society in order to prosper, thrive, and continue to strengthen the heart of our Imperial nation."

"As Rector of the Jikyo-koku Central Committee, I want you to know that I personally appreciate your generous contributions to our building fund. They will help us build a better faith and a better Nation. But you must not think of your contribution as a gift. It is an investment! Your lives will be improved. You will find good things happening to you because of this contribution. Mark my words!" he said with rising voice. "See if your business does not prosper. See if your children do not flourish. Trust me." The guests clearly did trust him. They leaned forward in their seats with sincere concentration.

"Our new Shrine will be completed soon, but without its treasures, the new building will be an empty shell. Our teacher, Takahashi-sensei, drew great lessons from the objects that fate brought to the Shrine. For that reason I am devoting all of my energies to restoring the Shrine's treasures. I hope I will have some important announcements in that regard soon, but for now all I can say is that you can trust me to put all my efforts into this important work."

The guests nodded approvingly at these cryptic comments, but Odagiri did not let them sink in. "The press of other matters makes it impossible for me to enjoy lunch with you, but my assistant, Deacon Suzuki Fumitoshi," Odagiri motioned toward his assistant waiting attentively near the rear of the room, "will now take you to a special lunch which has been set for you in my executive lunch room."

Odagiri turned to his assistant, "Deacon, entertain these friends well. Listen to both their opinions and their concerns and be prepared to report them to me. Do you understand?"

The assistant bowed gravely and said, "Hai, wakarimashita!"

With that Odagiri left the group with a bow and smile.

In the short time before lunch, Odagiri attended to a couple of minor business matters, responding to a fax from one of his agents in Singapore, calling the manager of one of his car dealerships to iron out a problem with sales goals for the coming year. In light of the economic conditions, the manager wanted the expectations lowered. Odagiri told him that would not be acceptable. Next, he read a real estate prospectus on a large apartment complex in Los Angeles. It was an attractive offering, but Odagiri decided against it, noting that his investigators reported a significant number of Blacks and Koreans in the area of the complex.

Shortly before noon, Odagiri's secretary buzzed to say that his car was waiting to take him to his luncheon meeting. The route had been checked so that the ride to the new Cafe Francaise took only a few minutes. The maitre d' was expecting him and Odagiri was ushered immediately into a sumptuous paneled room. The paneling had been removed from a 17th century French chateau and the table and chairs were antiques. There were several large bouquets of fresh flowers in the room. His hosts were waiting for him.

"Ah, Counselor. Thank you for joining us," Ogawa Kenichi said as he and his companions rose to greet Odagiri.

Odagiri had served two terms in the Diet in the 1970s. He had stepped down, but retained a leadership position in the Jikyo-tai party which had twenty-eight members in the Diet. In political circles he was still called by his Diet member's title.

Bowing to his hosts, Odagiri said, "Ogawa-san, it is a pleasure to see you," and the luncheon began. Ogawa, who was President of Central Japan Construction Corporation introduced his two associates and the three attractive young women who graced the table. He also explained he had taken the liberty of asking the chef-- who had recently returned to Japan from training in Paris--to prepare a menu. "That way we won't have to be embarrassed by our bad pronunciation," he explained to everyone's polite chuckle.

The meal arrived in a number of courses and it was, indeed, outstanding. There were a couple of different wines and a wonderful array of perfectly prepared light dishes served by two waiters. As the meal progressed, Odagiri and the others engaged in pleasant conversation. They talked about the weather and the general conditions for construction in Tokyo. Odagiri shared some gossip about the doings of various members of the Diet and teased one of the young ladies about the high hemlines that were coming into fashion.

As one of waiters was clearing the plates for the fruit course, Odagiri asked, "How are prospects for your firm, Ogawa-san?"

"Oh, I think our prospects are quite good," Ogawa replied in an offhand manner. "Of course, we are hoping to submit the winning bid on the new National Office complex being planned in Sakura City."

"That will certainly be a major project," Odagiri replied. "You feel your firm is well prepared to do the work?"

"Oh, absolutely, Counselor. We are the right firm for that job," Ogawa said.

"Well, I'm glad to know of your interest. If you have no objection, I'll mention it to the members of the Jikyo-tai caucus," Odagiri said as he sliced into a fresh pear.

"That would be nice," Ogawa said.

As soon as his pear was eaten, Odagiri placed his napkin on the table and apologized for having to return to his office. As he rose, the others got up and the women bowed toward him. Ogawa-san thanked him for making time for what had been a very pleasant lunch. As Odagiri stepped toward the door and bowed to the group one last time, Ogawa gave him a small, neatly wrapped package. There was another round of bows as Odagiri stood in the door and then he left.

In the back seat of his car, on the way to his next appointment, Odagiri opened Ogawa's package to find the equivalent of $85,000-- about what he had expected. He placed the money in his briefcase and gave his driver directions for the next appointment. It, too, would be a private meeting. So private, indeed, that Odagiri did not wish to arrive in his own car. Instead, he directed his driver to the pleasant old neighborhood near Ueno Park. Once there, Odagiri left the driver with orders to return to Odagiri Building Number Seven.

Like all of Tokyo, the Ueno area had grown dramatically in recent years, but Odagiri still recognized the family-owned shops, private residences, and neighborhood shrines that were characteristic of old downtown Tokyo. Odagiri walked among these for nearly twenty minutes, enjoying his anonymity on the city street, the pleasant weather, and a mild stroll after lunch.

Shortly before 2:30, Odagiri used his cellular phone to call a cab.

It arrived in only a few minutes. The driver greeted him by name and without asking directions, drove to the Kikusui, a traditional Japanese restaurant in the area behind Asakusa Shrine. Both the 1923 earthquake and the fire bombings of 1945 had devastated this area. The Kikusui had been built in the early post-war year. Like other structures of that age, it had both rustic charm and a perimeter wall that made it very private.

At the door, Odagiri was met by a middle-aged woman in a silk kimono who welcomed him with a deep bow and a pair of slippers. As he stepped out of his shoes, he noted three pairs of pointed black shoes neatly arranged at the side of the vestibule indicating the others had already arrived.

Stepping up to the polished wood floors of the restaurant, he followed the woman through a complex of rooms defined by paper panels. Near the rear of the building they were met by a stocky man wearing a loosely cut double-breasted suit. The woman bowed and he slid open the screen he had been guarding.

"Odagiri-san, come in, come in," said Tsuji Takeru, who was seated at a low table on the floor of a Japanese style room. As Odagiri took his seat on a zabuton cushion, he saw that the room had been opened to double size and that the screens along the exterior wall had been slid back so their room itself opened onto a small garden.

"Odagiri-san, let me introduce my kobun, Hatamura Joji. I have recently made him the head of one of my branch houses, he is a very skilled young man." Like Tsuji, Hatamura wore his hair in a crisp crew cut. Unlike his superior, however, the younger man was not wearing a suit. Instead he had on a filmy silk shirt that let the polychrome tattoos on his arms and shoulders show through.

"Your ride here was satisfactory?" asked Tsuji.

"Yes, of course. I have always been pleased with the service provided by Tokyo Transport taxis," said Odagiri with a bow.

"Thank you, Odagiri-san. My brothers at Tokyo Transport try to impress the importance of courteous service to all of their drivers," replied Tsuji with a wide smile.

The woman reappeared and set an array of small plates in front of each of the three men.

"I ordered a few treats. Be sure to try the ba-zashi. It's a specialty of the house," Tsuji said, helping himself to a piece of the marinated raw horsemeat. He smacked his lips and set his chopsticks down as he motioned to Hatamura to pour beer for the group.

Odagiri took a long drink from his glass. "Ah, that's good." Setting his glass down, he leaned one elbow on the table. "Tsuji-san, thank you for being available for a meeting."

"The pleasure is mine, Counselor," Tsuji replied. "I can offer very little to an important man like yourself, but I value the help you have given to me and my associates."

"You embarrass me, Tsuji-san."

"You should feel no embarrassment, Counselor. The members of the Kawabayashi Brotherhood preserve the purest values of our country and have much in common with your Jikyo-koku faith. I would be more public in my support, but we both know Leftists and journalists have confused the general public about us," Tsuji said earnestly.

"I have always valued your assistance," Odagiri said with a small bow.

"Counselor, my men and I look forward to working with you. How can I help?"

"Tsuji-san, you are dependable friend," said Odagiri to Tsuji's obvious satisfaction. "Again, this year, I will need your help in transferring funds into the accounts of the American students who work in my schools," he continued.

"That will be no problem. My friends in America will handle it as usual."

"Beyond that, there is another issue I would like to discuss with you."

Tsuji listened intently as Odagiri continued.

"As you know, construction of the headquarters of the Jikyo-koku faith is well under way. You are aware of the project, of course," Odagiri said.

Tsuji nodded gravely, recalling that Odagiri had asked him to step in when one of the concrete suppliers for the project had balked at the price he was being offered. After Tsuji sent men to burn three of the supplier's trucks and beat two of his key employees, the offer had been accepted and the project had moved ahead smoothly.

"The faithful will come in crowds and be moved by the beauty of the center we are creating, but I am still deeply disappointed that the heart of the our Shrine is missing." Odagiri continued.

"How is that, Counselor?" Tsuji asked with concern.

"Shortly after the end of the Pacific War, American soldiers stole two treasure swords from the Shrine," Odagiri explained.

Tsuji clicks his lips and shook his head.

"Some time ago I asked the National Police to investigate," Odagiri continued, "but they claim to have come up with nothing."

"And now you would like the Kawabayashi Brotherhood to join the search," Tsuji said.

"Yes," admitted Odagiri.

"Counselor, my friends and I will certainly help. I only wish that you had asked me earlier."

Odagiri nodded. "It was foolish to begin with the National Police, I know. I hope you can have more success since I have heard you have recovered many priceless swords."

"Our Brotherhood has many contacts," Tsuji said thoughtfully. "And my sword return operation has had many successes. I may well be able to help with your search."

"The swords themselves are priceless. One was declared a National Treasure in the prewar years. The other was recognized as an Important Cultural Asset. Both are magnificent as art objects, but their spiritual value is even greater since they demonstrate the mystical power of the Shrine. I want to return them as a reflection of my devotion. Frankly, I also fear that if they ever do surface, the Leftist bureaucrats in the Central Government will try to keep them in the National Museum," Odagiri was speaking with both emotion and sincerity. "I will pay any price and give any favor within my power for those swords."

"Counselor, your generosity and dedication are admirable, but all you need to do is ask," Tsuji said soothingly. "My Brothers and I will be honored to help you on this matter. Just send me whatever materials you have on the swords and put your mind at ease."

"I knew I could count on you, Tsuji-san," Odagiri smiled.

Turning to Hatamura, Tsuji continued, "After the usual problems I have to deal with, embarking on a activity like this will be a pleasant break. Don't you agree, my son?"

"Indeed, father," the younger man replied seriously.

Recognizing that Tsuji was now turning the conversation in a direction that would explain what he wanted in return for his help, Odagiri asked, "What sorts of projects are you involved in these days, Tsuji-san?"

"Counselor, we are both businessmen," Tsuji said taking another piece of horsemeat. "You understand the problems of managing both projects and people."

"Indeed, I do," said Odagiri, breaking apart his chopsticks and helping himself to a piece of horsemeat as well.

"Right now, I am working with a construction firm that has wonderful plans for a development on the west shore of Lake Biwa."

"Near the old Tokkaido Highway district?" asked Odagiri.

"Exactly. I helped them acquire rights to nearly a kilometer of lakefront property," Tsuji said. Odagiri could imagine the methods Tsuji and his men must have used, but chose not to dwell on those thoughts.

"The funding is all in place and plans are complete for a major new complex of residential and resort apartments. They will also develop a colorful theme park for people to enjoy. It will be very popular," Tsuji added positively.

"But there is a problem," he continued. "The Cultural Affairs Ministry is blocking the entire project."

"Is that so?" said Odagiri.

"Indeed, it is. You see, right now the area is taken up with dozens of old wooden houses and city covenant limits buildings to a total height of thirty meters," Tsuji explained shaking his head. "Now, maybe in the old days, a rule like that made sense, but the developers can't make any money with such small buildings," he scoffed.

Odagiri listened quietly.

"We can usually handle disagreements like these," Tsuji said, "but this case has gotten complicated because a bunch of leftists who call themselves historic preservationists have gotten the Cultural Affairs people from here in Tokyo involved. These preservationists say the area is the last section of the old Tokkaido Highway and they want it preserved. They also say high buildings will ruin the view of the Lake." He was obviously vexed by the situation. "We can't even reason with them," he said. "But the whole issue could be settled with an act of the Diet."

Odagiri pursed his lip thoughtfully and said, "It could, but passing such a bill would be very difficult and would have great costs." He paused thoughtfully. "Still, I think it could be done. Please keep me informed about this project." Then, to make sure that both sides understood the deal that was being struck, "And I'll be interested in anything you find out about the lost treasure swords."

4 | Maeda Nobuhide

In which creation of a treasure preserves two families.

Furukawa, Japan - 1587

Maeda Nobuhide, successful warrior who has assembled an alliance of local leaders to become Supreme Military Commander of Japan

Kutani Shinichi, one of Maeda's allies with aspirations of his own.

Tsunami Nishu, Lord Kutani's Keeper of Swords

Noda Shuichi, general in the armies of Lord Maeda's defeated enemy, Araya Kanenobu.

"Is there anything like the smell of a new castle?" Maeda Nobuhide asked his companions expansively. "I've spent most of my life burning castles down, but now I'm struck by the satisfaction I get from building them up again. Do you suppose that means I'm getting old?" he added with a smile.

The four men seated around Maeda on the *tatami* mats of the topmost floor of the newly rebuilt Furukawa castle chuckled politely. One of Maeda's armies had laid siege to the castle four years previously. Before they finally took it a year later, they had burned most of it to the ground. Since that time, Maeda had assigned his ally, Kutani Shinichi, the task of rebuilding the castle and establishing control over the district it commanded. On this early fall afternoon, a pleasant breeze passed through the new room and Maeda and the others could look out through the raised shutters to see the expanse of flat land that surrounded the castle.

"Lord Kutani, you have done a fine job. Furukawa castle is far better than it ever was. Adding these three stories to the keep improves the building's lines and affords a view of both the far distance and the south approach. Was the change difficult?" Maeda asked.

"Not really, sire. I gave the idea to Master Builder Sumida and he came up with this plan. We've given him a great deal of business, so he should be skilled at such things." The entire group laughed.

Reaching for one of the salted plums from a small plate on the lacquered tray that had been placed at his side, Maeda asked, "How many men did you have working on the project?"

"I knew you wanted the castle ready for use as soon as possible, so I had as many as three thousand hands working here last winter. I had to let some of the peasants go as rice planting time arrived, but there are still over a thousand finishing the work. The structure will be done this month. Then it will be simple decorating and fixture work. I'll have a crew of painters from the Kano school here this winter. They will embellish walls and screens. I also found that the local smiths could not manage the iron and copper trim so I've arranged for specialists to be brought in from the metal- working district of Nagoya."

The others nodded their approval of these details and of the industry Kutani had demonstrated in making Furukawa a comfortable, yet battle-worthy bastion in such a short time.

"Whoever falls heir to the Furukawa domain will certainly appreciate your efforts, Kutani." Maeda said smoothly, but with the clear implication to Kutani and the others that he had not yet decided how he would divide up the spoils of the victories he was overseeing. In fact, Maeda did not intend to let Kutani keep a rich estate like Furukawa. He had come to the Maeda side far too late to be treated like a close ally. He had stood firm at the battle of Sozudai, but many had done the same. He had entirely avoided the nasty business at Hoshino and had arrived a day late at the nearly fateful battle of Iwajuku where twenty thousand men died. Kutani had some value, but he was certainly an expendable minion in Maeda's view.

"Our forces in the south will be needing supplies this winter." Maeda said, directing the conversation to practical matters, "How are rice yields in this region?"

"Not at all good," Kutani replied with a wrinkled brow. "The warfare devastated much of the countryside and I've had to press the peasants into other service. Last winter saw the real famine. This year should be better, so I think we'll be able to ship at last year's level."

"That won't be good enough," Maeda replied sharply. "Our victories along the Inland Sea were all supported by resources I've had sent to the troops. If you think the fighting here was intense, you have seen nothing. Huge areas in the south have been laid bare. It's the cost of victory." There was a pause before he continued. "While others are proving their loyalty to me with blood, the least you can do is squeeze some more out of the comfortable backwater I've sent you to."

The rapid change in Maeda's mood had caught Kutani off guard. He bowed at the waist and said, "Sire, you must know that I will do everything you ask of me. While I am here, all of the resources of Furukawa will be directed to our victory." Regaining his composure, Kutani squared his shoulders and continued with lowered eyes but a hint of an edge in his voice. "Great Lord, I am a soldier and I seek only to serve you. Say the word and I will lead my troops against any enemy you identify."

"I am sure you will, Lord Kutani, I am sure you will. You may rest assured that I will use your soldierly talents," Maeda replied, smiling and bowing slightly toward Kutani.

There was a brief pause before Maeda turned his attention and the conversation to the administrative tasks that had brought him to Furukawa. With the help of his allies, Maeda arranged for arms to be acquired and shipped to the forces in the south. A cheap new style of flat helmet was examined and judged to be adequate for the regiments of farm boys being recruited as riflemen. Titles and duties for supporters of the Maeda faction were discussed. A couple of old friends were rewarded with august titles and reduced demands. Maeda noted the excellent service that had been given by Ito Nobuo, who had come to his side only the previous spring. Looking over the tabular accounts of a fierce battle fought the previous month he said, "Our new friend Ito accounted himself marvelously at Numazu. I wasn't sure about his ability to occupy the middle of that line, but he did well. His action certainly let Lord Hiida take the flank." Scanning the maps and documents that had been sent to him, he added, "Not everyone would rush that line with only fifteen hundred men." After a pause he continued, "Had he lived, I would make him a Duke!" The others chuckled politely before moving on to other matters.

By late in the afternoon, Maeda and his councilors had turned their attention to setting the levies to be demanded of his supporters. Maeda scoffed at virtually every one of the accounts and production estimates that had been sent to him. Several times he said, "I need more," and "That's not enough." In virtually every case, he increased his expectations for the coming year, assuring famine and forced enlistments in all the territories he controlled.

As this numbing work was winding up and the light was fading, Maeda ordered the evening meal. He had the papers removed and Kutani had a cask of good *sake* brought in. The mood was loosening when the watcher above the main gate sang out in the prescribed manner, "Dispatch rider coming!"

Maeda turned to Kutani, "Were you expecting something?"

"Indeed, I was not, sire," Kutani replied as he rose and went to the window. Seeing that the rider was already in the yard, he said, "The rider wears your crest, sire, and carries a special dispatch pennant."

"Makino must have sent him with news from the far south," Maeda said. "Bring him to me immediately."

When the dispatch rider appeared before his master he was disheveled and entirely exhausted. His face showed that he had not rested for days. Maeda ordered him to sit down and had *sake* and food brought to him.

Without waiting, the rider began to deliver his dispatch. He said he was a brigade lieutenant from one of Maeda's elite units. Maeda had never met him, but he was familiar with both the man's family and his unit. Maeda knew that a man of this rank would have to bring important news.

Continuing without a pause, the rider said, "Great Lord, I have ridden five days without stop to report that Araya castle has been taken."

"Excellent!" Maeda exclaimed. "Tell me about it."

"Sire, after we breached the outer defense last month, the Shiroishi brigade was lucky enough to start a fire in the main gate. With gunfire we were able to block their attempts to stop the flames. Six days ago, Araya asked for a conference. My liege, Lord Makino, met with him and accepted his terms. He dispatched me to report these events to you." Slowly the rider's voice was gaining strength. He gulped a cup of *sake* before continuing.

"What were the terms?" Maeda demanded.

"Sire, Araya wanted to die in his own castle, but he begged the privilege of saving his family treasure swords from the flames."

"That is laudable," Maeda said. "Lord Makino was wise to accept the request."

"He was sure you would agree, sire," the lieutenant said. "Lord Araya also asked permission to dispatch his aide General Noda to bring one blade to you. Lord Makino let him leave the castle under a surrender banner as the flames engulfed the keep. He is making his way to Furukawa as we speak."

"What blade is he bringing me?" Maeda asked.

"Great Lord, it is a dagger by the swordsmith Muramasa," the lieutenant replied earnestly.

"What!" Maeda raged. Jumping to his feet he bellowed, "They're trying to give me the Muramasa Son Killer. Where is Noda now?" He was extremely agitated.

Bewildered by this change of mood, the lieutenant said, "Great sire, he and his escort are traveling by foot along the Upland Road. He is perhaps three days behind me."

Maeda's eyes were aflame and his jaw was set as he stroked his temple nervously. His aides had never seen him this agitated. After a moment of pacing, he turned to Kutani.

"Kutani, now is the time you earn your keep," Maeda said in a commanding voice. "Find Noda and stop him. Do whatever you must, but make him give that tanto to someone else, anyone else. I will not take it. Do you understand?"

Kutani did not understand his master's violent reaction, but the order was clear and he said, "I understand, Master."

"Do it, Kutani! Do it now! If that dagger gets anywhere near me, your sons will be killed, your wife will be defiled, and your estates given to your enemies."

Kutani took leave of Lord Maeda and the others and hurried to his assigned task. He did not understand the crisis, but had no question about Maeda's sincerity. He began to issue orders as he made his way through the new castle.

Kutani dispatched emergency runners along all of the highways of the district. These men, who were on constant alert, were trained to run at full speed along a well-established network. They would alert every checkpoint within 100 miles of the castle. By the next morning, all traffic in the district would be stopped.

Before he reached his own chambers, Kutani also sent out a party of fast dispatch riders to locate Noda. They were ordered to return word of his whereabouts to the company of light cavalry who would be following them as closely as possible. The cavalry commander was ordered to hold Noda wherever he was found.

As his valet unpacked his battle dress, Kutani ordered his personal company to arms. By the time he was selecting the arms he would carry, he could hear the commotion of preparations that had begun in the castle yard. He took satisfaction in knowing that Lord Maeda would also have to be aware of the activity and impressed with his decisiveness.

As soon as his battle kit was selected and laid out, and as the shouts of his soldiers preparing for the campaign rang through the castle, Kutani stopped to gather his thoughts. He had a cup of tea brought to him and he sat down to consider the other preparations this task would require. Sipping his tea in contemplation, he sent for one of his company commanders and a keeper from his armory.

The company commander had been aroused by the call to arms and so tapped on the sliding screens of the master's chamber in only a few moments.

Without rising or offering the man tea, Kutani gave him a series of orders. The officer nodded his understanding of each task as it was assigned. When Kutani was done, he asked if the orders were clear. The officer indicated he had understood and left immediately.

As the commander was leaving, Tsunami Nishu, Kutani's Keeper of Swords, arrived. Tsunami had also heard the call to arms -- it had aroused the entire castle -- but the summons to his master's chamber had been a surprise. Tsunami was a samurai and trained in all the warrior's skills, but he rarely took part in field campaigns and had not expected to travel with the company that had suddenly been called up.

Lord Kutani had a huge arsenal and was constantly receiving and dispersing swords. Overseeing these weapons was Tsunami's responsibility. He had to judge their quality and see that they were polished and rigged properly, and he kept inventory records that allowed the swords to be issued where and when needed. For a feudal estate at war, these were important duties and Tsunami approached them with intensity.

Most of the swords Tsunami handled were new. The demands of a nation at war had encouraged many swordsmiths to turn out mass-produced weapons that lacked the grace and quality of real swords. Tsunami made sure these were issued to low class fighters and peasants who were being recruited in increasing numbers. Tsunami was deeply disturbed by the damage that was being done to the swordsmith's art. To assure that Lord Kutani had some blades of quality, he was also charged with selecting smiths who were commissioned to create art swords. He considered this work important because it preserved a craft that was at the spiritual heart of the country.

The work Tsunami loved most was caring for Lord Kutani's personal weapons. At all times, his master kept at least four hundred fine old swords for his own use and to give as special gifts to other military leaders. As a powerful warrior, the Master was continually giving and receiving swords. Some came as war booty and a few were purchased at great expense from sword dealers in Kyoto or elsewhere, but most were presented to Lord Kutani by other nobles. Nothing marked an important occasion as surely as the exchange of fine blades. The ability to select just the right sword for an underling or a superior was a mark of a refined leader and Tsunami was proud of the many recommendations he had made to his master.

Arriving at the Kutani's chamber, Tsunami was surprised by the warmth and relaxed tone of his welcome. "Ah, Keeper Tsunami. Thank you for coming. Please join me in a cup of tea," Lord Kutani said as if he were entirely unaware of the commotion in the rest of the castle.

"Master, I am honored to be called," Tsunami said as he knelt on the cushion the master directed him to.

"Before I ride on a mission of great importance to this estate and to our liege, Lord Maeda, I need your insights." Now the lord's tone was slightly more businesslike and Tsunami knew he should ignore the cup of green tea that was placed at his side.

"Of course, you are familiar with the swordsmith Muramasa," the master continued.

"Indeed, I am, master," Tsunami said.

"Tell me about him," Lord Kutani said.

Tsunami was mystified by his master's request. Muramasa was famous and Tsunami was sure Lord Kutani was aware of his history, but this was not the time to question his master's judgment.

"Muramasa lived during the Kokoku era and was last student of the great swordsmith Munemasa. His father, the smith Muratoshi of the Yasuda school, died when his son was a boy. Muramasa was then apprenticed to Munemasa. After ten years, the boy was awarded one character of the great Master's signature. That is how he came to have the name Muramasa. He established his own forge back in his home district of Yasuda and had two sons, both of whom became swordsmiths. The oldest took the name Muramasa and was the second in a line of four smiths with that name." Tsunami was proud of the store of information he could remember about notable swordsmiths, but he paused to see if he was presenting what Lord Kutani wanted.

"Yes," the Master said. "Please go on."

As if talking to one of his own apprentices, Tsunami said. "Muramasa made swords of the highest quality. He could work in any of the five great traditions, but he was at his finest when using the secrets of his own teacher, Munemasa. His swords have fine wood grain structure and a tempered edge in the form of waves and clouds. Connoisseurs find his blades easy to appreciate and they are said to be strong in battle, although they are preferred by few of the leaderly class. I think you know, sire, there are no swords by Muramasa in your own arsenal. Many students of the sword feel that Muramasa blades do not deserve the unfortunate reputation they carry."

"Tell me about that reputation," Lord Kutani said.

"These are dark subjects, sire," Tsunami continued, "well outside my expertise. Still, it seems that a great many Muramasa blades have been used in sorry acts. This has led some to say they have acquired strong powers, even that the swords themselves are bloodthirsty."

Again, Tsunami waited to be sure that the conversation was going in the direction his master wanted. He received no indication he should stop.

"My teacher, Nomura Taihenjiro, studied with old style sword augurs. These were men who sought to read the auspiciousness of blades. Nomura-sensei told me many stories he had learned. As I recall, the Shogun Ashikaga Tomonao, severely cut his hand while he was examining a Muramasa tachi. And the famous fighter, Takeuchi Heiji, died with a Muramasa blade in his hand at the Battle of Namikawa Bridge during the reign of the Emperor Gokomatsu. Many such stories are remembered about Muramasa blades."

"Have you heard of a sword called the "Son Killer?" the master asked.

Nodding slightly and knitting his brow, Tsunami said, "Its a dagger. Yes, I know the story of the Muramasa Son Killer."

"Tell me," Kutani commanded.

"The Son Killer is a small tanto. I have never seen it, of course, but it is described as a masterpiece in the best style of the Master Munemasa. According to the story, it was made for Natsushima Koka who ordered it as a weapon to carry in his retirement. Koka was the son and heir of the great general Natsushima Genko who ended the Go-Tembo Rebellion by defeating Ashiya Hidetaka. Because Munemasa had been associated with the forces of the Emperor Go-Tembo, the younger Natsushima wanted a Munemasa blade to show his family's domination of their enemies. By that time, however, Munemasa was dead so Koka turned to his greatest student, Muramasa."

Tsunami was trying hard to remember the facts of this case and present them clearly. Seeing that his master was still listening, he pushed on.

"Some say Muramasa may have hexed the dagger. The old battle tales even claim he made the blade in league with the Fox God so it carries a magical force. However that may be, Koka's son and heir died within weeks of the time his father received the dagger. Koka made his second son his heir, but he, too, died suddenly."

"What happened to the dagger after that?" Lord Kutani asked with great interest.

Tsunami paused to recollect all he knew so that no part of the history would be left out. He still did not understand his master's interest, but it was clearly a matter of great importance. "As you know, sire, the House of Natsushima did not last. Before Koka died, he was defeated in many battles. Ultimately, his estate was taken by the Uesugi family who acquired the dagger. The Uesugis were also crushed in the chaos of their age and the dagger disappeared. After some years, the Muramasa tanto surfaced again in the arsenal of the Warrior Igusa Daimaru who controlled most of the Inland Sea District during the Oei era. He liked the blade because of its beauty and had it remounted so that he could carry it for personal protection. As soon as Igusa began to wear the dagger, his oldest son was killed in battle. It was Igusa who gave the dagger the name "Son Killer." He had it blessed by priests and abbots, and retired it to his arsenals. I assume it remains there even now."

"No," Kutani said, shaking his head slowly as if in deep thought. "When Lord Araya swept across the Inland Seas district 12 years ago, he would have acquired the dagger with what was left of the Igusa domain," Kutani looked up as if requesting confirmation from Tsunami who shifted uncomfortably on his cushion.

"That I do not know, master," Tsunami said. "If you wish I will search my records for more information. I am deeply embarrassed that I have been unable to answer all of my Lord's questions."

"You have done well, Tsunami. Please go now and prepare to ride with the party I will be leading out," Kutani said. "I may need your help again."

Lord Kutani's forces found Lord Noda and his small party at a spot along the secondary road up the Sumitani valley. As ordered, the cavalry vanguard had stopped Noda where they found him and waited for Lord Kutani. Once Noda's whereabouts were known, Kutani showed no need to hurry. Five days after leaving Furukawa castle, he and his company arrived at the spot where Noda had been halted. He had his bivouac set up across the road so that Noda could have no question about his presence or intentions. After his camp was entirely set, he sent his greetings to Lord Noda and begged an audience with him. Noda replied that his business was with Lord Maeda and abjectly refused Kutani's request. Two more exchanges followed before Noda finally indicated his willingness to meet.

Noda was traveling with only a few men and essentially no equipment so he could not host a proper meeting. Still, when Kutani arrived, Noda was seated on a commander's stool and held a general's war fan. Kutani carried a similar iron fan and took his own seat as soon as his aide opened it directly in front of Noda.

"Lord Noda, it is a pleasure to see you again. We last met at Hirosato as I recall," Kutani started.

There was a pause before Noda answered. "Yes, it was at Hirosato and at that time we were on the same side."

"Things change," Kutani replied. "I have served Lord Maeda as my liege and Lord since before the Battle of Sozudai and with his support, my house has flourished. But enough of that. How can I help you here today?" Kutani asked abruptly, but with a pleasant smile.

Noda knew that he should be offended by Kutani's gracelessness. As a war leader, Noda deserved respect even in defeat. Kutani's lack of tact was certainly calculated to throw him off balance, but Noda knew there was nothing he could do. After a moment, he spoke.

"Your graciousness exceeds even your reputation, Lord Kutani. I will accept no assistance and trouble you only to let me pass and make my way to a meeting with Lord Maeda."

"My liege, Lord Maeda, has left Furukawa castle and will not be available," Kutani replied.

"Then I will follow and meet him elsewhere," continued Noda. "My Lord Araya ordered me to bring the Great Lord a sword of surrender. Your ally, Lord Makino, accepted the sword for Lord Maeda and extended a safe conduct pass to me so that I can deliver it to the Great Lord himself."

"We are aware of developments at Araya castle," Kutani interrupted. "Lord Makino accepted five of Lord Araya's treasure swords and agreed to let you carry another blade - a tanto - on to Lord Maeda. The dagger you carry has been accepted by no one and remains either the property of Lord Araya or yourself," Kutani corrected sharply.

Noda knew these details were correct. "I carry the dagger - a work of great beauty by the master swordsmith Muramasa - on behalf of Lord Araya. It was his last command that I carry it for him to Lord Maeda. I am compelled by loyalty to carry out my master's order," Noda said. "If you will clear the way, I will do so."

"Lord Maeda will not accept the blade you carry," Kutani said with finality.

"One way or another, delivering this dagger will be the act that ends my life, Lord Kutani. If you do not let me continue, I will perform *seppukku* here on the Sumitani Road after dedicating the dagger to Lord Maeda. My dedication of the blade will make it the

Great Lord's property and responsibility even if I do not meet him face to face. You cannot stop me from carrying out my master's last order." Noda spoke with sincerity and resignation.

"I admire your filial dedication, Lord Noda. You bring great honor to your family." As soon as Kutani had said this, he beckoned to a party of soldiers who were waiting slightly apart from the rest of his troops. With a company commander directing, three men carrying lacquer boxes approached the generals. Solemnly, they set the boxes in front of Lord Noda and stepped back. The commander turned to Kutani who said, simply, "Open them."

Noda could not stifle a gasp as the first was opened. Untying the silk-wrapped bundle that was in the box, the commander exposed the severed head of Noda's wife and set it on a small mat. Moving on to the second box, he removed the head of Noda's teenage daughter and set it out so that her father could identify it with certainty.

As the commander stepped to the third box, Kutani said, "Lord Noda, my men have not yet filled the third box." The commander gave a sharp order to a party of guards who were standing in front of the rest of Kutani's troops. They parted to show a young boy wearing the Noda family crest.

"Lord Noda, yours is an ancient family with a proud history," said Kutani, "but you can end it today."

In anguish Noda said, "What do you want?"

"Abandon your attempt to carry Araya's dagger to Lord Maeda. If you do so, I will see that your son is raised as a samurai so that your name may continue." There was no need to explain an alternative.

There was a long silence before Noda asked softly, "What should I do?"

"The *torii* gate we can see in the woods across the valley marks a national shrine in that small village," Kutani said pointing toward collections of farm houses at the base of the wooded hills. "Present Lord Araya's dagger as an offering to that shrine and I will see that your son survives and that your own ashes are buried with those of your wife and your daughter."

After a moment of silence, Noda said, "Very well."

5 | Tsuji Takeru
In which a treasure gets a new claimant.

Tokyo - present day

Tsuji Takeru, Director of the Greater Japan Imperial League and senior member of the Kawabayashi Brotherhood

Hatamura Joji, Tsuji's *kobun* or "son" within the Kawabayashi Brotherhood

Sato Yoshimasa, an earnest student of Master Ozawa Seiken, "last of the ninja"

Okamura Yoshio, Tsuji's patron and a retired leader within the Kawabayashi Brotherhood

Takahata Sachiko, a former bar hostess who is now Okamura's residential companion

Speaking over his shoulder, Tsuji Takeru's chauffeur said, "There's a *pori-ko* outside the office, Sir. Do you want me to go around?"

Tsuji leaned forward and craned his neck to see a uniformed police officer with a clipboard and camera standing directly across the street from the offices of the Greater Japan Imperial League. "Those pukes," he said in disgust. "Are you carrying a *chaka*?"

"No, sir."

"Neither am I. Pull up to the door. He can't arrest me for going to work."

The Imperial League office is located on a side street in Tsukiji, one of Tokyo's commercial neighborhoods near the harbor. New high rise buildings are appearing in the area, but most of the buildings are three or four stories high and unremarkable. The League office blends in with the shops, offices, and businesses around it. Parking is, of course, not permitted on the street in front of the office, but there is little through traffic and, in any case, no one complains when Tsuji's driver parks the car on the white stripe that defines the walkway in front of the office. Today, that might not be a wise idea.

As soon as the driver stopped the limousine, Tsuji stepped out of the back seat and bowed toward the officer. Speaking in a voice loud enough to be heard across the street, he said, "Good morning, officer. I am glad to see that you are here protecting the peace of our neighborhood." He made another deep bow to the officer who uncomfortably returned a polite nod.

Tsuji then walked confidently toward the policeman. As he entered the street his driver hurried to accompany him and officiously moved to halt any traffic that might have been on the street. Tsuji ignored this and approached the policeman with a broad smile.

"I don't believe that I recognize you, officer.. . ." Tsuji paused to read the policeman's name tag, "Takahashi. Are you new to this precinct?"

"No, sir. I am assigned to the Research Division of the Tokyo Metropolitan Police Department," the young man said crisply.

"Well, that's wonderful, officer Takahashi. But what brings you to this quiet street?"

"Sir, I am conducting a traffic flow survey."

"Wonderful, wonderful," said Tsuji pleasantly. "Will we have you here all day?"

"Sir, I cannot say," the officer said as Tsuji leaned a bit too close to him.

"Of course. I know how hard it is to schedule police work. I want you to know that we here in Tsukiji appreciate the fine work of the Metropolitan Police Department."

The policeman glanced at Tsuji uncertainly.

"We certainly do, officer," continued Tsuji. "And we know how important traffic flow surveys are. You let me know if there is anything I can do to help."

"Thank you, sir" said the officer.

"Anything at all, officer. You just let us know," Tsuji paused. "And officer, when you have to piss or even shit, you feel free to come over and use the toilet in my office, okay? It wouldn't do to have a member of the Metropolitan Police Department pissing in the street, would it?"

The policeman set his jaw firmly, but said nothing as Tsuji turned to go. Again, his driver made sure that all traffic was stopped as Tsuji strode across the street. When he got to his car, Tsuji turned back toward the policeman and said, "Officer, my driver needs to pick up some things in my office. You don't mind if we park here for just a moment do you?" The policeman said nothing.

Inside the office door, Tsuji looked back at the policeman and said, "I don't think that snot is going to be writing parking tickets today, but watch him just in case. Leave the car right where it is unless he comes across the street. Then he can go out and move it." The driver nodded and took a place just inside the door.

The front office of the Greater Japan Imperial League was a congested area with many desks crowed together in an undivided space. The office workers had been watching Tsuji's activities silently. When he turned to face the office, the three office girls rose from their desks and bowed toward him. "Good morning!" Tsuji said and in unison they said, "Good Morning, Mr. Director."

All the girls were dressed in blue skirts, starched white blouses, and neatly designed striped jumper tops. On their left breast they also wore feminine versions of the Imperial League membership pins.

"I see we have company this morning," Tsuji said lightly.

The girls all looked serious, knitted their eyebrows, and shook their heads.

"Well, let's be sure to make Officer Takahashi welcome," Tsuji said with affected sweetness in his voice. "Atsuko-chan, please bring him some tea right now and refill it every forty-five minutes."

The youngest of the girls said, "*Hai, Kaicho-san!*"

"And see if you can't get some nice pastries to bring him from time to time," he added. Again she said, "Yes, Director."

Turning to the oldest of the three girls he asked, "Miko-chan, is Hatamura-san already here?"

The senior office girl was an attractive woman of twenty-five. Like her younger co-worker she said, "Yes, Director," as she bowed smartly.

"Have him meet me in the conference area."

Miko left to get Hatamura and Tsuji took one of the upholstered easy chairs around a low coffee table near the rear of the office. He lit a cigarette and opened one of the newspapers on the table. As he did this, the third office girl jumped to bring him a large ashtray and then scurried off to get a cup of green tea. He took these without acknowledging them and read the paper until his assistant appeared.

When Hatamura arrived, Tsuji looked up from his paper. "Ahh, Hatamura-kun. You notice we have company this morning."

"Yes, Father," replied the younger man.

"Do you know why they decided to do this today?"

"I have no idea, sir."

"Did we do anything unusual last night?"

"Not really," the younger man said absently. "A couple of the men had to encourage that deadbeat who runs the Meibo Club to settle his accounts, but I don't think the *pori* were even called."

"I think they're just harassing us," Tsuji said.

"That's probably all it is, Father."

"Whatever they're up to, I'm going to have to change my plans for the day," Tsuji said annoyed. "But we can't let them get away with this sort of thing."

"Please tell me what you want me to do, Father," Hatamura asked leaning toward Tsuji.

"There's no need for violence," Tsuji warned. "Make sure that all the men know that." The young man relaxed slightly and nodded.

"I simply want you to make sure that everybody we know drops by today, all the local merchants and household heads. Offer treats to the old folks who meet in the neighborhood temple. Is the expectant mother's group meeting there today?"

"It is, Father, and the young men's *kendo* association meets this afternoon as well."

"Fine. Have them all come by the League Office to pick up some of our Anti-Stimulants posters. In fact, see if you can't get some of the teachers from the high school to come by so we can make a contribution to the Student Activities Fund. Tell the priest we have decided to make another contribution to the temple."

"I'll take care of it, Father." The young man smiled as his task became clear.

"And get a newspaper photographer or maybe some of those television guys down here," said Tsuji. "See if you can't get a picture of Atsuko-chan giving the *pori-ko* some pastries. That should make us look like good citizens." Tsuji and Hatamura shared a chuckle at that thought, before Hatamura left to begin his tasks.

Tsuji moved to his desk located with the others near the center of the crowded office. When he sat down, the youngest office girl brought him another cup of tea on a small saucer. As she did he said,

"Atsuko-chan, rub my neck. I feel stiff today." Setting down her tray, the girl did as she was told, using a number of mild pounding and poking techniques to massage Tsuji's neck and shoulders.

"Fine, that feels much better," Tsuji said putting another cigarette to his lips. As he did, Atsuko held a lighter for him and he said, "Miko-chan, I'm supposed to meet someone at 11:00. A person named Sato. I don't think it should take long, but we will meet in the private room."

"Very well, Director," she responded.

"I had a couple of other appointments for this afternoon, but I want them canceled."

"Fine, Director."

A few minutes before 11:00 an entirely nondescript man in his late twenties entered the office. In every respect he looked to be your typical lower level Tokyo office worker, light grey slacks and suit coat, white shirt, light tie. He was not fat, but he had a round softness and sweaty pallor that seems to go with life in the modern Japanese capital.

As soon as he entered, the three girls said, "Welcome," in unison and Atsuko rose to meet him.

"I am very sorry," he said. "I am Sato Yoshimasa, here to meet with Director Tsuji. I am slightly early and I am very sorry."

"Good morning. Mr. Tsuji is expecting you. Please come this way," and she led the visitor past the main office area to a small Japanese style private meeting room.

When she returned to the office area, she told Tsuji, "Sato-san is in the meeting room. Would you like tea?"

"Yes. Bring him tea. I'll go down there in a minute."

The Director finished his cigarette and closed the account book he had been looking at when Sato arrived. Before leaving his desk he took a nickel-plated automatic pistol from one of the side drawers of his desk. He pushed the gun into his belt so it was hidden by his suitcoat.

As Tsuji entered the meeting room, Sato, who had been sitting on the floor, fell to full bow. With his forehead on the straw mats, he said, "Tsuji-sama. It is a deep pleasure and a great honor to meet you. Words cannot express the deep gratitude I feel for this opportunity."

"Please, please. Relax and make yourself comfortable," Tsuji said taking a cushion at the side of a low table in the middle of the floor.

Kneeling on his cushion, Sato nervously held a business card to Tsuji who took it and read the handwritten message it contained.

"I understand that you are an acquaintance of my friend President Aida of the Central Japan Construction. He called to tell me that you wanted to meet with me." Aida was a relatively minor building contractor who had used the services of the Kawabayashi Brotherhood. He was a contact worth keeping, so Tsuji had agreed to this meeting.

"Indeed I am, Director Tsuji," Sato said. "I attended English class with President Aida's nephew." In fact, Sato had met the nephew in an evening 'cram class' they had attended because they had failed to gain admission to worthwhile universities.

"I see," said Tsuji, returning Mr. Aida's business card to Sato. "Aida-san did not explain what exactly it was you wished to speak with me about."

"Director Tsuji," Sato began anxiously, "it is my fondest wish that you can make use of my services."

"And what exactly do you do, Sato-san?"

Sato offered Tsuji-san his own business card. "Director, I am the last practicing disciple of the ninja Master Ozawa Seiken. Professionally, I go by the name Osatsu Juken." He bowed to the floor.

Tsuji was mildly surprised. "So you are a ninja?"

"Yes, Director. I am."

"I've never met a ninja before," said Tsuji. "In fact, the only things I know about ninja come from old movies and comic books." Tsuji raised an eyebrow skeptically.

"That does not surprise me, Director. In fact, most people's ideas of ninja come from those sources. True ninja have always been unusual and misunderstood. At their peak during the Edo period, when Japan was strong and peaceful, there were never more than 50 true ninja. My Master Ozawa Seiken received the secrets of *ninjitsu* as a boy and preserved them until today. Five years ago, when I was a second year student at Greater Tokyo Commercial University, Master Ozawa accepted me as an apprentice and with his guidance I have developed the arts and crafts of the ninja." As he said this, he knelt on the floor with his head bowed forward and he hands resting on this thighs.

Tsuji considered himself a traditionalist, but he had never given any serious thought to ninja or to the craft they were supposed to practice, *ninjitsu*. If he thought of it at all, he viewed these topics as fantastic fables that existed only in the *manga* comic books his men read with such dedication. Still, the improbability of this earnest young man's story interested him.

"So tell me, Sato-san. What value does a ninja have for me, for my business?"

"Sir, the central skill of *ninjitsu* is inconspicuous movement. Master Ozawa has told me that no man can be truly become invisible, but with his help I have learned how to become inconspicuous. I know the art of misdirection. I have trained myself to see well in the dark and to move between shadows. I can remain motionless for long periods and can climb walls and trees. I have studied locks and keys so that I can open doors that halt others." There was a touch of arrogance as Sato explained this, but Tsuji chose to ignore it.

"So you are a sneak thief?" he said.

Sato shifted on his cushion, careful to contain his irritation. "A ninja works for a patron and carries out tasks assigned to him," he explained. "Like the samurai of old, the ninja is loyal to his patron and can retrieve objects he is directed to. But a true ninja would not steal for simple personal gain."

"I see," said Tsuji. "And I suppose that you are also skilled in the martial arts?"

"Yes sir, I am, but I have focused on the traditional martial skills." In saying this, Sato spoke with a rehearsed tone as if he had made the statements many times before. "Most of the modern martial arts, kendo, judo, karate, and aikido are *not* traditional at all, but sports, hobbies for children and businessmen." The disdain in Sato's voice was evident. "They have nothing to do with the Japan's real martial tradition. I believe in Japan's real fighting skills as they were developed by the warriors of old Japan."

"And what are those skills, Sato-san?"

With a practiced movement, Sato reached into his shirt pocket and pulled out a steel disk with eight pointed projections. In an easy move, he flicked his wrist toward the calendar and sent the disk on its way. It landed true and stuck firmly. Continuing his smooth movements, Sato pulled four smaller disks from his belt and with four quick sweeps of his hand he sent these toward the same post. They stuck in a cluster near the center of the calendar. By the time the fourth struck the surface, Sato had produced four more disks from the pockets of his suit coat and threw them one at a time. They stuck firmly in the corners of the calendar and Sato turned to Tsuji with a satisfied look.

"Very interesting, Sato-san, very interesting," said Tsuji.

Sato bowed deeply. "Thank you."

"Have you studied firearms?" asked Tsuji, genuinely intrigued by the strange person who was presenting himself.

"I am familiar with most types of modern firearms, sir," said Sato pleased that Tsuji was showing enough interest to question him. "But I believe that firearms are not truly Japanese. I have fired *tanegashima*, the matchlock guns used by many samurai, but they have no place in the quiet movement of the ninja. Beside, I feel no need to carry a gun. My traditional weapons are all I need to fulfill my responsibilities as a ninja."

"Most of my men find they need guns in the modern world," Tsuji said skeptically. "With all the guns around nowadays, aren't you afraid your enemies will just shoot you?"

Sato seemed ready for this question. "The true ninja tries to avoid discovery and must be willing to match his skills against those of the gunman. Beyond that, my master has prepared me spiritually. The way of *ninjitsu* builds on the mystical secrets I cannot easily explain. I can say, however, that I have studied texts from China and the spiritual teaching of the ninja of old. They will protect me so I cannot be harmed by anything but a magic bullet."

Tsuji found the conversation turning silly. As devoted as he was to the traditional values of Japan, this kind of mysticism made no sense to him. "Sato-san, all of this is very interesting, but please, how could you be of use to either the Greater Japan Imperial League or any of my other enterprises?"

"Esteemed Director, I would be honored to serve you in any way I could," Sato said with another deep bow.

"I see," Tsuji said sighing. "Well, tell me what sorts of activities you have undertaken."

"Director, I am sad to say that there is currently little demand for the skills of *ninjitsu*. For the past two years, I have worked full time as a demonstrator at Ninja Village which Ozawa-sensei operates near Atami. That work has let me perfect my technical skills, but it offers no challenge. I long to use my abilities in real ways."

Tsuji had heard of Ninja Village. It was a moderately popular tourist attraction located near the recently built expressway between Tokyo and Nagoya.

Sensing that Tsuji was loosing interest, Sato said, "I can carry messages and follow people and could easily retrieve objects of value if you request." He paused hoping Tsuji would ask for details. When he did not, Sato continued with a tone of desperation in his voice. "I have also studied English and have traveled abroad. Before joining Ozawa-sensei at Ninja Village, I worked as a travel agent. I led tour groups to both Hawaii and California so I could operate in America. I am willing to travel anywhere and for the honor of working for the Kawabayashi Brotherhood, I would do anything within my power."

Tsuji looked sternly at his guest. He had not mentioned the Brotherhood and it was totally inappropriate for anyone outside the organization to refer to it by name. It was conceivable that a person like Sato could have some uses, but he had just worn out his welcome.

"Sato-san, I am sure that you are a very busy person and I do not wish to take too much of your time."

Sato wilted as Tsuji said this.

"Please give me your card, Sato-san. I will keep it and call on you whenever an appropriate project presents itself." Tsuji intentional used a positive tone as he said this, but it was clear he was eager to end the conversation.

Sato gave Tsuji card. "Thank you, Director. I sincerely hope that you will find a way to use my skills." He wanted to say more, but Tsuji rose and pleasantly but firmly drew him toward the door.

When Tsuji and Sato reached the office area, they found Hatamura waiting. Sato realized that he could ask for no more of the Director's time and simply said, "Good bye, Director. Thank you for making time for me," and he bowed deeply.

"Yes, yes, Sato-san. Thank you for dropping by," Tsuji said offhandedly. Then turning to him he added in a teasing tone, "You might want to use your *ninja* skills to make sure that the *pori-ko* across the street doesn't see you as you leave."

Sato looked toward the windows and saw the policeman standing on the far side of the street. Without saying anymore, he walked to the side of the front door. Standing to one side so that the policeman could not see him, he waited for a moment until he saw a garbage truck making its way down the street. When it was directly in front of the League office and between himself and the police office, Sato stepped out of the office.

"Father, as you requested, I have arranged for several of our neighbors to visit us this afternoon," Hatamura told Tsuji as soon as Sato left.

"Very good," Tsuji replied positively.

"And there will be two photographers."

"Two?"

"Yes," Hatamura said proudly. "At 1:30 *Japanese Sports* will be here to take a picture of you handing out anti-drug posters to the boys of the junior high baseball team. Then *Economics Weekly* is coming down to get picture of Atsuko and the copper. He thought it was a great idea so it may not even cost us anything."

Hatamura described these arrangements proudly and his boss nodded his approval. Like many younger members of the Japanese underworld, Hatamura usually wore flamboyant clothing. He liked tight pants and very long, pointed shoes. Unless it was very cold he preferred filmy silk shirts that showed both the knit belly band he wore around his abdomen and the colorful tattoos that covered his upper arms and shoulders. Today, however, Tsuji noted that his young associate was wearing a neatly tailored silk shirt and a rather conservative pinstripe suit.

"You have made excellent arrangements, Son. You make me proud of our association," said the older man.

"Thank you, Father," Hatamura said with a sincere tone and a polite nod.

"And you look good today," added Tsuji. "That's a real business suit you've got on. You're not a *bakuto* anymore, Son. It's time you gave up those streetfighter's outfits. Next time we have to bring in a group of girls from Thailand, I want you to spend a couple of extra days in Hong Kong so you can buy some more suits like that one."

"Very well, sir."

Tsuji spent the rest of the workday in the Imperial League office. He greeted the visitors and guests who dropped by and kept careful track of the police officer outside his door. Just after noon, Tsuji had his limousine moved and at 2:30 Officer Takahashi was replaced by another uniformed officer and a man in plain clothes. They continued to photograph all of the people who entered the League office, but they took no other action. Tsuji called a couple of newspaper reporters and other contacts who might have gotten word of an impending operation against organizations like Tsuji's. None of his contacts had heard anything to indicate that the police were embarking on a campaign of harassment, so he decided to go ahead with some activities that needed his attention.

At 4:00 Tsuji and Hatamura left the League office by the back door and met his driver around the corner. They drove to an area of fashionable residences between Yoyogi and Shinjuku. As they made their way through the congestion of early rush hour traffic, Tsuji explained to his assistant that he was taking him to meet Okamura Yoshio, a retired elder of the Kawabayashi Brotherhood.

He explained that the meeting had two goals. First Okamura had been a leader of the Brotherhood during the 1940s 50s and early 60s. He had sponsored Tsuji's membership and was, therefore, Hatamura's grandfather in the organization. Okamura was now old and frail and Tsuji wanted Hatamura to meet the old man to pay his respects. Beyond that, Tsuji explained that there were issues he needed to discuss with his old friend.

Okamura's house was located on a sloping lot in the shadow of a new elevated expressway. It was separated from the neighboring lots by a plain stuccoed wall, but when the limousine drove through the gate, Hatamura saw that it was a newly built structure with a well-kept Japanese garden commanding a wonderful view of the central Tokyo skyline. An attractive woman wearing a light grey silk kimono was waiting at the door of the vestibule as the men got out of the car. She could have been in her early forties, although Tsuji knew she was actually sixty-three.

"Tsuji-san, Welcome. It is so good to see you again," said the woman with an easy bow. "Grandfather has been looking forward to your visit."

"As have I, Sachiko-san, as have I," Tsuji said, returning her bow. "How is the old man?"

"Some days are better than others," she replied with a pleasant smile and another easy bow. "Today he is full of pep because of your visit."

"You are looking very well, Sachiko-san. I want you to know that I truly appreciate the help you have given to the old man."

"And we both appreciate your many kindnesses to us." Again she bowed but this was a more polite, formal bow and her face took on a serious look.

"I brought you a small gift," Tsuji said, giving her two neatly wrapped packages. The smaller of them contained a bottle of very expensive French perfume. "There is also a box of the sweet bean paste from the Takase district that the old man likes. Would you open it and bring it to us?"

"Of course, Tsuji-san. You are very kind," and she took the packages with another bow. "Grandfather is waiting inside."

Leaving their shoes in the vestibule, Tsuji and Hatamura followed Sachiko to a room that was opened to the garden. Okamura was dressed in a padded kimono over a cardigan sweater and a wool union suit. He was seated on the tatami floor at a low table with a quilt covering his legs and feet. When he saw Tsuji he looked up with bright eyes and a broad smile.

"My son, my son. Welcome and come in. It is a pleasure to see you." The old man's voice crackled with a phlegmy cough, but he was clearly very pleased to see his guests.

Tsuji dropped to his knees and bowed deeply to the old man. "Father, forgive me for not being more attentive."

"No, no. It is I who has had too little contact."

Sachiko placed two cushions on the floor beside the table. Tsuji took one and said, "Father, I want you to meet one of my newest *kobun*. This is Hatamura Joji. He has proven to be a dependable supporter. I think he has a great future within our Brotherhood."

Hatamura knelt in a deep bow to the old man who squared his shoulders and gave as deep a bow as he was able from his seated position.

Speaking to Hatamura, the old man said, "Welcome to my house and to our Brotherhood. I have complete faith in my son's decisions. I am sure you will do well and I wish you well within our community."

"Grandfather, I am honored to meet a man who is famous throughout Japan," said Hatamura. "I only hope that I can serve the Brotherhood with your dedication and wisdom."

From the doorway Sachiko said, "Tsuji-san brought us some Takase bean paste, Grandpa. I'll set it out and bring some tea."

"I also brought you some of the good Cuban cigars I know you like, Father," said Tsuji setting a gift wrapped box on the table. "I know Sachiko won't let you have them often, but I think one will do you no harm."

The old man chuckled at this levity and took the package. "You are too generous, Son. Thank you. Sachiko said you had some business to discuss with me. What can I do to help?"

"Father there is a matter you must advise me on," Tsuji began seriously. The old man leaned forward and looked at him intently.

"I am sorry to report that Sergeant Vincent Torelli has died."

The old man set his face with a serious look and nodded sagely. "That is sad news. Vince-san was a loyal friend and an important contact for our organization. When did you hear?"

"Our contact in New York faxed me the message last night, sir. He died yesterday in a hospital in his hometown of Hoboken. That is somewhere near New York City."

"I don't think that I can travel to the funeral," the old man said, "but we must send a representative. Will you go?"

"Father, I never met Sergeant Torelli although I hosted both his son and his daughter when they studied here in Japan. They were polite young people." Tsuji said no more because he did not wish to contradict Okamura's positive comments about the American. In fact, Tsuji had been very disappointed in the two clean cut Ivy League students Torelli had sent to Japan in the 1960s. Both seemed like serious students but they had not been interested in the business contacts Tsuji had been willing to arrange.

"Our Brotherhood must be represented," the old man said firmly. "Send a good man and make sure he brings many large bouquets." The old man gave this as an order and Tsuji replied politely.

"Yes, Father. Most of my contacts with Sergeant Torelli's organization have been handled through intermediaries, but I have one man in America who has had some contact with his people. I will send him as our representative."

"Is he a good man? Does he know how to present himself and us?" the old man asked sternly.

"Don't worry, Father. He has run our sword return operation for some time so he understands Americans. He'll do fine."

"That will be fine." The old man no longer gave many orders, but a lifetime spent in the rigid hierarchy of the Kawabayashi Brotherhood made his expectation of total obedience automatic. Tsuji was happy to comply with the directive he had been given, but Okamura continued as if he had to explain his actions.

"In the days of poverty and disorganization after the war, our Brotherhood worked hard to organize our country. Our greatest challenge was working with the Americans. Many of them were shamelessly greedy and dishonest. The rest were either stupid or unrealistic. We simply couldn't work with them. Vince-san was different. He was honorable. He knew how to accept a gift. He remembered his friends and his word was always good."

Tsuji was pleased to find his friend and patron in the Kawabayashi Brotherhood hearty and talkative. The last time they had met, Okamura had been frail and uncertain, not at all like the vigorous middle-aged man who had befriended Tsuji when he was an orphaned teenager after the war. Reminiscing about the days when he had been one of the major players in the Japanese underworld was clearly good for the old man so Tsuji let conversation continue.

"Vince-san was a *shira-nabe*," the old man said using the post-war slang for an American Military Policeman who were called "white pots" because of the shiny white helmet liners they wore. "In the years before the Korean War, he patrolled the district around the Tokyo PX. We met him there and after we got acquainted, he helped us acquire things we needed - gasoline, tires. It was through Vince-san that we got to know many of the other MP's as well." The old man leaned forward on one elbow.

"I was very disappointed when his enlistment was up and he went back to America," he said. He looked over to Sachiko who had returned to the room. "I was not the only one. Vince wanted to marry Sachiko." The old man said this with a playful tone in his voice, but Tsuji saw that Sachiko suddenly looked sad. She turned her face from his gaze.

"In fact, Vince-san proved even more useful to us after he went home. He had very good contacts in the New York area. Nowadays I know you get your guns from the Philippines and China, but we couldn't do that back then. When we had to acquire *chaka* in the years after the Korean War, Vince got us what we needed and shipped everything to us through friends in the Army. We also worked with him and his associates to get shipments of transistor radios through the port of New York for our friends at Imperial Electronics. Sergeant Torelli helped solve serious shipping problems and made our friends at Imperial very successful in America," the old man chuckled.

Tsuji didn't want to let Okamura grow tired, but he was glad Hatamura was getting a chance to listen to the old man's recollections.

"Father, thank you for explaining these things to us. I appreciate the insights, and you may rest assured that the Kawabayashi Brotherhood will be represented at Sergeant Torelli's funeral." The old man accepted this filial expression with a nod, but he seemed interested in talking some more.

"Tell me how things are going, my son. What problems are you working on?" With a wave of his hand he motioned Sachiko to fill the teacup again.

"Father, you know life in the Brotherhood. There is always something. From here, Hatamura-san and I have to attend to a shipment just arrived from overseas."

"More *chaka*?" the old man asked. When Tsuji nodded his answer, he grimaced his disapproval. "I don't like all the guns you young men are letting into our country. They will fall into the wrong hands. In the old days if we needed more than our fists, the Brothers used swords.

Tsuji knew the old man would not approve of importing more guns and he held no hope of explaining the modern world the Brotherhood found itself within. He wanted to avoid an argument.

"The Brotherhood is still committed to the sword, Father. Our sword return operation has brought thousands of blades back into the country. In so doing we've made a good profit and become well-armed."

"I am pleased you have kept the Brotherhood interested in swords. Swords have always been important to us, son." The old man seemed glad he did not have to continue his scolding tone.

"When I was a young man coming up, we all carried swords. And we could use them, too. You should have seen how the strikers would run when they saw us open our *happi* coats to show our swords."

"When was that, Grandfather?" asked Hatamura.

"There were lots of modern troublemakers in the years after the new Emperor took the throne." The old man had been speaking fairly standard Tokyo Japanese, but as he continued he began to reverse the syllables of some common words and used others in nonstandard ways. Tsuji hadn't heard anyone use this old style underworld slang in years and he felt a wave of nostalgia.

"Foreign ideas were everywhere in those years and both Chinese and Koreans were flooding into the country. We got lots of business from companies, and even the major combines, protecting their factories. That's how I got my start in the Brotherhood."

Again the old man was sharing interesting reminiscences that Tsuji was glad to hear.

"I was seventeen and working as a carter so I was strong and knew my way through the city. A street organizer named Noda asked me to help break up a strike at the Imperial Heavy Industries plant. He offered to pay me as much every day as I'd been making in a week and he gave me a *wakizashi* to use." The old man's eyes were twinkling.

"I took the job for the money, but I made a name for myself my first night out. I cut the arm off one of the strikers." As he said this the old man used his open hand to make a slight slashing motion and let his smile turn into soft chuckle.

"With the stump of his arm spurting blood he ran toward the crowd yelling that he was hurt." Holding his left arm above his head, the old man made a silly face and bounced to show how the striker had looked. All three of the men laughed and even Sachiko smiled. After a moment, the old man continued.

"That brought me to the attention of Yamanouchi Toshihiro who became my *Oyabun* and brought me into the Kawabayashi Brotherhood,"

Okamura sipped his tea, then continued.

"Right after the war, swords again became very important to the Brotherhood. The Americans supported the police so things were peaceful, but nobody had any money. We got involved in collecting swords and other old things simply because they were valuable."

"I don't understand, Grandfather. What did the Brotherhood do with the swords you collected?" Hatamura asked genuinely uncertain about what the old man was describing.

"The same thing we do with everything else we get. We used them to support the Brothers and their friends. Many we sold, some we used ourselves. We also gathered some treasures on commission for others who were worried they would be lost."

"Forgive me, Grandfather, but how did the Brotherhood assemble the treasures," Hatamura asked.

"How does the Brotherhood ever assemble treasures?" the old man asked. "We took them! You weren't even born then, and Tsuji-kun was just a kid, but he remembers what things were like. The country was destroyed. There was no food, no money, and only the Americans in charge. The Brotherhood had to step in to get things moving. We had to preserve what would have been lost. Art objects were the only things of value so we used to trade them for what we needed. There were some people in government and industry wanted to protect the country's treasures and swords were a special problem. The Americans were rounding them up and throwing them in the ocean! We had to do something."

Tsuji suddenly remembered Counselor Odagiri's request. "Father, what happened to the swords and other things the Brotherhood assembled?"

"Most of the great treasures made their way into the hands of men from old families and big industries. I assume that's where they still are." The old man stopped to wipe his mouth with a napkin.

"The old leaders were afraid of the Americans, but we were not. The Americans had what everybody needed and we were willing to undertake tasks the old leaders were afraid to. It worked well. Powerful people got what they wanted and so did the Brothers," the old man shrugged.

"Treasure swords we grabbed for others were only part of it, of course. We got lots more. Some we kept, but we sold most of them. All the GIs wanted swords as souvenirs, so many went to them. Of course, soldiers were confiscating swords on their own and stole a great many more after they had been turned in. Later on the officers' wives bought pottery and pictures and other things, but right after the war, swords were valuable when nothing else was." He paused before adding as an afterthought, "I sold Vince-san a couple of swords. They may have been pretty good."

Okamura paused deep in thought. He turned to Sachiko and said, "Fetch my *tanto*." As she left the room, he said, "I never carried a *chaka*, but I always had a blade. Even now, I feel uncomfortable without one."

Sachiko returned with a short silk brocade bag which she gave to the old man. His fingers were unsure as he loosened the cord that closed it, but when the knot fell away, he slid a short wooden storage mount from the bag and passed it to Hatamura.

The young man took the dagger with a bow to the old man. Anxious to show he understood sword etiquette, Hatamura began by inspecting the wooden mounting. He saw that it was of top quality but that it had no ink inscription describing the blade it contained.

"This is a beautiful *shira-saya*, Grandfather."

"Thank you," the old man said with a nod of acknowledgment. "The dagger was polished by Odaira Kiichi just before he became a Living National Treasure. He had the fitting made and also had me register it with the police." Hatamura looked at the sword registration card which was in a clear plastic case attached to the scabbard by a rubber band.

"After all the years I'd carried it in my belt, I didn't like letting the *pori* know about it, but the polisher was very afraid. He wouldn't have it in his shop unless it was registered. We had to register it in Sachiko's name because the *pori* would never let me have a sword. It's Sachiko's now," the old man laughed. "At least, I got a 'black number,'" he added with an ironic tone.

Hatamura saw that the registration number on the card in the case was printed in black ink. Like all other swords, blades brought back to Japan from abroad have to be registered with the police, but unlike blades that had never left the country, imported swords were registered with red numbers that carry a mild stigma.

Hatamura read the blade's signature from the card. "This is a Masahide blade," he said..

"Indeed. Please take a look," Okamura said with a wave of his hand.

The younger man put the dagger down on the table and placed a paper napkin between his teeth. This would catch the moisture of his breathe so that it would not condense on the blade. With the napkin in place, he brought the dagger to the level of his face and bowed toward it. Carefully, he pulled the blade from the scabbard. The fit was tight so he had to pull hard, but when it was free he could see that it was a fine blade with an absolutely flawless polish. The wood-grained structure within the steel stood out boldly and the wavy heat-treated edge formed a beautiful milky surface. "It's fabulous, Grandfather."

"Sachiko, get him a hammer. He needs to see the signature." Sachiko got a small brass hammer from a drawer in one of the iron-mounted chests in the room. Replacing the blade in the scabbard, Hatamura unscrewed the short punch from the end of the hammer and with it carefully drove the bamboo peg out of the handle of the mounting. This peg held the tang in the handle so that when it was removed, Hatamura was able to slip the blade out of the handle.

Setting the handle aside, he looked at the finely cut characters on the tang. "These are difficult old characters, Grandfather."

"They say the blade was made in Edo by Masahide for the Great Lord Shimoda. On the reverse, the date shows it was made in the third year of Bunka, nearly 185 years ago."

Hatamura spent several minutes examining the blade. He was not a serious student of swords and did not understand all of what he was looking at, but to have looked more briefly at the sword would have been impolite. After what he felt was an appropriate length of time, he passed the dagger blade to Tsuji who accepted it with a bow. Holding it only by the tang, Tsuji looked at the blade and said, "This was the first fine sword I saw. I remember when you carried it, Father." He returned the blade to Hatamura who put it back in its mounts.

"Father, I have recently been presented with another problem that you might be able to help me with. At least it will be of interest," Tsuji said.

The old man again leaned forward with a look of sincere concern. "What is it, my son?"

"Because of the success of our sword return operation, I was recently asked to search for some specific swords that were lost after the war."

The old man nodded. "Which swords have you been asked to find?"

"A pair taken from the Omon Hachiman Shrine in Takasaka after the war."

"Ah yes, the Omon swords," Okamura nodded. "I remember them. We were very upset when they were stolen from us. Who wants them now?"

" Odagiri Satoshi, the politician. He wants them returned to the shrine his organization is rebuilding at Takasaka."

"Those swords were lying about ignored after the war," the old man scoffed. "They were just out there at that country shrine when we decided to pick them up. I don't even think we had a commission for them, but after we selected them, they were stolen from us!" he said with force that surprised Tsuji.

Tsuji looked quizzically at his patron. "Explain that to me, Father," he asked.

"We often worked with the Americans, but sometimes there were problems. That's what happened at Omon."

"How did you work with the Americans?"

"Mostly we just provided the labor for them," Okamura explained. "In the very early days, they were picking up weapons, but they didn't know how to talk with people and didn't know where things were. We helped them."

"Weren't those contacts and arrangements difficult, Father?"

"Not really. The civil authorities would set things up," the old man explained. "The Americans would tell the police or the city officials to send them helpers. The leaders would select us." The old man shrugged. "It was a good arrangement. Nobody else wanted to work for the foreigners and we knew where things were. The Americans didn't care. If anything, they liked us because we were organized and could get things done! We let the leaders know what the Americans were up to. We could keep them away from things they didn't need to know about and, occasionally, we could help ourselves to the things we were handling." With a chuckle, the old man grinned, "If there had been anything to eat, it could have been a great time."

"What happened at Takasaka, Father?" Tsuji pressed.

"I don't remember the details, but I think in that case we had an Army officer who would pick up things we wanted. We let him keep some things he wanted and we kept quiet about his visits to young men. When he got greedy, we had to take care of him, but his men made off with the swords we wanted from Omon."

"What happened to the swords, Father?"

"I don't think we ever found out. I suppose we tried to get them back, but it came to nothing." The old man put this fist over his mouth so that he could clear his throat, but when he did it set off a spasm of coughing that he could barely control. Sachiko came to his side and helped him take a sip of tea. Tsuji was alarmed.

"Father, we have stayed far too long," Tsuji said. "We must be going."

Okamura motioned him to remain as he caught his breath and regained his composure. After a moment and a sip of tea, he continued.

"Things changed very quickly in those years. We didn't have time to worry about lost opportunities. We had to move on to other matters. Someone had to organize the bars and clubs and with all the Americans there was tremendous need for brothels. Then we got involved with construction and land acquisition." The old man paused again. "Those became the new treasures. They made us rich and put us in contact with important people. We had to ignore the ancient treasures then, but we must remember our past. If Odagiri wants the Takasaka swords badly enough, let him have them, but you should find them because they are ours."

Again the old man began coughing. As Sachiko comforted him, she shared a worried glance with Tsuji.

"Father, Hatamura-kun and I will go now and leave you and Sachiko in peace. We have enjoyed your insights and appreciate your generosity."

Tsuji and Hatamura moved toward the door. The old man returned their bow as he fought to control his coughing. When he was able he smiled and said, "Thank you both for coming. It has been a pleasure to remember old times and to realize the our Brotherhood is in good hands."

"Thank you, Father," said Tsuji before he directed Hatamura out of the room and then followed him. Sachiko accompanied the men to the front door.

"I am sorry we stayed so long, Sachiko-san. I fear we wore the old man out."

"He was very pleased to see to see you, but I think he will sleep soundly. Thank you for coming and for the wonderful gifts you brought us both. You are extremely generous."

"Nonsense, Sachiko-san. I always enjoy the old man and this evening he has given me some especially useful information."

6 | Ken Sawada

In which we observe the search for treasures.

Peoria, Illinois - present day

Ken Sawada, cosmopolitan Japanese who spends most weekends in American motels buying Japanese swords and other "military antiques"

"Where do over-size bags come out?" Ken Sawada asked of the only employee he could find in the Peoria, Illinois airport.

"Pardon me," the young woman behind the United Airlines counter asked as she jotted down the number of tickets she had counted before Ken had interrupted her.

"Over-size bags. Where do they come out?" he asked again when she looked up. Ken disliked repeating himself. He knew his English pronunciation was less than perfect but suspected some Americans misunderstood him on purpose.

"You mean over-size luggage from the Chicago flight?" the woman asked pleasantly, but with a slightly patronizing tone.

"Yeah. I have four gun cases, but they are not on the conveyer." Ken spoke slowly and clearly. The woman seemed to understand. Business trips brought Ken to lots of small towns and he was used to dealing with unsophisticated Americans. Small town airport personnel tended to treat him with pleasant disdain. Motel employees and rental car workers, who were even less sophisticated, often reacted with irritation or dumbfounded uncertainty when they had trouble with either Ken's English or his requests. Ken tried to not let it bother him, but it was among the worst parts of his life.

"Things too big for the conveyer will be brought to the double doors at the center of the back wall of the lobby." The young woman smiled reflexively as she said this and used her open hand to point to the back wall.

"Thanks," Ken responded with his own smile. There had been a time when he had found girls like this one very attractive, but that had passed. Dealing with American women was simply too difficult.

The liaisons he had had on his trips had all been uninteresting and difficult.

Before Ken got to the double doors, a man in coveralls had opened them and pushed four orange plastic gun cases toward the luggage conveyer. Ken placed the cases with the two suitcases that had already arrived, and since there were no porters, he left the six pieces in a pile near the conveyer. Taking only his attaché case, he proceeded to the car rental counter. His travel agent made a reservation for a car to be waiting. He showed the agent his Oregon driver's license and, to guarantee payment, his one and only credit card. He made a point of telling the agent he would be paying the bill with cash. She assured him that would be no problem. Ken paid for everything with cash. It was the way he did business, but he always liked to make sure that cash would be acceptable. Experience had taught him that most American clerks preferred the cashless transactions of credit cards because it made their accounting easier.

On his way to the car, Ken picked up a copy of the local newspaper to make sure his ad had appeared properly. An agency in New Jersey placed the ads and made all of his travel arrangements. He simply told them where he would be going and when he wanted to travel. They did the rest. There were rarely any problems.

Ken paged through the paper until he found the ad on page twelve. It was one of his standard ads filling a quarter page directly in front of the classified section. Large type across the top announced that a Japanese buyer would be in the area offering cash for Japanese swords, military antiques and Japanese art objects. Below were pictures of a *tachi*, a *tsuba*, a Nazi dagger, and the outline of an Iron Cross. The next lines explained that Mr. Ken Sawada was a Japanese sword expert interested in bringing family heirlooms back to Japan. This version of the ad did not have a smiling picture of Ken, but it did mention he was prepared to pay up to $200,000 for a single sword. Large dollar signs were in each corner to emphasize the point.

In the middle of the ad there was a long list of things Ken was willing to buy. In addition to Japanese swords, armor, and matchlock rifles, it included German daggers, pins and badges, helmets, and uniforms and Japanese art objects like woodblock prints, lacquered trays, and ceramics.

Mentioning the Japanese art objects in the ads was a recent addition Ken was still trying out. So far it hadn't brought in much. One woman in Colorado had brought in a pile of dishes marked 'Nippon' and had been very upset when Ken would not even make an offer for them. That sort of thing could be a hassle, but the previous spring, Ken had given a colonel's widow four hundred dollars for a lacquer box that sold for eighteen thousand in Tokyo. Buys like that were good enough to make sifting through the junk worthwhile.

Ken had forgotten this weekend's ad mentioned both German and Japanese war souvenirs. Mentioning German things was definitely optional in Ken's view because in big cities there were enough Japanese swords to keep him busy. He also worried that mentioning Nazi regalia might put people off. That had never been a problem in the Midwest and Nazi souvenirs were so common and so valuable they were hard to ignore. Ken faced a minor problem now, however; he had not brought any Nazi things with him.

Over the years, Ken found it was easiest for people to part with their souvenirs if he could show them things others had already sold. For that reason, he always began his buying weekends with some pieces he could claim to have "just bought." There were a couple of swords in one of his gun cases for that purpose. With no German items, he would have to fake it until he had acquired a couple of souvenirs he could legitimately show off.

The bottom third of the ad outlined Ken's schedule for the coming days. He checked this part of the ad most carefully. Tonight and tomorrow he would be in the Holiday Inn in Peoria. On Saturday, he would go to the Holiday Inn in Bloomington before spending Sunday at The Illini Motel in Champaign. He was scheduled to fly back to Oregon on Monday evening. It would be a busy weekend, but the dates in the ad were what Ken had expected and he was satisfied that the weekend would go smoothly.

The clerk at the Holiday Inn was ready for Ken. She gave him the slips on a couple of calls that had already come in for him and she was eager to show how the front meeting room had been set up for his use. As she prepared the registration, Ken explained he would be paying cash. She assured him that would be fine, but she asked for a credit card to guarantee the bill. Ken grudgingly gave her his card and shuffled through the message slips. Four were from people who called in response to the ad. The fifth, from his answering service, was marked urgent.

The ad said Ken would begin his buying at 3:00 PM. and experience indicated that people would begin arriving then or sooner so he had to hurry. He asked the clerk to have all six of his bags brought to the meeting room while he went to the room where he would be staying. As soon as he got there, he called his answering service. The operator read him a message that had come in some hours earlier.

"Mr. Sawada, you got a call from a Mr. Oyabun in Tokyo. I'm not sure I understood it right, but he said he wants your fax number right away. He said 'Very important' a couple of times. I asked for a number, but he said you'd have it. Does that make any sense?"

Ken said it did and thanked her. As soon as he hung up, he ran to the front desk, got the motel's fax number, and ran back to his room where he punched in the numbers for an overseas call. He reached a sleepy voice in Tokyo who took his name and his fax number, but offered nothing that might explain why Tsuji-san wanted to contact him.

Ken hoped there were no problems. He worried that he might have done something wrong at the funeral, even though everything had seemed to have gone well. Certainly, no one had communicated any displeasure to him while he was there, but Ken had never been at an Italian funeral before. If he had committed some error and word of a problem had gotten back to Tsuji-san it could be very serious.

Ken was genuinely worried, but there was nothing he could do and, since it was after 2:30, he had to get ready for business. The clerk had a man in gray work clothes show Ken the meeting room he had rented. Ken scanned it with approval. Since it was right off the main lobby, people would have no trouble finding their way in. It was well lit and large enough so people would not feel cramped. He asked only to have more ashtrays and an easel brought to the room. After the man left, Ken called the front desk to order a pot of coffee, some ice water, and a dozen cups. When all of that was done, he got his folding sign and some balloons out of his largest suitcase. The sign said, "**SWORD BUYER**" in large letters and it would be placed on the easel outside the door. Ken always put a few balloons at the top of the easel as a festive attention getter. Ken took the pair of swords he had brought with him out of the gun cases and set them in plain view on one of the tables against the back wall. Just as he was finishing these preparations his first visitors of the day arrived at the door.

Turning to see two men at the door, Ken said, "Hello. Please come in." He smiled and extended his hand to the older of the men as he said, "I'm Ken Sawada."

"How do you do? I'm Lester Jacobson and this is my son-in-law Mark Wilson."

Ken shook hands with Mark and invited them to sit at the table near the front of the room. He saw that the older man had a small parcel and that the son-in-law was carrying a sword wrapped in a terry cloth towel. The older man was old enough to be a World War II veteran and the younger man may have been in his forties. Both men wore khaki pants and flannel shirts.

As soon as Ken sat down opposite the men, he got right to work. "I see you got a sword there," he said.

"Yes," Mr. Jacobson said, "I got this in Japan after the war," and he began to remove the rubber bands that held the towel in place. "Now, you call it a sword, but they told me at the time that this was a 'saber.'"

"Yeah, there are lots of words for swords," said Ken trying to avoid either an argument or a lecture. Veterans were almost always eager to tell stories about the things they brought to Ken. If they needed time to make up their minds or show him all their things, Ken would let them talk. When he could, he tried to keep the conversations as short as possible.

When the towel fell free, Ken saw that the sword was a standard Army officer's sword. Most of these contain mass-produced blades with no collectors' appeal. Ken couldn't ignore them, however, because some officers had had fine old blades remounted as army swords.

Ken took the sword as soon as Mr. Jacobson laid it on the table. While he examined it, the old man spoke.

"I got that saber after the war. They made me a clerk so I didn't get out much, but I grabbed that one, because a Jap boy who was working for us said it was a good one."

"Really?" asked Ken as he looked up from the sword. "This is a military sword, made during the war." The old man nodded blankly and Ken proceeded to dismount the weapon. He took a brass punch and a small hammer from his attaché case and used them to drive the bamboo peg out of the handle. It came free easily which Ken took to mean that the sword had been inspected by others. "Is the blade signed?" he asked.

"Yeah. There's some writing in the end of the blade, there," acknowledged the old man.

With the peg removed. Ken unlatched his wristwatch band and rapped his left wrist sharply as he held the sword with the blade pointed away from them. One firm blow was all that was necessary for the blade to jump lose of the mounting. Ken grasped the blade by its small brass collar and slipped it out of the handle.

"It's really somethin' how those things just come apart like that," the son-in-law said. Ken did not look up, but noted the young man's familiarity and assumed it meant that the old man had more swords than the one that had been presented.

"Yeah. This sword was made in August 1943," Ken said showing the dated side of the tang to the two men. Turning it over to examine the signature of the maker he said, "This side says it was made by a swordsmith named 'Masatoshi.' He lived in a town called Seki. There were lots of swords made there during the War."

Then, holding the tang so the men could see it clearly, he pointed to a small stamped mark above the signature. "See this stamp? It says 'kan' and that means this sword was made with factory steel. This is a military sword, not an art sword. It's in good condition, though, very clean."

"Do you buy swords like this one?" the old man asked pointedly.

"Well, I can use these, but military swords can't go back to Japan so I can't pay too much. You have others?"

"Let's talk about this one. What's somethin' like that worth?" the old man said firmly.

Some veterans brought their swords in simply to talk about them. Some lonely old men just wanted an audience for their recollections. Ken was even sure that some of the men who responded to his ads simply wanted to irritate their old enemies by showing off war trophies they would never sell. Some brought their souvenirs in for a free appraisal. That might be why this old man was here, but the fact that he had brought his son-in-law seemed to mean that he was ready to act. In any case, Ken was sure the sword he been shown was a test of his knowledge and seriousness. It had almost certainly been shown to other collectors and dealers and the old man probably knew something about its age and value. If Ken could beat the other offers the old man had received for this sword, he was sure that he would be able to see other swords.

"This a nice clean sword. I can pay you, four-fifty for it." In fact, Ken would barely sell it for that price, but he felt he had to make a maximum offer. His strategy worked. The old man looked at his son-in-law who nodded with raised eye brows. There was a whispered exchange that ended when the old man gave his car keys to the younger.

"I've got a couple of other swords you might want to see."

Ken poured a cup for the old man and asked him when he been in Japan. He didn't want to encourage him to become too conversational, but had to keep him busy until his son-in-law returned. It might also be useful to know where the swords had been acquired.

"I was at Yazuyama from September of '45 until the April of '46. They wanted me to stay in, but I wanted to get home so I got out when I could."

Ken had never heard of Yazuyama. If the old man remembered the name correctly, it was probably an obscure neighborhood or a suburb that had long since been absorbed into one of modern Japan's cities, so Ken moved the conversation in another direction. "You were in the army?" he asked.

"Yes. I went in in 1943 and trained for Europe, but they sent me to the Philippines. I landed at Okinawa on the fifth day of the invasion. I stayed there 'til the war was over and then they sent us up to Japan. I was a Technical Sergeant in a Depot Battalion."

"Really!" said Ken. He was not merely being polite. Working in depots meant that the old man had been in a position to acquire swords as they were being surrendered to the Americans. Most of what he had access to would have been military swords, but amongst them there could have been some good older weapons. The trouble was, of course, that GIs hadn't known the good swords from the bad. The swords Ken was waiting for could be anything and he didn't want to let his hopes get too high.

When the conversation lagged as they waited for the son-in-law to return, Ken couldn't help wondering about the message from Tokyo. He had no idea what Tsuji-san wanted and he could only hope there was no problem. The funeral seemed to have gone well, but who can know about such things. Perhaps he had done something offensive or embarrassing and word had gotten back to the *Oyabun*.

When the son-in-law returned, he had a blanket-wrapped bundle under his arm. Ken had him put it on the table where he unrolled it to reveal four swords.

In these situations Ken always tried to start with the worst sword since it encouraged people to have low expectations. Sometimes it was hard to pick out an obviously bad piece, but in this case the choice was easy. Ken picked up a light sword with a chromed scabbard and a European style handle. "This is a machine made parade sword for an Army officer," he said.

"Now, a fellow I talked to said that was a police sword," the old man replied.

"No. It's not police. Police swords look kind of like this, but they have the police crest right here," Ken said pointing to the back of the handle. He used a firm tone to sound authoritative and to discourage the old man from arguing. Ken put the parade sword down without looking at it. The old man waited for him to proceed.

Next, Ken selected another officer's sword. He held it edge upward and smoothly pulled the blade out of the scabbard. For a moment he held the bare blade at arms length to consider its shape before bringing it closer so he could examine its surface.

"This is a nice blade," he said. "It was made by a rear swordsmith during the War. It not very old, but it's a nice sword. I can use these."

Without asking permission or even looking at the men, Ken proceeded to push the peg out of the handle and remove the blade as he had done with the other sword. Ken wanted to remain in charge and authoritative so he moved confidently. When the tang of the blade was exposed, he inspected it and was pleased with what he saw.

"This blade is not dated, but I think it was made in about 1941. Not very old. It's signed by a sword maker who lived in Tokyo. His name 'Yasunori.'" Ken looked at the men as he explained this, but as soon as he was done, he reassembled the sword and set it aside. This sword had been made by one of the leaders of the group of smiths who worked at the forge set up to make army swords at the Yasukuni Shrine in Tokyo. Even though it dated from the war years, it was much more valuable than the arsenal sword Ken had looked at first because, as a hand-crafted sword, it could be returned to Japan. Beyond that, with their strong nationalistic associations, the Yasukuni Shrine swords were becoming quite collectible. Of course, Ken felt no need to explain any of this to the old man and didn't want him to know its greater worth. He simply reassembled the sword and set it aside.

Both of the swords Ken had left until last appeared to be interesting. One was a long sword, or *katana*, in a plain wood storage mount. The fitting was dirty and had been repaired with black plastic tape, but Ken saw that there was an old attribution written on the scabbard. He selected it next and, as he slid the blade out of the scabbard, was pleased to see that even though the mountings were dirty, the blade was clean and in very good polish. As before, he began by holding the bare blade at arm's length to check its shape. Next, he hooked the end of a steel tape measure on the point of the sword to measure its length. At seventy-two centimeters or twenty-eight inches, it was a desirable length. With only this much inspection, Ken had seen enough to know that this was a well-made old sword.

Ken was not a trained *kantei-ka*, but he had seen a great many swords over the past six years. Even if he could not immediately identify the age and maker of every sword he saw, he was a good judge of quality and this sword was worth a lot.

"This is another nice sword," Ken said turning to his visitors. Using only his brass punch, he was able to push out the bamboo peg that held the wooden handle. With a few light taps to his wrist, the blade slid free. It had a nice old tang, with deep black rust that showed the sword's age. A couple of characters were faintly visible on one side.

"This says 'Nobuyoshi'. He's not too famous, but he made swords in the 1400s." In fact Ken was not familiar with this name, but that was not necessarily bad. Too often if he found a well-known swordsmith's name on a tang, it turned out to be a fake signature. The names of nearly seventeen thousand swordsmiths are recorded in Japan and Ken didn't feel he had to remember all of them. There were a couple of egg-heads in Tokyo who probably knew them all, but in Ken's world that would be a waste of effort.

"It's really something how those blades stay so shiny," the son-in-law said. "They must have been made out of real good steel."

"Yeah, the steel is very good, but they also kept them polished," Ken explained as he quickly checked the blade to make sure he had not missed any serious flaws. He scanned the edge to make sure there were no *ha-giri*, or edge cracks. These might be no bigger than a whisker, but one of them would destroy the value of a sword. Ken also let light reflect off one side of the blade and then the other to be sure that there were no *fukure*, blisters caused when rust creeps between the laminations of the steel. When he was sure the sword was sound, he quickly put it back in its mounts and turned to the last blade.

It was a *kyu-gunto,* an old army sword, carried by Japanese officers from the late 19th century through the 1930s. These fittings were a modified European design with a nickled scabbard and long D-shaped handle. Regulations were relaxed at that time and all of the swords had been the private purchase of individual officers so they varied greatly. A collectors' interest was developing in these old style mountings and Ken knew they often contained very good blades. This particular sword was a good deal smaller and more delicate than some *kyu-gunto*. As Ken picked it up he also saw that it had and extra engraved embellishment along the backstrap of the handle indicating it had been carried by a general officer.

"This is an old army sword. The type carried around 1900 when Japan was fighting Russia." Ken gave this information in an offhand manner as he examined the blade. His primary goal was simply to stay in contact with the old man.

"Now, is that one different from the one you called a parade sword?" Jacobson asked.

"Yes. It was made before the war and the blade is old." In fact, Ken could see that the blade was a fine one in very good condition. As he began to take its handle off, the old man leaned forward to see what he was doing.

"Now, does the handle come off of that one, too?" he asked as Ken drove the peg out of its handle and began to dislodge the blade. This blade was very securely set in the handle. Unlike the old man's other swords, this handle appeared to have been on since 1945.

"Well, I'll be darned," the old man said as it became obvious that Ken knew what he was doing. "I never knew that one came apart." He cocked his head to bring his bifocals into focus.

Ken had to pound on his wrist several times to get the blade loose and when he started to work free he had to work it back and forth because the fit was tight. When it was finally out, Ken set the handle aside and examined the signature.

"This is another nice sword. I like it. It's signed 'Yamashiro Daijo Fujiwara Kunikane'. He made sword in a town called Sendai in the 1600s, maybe about 1620. Yeah, this is a nice sword." The old man was craning to look at the tang that Ken had exposed, but Ken started to reassemble it immediately. If the old man asked any questions, Ken would answer them, but as a rule, he volunteered very little information. Having satisfied himself that he wanted the swords, any more examination would simply get in the way of the transaction he now had to complete.

"I would like to buy these." Ken had found that a direct approach was best at this point.

"Well, they aren't doing me any good and our daughter Elaine doesn't want them around the house. So I would sell them, if I got what seemed like a fair price." said Jacobson with a couple of shrugs.

"You got a price in mind?" Ken asked. The old man appeared ready to sell and he wanted to keep the pressure on him.

"Well, I don't know what they're worth," the old man shrugged. "Are you a collector or are you buying these things for the families, or what?"

Ken wouldn't go into detail, but he was used to this question. "I work for an investors' group in Japan."

"Do you live in Japan, then and just come to America to buy swords?" the old man continued.

"I live in Oregon. My wife is American."

As Ken said this, another older man appeared at the door. His timing could not have been better and Ken was pleased to see he was carrying both a sword and a cloth shopping bag. "Hello, please come in." Ken smiled to the man and motioned him to a seat by the door. "Please, help yourself to coffee. I'll be with you in just a minute."

"What do you want to give me for the swords?" Jacobson asked in a slightly lowered voice. Ken moved closer to him and lined up all five of the man's swords. He considered them seriously and rubbed the back of his head before looking up.

"I can give you four thousand, five hundred dollars for all five sword," Ken said firmly but in a soft voice that the new man could not hear.

The old man was clearly impressed. He exhaled and stroked his chin and then turned to the young man. "What do you think, Mark?"

"It's up to you, Les. Lainny doesn't want them and that's a lot more money than that other guy offered you. You go ahead if you want to." Ken knew the deal was as good as closed.

"You'd pay with a check, then, or how would you pay me?" Jacobson asked turning back to Ken.

"Cash. No problem. I'll pay right now." Then to put just a little more pressure on the old man along he looked over to the other man who was still waiting beside the door. "I'll be right with you."

"I think that's a good price," Ken said. "Nobody else will pay more and I've got cash. Let's make a deal." This was one of a number of expressions Ken had learned from an East Coast dealer. Ken had hired the man to teach him colloquial expressions that would be polite but direct.

"Yeah, I think I will. I'll sell'em. Give me the money."

Ken immediately took a packet from his attaché case. He opened it to reveal a large stack of bills. He removed five paper-clipped packets of hundred dollar bills. He opened each one and counted them in front of the old man. When there were four piles of ten bills each and one with five laid out on the table, Ken said, "Please count them again."

The old man recounted the money methodically stopping occasionally to run his hand along his forehead or temple. "Gee, this is a lot of money," he said when he was done. Ken rose and held his hand out to the old man.

"I know you got to get on to the next person, but these are a couple of other things I brought home." He pushed a small paper sack toward Ken. "There's nothing much in there, but you can go ahead and have this stuff, too. I'll just throw it in on the deal."

"Great," Ken said taking the bag. "Thanks. Here's my card. If you've got other swords or friends who have things to sell, I'll be happy to buy it. Okay? Call me."

Ken shook hands with both men and walked them to the door. "Thanks again, You have a nice day," he said as he turned to the man who had been waiting. "I got to make just one call. I'll be right with you."

Ken used the phone at the back of the meeting room to call the front desk. They had no messages for him and said no fax had been received so Ken returned to the man waiting patiently at the front table.

"Sorry," Ken said as he sat down across the table from the man. "I'm waiting for an important call. Let's take a look at your sword."

The man placed it on the table and slid it toward Ken.

The sword was another *katana*, but nicely mounted in traditional fittings. At first glance, it seemed plain, but Ken saw immediately that was not the case. Its black scabbard was essentially unembellished and it had a plain iron guard or *tsuba* and handle with excellent fittings. Only members of the samurai class had been allowed to carry swords of this size and the mounts were of top quality. They showed the austere beauty that was the hallmark of samurai taste. Ken judged the fittings to date from the early Nineteenth century. The blade could, of course, be older.

"This is a pretty sword," Ken said pleasantly. "Where did you get it?" Again, he did not want to involve the owner in a long discussion, but the sword was good enough to suggest it might have some history.

"A gentleman in Tokyo gave it to me in 1953," the man said.

"Really?" Ken said.

"Yes. His name was Takahashi-san and we got to know him because he ran a small electrical shop near our quarters at Tachikawa. My wife took a flower arrangement class from his wife and we visited them several times. When we were getting ready to rotate back to the States, he gave me this."

"You were in the army?" Ken asked.

"Air Force," the man corrected. "I flew B-29's during the Korean War."

"I see," said Ken and turned his attention to the sword. He found the blade slightly scuffed but apparently well-made. He pushed the peg out of the handle and exposed the tang as the man looked on.

Looking at the signature, Ken said, "This blade was made by a swordsmith named Sadatoshi. He lived in Tokyo. He put a date on, too." With his free hand, Ken opened his attaché case to pull out a well-worn reference book. He thumbed through to a double page chart. "The date is the third year of *Tempo* which is the same as 1839. It's is just over 150 years old. Not too old," he smiled

"No," the man agreed. "Not too old for Japan."

Ken wanted to finish dealing with the sword, but the man put his shopping bag on the table and said. "Beside the sword, my wife and I brought home several other things." Ken had no choice, but to look at what was in the bag. There were a couple of framed woodblock prints, a set of antique blue and white teacups, and simple wooden box closed with a black braid. Ken untied the cord and opened the box to find a rustic old tea bowl wrapped in a silk cloth. The written inscription on the inside of the cover said the tea bowl dated from the Momoyama period and was from the kilns at Tamba. The inscription itself was dated in the third year of the *Meiji* period, 1870. Ken didn't translate any of this or even mention he had seen the inscription. Experience had told him that these sorts of things had some value, but that they are fragile and a nuisance to carry. He would have to be polite about the pottery and the prints, but his challenge would be buying the sword without having to take the other things.

"My wife passed away last year and I'm getting ready to move to a smaller place so it's time to get rid of some things."

Ken appreciated the man's directness. "Do you have a price in mind?"

"No, not really. A man from Chicago offered me twelve hundred dollars for the sword a couple of years ago, so I suppose it's worth at least that much."

"Oh yeah. It's worth more," Ken said setting the sword aside so he could look again at the teacups. Now that he had an idea of what the man was expecting, he realized it would be easier to simply make a package price and throw the pottery away than try to buy just the sword. After considering the things a few minutes, Ken looked up at the man and said, "I can give you thirty-four hundred for everything."

"That sounds fair," the man said, looking over the rather small pile of things on the table. "Let's do it."

Ken was not sure what that meant, but assuming it was positive, he opened his attaché case again and counted out three packets of hundred dollar bills and four single bills. Again, he opened each packet and counted the contents, then had the man recount them himself. When he was done, the man jogged the bills into a neat pile, rose, shook Ken's hand and left without even taking one of Ken's cards.

A steady stream of people kept Ken busy throughout the afternoon. A man who had been waiting outside the meeting room until the second man left sold Ken a German Army dagger, a canteen and a German helmet for $150. Another veteran brought in a German uniform and three more people brought in Japanese swords. One of these had been a young man who studied *iai-do*, Japanese swordsmanship. He tried to sell Ken a sword that had been sold to him by his martial arts instructor. Ken declined because it was a very inferior old sword that had been skillessly remounted in America. When Ken declined, the young man had pushed for an offer. To send him on his way, Ken had offered $125 simply because he was certain the American instructor had charged far more than that. The young man was crestfallen when he left with his sword. Aside from that all of the other transactions had been successful. Ken had spent more than $16,000 before dinner. At the usual rates, that would mean that he had made about three times that much for his Tokyo sponsors.

At just before 6:00 the front desk clerk came to the room with a two-page fax message that had been received for Ken. The first sheet was a short page of written Japanese. Ken took it with relief and scanned it hurriedly:

"We have been commissioned to find two swords stolen from the Takasaka Shrine in 1945. One is a tanto signed 'Muramasa.' The other is an unsigned long sword by 'Munemasa.' Do all you can to find these swords. Inform me as soon as you have any news. This is of utmost importance."

The second page was a rubbing of the dagger's tang. Rubbing a soft ink stick across a piece of fine paper held over the surface of the tang makes an exact, high contrast copy of the signature and all the other irregularities of the tang surface and shape. These rubbings or *oshigata* have been the standard way of recording sword signatures for centuries and continue to be popular because they reproduce well with either photocopy or fax.

The faxed rubbing was one that had been attached to an official inventory form before the war. The prewar characters printed on the margins of the form were not crisp, but the rubbing itself was sharp enough to read. It was a simple, two character signature. Blades by Muramasa are not common, but over the years Ken had seen some. That was probably why the rubbing looked familiar. Before he was able to consider the matter further a pair of old men entered the meeting room and Ken had to turn his attention to them.

One of the old men had a Japanese Army officer's sword with a wartime blade and a Type 94 pistol. Ken did not ordinarily buy firearms, but the old man was fairly insistent about selling both pieces so Ken bought it and the sword for $400. The other old man had only a couple of odd knives he had brought home from the Philippines. Ken did not want these and refused to make any kind of an offer for them, even though it was clear the man was disappointed.

When that pair left, Ken went to the dining room to get a dinner he could bring back to the buying room. As he ate, he looked through the bag of small items the first man of the day had left with him. There were several American badges and pins in the bag that Ken separated out as worthless. If space became tight, he would simply throw them away at the end of the weekend.

Far more interesting was a nice group of Japanese uniform insignia and badges. Ken had no interest in these sorts of things, but a couple of dealers in Tokyo were reporting strong interest in Imperial Army militaria among younger Japanese, so Ken bought such items when he could. The pieces in the bag included a Navy specialty badge in its original wooden box, an Army War College graduates breast badge, a sixth class Order of the Rising Sun without a box, and, best of all, a boxed breast badge for a third class Order of the Golden Kite. Ken had to shake his head in amazement as he realized that this bag of trinkets would probably pay for the entire weekend.

As he was finishing his dinner, another older couple dropped by with some German items, a helmet, a bayonet and some miscellaneous field gear Ken didn't recognize at all. He offered a hundred dollars for the lot and the couple left happy.

At that point there was a brief lull that allowed Ken to follow up the phone calls that had been waiting for him. He answered four calls that came in before he arrived and returned three that had come in since then. This process took a lot of time and energy and produced only marginal results. One woman apparently had a couple of Japanese swords that her husband had brought home. Ken made arrangements to visit her the next morning. None of the other calls were worthwhile. One man had asked if Ken had anything for sale. Another was angry that Ken was buying things in "his" area. This happened to Ken virtually every weekend. It was hard not to find them annoying, but they seemed to be part of his job. If Ken was to have any hope of reestablishing himself within the Kawabayashi Brotherhood, he would simply have to put up with these and all the other problems of his operation.

When 9:00 came, Ken was glad to be able to close the buying room. He called the front desk to request a cart. When it arrived, he assembled his purchases and other luggage so he could get back to his room to do what he had to before he could get to sleep. On his way past the front desk, Ken asked if they had any boxes since he knew he had bought many more things than he could carry in his luggage.

In his room, Ken arranged the swords he had bought during the afternoon into two piles. The smaller pile contained the six military swords with wartime blades. Some of these were quite handsome, but they were not what Ken was after because Japanese customs regulations block them from entering Japan because they are classified as mass-produced blades as "weapons" rather than "art objects." Since all officers in the Imperial Army and Navy had to wear swords, however, military swords formed the bulk of the blades that had been available to American GIs. They are so common that Ken could not avoid buying them. They had never been profitable and had even presented a marketing problem until a year and a half ago when Ken met a German dealer at the Baltimore

Gun Show. The German had agreed to pay four hundred dollars apiece for as many military swords as Ken could supply. That price barely allowed a profit, but the German had agreed to take possession of the swords in New York *and* he had been willing to make his payment into a German account. The sheer convenience of the deal had made it appealing to Ken. After Ken had explained it, Tsuji-san had also been very positive about the banking arrangements. Ken had no idea how the money was used, but Tsuji-san periodically informed him of new accounts he wanted the German to use. He also urged Ken to supply the German with as many swords as possible.

The other pile, with twelve swords, held the pieces Ken would be sending to Japan. He hung a paper tag on each of them, and after consulting his pocket notebook, numbered them from 637 to 648. Some records were unavoidable, but Tsuji-san had instructed Ken to create as small a paper trail as possible so he had developed a very cryptic recording system built around irregular blocks of numbers. Occasionally he used names instead of numbers and also used a variety of different tags so that customs inspectors could not easily identify the swords as coming from a single source.

Virtually all of the swords he sent to Japan were legally imported, but to make the scope of his activities less apparent to Japanese officials, Ken shipped swords in many different ways to a variety of individuals. This added to the headaches of record keeping, but it was the way Tsuji-san wanted it. As far as Ken could tell, no swords had ever been lost, but he had no real idea of what happened to them after he sent them on their way. Now that he was handling things other than swords, and recycling many of his purchases in America, Ken's accounting problems were even greater.

But he tried not to worry about the complexity of his operation. All the evidence he had told him his work was going along well. Tsuji-san made occasional contact with him and always seemed pleased. Still, as Ken listed this group of swords into his notebook, he had a familiar feeling of powerlessness. He did not mind the long hours or the constant travel. He certainly didn't mind being away from his wife who seemed to be equally happy living essentially alone in Portland. After a day like this Ken had to wonder if Tsuji-san really appreciated Ken's good work. The *Oyabun* had never shown deep interest in the swords Ken was shipping back to Japan. Ken also doubted that he understood that he was paying for most of his overhead costs by recycling so many of purchases right in America. No one, in fact, seemed interested in the details of Ken's operation and Tsuji-san rarely gave him any encouragement beyond simply telling him to keep up the good work.

As Ken listed the day's purchases, he couldn't help wondering what would happen to the swords he was sending home. He was not sure how they were marketed or even who handled them for the Brotherhood. The few sword dealers Ken had met in Japan and at American sword gatherings had all been haughty and disrespectful even though Ken was sure he was dealing in more and better swords than most of them. He had mentioned this to Tsuji-san during one of his trips back to Japan. The *Oyabun* had shown some sympathy but went no farther than assuring Ken that members of Brotherhood had to expect such treatment from the public. Ken couldn't help feeling alone and unappreciated.

At the very least, he wished Tsuji-san would let him know more about the financial side of his operation. After nearly nine years of buying swords in America, Ken knew nothing about where his money came from or how the profits he had to be generating were being used. Whenever his supply of cash was running low, he simply mentioned the need for "supplies" to his travel agent. A few days later an airplane ticket and other travel arrangements would be delivered to wherever Ken happened to be. The ticket was usually for a midweek trip to either New York or New Jersey. At some point along the way, a package containing two hundred thousand dollars in cash would be delivered to him. Sometimes a man would bring it to Ken's room. Occasionally he was instructed to pick it up at a restaurant or a business office of some kind. Often it arrived as a package brought by UPS or a taxi driver. The money was always neatly packed in paper-clipped, thousand dollar units of clean used bills. Ken preferred hundreds and hated twenties.

This system had been working smoothly for several years, so the only problem Ken ever encountered was scheduling his trips to make sure that he was never without working capital. He rarely visited his travel agent's office and when he did he spoke only with a middle aged blond woman who seemed to know him only as a client. Ken couldn't believe she was involved in the money transfers.

He realized it was best if he did not to know the details of that side of his operations. Still, if Tsuji-san really trusted Ken, he would confide in him.

After he had finished his notes, Ken thought about looking again at a couple of the blades he had just bought. The Kunikane sword in the *kyu-gunto* mounts he had bought early in the day was potentially a very important sword. It deserved more careful study, but he was very tired and did not want to take the time. Instead, he simply taped it closed as he had the other swords in the group and stacked it in a gun case. The swords he had bought filled all four of the cases he had brought so he would have to stop by a sporting goods shop on the way to Bloomington to buy a couple more.

The day was becoming long and Ken wished he could soak himself in a deep, steamy *ofuro*. The hot shower he took instead simply could not compare with a Japanese bath. Had the motel had room service, he would have called for a double shot of whiskey. Going to the to the bar to have a solitary drink was not an appealing prospect, so Ken simply donned his pajamas and packed the day's miscellaneous purchases into the cardboard box he brought to the room. His odds and ends nearly filled the box that he would carry with him until Monday. If the next two days were as productive as this stop had been, Ken would ask the last motel to ship the boxed goods to his Oregon address. The pistol and the ceramics he bought from the B29 pilot remained problems, but Ken was too tired to deal with them.

As he slipped into bed he had to wonder if Tsuji-san had any idea how hard he worked. To clear his mind of that thought and help himself relax, Ken made a mental checklist of the things he would have to do tomorrow. He was scheduled to begin buying at Bloomington at noon and before that he had to visit the widow who had called the motel. If he saw a sporting goods store, he wanted to buy a couple of extra plastic gun cases. Tomorrow morning would also be the only time he could call his local contacts. He exhaled sharply as a wave of stress swept over him.

Ken had worked hard to establish good relations with gun dealers and collectors throughout America. He always made a point of calling the people he knew in the areas he visited on his buying trips. Because of the funeral in New Jersey, however, time had been short and Ken had forgotten to call any of his contacts in Illinois.

He had been very sleepy only a few minutes earlier, but neglecting an important step of his operation brought Ken fully awake. He switched on the lights and got up to get the contacts book out of his attaché case. He nervously checked his wrist watch to see that it was just after 10:00 PM. Ken kept his traveling files in a compact Japanese ring binder. He had never seen one like it in America and he liked it because it let him arrange the names both alphabetically and by state. Turning to the Illinois section, Ken was surprised to see that it was quite large because of all the collectors in the Chicago area. After consulting the map in the phone book, Ken decided there was no need to contact any of those people. That made his list more manageable and as he scanned it he recognized only a couple of men who had actually been good contacts in the past.

As he ran his finger down the list one name jumped out at him. Jim Sime, in Springfield, had sold him a number of swords and had made some shipments to Japan that Ken had found useful. Following a hunch, Ken looked for Sime's name on the alphabetical list. When he found it, he clinched his fists and exclaimed, "*Kachimashita!*"

Beside Sime's name was a notation written in Japanese characters saying "Muramasa tanto." As soon as Ken saw it he realized why the rubbing that had been faxed to him from Tokyo had looked familiar. It had to be the same blade Jim Sime had told him about earlier in the summer. Ken couldn't recall the details, but he remembered calling both Sime and someone else about the dagger. He couldn't remember where the deal stood now, but he was sure he had information filed on it in his permanent files. As he looked once again at the faxed rubbing, he became absolutely convinced that the blade Tsuji-san wanted was the dagger Sime had found.

Ken was full of nervous excitement as he punched the numbers of Jim Sime's home telephone. As he listened to the phone ring he again checked his watch. It was 10:25 and perhaps a bit late, but he was sure that Sime would be either awake or only recently retired. In either case, Ken had spent so much money with the American that he would forgive a late night call. A man's voice answered after the fifth ring.

"Hello, Jim! This is Ken Sawada. Did I wake you?"

"No, no. Ken. I was just watching TV. I saw your newspaper ads so I knew you were in the area. Are you down in Peoria?"

"Yeah, I've been very busy. I'm sorry I didn't call you earlier. How you been?" Ken was buoyant and his voice was full of pep.

"Fine, Ken. I been finding some stuff and keeping busy," Jim replied vaguely. "How have things been going' with you?"

"Oh busy, busy, busy. I travel every week these days."

"How's your buy going' down there? Are you doing all right in Peoria?" Ken asked.

"Not so good," Ken replied drawing his breath across his teeth in a soft hiss. "Not so much stuff around like it used to be. You got any swords for me?"

"Well, let's see." He paused for effect. "I got a short sword that's pretty nice and a couple of military swords, but I got to tell you that I had to pay quite a bit for them."

"That's all right. I'll pay more. You know that, Jim. I'd like to see them." The conversation was going perfectly but Ken tried to keep from betraying the excitement he felt.

"Can you come on up to the shop tomorrow? It's only about fifty miles."

"No. I can't do that, Jim. I got to drive to Bloomington. But I tell you what. Today, I bought a gun I can't keep. You drive down there, I'll give it to you. I got some German stuff for you, too, couple daggers and helmets," Ken added.

"What kind of gun is it?"

"It's a Type 94 pistol. Nice shape, but I don't like guns. You can use it. I want you to take some woodblock prints and old dishes, too. All good stuff, but hard for me to carry."

"Sure, Ken. What the hell. I'll run on down tomorrow afternoon," Jim replied.

"Great! I'll be glad to see you," Ken said pleasantly. "Since you're coming, let me ask two other things," he continued without allowing Jim time to protest. "First, I need a couple of plastic gun cases. You got some?"

"You mean the cheap ones, about twenty-nine bucks a pop? Yeah, we got a bunch."

"Great. Bring me four. I'll pay you when you get here."

"Sure, Ken, that won't be a problem."

"And then, remember a couple of months ago, you sent me a rubbing from a tanto you found? Did you get that tanto yet?" Ken was being careful not to sound too interested.

"Ahh, let's see," Jim paused. "Yeah, I remember. I made the rubbing up at the Des Moines Show. It was a nice little rig that Ric Mallow up in Minneapolis found. I haven't done anything with it beside telling you about it."

"I called the guy, what's his name?" Ken asked.

"Mallow, Eric Mallow," Jim said.

"Yeah, Marrow. Does he live around here?"

"No, no, Ken. He lives way up in Minneapolis. That's like six hundred miles from here."

"Oh yeah, right," said Ken. "I called him a couple of times, but he wouldn't sell the tanto. Too, bad, I could really use it. You think you could buy?"

"I don't think I could get it if you couldn't Ken. Did you offer him enough money? You didn't try to jew him down or anything, did you. Ken?" Jim asked teasingly

"I'm no Jew!" Ken replied with a playful tone. "I offer him lot of money, but he wouldn't sell."

"I don't know what to tell you, Ken," Jim said blankly.

"You got a copy of that rubbing. I'd like to see it again since I'm in this area."

"Yeah, I'll bet I do. You want me to bring it with when I come tomorrow?"

"That would be nice. I'll see you in the afternoon, okay?"

"Great, Ken. See you tomorrow."

"Good night," Ken replied.

Without putting the receiver down, Ken pressed the return and punched an overseas call into the telephone. It went through smoothly and a young female voice answered in Japanese.

"Good morning. Thank you for calling The Greater Japan Imperial League."

"This is Sawada in America," Ken said crisply. "If it is at all possible I would beg to speak to the Director on an matter of great importance." Ken selected his words carefully to be polite in his request, but authoritative in his level of address.

"I will communicate your request to Director Tsuji immediately. Please hold," and the line went to saccharine Japanese Muzak. Ken waited nervously.

"Sawada-kun," Tsuji-san's voice boomed on the line. "It's a pleasure to hear from you. I hope everything is all right. Are you well?" Certainly, his tone was very positive and level of address was very warm. Still, by referring to him as "kun" he set the conversation at merely a friendly level. Ken hoped he was not angry.

"President, I beg your forgiveness for disturbing you. I know you are far to busy to take trivial calls."

"Nonsense, my son. I look forward to your contacts as I would those of any of our Brothers." Now the Tsuji-san was using the special words of the Kawabayashi Brotherhood and Ken felt deep relief.

"Father, earlier today I received your faxed instructions to find a dagger signed by Muramasa. I am currently in the midst of a buying expedition in a small American city so I do not have my complete files. Still, the *oshigata* you included was very clear and I believe that I know where this sword is located."

"Excellent! Excellent. I am very pleased my son. Once again, you have done excellent work. When can you get it for me?"

This enthusiasm made Ken uncomfortable. "President, there is more work I must do to acquire the tanto. Of course, I will do all I can, but at this point I am not sure how I will acquire the dagger for you."

"We need that dagger, Sawada-san," the Oyabun said with an icy tone and a formal term of address. "Is it a matter of money? Pay whatever you have to."

"Thank you for your support, President, but it is not simply money. I must first be sure the blade I have found is the one you are searching. Beyond that, the man who holds the dagger seems unwilling to part with it. I will have to work hard to convince him of my interest."

"I see," said Tsuji. He paused for a moment before continuing. "My son, we need to talk about this and other matters. I want you to come to Tokyo. Can you make it next week?"

"I have placed expensive ads in a town called Albuquerque, President. It would be better if you would allow me to arrive in two weeks, if that would meet with your schedule." Ken bowed reflexively toward his telephone.

"That will be fine. I'll do some work at this end and you do what you can to make sure that the blade you have found is the one we are looking for. Do you need a clearer *oshigata*?"

"That would be very useful, Director. I will also try again to convince the man who has the dagger to part with it."

"Do that, my son. Do that. The dagger will be very useful to me and to the Brotherhood. Please try to convince him we are very serious." Tsuji paused. "Make sure he understands that the Kawabayashi Brotherhood can be very convincing."

7 | Dave Stalgaard

In which a treasure begins to be appreciated.

Minneapolis - present day
Dave Stalgaard, "art dealer" with special interest in Japanese swords
Eric Mallow, gun collector with many friends
Dawn Watanabe, Eric's friend

Eric's trip back to Minneapolis was flawless. His flight took off and arrived on schedule and he picked up his luggage as soon as he got to the carousel. Best of all, Dawn was in her car waiting for him when he stepped out of the terminal door.

"Hi'ya," he said as he slid into the passenger's seat. "That's what I call perfect timing."

"Well, your timing can be pretty good too," she said playfully and pulled into traffic. "How was your weekend?"

"Great. I had a good time and bought some great stuff."

"I can just imagine. More guns!" she teased as she looked over her shoulder to change lanes.

"I did pick up a couple of neat guns, but that's not all. Guess what else I found," Eric said.

"Found! You always make it sound like you've been out looking for agates or arrowheads or something. Didn't you pay for these things?"

"Well, of course, I paid for them, but in serious collecting, money is never enough. You've got to be lucky."

"And you were lucky in Des Moines?"

"You betcha' I was. Now if I can get lucky this evening, it'll be a perfect weekend," Eric added with a wink.

Dawn giggled. "Well, maybe you will, but nothing's going to happen until you've taken me to dinner at the Athenia. I'm in the mood for grape leaves."

"Hey, great idea!"

"I knew you'd like it. I'm ready for some time off, myself. I spent the entire weekend setting up the Twin Cities Cement Finishers'

Association Newsletter. Would you believe it's called The Mixing Trough! Anytime I want to think about freelancing full time, a job like this brings me back to reality."

"Pretty boring?"

"Deadly! And you wouldn't believe the sexist bullshit they put in there. Cement finishers definitely aren't ready for liberation."

"Did you get it all done?"

"I sure did and it looks great, but I want to forget it over a glass of retsina. Regale me with your adventures."

"I told you to guess what I found."

"Some guns, I suppose. Who knows?"

"No, besides the guns. Guess."

"Eric. Who knows what kind of stuff you dragged home? Just tell me."

"Okay, if you insist. I got a samurai sword and a really groovy Japanese dagger."

"Eric, please. You aren't going to start collecting those things, now, too," Dawn rolled her eyes.

"Why not? A lot of guys make great money with Japanese swords and, who knows, maybe your dad will think they're cool."

"Dad wouldn't know a samurai sword from a Toyota clutch and I don't think he'd care. Besides, you don't need to impress him. He thinks you're terrific anyway and he'd love it if I married a dentist." Dawn laughed and took a hand off the wheel to poke Eric in the side.

"We'll talk about that some other time," Eric said playfully. "Right now, I've got to find out something about these swords."

"Why'd you buy them if you don't know anything about them?"

"Well, sometimes you've just got to take a risk. They also kind of came with some other stuff I did want."

"So how much did you pay for these treasures?"

"I actually only own the long one. It was part of a package deal that has already paid for itself. The lady who had the stuff in her attic didn't show me the dagger until after I'd spent all my money. She was real anxious to get rid of it, though, so I told her I'd sell it for her."

"Sounds complicated. What kind of swords are they?"

"A long one and a short one. That's the limit of my knowledge."

"So how are you going to find out where to sell them?"

"Selling them won't be hard at all. The woods are full of guys who buy Japanese swords. The hard part will be finding out what

122

they're really worth."

"How are you going to do that?"

"I know a couple of guys who are into Japanese stuff. One may even be honest enough to give me the straight scoop."

"So, are you going to show me these treasures after dinner?"

"Sorry, I asked a friend to bring them back to the Cities for me because they didn't fit in my bags. We'll just have to think of something else to do after dinner."

A week after returning from Des Moines, Eric's phone rang while he was spending a quiet evening at home.

"Hi. This is Dave Stalgaard. You left a message on my machine about a couple of Japanese swords."

"Thanks for calling back, Dave."

"Is this a good time? I'm always ready to talk about Japanese swords, but I don't want to interrupt you."

"No, this is perfect," Eric said. "I don't know if you remember, but we've met a couple of times at gun shows in this area. I collect automatic pistols and some other things."

"Sure, Ric. I remember. You had the cased flintlocks on display last year at the Armory show," the voice on the telephone replied.

"Yup, that was me. I called you because everybody says you're the guy I should talk to about a couple of Japanese swords I picked up last week in Des Moines."

"All right! I'll sure help if I can, Ric. What did you score?"

"I'm not really sure. I got the swords in a deal with some other stuff. I don't know much about them, but I'm beginning to think one of them is pretty good."

"It sure could be. There are still a lot of good swords out there in closets and attics," Dave said trying to sound positive. "What kind of swords are they?"

"You'll have to help me with that, Dave," Eric said. "One's a long sword. I think it's a garden variety sort of thing. The other one is a dagger in a nicely made plain wooden mounting."

"That's a storage mount called a shira-saya," explained Dave. "That's how I like to keep my blades."

"Yeah, well, in fact, the dagger isn't really mine. I'm holding it for the old lady who had the stuff. It was kind of complicated, but I think that's the one that may be pretty good."

"Why do you say that?"

"I showed the dagger to one of the gun slicks at the Des Moines show. Apparently, he sent a rubbing of the dagger's signature to a Japanese sword dealer who called me the night before last. He offered me five thousand for it."

"That would get my attention. What's the signature?"

"I can't tell you, Dave. I took a look at the tang so I know there's something there, but it's strictly chicken scratching as far as I'm concerned."

"But a five thousand dollar offer convinced you to do a little bit of investigation."

"Exactly," said Eric.

"I got to tell you, Ric, you might want to be a little careful of guys who offer big money over the phone. There are more than a few hustlers buying Japanese swords these days."

"Oh, I'm sure there are, but this offer seemed serious. The guy said he'd send me a cashier's check up front and he only asked for a one day inspection privilege. That struck me as reasonable."

"It sounds like you got something the dude wants. Who is he?"

"His name is Ken Sawada."

"Oh," Dave said thoughtfully. "Ken's a heavy hitter, but I thought he was only setting up in motels these days. I think you better find out what you've got and get some other offers.

"That's why I called you, Dave. Are you interested in wading into this deal?"

"A dagger that Ken Sawada offered five G's for? You bet I'm interested."

"Great. Can we meet some place or can I bring it over to your home?"

"Gee, Ric, my pad's a little rustic. I'd actually rather go over to your place if you don't mind."

"That's cool. I just had a walk-in gun safe installed so I can keep my stuff here and there's plenty of room. Can you make it some night this week?"

"How's tomorrow?"

"Fine," Eric said and gave Dave directions to his place, and instructions about the security system his neighbors insisted on.

Dave's apartment was certainly not designed for entertaining. He lived in the rear portion of a building that had been a wholesale hardware warehouse in an older section of north Minneapolis. As a minimally finished storage space in an industrial area, it was not very presentable. Dave was also not a tidy housekeeper, but the cluttered, open space fit his needs. It was safe, big, and cheap.

Reasoning that no one would expect to find anything of value in a place like his apartment, Dave felt free to leave good swords and other valuable objects there. Over the years, he had accumulated several old safes which he used to lock up particularly valuable items, but Dave liked to think the squalor of the place was his best defense against theft.

The old warehouse also afforded Dave ample storage and work space. His immediate living area was ringed by a relatively orderly research library on subjects of his interest. It included more than two thousand volumes on Japanese swords. Dave rarely dealt in furniture anymore, but in the past he had been able to bring home things as big as an immigrant Norwegian church altar and a World War II Japanese howitzer. In one part of the space he also had a workshop set up with a variety of tools, including a large belt sander and a full set of polishing stones Dave used to clean and reshape Japanese swords that had been abused or allowed to become rusty.

In a more convenient neighborhood, the warehouse would be a prime candidate for gentrification, but in this location, the building commanded very low rent, which was important for Dave who often faced cash flow problems. He had had a couple of jobs after dropping out of the University of Minnesota in the late 1960s, but since his discharge from the army, he had supported himself entirely by dealings in interesting old things.

For tax purposes, Dave described himself as an art dealer although he knew it was not a very adequate description of what he did for a living. He tried to avoid dealing in material that was explicitly illegal, but beyond that he would buy almost anything that could be sold for a profit. He had dealt in things as diverse as colored gem stones and bulk carpeting, and regularly traded in folk art, old guns, militaria, ethnographic materials, oil paintings, and oriental ceramics. All of these were secondary interests, however. For more than twenty-five years, dealing in Japanese swords had been the center of Dave's life.

Dave had learned about Japanese swords while still in high school when he enrolled in a karate class. His interest in the martial arts faded after he earned a brown belt, but the complexity of Japanese swords had remained intriguing. By the time he was twenty, Dave began acquiring Japanese blades and initiated correspondence with other collectors in both America and Japan. At that time, Japanese swords held little interest for American collectors. They were nothing more than war souvenirs with no particular value, so Dave was able to buy them at gun shops and antiques stores for a few dollars a piece. When he discovered that swords were traded with other kinds of weapons at gun shows, attending them became a regular part of his life.

Over the years, Dave developed a deep familiarity with all aspects of Japanese swords and their fittings. He learned to identify subtle differences of shape and construction so that he could judge the quality of a blade and tell where and when it had been made without looking at its signature. Before dropping out of the University, Dave had taken a couple of Japanese classes and after his military service in Viet Nam, he spent a year in Japan, recovering and teaching English. Those experiences allowed him to read--or at least puzzle through--the arcane literature on swords. While acquiring these skills, Dave also built a large network of contacts who knew of his interest in swords. His knowledge and contacts together with a reputation for honesty allowed Dave to make a living trading in Japanese swords.

As the World War II generation passed and the strength of the Japanese economy drew swords back to Japan, many people assumed that Dave would eventually run out of swords. Certainly, the supply of swords had changed in the years he had dealt in them, but he still found lots of interesting pieces. The major trend he observed was a dramatic increase in prices. Swords that had been worth a few dollars when he was starting out now commanded thousands. As prices rose, collectors had become more discriminating so that the risks of dealing had grown considerably. Nowadays a bad purchase meant a serious financial loss, but Dave did not mind increased risk.

Dave looked for swords whenever he could. He continued to attend gun shows since a trickle of old war souvenirs continued to surface there. He was also a regular at the half dozen or so Japanese sword shows that were annually organized in different parts of North America.

Increasingly, he had to find other strategies and travel much farther to find merchandise. On a couple of occasions, Dave had made very good money helping curators "deaccession" swords that sat unappreciated in museum collections. He also placed ads in national and local publications and occasionally blanketed particular areas with newspaper ads announcing that he would be buying swords in a particular motel room for the weekend. Having sold thousands of swords to collectors over the years, Dave knew where lots of blades were and he often worked with collectors who were thinning their collections or executors who were breaking up estates. As much as the risk, Dave loved the unpredictability of his profession.

Since Dave did much of his business by telephone, he found it convenient to keep his answering machine on at all times, even when he was at home. He had heard Eric's call, but had not picked up the phone because he was involved in refinishing a group of 287 tsuba, sword guards an antiques scout had found in Massachusetts.

Japanese curios had been popular in Europe and America from the 1880s through World War I. Japan exported newly made objects and common antiques in quantity at that time. The box of iron disks Dave was working on when Eric called had apparently been forgotten since then. Dave learned about the group from a collector who had selected a couple of nicer pieces, but rejected the rest as far too rusty to be interesting. Dave got the box for four thousand, which meant that each piece cost just over $14.00.

Sorting through the guards, Dave found they were overwhelmingly mass-produced pieces made for low class samurai and townsmen in the early Nineteenth century. They were legitimate antiques, but there were none of the ornamental guards high class samurai had worn on their swords as personal adornments, and they were also covered with scaly red rust. Setting aside a pile of eighteen pieces that warranted special treatment, Dave began to work on the rest of the tsuba. When Eric called, Dave had just started the process of soaking and pickling that would give them the rich surface of worn basalt or black marble. It would take about a week, but when it was over, Dave could expect to wholesale the guards for about a hundred dollars a piece.

The tsuba Dave set aside for special treatment included a couple of guards that had been embellished with silver and copper overlays that would not survive the batch processing he planned for the common pieces. The embellished guards were already in sorry condition and would never be worth more than the others in the collection, but Dave would finish them by hand simply to prevent further damage.

The rest of the selected tsuba were totally unembellished iron disks that most people would find among the least interesting of the lot. Dave recognized them as the kind of guard used by the samurai warriors during the Thirteenth and Fourteenth centuries. Elaborately decorated sword fittings had come into use only after about the mid-1500s. Before then, most fittings were made by the swordsmiths themselves and most swords had only a thin disk of steel between the handle and the blade. The best swordsmith guards of that period were trimmed with a few stylized silhouette cut-outs that fit the austere tastes of the early samurai and the technical capabilities of early swordsmiths. There were no pierced guards in the box Dave purchased, but he knew a fellow in San Francisco who specialized in adding pierced designs to unembellished older pieces. A phone call to him had sold eleven plain guards for twenty-five hundred dollars and convinced Dave to stay away from high end swordsmith tsuba for the next year or so.

Dave Stalgaard called Eric the next evening to say he had found a couple of interesting things at an auction and that he might be a little late. When it was almost ten, and Eric had decided that Dave had abandoned his planned visit altogether, the front door buzzer sounded.

"Ric, This is Dave Stalgaard. I hope I'm not too late," Dave's voice crackled through the intercom.

"I'd given up on you, Dave," Eric said as he pressed the button that would open the security door. "It's number 515."

Eric was waiting at his door when Dave got off the elevator and walked down the hall of the well-furnished condominium.

"I'm real sorry I'm so late, Ric. I went over to Mike's Thursday Night Sale and found a couple of interesting things," Dave said as he neared the door. "Mickey told me they'd come up early, but the damn sale went on and on."

"It's not a problem, Dave," Eric said as they shook hands. "Did you get what you were after?"

"Yeah. A couple of old Japanese tea bowls and a pretty nice piece of Korean celadon."

"So you're into Oriental ceramics, too?" Eric asked as he closed the door behind Dave.

"It's not my main thing, but a nice tea bowl or two goes well with any sword collection and, frankly, a lot of Oriental ceramics are seriously underpriced."

"So did you do pretty well with Mickey?"

"Not too bad," Dave said. "If you're interested, I'll go get the stuff."

"No, that's all right. I don't need to get interested in anything more at this point in my life," Eric said with a wave of his hand. "Can I get you a cup of coffee or a beer?"

"Coffee'd be great, Ric."

As Eric walked to the kitchen he said, "I'll grab it before we go downstairs to the gun room."

"Jees, you got a lot of room here, Ric," Dave said, looking around the spacious apartment. "What'd you do, put a couple of units together?"

"That's exactly what I did," Eric said as they walked down a short hall to a flight of stairs down to the paneled room on the floor below. It was comfortably furnished with overstuffed chairs and a thick rug. On the walls, lighted gun racks were interspersed with framed pictures.

"This is nice, Ric," Dave said as he apprised the room. "How'd did you get all this space?"

"It just kind of happened. I originally sublet this unit eight years ago when I was opening my practice and couldn't afford anything else. A couple of months later, it was offered to me as part of an estate settlement at a price I couldn't pass up. A year later the two units right upstairs came on the market so I bought them and had the place remodeled," Eric said. "I'm the youngest person in the building, but that's all right. Most of the rest of the folks are retired so they take real good care of the building."

"Little old ladies can be a great security system," Dave agreed.

"You bet. If somebody unusual shows up in the building, they're on the phone like that," Eric said snapping his fingers.

"You got some good stuff here, Ric," Dave said walking toward a western oil painting. "And it looks like you've a real secure spot."

"I think it used to be more fun when stuff was cheap and we didn't have to worry about it. I just had a walk-in safe added in what used to be the bedroom closet. It would take a jack hammer to get stuff out of here."

Looking at the painting, Dave said, "This looks like a real Olaf

Stelzer you got here, Ric."

Eric was surprised that Dave so easily identified the work, having assumed his only interests were in Japanese swords.

"Everybody says it is. I got it in a trade with Rex Watson who dug it out of the woodwork in Montana."

"It's very nice."

"Sometime I'll have to show you the rest of my stuff, but let's take a look at this dagger. Just getting it here has turned out to be an adventure."

"How's that?" asked Dave.

"I flew down to Des Moines and didn't have a case big enough to carry the swords and stuff I picked up down there, so I asked Terry Carlson to bring it back to the Cities for me."

"The guy who does Civil War guns?" Dave asked. "I heard he just wrecked his car."

"On the way home from Des Moines, a truck rear-ended him. He's all right, but his van was totaled. He showed me pictures when I picked up the swords from him. I don't see how he walked away from the wreck, but he's okay and the stuff he was carrying for me came through just fine." Eric took the wooden box containing the dagger from a sideboard and placed it on the coffee table.

Dave sat down at the table and got out a pair of reading glasses before looking at the writing on the top of the box. "This is very interesting," he said.

"What does it say?"

"This flowing script is a little tough to figure out, but this is clearly a date," he said running his finger over a block of writing in the lower left hand corner of the lid.

"How old is it?" asked Eric.

"The date is a lucky day in sixth month of the 13th year of Showa. That's May 1938."

"Are you kidding?" Eric asked in disbelief. "You mean its like sixty years old?"

"No, that's just when the box was made," Dave said, still pondering the inscription. "Across the top here it says it's a gold mounted tanto by Muramasa. And this says 'Important Cultural Property' and that's the signature of the guy who made the evaluation. His name was 'Tsunami Tobiguchi'."

"So what does it mean?"

"It's very cool, Ric. The box was made in 1938 for a gold-mounted dagger that had been made by a swordsmith named Muramasa. He's a very famous smith who worked in the late 1300s. It looks like the dagger was designated an Important Cultural Property by the Japanese government. I assume that was done in 1938 when the box was made."

"What's an Important Cultural Property?" Eric smiled over the formality of the title.

"The Japanese government has a system for recognizing places, things, and even people that are worth preserving. There are craftsmen who are called Living National Treasures because they have some skill the government feels is important to Japanese culture. Things can be treated the same way."

"So you're saying this dagger is a national treasure?"

"Well, not exactly. A 'National Treasure' is the top ranking and this box uses the term 'Important Cultural Property' which is a lower ranking."

"Only two stars and no bullet."

"Exactly. Nice lyric, easy to dance to, but not at the top of the charts."

"There's another problem, Dave."

"What's that?

"The wrong dagger is in there. Take a look," Eric said, "it's not gold-mounted."

Dave turned back to the box and slipped off the lid. Laying it on the table, it was obvious that the box had been made to accommodate two daggers, only one of which was present.

"Somebody appears to have grabbed the goodies," Eric said ruefully.

Dave said nothing, but picked up the tanto in the plain wooden mounts. Examining the blade, he said, "They didn't get it all. If this isn't a Muramasa blade, I'll eat it."

Using a brass punch attached to his key ring, he pushed out the bamboo peg that held the handle onto the tang of the blade. With a few strong raps of his right hand to his left hand grasping the dagger, he loosened the blade from the handle so he could slide it free. Careful to touch only the rusty tang, he held the blade in the light of the lamp at his side. The short inscription was clearly visible.

"It says Muramasa big as life," Dave said holding the tang so that Eric could see it too. "I'm sure this is the blade that's supposed to be in the box."

"So Muramasa's a big deal?" Eric asked looking at the signature Dave showed him.

"Yeah, he is," Dave said, trying to recall what he had read about the smith. "His teacher was even bigger, a dude named Munemasa. I've seen a couple of Muramasa's blades and they're pretty good. But he's mainly famous for making blades that are kind of hoodoo. Blades that have mystical powers. I don't think anybody takes that sort of thing seriously these days."

"What about the gold mounts?" asked Eric.

"Who knows? If I had to guess, I'd say that when the dagger was recognized as a cultural property, they repolished it and put it in this storage mount. Then to hold the fittings together, they probably made a wooden copy of the blade and put it in the mounts. It would have lain right here," Dave explained as he pointed to the empty niche in the box.

"Did they do that kind of thing?"

"All the time. The plain wooden shira-saya mounts are real stable so they're better for long term storage. The wooden blades are called tsunagi and since they can't corrode, they'll keep the mounts nice and clean."

"But the different parts can get separated?"

"I think that's what happened here, but you've got to remember that Japanese swords are made to be taken apart. The blade and the fittings are separate. Push out that little bamboo peg and the whole rig comes apart." Holding the blade up, he continued, "This thing right here is the sword. This is the Important Cultural Property. Whoever lifted the fittings missed the best part."

Dave held the bare blade under the lamp and examined it very carefully. He turned the blade to let the light play off the sides and back. After several minutes, he turned to Eric and said, "This is a fabulous blade, Ric. It's worth a great deal of money."

"Like how much?"

"I'll have to do some checking to find out about its designation as an Important Property. It might even be one of the blades that was listed among the "National Treasures" that disappeared after the War. If it's one of those, I'd have to assume that it would be worth like a hundred grand or more, maybe a lot more."

"Even without the fittings?" Eric asked in disbelief.

"They'd definitely help, but with Japanese swords, the blade is always the main thing. It would be great if we could find the fittings, but the blade is very salable as it is."

"Wow," said Eric, looking at the dagger.

"It looks like you made some money on this one," Dave smiled.

"Well, not really. You see, it still belongs to an old lady in Iowa. I agreed to sell it for her."

"So sell it for her. Tell her you had an offer of $5000 for the thing. That's a lot more than she'd get at a garage sale and it leaves a little bit in it for you."

"Yeah, ninety-five grand!" Eric shook his head. "Nahh, I couldn't do that."

"I know what you mean. I don't mind screwing other dealers at all, but I hate dealing with vets and widows. Is she in a hurry to get rid of it?"

"She doesn't want to keep it, but I don't think there is any particular rush."

"Then, let me do a little research on it. We should find out more about it before anything happens."

"Are you a buyer for this sort of thing?" Eric asked pointedly.

"I don't think I could afford to keep it myself, but I could put the deal together for you or her and we'd all make some money," Dave said as he put the blade back into the wooden handle and scabbard.

"You want to take it on the arm?"

"I could, but it would be just as easy for me to set the deal up. I'd want twenty percent on something like this, but once we got serious, I think we could have it sold in a couple of days."

"You've given me plenty to think about, Dave. I'm impressed that you've been real honest with me on this deal so let's work together on it. Do whatever research you can and try to figure out the best way to handle it. I'm not going to get back to the lady in Iowa 'til we're ready to move."

"Great! I'll try to make us all some money," said Dave. "You said there was another sword. Let's take a look at that?"

"Oh yeah, I nearly forgot," said Eric as got up to get the sword. It was in a soft shotgun case when he brought it to Dave. "I don't think this is the same kind of thing."

With the sword out of the gun case, Dave looked over the fittings. He scanned the outside of the sword carefully, examining each of the fittings and paying close attention to the lacquered scabbard.

"This style of mounting is called a tachi. It's an old style, formal sword, but I'd guess this one was made up sometime just before the war. Maybe in the 20s or 30s. You can tell from the metal work that it isn't real old and the lacquer is pretty thin." Dave pointed to an area of scaling finish on the scabbard as he said this. "I think a lot of these things were used as ceremonial offerings to shrines and things. They're collectible, but not as valuable as older swords."

At that, Dave held the sword with the cutting edge up so that he could draw the blade out along its back ridge. He set the scabbard aside to examine the blade. As he looked at the polished surface his eyes widened. "Holy shit," he said as he held the blade straight up at arm's length to consider its shape and curvature. "Holy shit."

"What's the matter?" asked Eric.

"This is a fabulous blade, Ric."

"You just said it was made in the 30s."

"I think that's when the fittings were put together, but this is a much older blade and it's fabulous."

Dave had to use a small hammer to removed the peg in the handle of the long sword and then had to work quite hard to get the blade free from the handle. It clearly had not been removed in a very long time.

"I'm really curious to see the signature," Eric said as Dave worked the blade loose.

"If it's what I think it is, it won't be signed," Dave said as the handle finally separated from the tang of the blade. Quickly scanning both sides of the tang, he said, "and it isn't!"

"I don't understand one damn thing about this stuff," said Eric in frustration. "You mean it's better if it's not signed"?

"In this case, it is. There was only one smith who could produce a blade this good--Munemasa--and he didn't sign his best swords because he figured no signature was necessary. Only he could make swords as good as this." Dave took a deep breath and said, "This has got to be one of his swords."

Dave spent the next hour alternately looking at the sword and showing Eric details of its construction. After cleaning the blade with a fine powder and a tissue, he showed Eric the perfect curvature of its sweeping shape and called attention to the way the blade narrowed from a delicate point to a base that was only slightly wider but massive in its feel.

Then Dave encouraged Eric to "look into the steel." Eric thought it sounded like mystic foolishness and he protested. "You're making this sound like something out of Karate Kid, Dave." But he did examine the surface of the blade and saw it had a complex structure that looked like wood grain. As he looked at the fine lines and swirls that covered the blade he asked, "What's all this stuff along the cutting edge?"

"That's the hamon, a heat-treated edge. I've never seen one like this." Dave explained the unique heat treating processes developed by Japanese swordsmiths. The process kept the body of a sword relatively flexible even though the steel at the edge was nearly glass hard. This combination made for an incredibly sharp blade that could stand up to the rigors of battle without breaking.

"Munemasa made swords that were strong and he also figured out how to heat treat them so that there were beautiful patterns in the hamon," Dave explained. He showed Eric the streaks of color and fine billowy forms present in milky steel along the cutting edge.

Dave seemed ready to spend all night looking at the sword, but Eric finally said, "Dave, it's after 1:00 AM. We better wrap this up or I'll be dead tomorrow.

"Okay, Ric, just let me make a rubbing so I can do some more research on this shooter." He placed a large piece of fine paper over the blade, holding it in place with several small magnets. When it was secured, he rubbed a small cake of dry ink along the edges of the sword and down the central ridge. He rubbed the entire tang even though it had no inscription. Finally, he skillfully traced the patterned of the hamon on to outline he had made so that he ended up with a full sized picture of the blade.

As the evening wore on, Eric had considered offering to let Dave take the swords, but he decided against it. They were secure here, and although Eric had been impressed by Dave's candor and expertise, he really didn't know him all that well.

"Now let me get this clear, Ric." Dave asked as he was reassembling the sword. "The little old lady in Iowa is the owner of both of these swords?"

"No," said Eric. "The dagger is still hers, but I bought the long one from her with a couple of guns. It's mine. I didn't know what it was and I figured it into the deal at a thousand bucks."

"I think you'll make some money on the deal."

"That's great, but it's too late to get into it now. The sword's not going anywhere, so we can talk about it later." Eric was tired.

"Okay, but I got to ask you Ric, does anybody but Ken Sawada know about these swords?"

"No. In fact, Sawada doesn't even know about the long sword. His offer was strictly for the dagger."

"That's probably just as well. I think you ought to keep kind of quiet about them for a while. There are people who'd kill for this kind of stuff."

8 | Sawada Kenji

In which the search for a treasure becomes focused and informed.

Tokyo - present day

Sawada Kenji, associate of the Kawabayashi Brotherhood hoping to rise above the unfortunate duty of recovering Japanese swords that have found their way to America

Tsuji Takeru, Director of the Greater Japan Imperial League and senior member of the Kawabayashi Brotherhood

Hatamura Joji, one of Tsuji's *kobun* or "sons" within the Kawabayashi Brotherhood

Sawada Kenji was unprepared for the greeting that awaited him in the reception area of Narita Airport. When he pushed through the double doors from customs clearance, he was met by a line of four men standing with their legs assertively spread and their arms folded on their chests. The reception area, as always, was crowded with arriving passengers and others there to greet and assist them, but the four men ignored all of the action around them. Their clothing varied in details, but all wore tight, slightly belled pants, wide lapel sports coats, and dark silk shirts. Their hair was closely cropped and all four wore extremely pointed shoes. Even though they were inside, three of the men wore dark glasses.

Sawada immediately recognized the men as gang members and hesitated briefly. In that instant one of them said, "That's him," and their demeanor changed from ominous intensity to buoyant goodwill. They broke into wide smiles and joined in a deep bow. The man in the center of the group turned to the others and said, "Hey-yo!" to which the group responded with a complicated clapping routine that ended with a shout of "Welcome Home, Sawada-san! Banzai!" Again the men bowed deeply toward Sawada, a gesture he returned with a deep smile and sincere appreciation. Members of the Brotherhood had never before welcomed him home at the airport and he was very pleased.

When Sawada finished his bow to the group, Hatamura Joji stepped forward and made another rather more relaxed bow. "Brother Sawada, Welcome to Tokyo. Chairman Tsuji sends his deepest regards."

"Your greeting is overwhelming, brothers. It makes me feel truly at home."

"That was our goal," said Hatamura before turning to his companions. "Takahashi-kun, get the car. Sato-kun, take brother Sawada's luggage. We've got to help our Brother relax after his long trip." One man disappeared into the crowd and other two stepped forward to take Sawada's bags. Before Sawada surrendered his bag of duty free goods, he removed a boxed bottle of whiskey and gave it to Hatamura.

"Hatamura-kun, I want you to have this. I've acquired the taste for good bourbon while I've been in America. Wild Turkey is the best there is. See what you think."

"You're too kind, brother," Hatamura said with a crisp. short bow. "I've tried bourbon, but never acquired the taste. I'll 'study' this gift well," he laughed. "We should go now. Do you have anything else to pick up?"

"Indeed, I don't," Sawada shook his head. "I did not bring much because I must get all of the necessary work done in only three days."

"You brought no swords?" asked Hatamura.

"I haven't carried swords with me in years," he said with a wave of his hand. "The customs inspectors would tie them up for sure."

"I see," Hatamura said quickly. "The Director has told me little about your operation. It all sounds very complex, but I would like to know more. Perhaps you can tell me about your work as we drive back to the city. The car should be here by now. Shall we go?" He motioned Sawada toward the main exit.

The two men carrying Sawada's luggage formed a wedge that led straight toward the main exit. At the curb, in a place reserved for cabs, a shiny dark blue BMW was waiting with its motor running. The man who had been sent to get it held the rear door open. The chauffeur jumped out of his seat as soon as Hatamura and Sawada left the terminal.

"Here we are," said Hatamura. "Well done, Takahashi-kun. Was there a problem?"

"None at all. The cabbies took care of things, and we should move along," the man said pointing discreetly toward a pair of police officers who were eyeing their activities.

"Indeed, we should," Hatamura said looking around to see the pair. He nodded toward them with a broad smile and, with a larger than necessary motion, said, "Put the bags in the trunk."

Before joining Sawada in the back seat of the car, Hatamura stopped to speak to the man who was holding the door. "I'm going to take Sawada-kun to have a nice hot bath. After that, we'll stop for drinks before having dinner at the *Kikusui*. Meet us there."

The man bowed sharply and said, "*Hai! Kashikumari-mashita.*" When Hatamura took his seat, the man closed the door and lined up with the others to bow as the car drove off.

"How was the flight?" asked Hatamura.

"The flight is always a long one and the past couple of weeks have been truly hectic, but your greeting makes up for all that old business. It feels great to be back."

"I'm glad to hear that. The Director said that you would be with us only a couple of days and he told me to make you comfortable."

Sawada couldn't help being surprised. He had met Hatamura several times and knew him as one of Tsuji-san's *kobun*. Still, they had never been close and, since they were of the same generation, polite directness was all he could expect of their interactions. The gracious treatment he was receiving went well beyond what was necessary. Sawada was also surprised to learn that Tsuji-san himself was taking an interest in this visit. Normally, when he made his periodic trips to Japan the Director was friendly enough, but he rarely demonstrated special interest in Sawada's efforts.

"I'm deeply honored, Hatamura-san," Sawada said bowing as much as he could, sitting in the car. He spoke carefully now and referred to Hatamura with a politely neutral term. Hatamura had called Sawada "brother" when they were in the airport. He had not objected when Sawada returned the familiarity, but all of that had been in public and things might be different here in the privacy of the car. Sawada was intensely aware that Tsuji-san had never formally accepted him as a *kobun*.

"It's too bad that you have to return to America in only two days."

"I wish I could stay longer, but I've made arrangements for a major sword buying campaign in the area around the city of Atlanta. Several thousand dollars have been invested so I really must return."

"I see," Hatamura nodded. "You advertise your operations, then?"

Sawada noted that this was the second time Hatamura had asked about his activities in America. He was willing to tell what he could about his work, but it was hard to know where to begin. It seemed clear that Hatamura and the others here in Tokyo knew very little about what he did or the challenges he faced in America.

"Yes. Well-designed ads are a central part of the operation. You see, anyone can own swords in America so they can be anywhere. I travel to various parts of the country to buy them. Its more complex than it may sound, but I rent rooms in large motels and run ads telling people to bring me their swords. When they come in, I buy them."

"I see," Hatamura nodded blankly. "And you can just buy the swords? Legally?" he continued.

Sword ownership has always been restricted in Japan and since World War II registration requirements have been especially strict, so Sawada understood Hatamura's surprise. "Swords are entirely legal in America," Sawada said. "No one cares about them, so I can buy as many as I want."

Hatamura shook his head in disbelief. "You don't even have to register them or anything."

"Oh no. In fact, in most places, I could even buy guns if I wanted to."

"Pistols and rifles and everything?" Hatamura asked incredulously.

"That's right. Machine guns are absolutely out of the question as far as the law goes, although I have been offered them. There are some cities that have special regulations and now they're passing laws because the Blacks and others are getting very powerful guns. Aside from that, nobody cares about guns in America."

"Do Americans really carry guns? I mean just regular people?"

"Not everyone, and in most small towns they're not necessary." Sawada couldn't resist a bit of drama. "Still, you really need to be armed in much of the country. Americans just don't know how to get along and the Whites can no longer control things."

"I see," Hatamura said again. "Do you carry a gun when you're working?"

Sawada chuckled. "I do most of my traveling by airplane and that makes guns very difficult. If I drive to one of my buying operations, I bring a gun. Sometimes, when I'm working in a big city and have lots of money, I hire a security guard."

"Are Americans hard to deal with?" Hatamura asked sincerely.

"Yes and no," Sawada replied thoughtfully. "They don't know how to work together and they act impulsively so when you deal with them, you have to be flexible."

"Are they slippery?" asked Hatamura.

"Not really," replied Sawada somewhat surprised by all of this interest. "I think they're like children. They're honest, but they don't think about their actions and don't take care of what they have. They're very short-sighted."

"I see," nodded Hatamura. "Tsuji-san told me that you have been far more successful than any of the other sword return operations the Brotherhood has tried."

"I am deeply honored that the Director has bothered to take note of my activities." Sawada made a slight nod with his head and drew his breath across his teeth with a soft hissing sound. He tried not to betray his surprise at Hatamura's comment, but he had never heard that the Brotherhood had been involved in returning swords from America before he began buying them.

"I've never heard how you got started." asked Hatamura.

Sawada hesitated. His decision to move to America remained a source of uncertainty and he was not sure what Hatamura may have heard. "When I moved to America, I intended to enter the jewelry business, but I bought a couple swords at an antique shop. I presented them to the Director as a gift. He graciously encouraged me to acquire more. When I was able to find some more, he encouraged me to begin a systemic search for swords. He arranged financing and contacts here in Japan.

Perfecting the operation took some time, but I made contacts and developed procedures that now work quite well."

Sawada paused for a moment to recall the events that had brought him to his current situation. His father had operated a small liquor shop in a working class neighborhood of Chiba, an area of suburban Tokyo that has benefited hardly at all from the city's growth and modernization. As an independent businessman, he would have been a leading member of pre-War society, but by the 1960s he could feel himself being left out of new, corporate Japan. To increase their son's chances of success, Sawada's parents had enrolled him in one of Tokyo's better urban high schools. Sawada wanted to perform well, but the ninety minute commute he had to make twice a day kept him from putting in the extra work that would be required for real success. He was unable to rise above the mass of the other students and his teachers decided he was not a good prospect. If his family had more money, they might have been able to encourage his teachers with gifts and favors, but that had been impossible.

Sawada looked out the window and remembered the long rides to school and how he had dreaded them. Who would have guess that he would be riding in a chauffeur-driven car?

As a tenth grader, when it became apparent that he would not be among the top students, Sawada found himself being teased by a gang that included several members of the baseball team. He was never sure why they picked on him and he was not their only target, but once he had been selected, they made his life miserable. They waited outside of school to call him names and pelt him with rocks and garbage. Occasionally their roughhousing turned into serious beatings. As the bullies increased their intensity, Sawada found other students joining in. His teachers never took part in the harassment, but Sawada was sure they were aware of it and tolerated his embarrassment.

Shifting his gaze from the window to his companion, Sawada wondered how Hatamura had passed his teenage years. Had anyone tormented him, Sawada was sure Hatamura would have known how to respond.

At first, Sawada tried to ignore his tormentors or deflect their attention to others. Neither strategy worked. The harder he tried to avoid the gang's barbs, the more brazen they became. Had he lived closer to the school, he might have joined the baseball team. Had his parents let him, he would have transferred to another school. In desperation he had mentioned his distress to the only teacher who treated him with anything approaching warmth. The instructor offered no help, however, and simply counseled him to 'gaman-suru'--to persevere.

In his isolation and anger, Sawada was drawn to a small group of other students who shared his outcast status. They had little in common beyond poor prospects and ample anger, but when they were together as a group, the bullies on the baseball team left them alone. With their security established, the small clique sought identity by engaging in rebellious activities. At first, they simply listened to rock music and dabbled in drugs. With time, they began to dress in outlandish clothes and go to the park at Harajuku on Sunday afternoons to dance wildly with other teenagers. These activities earned them a reputation among their classmates, but their identity as rebels was ultimately established when they discovered right wing politics. Political activity of any kind was rare in their school, but espousing ultra-nationalistic views set Sawada and his friends apart from their classmates and had the added advantage of making their teachers very uncomfortable.

When the baseball players and other boys made a point of letting their school uniforms become rumpled and worn out, Sawada's group bought custom tailored uniform coats that were cut long enough to reach nearly to their knees. They kept these clean and pressed and wore them with obvious pride. Most other students wore soiled sneakers, but Sawada's friends preferred highly polished black shoes with very long pointed tips. Their teachers would tolerate no more than these extremes when they were at school. Away from campus, however, the boys went even farther. To show off their precise crew-cuts, they abandoned their school caps whenever they could, and wore dark glasses and arm bands supporting right wing causes.

They named their group "The Imperial Respect Cell" and registered as one of the school's official clubs which let them take part in school events. To be as outrageous as possible, they developed a number of chanted routines about the Emperor and racial purity. They practiced these on the playground after school and executed them with choreographic skills they had acquired while dancing at Harajuku.

These antics had three results. First they afforded Sawada and his friends considerable respect among the other students. No one teased them and many girls began to find them attractive. Second, the faculty's low opinion of the boys became fixed in a way that assured they would have no academic future. Finally their antics brought the boys to the attention of Tsuji-san who was at that time the Senior Assistant Director of the Greater Japan Imperial League.

Tsuji-san invited the boys to take part in campaign rallies he was organizing. They accepted willingly and found riding through the city on brightly painted sound trucks adequate reward. When Tsuji began to support the boys with new uniforms, a special drum, and finally with gifts of cash, they became permanent fixtures at Imperial League functions.

After high school, Sawada entered a small private college. He majored in English because he enjoyed the language. He also joined the campus sword study group out of diffuse interest, but he did not enjoy college life and spent very little time on campus. He graduated because he was more than smart enough to do the small amount of work assigned to him. In fact, Sawada was smart enough to realize that he could expect little out of his family and school connections. He also realized he did not want one of the low level office jobs he saw other students accepting. Tsuji-san offered a much more interesting option.

Initially, Tsuji-san encouraged Sawada to enter politics. He was a clean cut, good looking young man with no police record and a solid family background. Tsuji-san wanted him to prepare to run for a seat in the Diet. Sawada considered this advice politely and accepted a staff position within the Imperial League, but he was never very serious about politics. The League's positions were not easy to articulate and its powers, although considerable, did not include winning elections. Thus, Sawada's chances of ever gaining a seat in either the Diet or the City government were essentially nil. He was far too impatient to relish the idea of waiting 30 years or more for such a slim chance at success.

Tsuji-san had been reticent to bring Sawada into the actual work of the Kawabayashi Brotherhood because it would break Sawada family traditions and end any hope the young man might have of becoming an accepted member of middle class Japanese society. Sawada understood these reservations, although he never addressed them explicitly. He certainly never mentioned the name of the Brotherhood, but he never missed an opportunity to tell Tsuji-san that he was willing to help him in any way he could. After several such offers, the senior man relented by letting Sawada help with ticket scalping.

As the car traveled along the crowded Tokyo Expressway, Sawada recalled his adventures as a scalper. Truly, that is when his education had begun.

Like underworld organizations everywhere, the Kawabayashi Brotherhood made most of its money in small-scale activities that escaped the notice of the authorities and most citizens. One of Tsuji-san's associates, for example, did a good business selling hand towels and napkins at just above the going rate because he would not tolerate competition. As head of a small group called the 'construction section,' Hatamura spent most of his time working with cement producers, making sure that their trucks were not damaged and could arrive on time at road building construction. Tsuji-san had links to several taxi companies, but far more important were the personal relationships he maintained with virtually every car parts dealer in central Tokyo. These relationships added only a few yen to the cost of every spark plug and fan belt sold in the city, but they let Tsuiji-san ensure that parts distribution was never interrupted. His branch of the Brotherhood also supported the Japanese love of music by facilitating the distribution of concert tickets.

Sawada's first regular responsibility for Tsuji-san involved buying tickets to particularly popular performances. Whenever a big star came to Japan, Sawada would either arrive at the sales outlet before other customers or he would simply push his way to the head of the line and trust several burly gang members to make sure no one objected. Once in line, Sawada would buy all of the tickets for the best weekend dates and arrange for them to be resold at bars and informal outlets run by associates of the Kawabayashi Brotherhood. This drives prices up, often substantially, but the system is well-established because very few people object. Promoters get sold out performances and can usually count on a generous kickback. Fans can buy their tickets in convenient locations and, in the complex world of Japanese gift giving, higher prices are not necessarily bad. The gift of a couple of overpriced tickets to an associate's teenage children, for example, can be an effective way of getting his attention or repaying a favor. The profits of ticket sales are, of course, never reported to tax authorities and performers do not share in them, but those are not the Brotherhood's problems.

Sawada was a good worker with a good knowledge of popular music, so he did very well with the ticket operation. He also enjoyed the company of the men who worked for Tsuji-san and took great pride when they began to call him "Brother." Still, after two years of working full time for Tsuji-san, Sawada grew restless. In spite of the fact that he had already been given more power and responsibility than many other workers who had come through the ranks as day laborers and taxi drivers, he felt himself making very little progress within the organization. Beyond that, he met a remarkable American girl - Rebecca - who was teaching English in a private school in Shizuoka. After they met at a rock concert, they spent nearly every weekend together in Tokyo. Sawada showed Rebecca things that had not been addressed in her Japanese society classes at Southwold College and she amazed him with her relaxed sexuality. When her contract was completed, Rebecca convinced Sawada that he could be very successful in her father's jewelry business. Thus, without seeking Tsuji-san's advice, Sawada had married and move to Portland, Oregon.

"You took a big risk, but it appears to have paid off," Hatamura said. Sawada did not fully understand this statement and Hatamura may have made it with a judgmental tone, but there was no time for a response because Hatamura continued immediately. "I'm sure we'll be talking more about the sword return operation, but before we arrive in the city, I need to tell you about what we need to accomplish in the coming days."

"Of course," Sawada said attentively.

"First, the Director is eager to hear your report on the Muramasa *tanto* you have discovered. He wants to allow most of tomorrow for that purpose."

"Fine," said Sawada. "I'll tell him what I can about the blade, but it's a complicated situation."

"Yes, well, I think the Director may have some information for you," said Hatamura, obviously not wanting to discuss the issue.

"There is another matter I need to tell you about. It is of some importance."

Sawada listened closely. Hatamura cleared his throat.

"Director Tsuji has asked me to address the matter of your membership within our Brotherhood." Hatamura was speaking with great control and obvious care as he said this and Sawada was swept by a wave of frightened uncertainty. His chest tightened.

"The Director has instructed me to tell you that he deeply appreciates your efforts for him," Hatamura continued. "He is very pleased with your industry and the dedication you have demonstrated." Sawada was still not sure where the conversation was going, but Hatamura's tone let him relax.

"The Director has been deeply embarrassed by his inability to reward you adequately. He wants you to be able to take part in the operation and the success of the Brotherhood." Hatamura paused to let Sawada realize that he was being offered a position of leadership within the Kawabayashi Brotherhood. "Are you prepared to accept Director Tsuji as your patron?"

"I am overwhelmed. Tsuji-sama has always been generous. Formalizing our relationship has always been my hope."

"Excellent! Tsuji-sama will be very pleased," Hatamura smiled. "Because of your life in America and your busy schedule we have not been able to make all of the usual arrangements. Still, Tsuji-sama would like to accept you as his *kobun* this evening. We have prepared a small ceremony."

Sawada was nearly overcome. "I am deeply honored."

"Tsuji-sama has asked me to serve as *nakodo*." As he said this, Hatamura turned toward Sawada, placed his hands on his knees and he bent forward at the waist in a formal bow. His jaw was set and he did not relax until Sawada spoke.

"I am deeply honored," Sawada said with a bow that mirrored Hatamura's.

There was a pause as both men traded bows for a second time. Sawada was overwhelmed with emotion and not certain what he would have said had he been able to speak. Hatamura broke the silence.

"If you are up to it, the Director has arranged a dinner of initiation for this evening. Brothers from throughout the Kanto District."

Sawada shook his head in speechless emotion. "I am overwhelmed," he managed to say before realizing that he should acknowledge Hatamura's role as go-between. It helped him gain his composure.

"I am deeply honored that you have agreed to serve as *nakodo*. We have hardly had the opportunity to become well acquainted, but I respect Tsuji-sama's selection and I willingly acknowledge your generosity and senior status." Without thought, Sawada adopted both the formal speech and traditional vocabulary appropriate for members of the underworld.

Hatamura accepted his bow, but tried to change the tone of the conversation with a broad smile. "We must relax. There will be plenty of time for formality. You will also need to change clothes. I thought we'd drop by the *Ebisu* bathhouse for a good soaking. I feared you would not be traveling with all the clothing you might need, so I've also arranged for an appropriate outfit to be waiting at the room."

Hatamura and Sawada spent an hour enjoying the steamy warmth and good fellowship of one of Downtown Tokyo's few remaining traditional bathhouses. From there Hatamura had escorted Sawada to the *Unkonshi*, a first class *ryokan* near Ueno Station and left him in the care of one of the inn's porters before leaving to make his own preparations for the evening.

Sawada found a large room had been reserved in his name and that a complete *hakama haori* had been laid out for him. There was also an attendant waiting to help him into the complicated formal garment. Sawada had not worn *kimono* in years and had never had to tie and fold the layers and parts of the *haori*. The attendant deftly draped him with the parts of the garment and arranged them into a series of nested planes. The black *kimono* carried the crest of the Kawabayashi Brotherhood over both shoulders and in the center of the back. As he was being dressed, one of the serving women on the inn staff brought him green tea and a couple of preserved plums so that by the time Hatamura returned for him, Sawada felt truly pampered and wonderfully turned out.

Hatamura arrived wearing a formal *kimono* similar to Sawada's. His presence was announced by one of the inn porters and he waited outside Sawada's room until Sawada had had time to seat himself on a flat pillow. When he was ready, Sawada's attendant slid the paper door open for Hatamura, who knelt on the wooden floor outside of the room. Without looking up, he pushed a small bundle into the room and followed it on his knees. As the door was slid shut behind him, he knelt again on the straw *tatami* of the room and spoke in a deep formal tone.

"Brother, I have the honor of bringing you to your ceremony of introduction. Please distinguish me with your company."

Sawada knelt to a deep bow. It was the obvious thing to do, but as he returned this gesture, Sawada was uncertain what to do next. His relations with Tsuji-san and his employees had always been rather informal. During the years with the ticket sales operation he had seen others using the highly formalized words of *jingi*, but he had not grown up in the code of morality and the experiences he had had were all separated by his long years in America. Still, when he spoke, he fell comfortably into the formal style Hatamura had used.

"Elder brother, you do me great honor and embarrass me with generosity I will never be able to repay." Sawada's forehead was near the floor as he spoke.

Hatamura did not rise until he had pushed his bundle toward Sawada. When it was squarely in front of him, he assumed a formal kneeling position with his head slightly bowed, his shoulders squared, and his hands resting on his knees. His jaw was set and he remained tense as he spoke. "I have brought small gifts to mark this occasion and to symbolize my small part in your formal introduction to our Brotherhood."

Sawada rose from the floor to see a small parcel wrapped in gray silk *furoshiki*, a traditional Japanese wrapping cloth. "Please open it, simple as it is," Hatamura said.

Sawada loosened the knots that connected the corners of the *furoshiki* and pulled it open to reveal two small packages. He turned first to the one that was wrapped in a sheet of traditional Japanese gift paper. He loosened the red string that held it closed to find a long narrow bamboo leaf neatly folded around a pair of salted herring. The other box was wrapped in bright blue Western style paper. It contained a solid gold Rolex watch.

Sawada was silent for a moment until he realized he was prepared for an eventuality like this. Without saying anything, he rose and walked with short choppy steps to where his luggage had been laid out. From among the things he had brought from America, he selected a parcel he had wrapped in a *furoshiki*. Kneeling, he pushed the parcel forward. Hatamura loosened the cloth to find a plane wooden box closed with a neatly tied black braid. Inside was a roughly thrown tea bowl. Hatamura held it up admiringly with both hands and looked at the written attribution on the inside of the box cover. "Thank you, brother, for this elegant Tamba tea bowl."

"And thank you, elder brother for this gift I will wear with pride and recollection of our association." Both bowed once again.

From the inn, Hatamura and Sawada were driven to the *Kikusui*, an old style restaurant north of Asakusa Shrine. The entire front of the restaurant compound was lined with large wreaths of bright paper flowers. Each wreath was crossed by a paper banner bearing the name and address of the Brother who had donated it. Sawada did not know all the names, but the sheer number of wreaths and the fact that they came such distant cities as Sendai and Hakodate in the north, and Kurashiki and Kita-Kyushu, in the south, let him know that Tsuji-san was making his initiation a major event.

As they prepared to step out of the limousine, Hatamura pointed to a police officer across the street photographing people as they entered. "The *satsu* are probably pretty curious about this gathering. We might as well keep them guessing," he said and gave Sawada a large wicker basket to wear over his head as he stepped from the car into the building.

In the vestibule, Sawada was met by a delegation of four Kawabayashi members. After greeting him, they waited while a restaurant employee gave him a comb and mirror which he used to make sure his hair was perfect. Then, the group proceeded into the restaurant. A very large space had been created by removing most of the interior sliding partitions. The room was festively decorated and full of men dressed in black *kimono*. They were seated at low tables and had been enjoying *sake*. A great many small flasks stood on the tables together with many plates of food and treats. When Sawada entered the room, the group looked toward him and began a spontaneous round of applause. There were shouts of "Welcome, brother," "The guest of honor!" and "Here he is now." Many of the men raised their *sake* cups in his direction.

Sawada was brought to the front of the room. Hatamura invited him to be seated at a vacant place next to Tsuji-san. Only then did he take his own seat nearby. Sawada was not in the center of the room, but he was directly in front of the *tokonoma* where a complete suit of armor and a beautifully matched set of swords were on display. As he looked around the room everyone was smiling.

Tsuji-san drew the group to order by simply squaring his shoulders. When they were silent he said, "Brothers, I express my deepest appreciation for the generosity and respect you have shown by joining us here this evening." He paused to bow deeply toward the center of the room. "I have invited you to witness a birth and record a rite of paternity." He nodded to a Shinto priest who was waiting outside the door.

The priest was dressed in flowing brocade robes with a high black hat. He carried a large paper whisk as he strode to an altar that had been set up at the rear of the room. When he was positioned directly in front of it, he swept the whisk back and forth several times and began a chanted prayer. Twice he stopped to strike a small gong and sweep the whisk over offerings of fruit, *sake*, and flowers that had been set out in front of the altar. When he was done, he turned to the assembled crowded and bowed. The party had been quiet while the priest was chanting, but as soon as he was finished the men broke into boisterous conversation. Several threw coins on the altar. Others bowed their heads in its direction and slapped their hands together in relaxed reverence.

As the priest left, the room grew silent and everyone turned back to Tsuji-san.

"Brothers, friends, most deeply esteemed colleagues," he said grandly. "What makes us different from other men?" The room was silent. "Is it simply that we work harder than other Japanese? Are we bigger or stronger than others of our nation? Were we born to wealth and power? Have we been raised in culture and privilege?" There was soft muffled reaction from the group as several men scoffed at Tsuji-san's last suggestion.

"Of course not," Tsuji-san said. "We are simple Japanese. We have no power and little respect. Many in the country despise us because they have accepted foreign ideas and modern thoughts. Our lot is to preserve all that is best in the national character. Although others cannot understand, this is our chosen duty. Our burden and our privilege."

"Brother friends," he continued after a moment, "who practices the conduct of the samurai if we do not preserve it? Where is the morality of the warrior if not within our Brotherhood? Who can respect the grand traditions of the country if we let them pass?" There was nodded approval from the crowd.

"What is the key to our way of life and to our ability to preserve ourselves and the best part of our national spirit? It is loyalty," he said with rising voice. Again, several members of the assembled group nodded their strong agreement. None of these ideas were new to the men in the room. This was the rhetoric of virtually every formal meeting of the Kawabayashi-Gumi.

"Loyalty to one another, to our seniors, and to those who have been placed below us. That is the morality of the samurai and it is our special preserve," Tsuji-san continued. "Tonight you have come here to help forge a formal link of loyalty. You will witness Sawada Kenji accept my sponsorship and you will record my willingness to support Brother Sawada as I would a son."

Tsuji-san paused and looked around the room with a pleasant smile. When he spoke again his tone was slightly softer. "Brother Sawada is a long time member of our circle. For several years he has worked to establish our organization in America. By accepting one another as father and as son, we will be bringing the Kawabayashi Brotherhood into the future and in strong new directions." Tsuji-san lowered his head to indicate he was done. Everyone in the room waited in silence.

Hatamura squared his shoulders to let the group know he was about to speak. "It is my honor to serve as the conduit for the new alliance being made here tonight." He rose and walked to the front of the table where Tsuji-san and Sawada were sitting. Bowing to both of them, he knelt and picked up a large red lacquer *sake* cup that had been placed on the table. He held it toward Sawada who bowed intuitively. Then he held it toward Tsuji-san who made a similar gesture. Setting it down, Hatamura picked up a flask of *sake* that was waiting on the table. He filled the cup with several small pours. He set the flask aside and offered the cup to Tsuji-san. "This is the blood of a new relationship."

The older man accepted the cup with both hands, held it for a moment in front of his face before nearly draining it with several sips. When there was just a small amount left in the cup, he set it down and said, "Fill it for my newest son."

Hatamura moved the cup to Sawada and filled it with the same series of small pours he had used to the first time. He held the cup up to Sawada. "This is the blood of new relationship," he said in a loud voice. In a barely audible whisper he added, "Drink it all." Sawada did so in three separate sips. When he was done, he passed the cup back to Hatamura who turned to let the others in the room see that it was empty. Tsuji-san smiled broadly and the room broke into applause.

As Hatamura returned to his seat, Tsuji-san nodded to an older woman who had been waiting in the hall, and she stepped back to let a procession of women in *kimono* enter the room. They were carrying platters of artfully arranged treats. Several of these were set on each of the tables and fresh flasks of hot *sake* and large icy bottles of beer were brought into the room as well. The men helped themselves to skewers of marinated clams, *sushi*, slices of pickled radish, broiled chicken strips, and deep fried vegetables and shrimp. As they ate they poured one another cups of *sake* and glasses of beer.

When food and drink were placed on the table in front of Tsuji-san he held a *sake* flask up to Sawada who bowed and lifted a cup to be filled. Sawada took a small sip, set the cup aside and offered to fill Tsuji-san's cup. The senior man accepted the wine he was offered.

"Father, I am deeply moved by your generosity. I have long wanted to pledge my personal support to you, but this is far more than I ever could have hoped for."

"My son, this ceremony is overdue. You have earned far more than I am giving you this evening. Relax. Enjoy yourself. Get ready for full day of hard work tomorrow." He offered Sawada more *sake*. The younger man quickly held up his cup to accept the wine. "No, no, drain the cup," Tsuji-san said and he held the flask while Sawada drank what had been poured earlier. When the cup was empty, he filled it again.

"Father, I am eager to understand your comments about bringing the Brotherhood to America," Sawada asked with genuine curiosity.

Tsuji-san smiled and waved his hand. "My son, this evening is for you. We will discuss business tomorrow."

Sawada was now even more curious and uncertain, but he knew he would have to wait until tomorrow for clarification. One of the Brothers came to his table with a *sake* flask and offered to pour him a drink. Sawada accepted, but made sure that his cup was nearly full when he held it out. That would let him accept the offer without requiring that he drink too much.

The socializing continued for more than two hours. Food was periodically replaced and the flow of flasks of hot *sake* never stopped. Men moved through the room pouring one another drinks and engaging in relaxed conversation. Behind the informality there was, however, a definite order to the evening. The first man who offered Sawada a drink was followed by several others. Without apparent orchestration, about half of the men at the party came to Sawada's table, knelt and offered to fill his *sake* cup. After Sawada accepted their kindness, they all placed a small white packet on his table and bowed to Tsuji-san. Some stayed long enough to make a brief comment or two, but it was all small talk. One old man asked how Sawada liked American girls and another suggested that he must get lonely living in a foreign country. A younger man dressed like all the others in the room, came to Sawada's side and took charge of the gifts he was receiving. He also circulated a sign-in sheet to each of the men who had brought gifts.

Just before eleven a photographer arrived. He set up his equipment at one end of the room as the socializing continued. When he was ready the tables were quickly moved out of the way and the group gathered for a picture. Hatamura took charge of arranging the guests. He had Tsuji-san sit near the center of the room, and Sawada was placed in a group that sat on the floor around him. The rest of the group stood around and beside them. When everyone was in the right place, Hatamura sat down with the group next to Tsuiji-san and the photographer took his pictures. As soon as he was done, the group began to disperse.

"My son," Tsuji-san said to Sawada, "some of Hatamura's men are ready to show you the pleasures of *Kabuki-cho*. Will you join them?"

"Father, the trip and evening have been overwhelming. I appreciate the offer, but . . ." He let his voice trail off.

"A wise decision, son. We have a full day tomorrow. Get a good night's sleep and I will see you at the League office tomorrow at, shall we say, 9:00?"

Sawada awoke early the next morning. The smoky room and the eating and drinking of the night before might have left him feeling miserable, but he had remembered to remain moderate in the midst of an apparently excessive affair. He had accepted cups of wine from virtually every one of the Brothers who had attended his initiation ceremony, but he had been careful to take only a sip or two from most of the cups. He had used fresh cups whenever possible so that he had actually had very little to drink. He had also done little more than taste the rich, salty treats that were served to the group. For these reasons, he awoke refreshed and hungry.

As soon as he rolled out of his thick *futon*, he straightened the light *yukata* he had slept in and walked down the hall to wash his face and brush his teeth at the lavatory. He brought the small towel the inn had supplied with his robe, but left his American toiletry kits because he knew a new toothbrush and a razor would be waiting for him. As he washed and shaved, he greeted another guest who came to share the long tiled sink. This required no more than a pleasant nod, but it struck Sawada as a much more civilized way of beginning the day than the sterile isolation he had grown used to in American motels.

When he returned to his room, a middle-aged woman in a neatly pressed *kimono* brought him a cup of green tea and asked if he would like breakfast. He told her he would and she returned with a neatly arranged tray of lacquered containers and small ceramic plates. She laid these out on the low table in the room and knelt on a *zabuton* to chat with him as he ate. Sawada rarely ate breakfast in America, having never developed a taste for the greasy sweet morning meals served in America, but his mouth watered as the woman set out the dishes.

He slid his white wood *hashi* out of their paper cover and snapped them apart so he could mix his *miso* soup. There was a single small shrimp in the bottom of the lacquered bowl along with several pieces of creamy white *tofu*. As he savored one of them, he couldn't help remembering how ill he had become after eating a large helping of biscuits and gravy on a buying trip in Tennessee.

The woman did not intrude, but waited patiently as Sawada broke a raw egg into a small bowl and used his *hashi* to whip it with *shoyu*. After he poured this mixture over a bowl of steamy rice and took a large mouthful she spoke.

"Our guest is not from Tokyo?" she asked as Sawada dipped a small slip of seaweed in *shoyu* and wrapped it around a second mouthful of rice.

"No," answered Sawada. "I'm an *Eddoko*, but I've been living in America for some years."

"America! *Hora, nee*," she replied with raised eyebrows. "America, indeed. It must feel very good to be back home."

"It does, Auntie. It does." Sawada said with complete sincerity.

Sawada ate slowly, enjoying both his food and the woman's pleasant conversation, but it was still before 7:30 when he was done and the dishes had been cleared from his room. To fill the time until he was to meet with Tsuji-san, he thought about going down to the wholesale fish market area around Tsukiji. But the day's selling would be over soon and he found the crowded bustle of Tokyo so interesting he decided to simply spend a little time enjoying the city. As he walked along streets full of handsome people moving quickly along their way, Sawada couldn't help noticing Tokyo's beauty and dynamism.

There was construction proceeding everywhere, and the new buildings were quite attractive. Sawada also liked the older side streets and generally reveled in the crowded trimness of the city. At the Uguisudani station he bought a ticket for Shimbashi, but so enjoyed the feeling of the platform that he let two Yamanote trains go by before he boarded one. While waiting, he bought a copy of the *Yomiuri Shimbun* at the platform newsstand. The woman behind the counter understood him immediately and filled his request without hesitation. How different things were in America where every question was a challenge, everybody he met found him strange, and every interaction required an effort.

He stopped in a coffee shop near Shimbashi station to enjoy a cup of strong coffee and read his paper. The coffee cost the equivalent of $6.75, but Sawada understood the menu completely and the waiter brought his coffee without question or hesitation. By the time he arrived at the offices of the Greater Japan Imperial League, Sawada felt more relaxed than he had in years. He felt comfortably at home as he had never felt in America and now that he had a formal place within the Kawabayashi Brotherhood, he looked forward to someday soon being able to come home to Japan.

When Sawada stepped into the Greater Japan Imperial League, the uniformed young woman sitting closest to the front door rose, bowed toward him and said, "*Irrashyaimase.*" It had been years since he had been in the offices and he recognized none of the staff.

"Thank you," Sawada said with a bow. "Sawada Kenji, for Director Tsuji."

"Ahh, Sawada-san!" said the girl with a broad smile and a louder voice. When the other women heard her, they all rose and bowed politely in his direction. The women who had been sitting at the desk nearest the back of the work area immediately started toward the front of the room. She moved quickly, but, like everyone else, she wore light slippers so she slipped her feet along with a shuffling gate. When she got to the edge of the raised portion of the floor, she squared her shoulders, folded her hands over her groin and gave Sawada a deep formal bow.

"Sawada-san. Thank you for coming and welcome to our office," she said. "We have been expecting you. Please come in." The other girls formed a wedge behind her and all four joined in more bowing.

As Sawada stepped out of his shoes and up to the wooden floor, one of the girls scurried to give him a pair of slippers. All the others made attentive noises and small welcoming motions toward the couch and chairs in the back of the work area.

"The Director has told us about you," one of the women said and another added, "We have been eager to meet you."

"Thank you. It is a pleasure to be back after all these years," Sawada said as he walked toward the couch.

"The Director is working in the back room," the senior girl, Miko, said. "He is eager to see you. Atsuko-san, please tell Director Tsuji that Sawada-san has arrived." The younger girl scurried away.

Sawada sat down as Miko stood attentively by his side. "How have you found Tokyo? It must be very dull after all of your experience in America," she said.

"American can be an adventure, but it is a joy to be back in the country," Sawada said not trying to hide the pleasure he felt. "I look forward to spending more time here." Miko said nothing.

"Good morning, my son," Tsuji's voice boomed through the office. "I am glad to see that our party last night did not leave you too exhausted."

"Absolutely not, Father," Sawada said rising to greet his patron. "Had I known you would be here I could have arrived much earlier. I sincerely hope I have not kept you waiting." There was a hint of anxiety in Sawada's voice.

"Relax, relax, son," said Tsuji-san. "We all enjoyed last night and I especially wanted you to have a good time. We have a few things to do before you return to America, but there is plenty of time." He motioned for Atsuko to bring some tea and he sat back to light a cigarette. "You're probably ready to return to America now. Japan must strike you as backward and dull," he said as he snapped his lighter closed.

"On the contrary, Father," Sawada said earnestly. "I would be happy to stay right here in Japan for the rest of my life."

"Perhaps you would," Tsuji-san chuckled as if Sawada had made a small joke, "but if things go as I hope they will, your duty to the Brotherhood will keep you busy in America for years to come." Tsuji-san smiled broadly as he said this. "I'll explain all of that later. First I want to discuss the situation with the Muramasa dagger."

Sawada was taken back by Tsuji-san's comments. He had been expecting to discuss nothing but the dagger and the *Oyabun's* mention of other plans and long-term duties in America took him entirely by surprise. He was very curious, but he bowed reflexively and said, "Fine, Father."

"Please begin by reviewing the situation for me," Tsuji-san said crossing his legs. "How did you find out about the *tanto*?"

Sawada leaned forward in his chair and spoke seriously. "Father, over the years, I have built up a network of Americans who sell me swords. These are called 'pickers'." He used the English word, but pronounced it 'pikaa' so that Tsuji-san could understand it.

"Pikaa," Tsuji-san repeated thoughtfully.

"Yes, sir," said Sawada without trying to explain the word. The *Oyabun* repeated it once again as if he were trying to master it as a piece of potentially useful vocabulary.

"Some of the pickers have become quite loyal and they call me if they come across a good sword."

"Who are these pickers? Are they dealers?" Tsuji-san asked.

"Some are gun dealers, but most are private collectors who simply find swords from time to time."

Tsuji-san shook his head in mystification. "What a strange system," he said.

Sawada had to agree. "America really isn't very well organized."

"At any rate, one of these pickers found the dagger?" Tsuji-san asked to get the story moving again.

"Not quite," Sawada said pursing his lips. "My picker was at a gun show last spring when another man bought the dagger. The picker thought it might be a good one so he made an *oshigata* of the signature and sent it to me."

Tsuji-san stifled his urge to ask about gun shows and instead simply nodded to indicate that he was following.

"I always follow up leads like that one, so I called the man who had the dagger. He still had it, but wouldn't sell. Since I saw no special reason to pursue the blade, I simply filed the information away and let the matter drop until I got your fax two weeks ago. The *oshigata* you sent seemed familiar to me so I checked my records. When I realized that it was from the dagger my picker had found, I called you right back."

"Excellent, my son. Your attention to detail is outstanding" said Tsuiji-san.

"It was really a lucky fluke that I was able to make the match so quickly," Sawada said modestly. He continued after a brief pause. "Father, I'm very curious. Why is this dagger of special interest?"

The *Oyabun* leaned forward to flick his cigarette into the cast iron ashtray on the coffee table. "The situation is complicated and I'm still not sure I understand all of the details. A meeting I've arranged for later today may make things more clear." He leaned back and took a long drag on his cigarette. "At this point only three things seem certain. First, a powerful man wants the dagger and it is to our advantage to make it available to him. Second, the dagger disappeared with another very valuable sword. If it can lead us to that blade, the dagger becomes even more valuable." Again, Tsuji-san paused to clean the tip of his cigarette.

"Finally," Tsuji-san said with emphasis, "it seems that the dagger may have been Brotherhood property. It appears to have been stolen from us." He set his jaw and tapped the table hard with his index finger. "If it was ours, we must do everything in our power to recover it."

Sawada nodded his agreement and took a couple sheets of paper out of his brief case. He placed these on the table in front of Tsuji-san. "This is the rubbing you faxed to me and this is the rubbing my picker made. I think you can see that they are identical in every regard."

Tsuji-san leaned forward to inspect the rubbings. "I'm no expert on these matters," he said slipping on a pair of heavy-framed reading glasses. "They look very similar," he concluded after a moment. Turning to one of the office girls who was working just a few steps away, he said, "Atsuko-chan, make us some copies of these rubbings. Three will be enough." Turning back to Sawada as the girl took the papers from his hand he said, "We may want to show these to some other people."

"I'm sure they are from the same sword," the younger man said.

"Your opinion is good enough for me. Buy it. Pay whatever you have to."

"That's the problem, Father," Sawada said with a grimace. "The man who has the *tanto* refuses to sell. In addition to talking with him several months ago, I made three telephone calls to him in the past two weeks. He entirely refuses to listen to offers."

"Did you offer him enough money?"

"I think so," shrugged Sawada. "My first offer was five thousand dollars which is more than anyone else in America would have paid. Last week, I raised that to a hundred thousand."

"That's about Y10,000,000?"

When Sawada nodded Tsuji-san said, "Offer him more! I'd be happy to pay five times that much. Offer him whatever he wants."

"I don't think it's simply a matter of money, Father. I couldn't even get him to name a price. It's as if the man does not want to deal with me on this matter."

"What's the problem?"

"I'm not sure. Another dealer may have gotten involved." Sawada paused. "It is also possible that the man simply does not want to deal with Japanese people. Some Americans truly do hate us."

"I see," said Tsuji-san. "Have you met the man?"

"No, Father. He lives in Minneapolis. The situation has developed so quickly, I had no time to go there.

"If he won't listen to reason, can we get his attention some other way?"

"That's very difficult, Father," replied Sawada. "I have never developed any agents for that sort of work."

Tsuji scratched the back of his head as he pondered the situation. "No, of course you haven't." He paused again. "Do you suppose that Sergeant Torelli's people could help us in this situation?"

"Father, until you sent me to the funeral last month, I never had anything to do with Sergeant Torelli's organization. Even now I am not sure who I could work with or what I could ask them to do for us."

"That's my fault, my son. I should have involved you in those operations long ago." Tsuji-san knitted his brow. "That's another thing we need to discuss."

"In any case, Father, I am not sure the Torelli group could help us. The dagger is in Minneapolis and they may not operate so far from New York." Sawada let his voice trail off.

"You do know where the dagger is?" asked Tsuji-san.

"Yes, Father," said Sawada. "The man is keeping it in his home."

"So we know exactly where it is?" asked Tsuji-san.

"Yes, Father," Sawada nodded with a small shrug.

After a moment of contemplation, Tsuji-san said, "Sometimes, my son, direct action is the only answer."

"Do you have a plan, Father?" asked Sawada.

"Possibly," he said with a vague smile. "I recently met a man who might be able to help us in a situation like this." He paused again before looking up at Sawada. "Stay in contact with the person who has the dagger and before you leave, write down all the information you have concerning this matter. We will watch it closely," he added as he stubbed his cigarette firmly into the ashtray.

9 | Kutani Noburo

In which a few details of a treasure's loss are grudgingly revealed and plans for an expansive future are explained.

Tokyo - present day

Professor Kutani Noburo, retired Director of the Sumitaka Museum of Fine Arts and Emeritus Professor of Art History at Meidai Gakuin University, Tokyo

Professor Akashi Akira, Professor of Archeology and National History at Meidai Gakuin University, Tokyo

Tsuji Takeru, a Tokyo businessman pursuing some personal research interests

Sawada Kenji, one of Mr. Tsuji's associates

"I'm very unhappy about this!" Professor Kutani Noburo said petulantly as he looked nervously around his office. "You've just forced me into this meeting and I'm quite angry!" He paused to purse his lips and fold his arms tightly across this chest. "And I'm just very sure these are vulgar men," he continued as he unfolded his arms and ran one hand across his hair which was swept back in a flamboyant pompadour.

As an emeritus member of the Department of Art History at Meidai Gakuin University, Professor Kutani was not a close colleague of Professor Akashi. Still, the older man was a famous scholar and a longtime member of the Meidai Faculty of Arts and Letters so that Akashi had known him for many years. They had worked together on committees and attended a great many meetings together. Akashi was well aware of Professor Kutani's reputation as a fidgety old pedant given to moods and strong opinions, but in all their contacts, he had never seen the old man so agitated.

"Sensei," the archeologist said soothingly, "I appreciate the assistance you have extended to me by agreeing to this meeting. Had I any idea it would be so distressing, I would never have imposed."

Akashi was not being entirely candid, but said this to relax Kutani. He had been under great pressure to arrange the meeting and had been quite willing to impose on his senior colleague. A highway contractor had asked Akashi to arrange the meeting. Akashi acquiesced without thought because it seemed like a minor matter. He hadn't given it any priority until the contractor called back to say that if the meeting was not arranged soon funding would be terminated for a large salvage excavation Akashi was overseeing in advance of a major new expressway being built in Tokyo's western suburbs. That got Akashi's attention and he called Professor Kutani immediately.

At first the old man had been collegial and willing to help. When he heard the name of the man who wanted to meet with him, however, he broke off the conversation and refused Akashi's subsequent calls. The contractor seemed serious about ending the excavation funding and even began to take steps in that direction so Akashi had asked his Dean to intervene. The excavation was bringing more than a hundred million yen into the university so the Dean was very willing to help. Even after he joined the discussion, however, Professor Kutani remained uncooperative. At first, he claimed to be too busy and then he was under the weather. At one point he even made a sudden trip to Boston to check on plans for a traveling exhibition of Kano School paintings. The Dean kept up the pressure by pointing out that as an emeritus faculty member, Kutani might have to be asked to give up his office space. This threat brought him into line and he finally acceded to the meeting, but he insisted it had be as short as possible and he wanted it held in his office. Those conditions were acceptable to the road builder and Akashi was relieved his research would not be interrupted.

"Professor Kutani, I don't think Tsuji-san is a person of quality, but I have been assured he will not burden you. Let me explain again he is a businessman engaged in a personal historical investigation. He merely wants to speak with you in the hope that your deep expertise can be of help."

Professor Kutani sighed nervously and pursed his lips. He looked briefly at his fingernails before refolding his arms once again. "They always want something, these people," he said.

Akashi did not understand that comment or the basis of Kutani's distress. He simply wanted to avoid any further problems. "Please, Sensei. Put your mind at rest," he said trying to sound relaxed. "I have been assured that Tsuji will not pressure you in any way. He is not concerned with any judgment currently being made by the Cultural Properties Board."

"I hope not," the older man said sharply. "I've served on the Cultural Properties Board for twenty-three years and in that time I've never let my assessments be influenced by money or power or threats."

"No one would ever suggest that you have, Sensei. Your reputation for probity is well-established." This reassurance and his younger colleague's soothing tone appeared to help the older man relax. "I assure you the meeting will be as brief as possible and that you will not be placed in a position of discomfort. I truly believe Tsuji's desire to meet with you is sincere."

The older man unfolded his arms and looked up at Akashi. "I don't want you here when I meet with him."

"As you prefer, Sensei. Would you like me to wait outside until he leaves?"

"Absolutely not! You may show him in if you must, but then I want you away from here," he said dismissively.

As Akashi nodded, there was a soft knock on the door.

"You look tired, my son. I think you're still on American time."

Sawada Kenji was in the middle of a broad yawn he couldn't stifle even when he realized both Hatamura and Tsuji-san were watching him. He did, however, let it combine with an embarrassed smile and relaxed chuckle. "I slept well last night, Father, but I'm still finding myself a little tired. It's always like this for a few days after I arrive back home."

"These flights across the ocean must put a great strain on your health, my son. I wish we could avoid them," Tsuji-san said with fatherly concern. "This meeting should not take long and when it's done we'll let you take a nap."

The older man leaned forward to divide his attention between Hatamura who was in the front seat next to the driver and Sawada who sat with him in the back seat.

"We're going to meet with a man who may be able to give us some information on the disappearance of the Takasaka swords. The trail is somewhat cold, but we must explore all the avenues we find."

"Of course," Sawada said nodding his agreement. "Is this man one of our Brothers?"

"Not hardly," Hatamura scoffed.

"Be generous, my son," the older man cautioned with a wave of his hand. Turning to Sawada, he said, "He's a teacher at Meidai Gakuin University and quite famous. Kutani Noburo. You may have heard of him."

Sawada shook his head.

"It doesn't matter," Tsuji-san said. "He's a *bunka-jin*," he added dismissively. "For several years he ran that big art gallery the Sumitaka Company built downtown. He still gets his picture in the paper a lot." Tsuji-san paused before adding, "An *O-kama*," as an afterthought to indicate Kutani's homosexuality.

"I see," Sawada said. "Is he an authority on swords?"

"No," Tsuji-san said shaking his head. "He just seems to know about art and the like."

"Why do you think he can help us with the Takasaka swords, Father?" asked Sawada.

"It's really just a guess," Tsuji-san said leaning back in his seat. "I'm sure he'll try to deny it now, but the Brotherhood used Kutani to sort through things that were being gathered up in the days right after the Pacific War. He's been trying to avoid all contact with us for some time. His type knows nothing of gratitude or loyalty, but a couple of the senior men have mentioned working with him in the old days. He may know something about what happened at Takasaka. The hard part will be getting him to tell us what he knows."

"Have you met him, Father?" asked Sawada.

"Once, many years ago," Tsuji-san said. "He was an arrogant worm. I doubt if he'd recall me."

Both Sawada and Hatamura remained silent to encourage their patron to continue. After a brief pause he did.

"It was in the twenty-ninth year of Showa, just after the Korean War when things were getting organized. The Americans were still around, of course, but no longer running the government. I was a street organizer with only a couple of my own work crews, but I was earning a reputation for being able to get jobs done. My *Oyabun*, Okamura Yoshio, assigned me the job of retrieving some paintings one of the senior Brothers had in storage in a country *kura* out by Furukawa."

"It wasn't a big job. The paintings were on movable wall panels so all I had to do was get them loaded onto one of Okamura-sama's trucks and bring them back to the big museum over in Ueno Park. I used one of my own work crews and they treated it like a holiday." Tsuji-san paused to light a cigarette.

"I certainly could have handled the job by myself, but Okamura-sama had me take Kutani along to oversee the job. He stayed out of my way while we were doing the work. When we got back to Tokyo, though, there were a bunch of newspaper photographers and reporters waiting for us, and Kutani started to act like he was in charge. He stood where everyone could see him and he ordered us around." Tsuji-san scowled officiously and pointed in a couple of different directions to show how Kutani had ordered them about. The slight may have been more than forty years old, but it was obvious that Tsuji-san still remembered it with irritation.

"I didn't like his manner at all, but I didn't do anything about it because there were so many witnesses. Afterward, I asked Okamura-sama about it. He explained things." Tsuji-san took a drag from his cigarette.

"The paintings, it turned out, were from the old castle at Furukawa, that had gotten firebombed late in the war. I've never been sure how the Brotherhood got the paintings. It's possible we salvaged them after the bombers did their work, but I rather suspect one or another of the Brothers had them in storage even before the damage was done." Tsuji-san adopted a conspiratorial tone for this part of the story.

"With the Americans out of the government, the senior Brothers decided it was time to get rid of the paintings," Tsuji-san continued. "Looking back, it may not have been a good time to sell such things. Certainly, they'd be worth far more now. But that's all hindsight and you've got to remember that we really needed cash in those days. There was lots of building going on and still a little bit of land being traded so the Brotherhood needed cash. That was also, of course, just when the brothels were closed down so a major source of income had been cut off."

The younger men listened with interest to these details. Tsuji-san enjoyed their attention and approved of their interest in Brotherhood affairs.

"The senior Brothers made all of the arrangements to sell the paintings to the Sumitaka Company, but all of that had to be kept secret. The Brotherhood couldn't explain how they came to have the paintings and the Sumitaka people certainly didn't want to be publicly associated with us. Someone had to front the transfer and that's why Kutani had been brought in. The newspapers were told that no one had known about the paintings until Kutani had 'found' them out in that country storehouse." Tsuji-san took a drag from his cigarette before continuing. "It was all a dodge, but it made big news at the time. People bought the story."

"The dealings were done by another branch of the Brotherhood so I'm not sure what we got, but whatever the Sumitaka people paid was cheap. At the time, they got credit for preserving a National Treasure. Later, those paintings became the centerpiece of their museum. They've also been able to cart them out whenever they've needed good press. When they were accused of pouring poison into the ocean down there in Minosui, for example, was just when they came out with a flashy book on the paintings."

Hatamura sucked his teeth with a soft smacking sound and nodded his head in admiration. "They made a wise investment," he said.

"Indeed, they did," Tsuji-san agreed. "I've always felt the Sumitaka group was very skilled. You've got to respect success. And Kutani also made the most of those paintings. We have to give him credit for that. I'm sure that affair was what got him lined up with the Sumitaka Company and with this fancy school we're going to. I hope he'll remember his obligations to us."

As he said this, Tsuji-san looked up to realize they were nearing the Meidai campus. He snuffed out his cigarette and turned to Hatamura. "We're getting close and should do a bit of planning. Somebody will meet us at the campus gate and take us to the Kutani's office. I expect no problems, but I want you to stay with the car. The Second Son will accompany me."

"I understand, Father," Hatamura said.

Sawada did not know what to expect at the meeting. Tsuji-san had never involved him in serious violence and as they walked across the park-like Meidai campus, Sawada hoped Tsuji-san wasn't planning to use force today. Still, Sawada realized that he was being brought as Tsuji-san's assistant and that he would have to carry out any orders he might be given. As he and Tsuji-san were led into the Humanities Building, Sawada felt himself becoming tense. When they arrived at Kutani's office, however, he was completely surprised by Tsuji-san's behavior. He had never seen his patron so explicitly polite and respectful.

As Akashi's assistant showed them into Kutani's office, the old professor's face was fixed in a hard scowl. He gave no hint of warmth or welcome, but Tsuji-san appeared not to notice this.
He bowed very deeply as he entered the room and kept his eyes diverted. He spoke with a soft voice and used extremely polite speech forms. He offered his business card to both of the men who had been waiting for them, but let Professor Akashi slip out of the office almost immediately. When they were alone, Tsuji-san waited for Professor Kutani to offer a seat. Kutani grudgingly pointed to the upholstered chairs around a low table in one corner of the office and Tsuji-san sat primly on the edge of his chair until his host was seated.

Tsuji-san opened the meeting by taking a neatly wrapped package out of the shopping bag he had carried. He pushed it toward the professor. "Esteemed Sensei, I sincerely hope you will accepted this humble expression of my respect." He bowed at the waist and held the position until Kutani took the package.

Kutani accepted the gift with a nod. "How very generous," he said with a tone that could have been either icy or sincere. Tsuji-san and Sawada watched as he unwrapped the package. When it was open, Tsuji-san spoke.

"For a discriminating authority like the Sensei, selecting gifts is very difficult. I hoped you would enjoy some Takase sweet bean paste. This is from a shop recently been recognized as an Intangible Cultural Asset by the prefectural government. This is from their first batch of the new season." Tsuji was in a half bow with his eyes diverted downward as he said this.

"Ahh yes, Takase bean paste," Kutani said as he inspected the package neatly tied in elegantly folded bamboo leaves. He made small flourishes with his hands and when he looked up Sawada felt his expression may have softened slightly.

Next, Tsuji-san produced another, larger, package from his shopping bag. "I also took the liberty of hoping that you would enjoy a bottle of scotch." He pushed the neatly wrapped package across the coffee table that separated him from Kutani. The professor opened it to reveal four bottles of thirty year old Ballantine Scotch.

"Oh my heavens, this is very nice," Kutani said with a tone that sounded truly sincere. "Thank you," he smiled.

Sawada was silent during these exchanges and tried to let his face betray nothing. He realized Tsuji-san's strategy was working, and couldn't help but feel great pride in his patron.

"Sensei, let me begin by begging a favor," Tsuji-san continued as he took a final object from his shopping bag. "The daughter of one of my associates is one of your great admirers," he said as he folded the bag to show it was now empty. "She is a serious student of art history and has several of your books. My associate asked me to inquire if you might be willing to extend his daughter the honor of autographing one of your volumes for her." He slid a book across the table to Kutani.

Kutani smiled as he leaned forward and adjusted his bifocals to bring the book into focus. "Oh, my, my," he said as he recognized the volume. "This is a very old book, indeed. A real antique. *The Kano School Paintings of Furukawa Castle.*"

He fanned through the pages of the book. "My, my, my. This is more than thirty years old now." As he held it open to the cover page, he took a large fountain pen out of his shirt pocket. "I currently have seventeen titles in print," he said with obvious pride. "How should I sign it?"

"Seventeen books, indeed," Tsuji-san repeated smoothly.

"Yes," Kutani smiled. "This was my first major volume. It got my career off to a solid start."

"I see," Tsuji-san said with a unctuous tone that Sawada was sure had been intended to be a parody of Kutani's speech, though the professor seemed not to notice. "You could probably say that you owe your career to the screens that were in that *kura* out in Furukawa."

Tsuji-san's face was set in a pleasant smile as he said this. His voice retained a very agreeable tone, but the words made Kutani look up with a start. He looked intently into Tsuji-san's face as if he were trying to place it in his memory.

Tsuji-san betrayed no emotions. "A simple signature will be ample, professor," he said, pointing to the open book in front of Kutani. "There is no need to personalize this."

Kutani hurriedly signed his name and returned the pen to his pocket before pushing the book back across the table. His face was now tightly set with slightly pursed lips and raised eyebrows. He nervously crossed his hands over his lap and waited for Tsuji-san to speak.

"Professor Kutani," Tsuji-san said in a gentle businesslike tone, "I know you are a busy man and I don't wish to take much of your time."

Kutani cleared his throat nervously.

"I am interested in finding a pair of swords that were lost in the days just after the Pacific War."

Sawada was watching Kutani closely and it seemed to him that the professor's expression softened slightly when Tsuji-san said this. Kutani knit his brows with nervous intensity and leaned forward before speaking himself.

"But Tsuji-san, I have no expertise with swords. I don't see how I can be of any help to you." He sounded genuinely sincere.

"Oh, I understand, Sensei," Tsuji-san said soothingly. "It's just that with your familiarity with art and your well-known ability to ferret out lost treasures, it occurred to me that you might be able to give us some clues."

"Well, I doubt if I can be of any help at all," Kutani whined.

"The swords we are seeking were lost from the Omon Hachiman Shrine in Takasaka."

Again Kutani seemed relieved. "I never had anything to do with Takasaka," he answered quickly. "I never went there. I was not involved in that affair whatsoever."

"But you were familiar with the situation?" asked Tsuji-san as he leaned forward to keep the conversation focused.

Kutani paused for a moment as he weighed the situation. The conversation was not going in as threatening a direction as he had feared it might. He decided to trust Tsuji-san.

"Those were dark days," he began softly. "Because of my training and my contacts with the Ministry of Cultural Affairs, I was employed by parties who were engaged in," he paused to find the right words, "gathering items that were in danger of rough treatment."

Tsuji-san leaned back in his chair. "I'm very interested in those operations. Who were you working with?"

"The situation was complex," Kutani began softly. "I did not know all of those involved." He leaned forward and looked Tsuji-san in the face as he continued. "In particular, I knew few of those individuals who may have been affiliated with," he paused to make it clear that he was speaking carefully, "your organization."

Kutani had been discrete. He had not mentioned the name of the Kawabayashi Brotherhood and he had been respectful in his tone. Still, his words were an acknowledgment of his association with the Brotherhood. This could only indicate willingness to remain subservient. It was now clear to everyone in the room that the conversation had become as open and candid as it could.

"Oh, I understand," Tsuji-san said smoothly. "The situation was complex, I'm sure." He waited for Kutani to go on.

"My contact was entirely through Hatami Saijiro who had operated an antiques shop near Yoyogi. Initially, he had only wanted me to check some information on file at the Ministry of Cultural Affairs."

"I see," said Tsuji-san, waiting for Kutani to continue.

He did so only after exhaling deeply. "Hatami wanted me to make of list of cultural properties that were in what you might call 'insecure storage.'"

"Ah, of course," Tsuji-san said with a tone that communicated no disapproval. Sawada nodded nonchalantly even though he realized that Kutani was telling them he had helped the Brotherhood set up burglaries.

"And the shrine at Takasaka was one of the places you identified?" Tsuji-san continued.

"I think it was," Kutani said, "but I really can't remember what in particular was held there. It certainly wasn't an important place."

"I see," repeated Tsuji-san, "go on."

"Hatami was also informally hired to assist an American army officer who was picking things up. The officer had some kind of official position and he was using it to gather up art objects. I had nothing to do with the disposition of what was secured. Hatami took me along on some of his trips but he made all the contacts. My job was simply to identify the objects we found."

"Did you work directly for the Americans?" asked Tsuji-san.

"No. I'm quite sure that Hatami's contacts were all," again Kutani paused to find the right word, "unofficial."

"Do you know the name of the American officer?"

This question caused Kutani to tighten up, but he answered it immediately. "His name was 'Breedmore, Lawrence Breedmore.' Hatami pushed us together and made me spend some time with him, but we were never close. He was kind and quite cultured and quite unlike the other Americans, but I never really cared for him and we were not together long." Then after a pause, he added, "I know nothing about what happened to him. I was not involved in any of that."

"What happened to him?" Tsuji-san asked flatly.

"He died. I always assumed someone killed him." Kutani was speaking freely now, and looking directly at his guests. "I knew he was becoming interested in the things he was handling and I think he may have angered his contacts because he was keeping things he was supposed to be passing on. You must understand I had nothing do to with that. I was not involved in that aspect of his life. I really don't know who he was working with or what trouble he may have gotten into, and I never took anything from him."

Kutani spoke with obvious conviction and a trace of fear so that Sawada felt he had to be telling the truth.

Tsuji-san may have agreed, but he had more questions. "Was this 'Breedmore' involved with the Takasaka swords?" he pushed.

"Tsuji-san, you must understand that all of this happened years ago," Kutani pleaded. "I was in Tokyo when he died. I was *not* involved with the matter," he said emphatically.

"Oh, I understand, Sensei," Tsuji-san said, obviously trying to be soothing. "But you may have heard something, anything, that might be of help."

Sawada again had to admire Tsuji-san's skill. He was clearly and effectively keeping the pressure on Kutani.

The professor sighed deeply and ran his hand across his brow. "When Hatami told me about Breedmore he mentioned something about Takasaka. I remember no details and do not know if it involved swords. I do remember that he wanted me to look for the enlisted men who had been working with Breedmore. He was eager to find them and was very upset. Maybe they had some of things from Takasaka. I really couldn't say."

"Did you look for the soldiers?"

"Of course not!" Kutani said emphatically. "I never had anything to do with them and wouldn't have known where to find them."

"Do you recall their names?"

"Absolutely not. They were entirely common people," the professor said with finality. Then as an afterthought he added, "One of then was a *Nisei* but he was just like the rest, very vulgar."

There was a pause as Tsuji-san searched for another question or another line of inquiry. "You couldn't suggest anyone else who might know something about the Takasaka swords?" he finally asked.

This question was so open-ended and Tsuji-san's tone so uncertain that Kutani was able to take back some initiative. "Absolutely no one, unless it would be someone you might know of."

As he said this, Kutani had adopted a tone that Sawada did not like, but Tsuji-san did not react to his change in manner. He said only, "Well, in that case, Sensei, I think you have helped us in every way you can. We'll leave you, but not until I again tell you how much I appreciate your help."

Kutani seemed surprised. "Is that the only matter you wished to discuss?" he asked.

"Yes," said Tsuji-san.

Kutani had clearly been expecting something more. After a moment of uncertainty, he said, "Well, I'm certainly sorry I was not able to be of more help with the Takasaka matter." He sounded very congenial. "I am a member of the Cultural Properties Board and I assumed there was something you wished to talk about in that regard."

"Oh, we are certainly aware of your position, Sensei. And periodically, I am involved in cultural properties, but I wouldn't wish to impose."

Sawada realized the conversation had now moved to another matter and he wondered if reestablishing a relationship with Kutani had been part of Tsuji-san's plan from the beginning.

"I appreciate that," said Kutani, "I certainly do. Still, I try to stay open and available to people who have sincere concerns they wish to share with me." He smiled affably.

"How very generous, professor," Tsuji-san said. "I'll keep that in mind." He slipped a thick white envelope out of the breast pocket of his suit coat and placed it in the center of the coffee table in front of the professor. "For now, though, I think we have taken enough of your time."

When Tsuji-san began to stand up, Sawada immediately joined him. Together they walked to the office door where they exchanged another round of farewells and bows before departing. Sawada was bursting with questions and eager to hear his patron's insights on the meeting that had just taken place. He was not sure where or how to begin so he waited for Tsuji-san to break the silence.

"Is this what your college was like?" Tsuji-san asked as he looked over a pair of well-dressed coeds on the way back to the car.

"Not really, Father," Sawada replied. He was quite sure Tsuji-san understood that as one of Tokyo's elite universities, Meidai was much more spacious and elegant than the cramped commercial school he had attended.

After a moment Tsuji-san broke the silence again. "That was disappointing. I had hoped Kutani could tell us something about what happened at Takasaka, but he knows nothing that can help us."

"I think he was telling the truth, Father," agreed Sawada. "I don't think he was hiding anything."

"Yes. He wasn't," Tsuji-san said answering the question in Japanese fashion.

"At least it seems clear we'll be able to work with Professor Kutani in the future. That should be positive, shouldn't it?" Sawada said trying to sound positive.

"Oh, it's always good to have friends on the Cultural Properties Committee," Tsuji-san said, "but formal recognition isn't worth nearly as much as it used to be. I left the money only because he had asked for it."

"I see," Sawada said, deciding from his tone that Tsuji-san did not wish to discuss the issue anymore. Their conversation lagged until they neared the campus gate and saw Hatamura waiting with the car. Then Tsuji-san smiled and said, "Don't look so depressed, my son. The meeting wasn't an entire waste. We'll sort it all out later. For now, though, I have some business to attend to and I promised you a nap. I want you to go back to your *ryokan* and get some rest. Take a nap and a nice bath. Then I want you to assemble all of the information you have on the Takasaka *tanto*. Everything. Tell me what you can about the man who has it. Tell me its exact location and whatever else you can think of. Write it all down so you can give it to me later this evening. Come back to the League Office at eight and we'll discuss it all then. There are also some other matters we need to talk about."

Sawada began to protest that he wasn't tired, but Tsuji-san cut him off by saying, "Hatamura-kun, call your brother a cab."

It took Sawada less than twenty minutes to assemble the few pieces of information he had on the Muramasa *tanto*. He neatly copied his notes and organized them in a sub-divided file. He included a copy of Eric Mallow's card in the file and copied his name neatly in English and in phonetic Japanese using both the *katakana* syllabary and *romaji*.

When that brief chore was done, Sawada took a nap and packed the things he would be bringing back to America. He telephoned a couple of friends and tried to read the evening newspapers. Time passed slowly, however, because he was eager to meet with Tsuji-san. He understood the *Oyabun* had more to discuss about the Takasaka swords, but the matter that had brought him back to Tokyo no longer held Sawada's interest. He wanted to hear what Tsuji-san had in mind for his future.

Sawada had come to Tokyo hoping only to reestablish himself with Tsuji-san. He had wanted no more than an invitation back to Japan and a place in one or another of the Kawabayashi operations. He was proud of his success with the sword return operation, but realized it couldn't go on forever. The supply of good swords in America would have to dry up eventually. Sawada had also begun to let himself acknowledge that he was very tired of life in America. He was tired of being a foreigner. He longed to be able to return to his home and would have been happy for any job--even overseeing the operation of one of the Brotherhood's bars or even a group of "love hotels."

The past two days had changed all of that and made Sawada very uncertain about his future. He was now one of Tsuji-san's personal associates. Suddenly, he held a position that could let him set his goals very high. The men Tsuji-san selected as *kobun* ran their own branch houses. They controlled whole neighborhoods or major businesses and maintained cadres of men in their own *gumi*. These were the kinds of men who had come to Sawada's initiation and he was pleased to be among them. The problem was, of course, that Sawada saw no way he would ever be able to assemble the kinds of resources those men had.

And beyond that, Sawada recalled Tsuji-san's comments about plans for the future. The *Oyabun* had said things about expanding operations in America and made unsettling comments about keeping Sawada in America. He needed to know what Tsuji-san had in mind. By 7:15 he could wait no longer, and he took a cab to the Imperial League office.

Only the senior office girl, Miko-chan, was still at work when he arrived. Sawada saw her sitting at her desk as he stepped through the front door. When he did, she looked up and said, "Ahh, Sawada-san!" and immediately came to greet him at the front of the office.

"Good evening," Sawada said looking around to see if anyone else was present. Except for Miko, the outer office was empty and the hallways leading to other parts of the building were all dark. He had been hoping to find Tsuji-san waiting for him so the empty office was a disappointment.

If Miko was aware of his dismay she did not acknowledge it. "Please come in," she said with bright-eyed enthusiasm and led him toward the chairs at the back of the room. When Sawada took a seat, she brought him a cup of tea.

"The Director told me to wait for you, but he said not to expect you until eight," she said pleasantly.

"I was done with all of my business and decided to get an early start on our meeting," Sawada said with a mildly officious tone.

"I see, I see," Miko said. "With your busy schedule you have a great deal on your mind."

"My plane leaves early tomorrow morning so time is short."

"We just don't know how you do it, Sawada-san," Miko said sympathetically. "The girls often marvel at your energy." Then to change the subject, she placed a neatly printed letter on the coffee table in front of Sawada. "Since you will be leaving tomorrow, the Director wanted me to get your approval for this letter of acknowledgment and thanks. If you approve, we will send it to all of those who participated in the recent rite of adoption."

Sawada read it and said, "This is very nice. Thank you."

Miko then gave him a list of names. "These are the gentlemen who attended the ceremony. Director Tsuji has indicated the name of four individuals who were especially generous to you. He asked me to remind you that personal acknowledgments would be appropriate."

"Yes, of course," Sawada said as he looked over the list.

"You may keep that copy," Miko said.

Sawada put the list into his bag. "Is the Director here?" he finally asked with only a hint of impatience.

"He is not," Miko said. "But he told me to ask you to proceed to the *Kikusui* where you will be having a private meeting." She checked her wristwatch. "It's still a bit early, but I think he may be there. If you wish, I'll give him a call."

Sawada wondered what to do. It was rather early and he did not want to interrupt Tsuji-san. As he thought the matter through, he looked down at the surface of the coffee table and ignored Miko who was standing in front of him.

In fact, most of the men who passed through the League office either ignored Miko or took her for granted. She was attractive enough and both bright and pleasant, but at work those qualities were hard to appreciate. Her uniform was neat and trim, but it did not set off her figure. She kept her hair in a neat but rather severe arrangement and never wore makeup. She was in charge of the other girls who worked in the office, but never exerted authority while men were present. Instead, she would always defer to the men around her and, of course, never objected to being referred to with the diminutive title, Miko-chan. Like all of the other men who visited the office, Sawada would have been very surprised to realize that as soon as Miko was done at the office this evening, she would be going to a disco in Roppongi, a new place called the Starlight. There, with her hair flowing down her back, she would spend the evening, dancing braless in a see-through blouse and a gold lame miniskirt.

Sawada knit his brow and took a sip of tea. "Yes, Miko-chan. Please give the Director a call."

When she returned from a brief phone conversation that Sawada had not been able to hear, she said, "Director Tsuji will be waiting for you and hopes you will meet him at the *Kikusui* as soon as possible."

As he rose and made his way to the front door of the office, Sawada could not entirely hide his irritation at having to make another trip.

"I'll call for a Tokyo Transport taxi. May I say you'll be waiting on the corner?" Miko asked as Sawada stepped into his shoes.

"Yes. Please do that," he said over his shoulder and stepped onto the street.

A middle aged hostess in *kimono* was waiting when the taxi pulled up to the *Kikusui*. She bowed low and said "*Irrashaimase*," as Sawada stepped into the vestibule. "It is our great pleasure to welcome you once again, Sawada-sama."

Sawada nodded to her and simply said, "Thank you," although her welcome had made him feel very special. No one had ever called him by the honorific title.

"Please do me the honor of following me to your party," the hostess said before leading him to a small private room at the far corner of the building. When they arrived, she knelt at the paper partition. "Please excuse me. A guest has arrived," she said and slid the paper screen open.

Sawada was pleased to find Tsuji-san was alone in the room. He was seated at a low table and smiled broadly when Sawada entered. "Come in, come in, my son," he said. "I'm glad you're here." He moved the papers he had been reading to one side. "We're ready for refreshments," he told the hostess. "Beer will be all right, won't it, my son?"

"Oh, excellent, Father. Just what I need."

"Did you rest?"

"Very well, Father. I'm all packed for my return trip."

"Excellent," beamed Tsuji-san.

Sawada knew he should wait for Tsuji-san to begin the business, but he wanted to move beyond the small talk. "As you requested, Father, I pulled together all of the information I have about the Muramasa *tanto*. There isn't much, I'm afraid." He passed the file to his patron.

As Tsuji-san took the file, the paper screen slid open and a waitress brought a tray containing two large beer bottles and a flat basket of chilled blanched soybeans.

Tsuji-san waited while the waitress put a pair of glasses on the table and then he held his up so that she could fill it with beer. When Sawada had done the same, the *Oyabun* let the woman leave before raising his glass to Sawada and saying, "*Kampai!*"

When they had both sipped the beer, Tsuji-san said, "Help yourself to some *eda-mame*. They've just come in so they're as fresh as can be." Sawada pulled a couple of the beans off the vine and squeezed the soft kernels out of their husks as Tsuji-san looked through the file.

After a moment, he looked up. "You're right. There isn't much, but I think it's enough. We know where the dagger is. We know who has it and you have determined that he doesn't wish to deal with us in a reasonable manner."

"I think that is correct, Father."

"I want you to stay in contact this man, Mallow," Tsuji-san said checking the file, "maybe he will change his mind."

"I don't think it's money, Father. No one in America would have offered him more than I have. I think he simply doesn't wish to deal with us," Sawada said.

"That may be the case and if it is, we'll have to employ other means. If it comes to that, though, I don't want you involved. You are not to be part of any direct action. I'll handle all of that from here."

"How, Father?"

"I have a few ideas, but I don't want you involved," Tsuji-san said taking a draw from his beer. "You, son, must maintain a spotless record. Stay away from the rough work. You've got more important work to do for the Brotherhood."

"I understand, Father," Sawada said knowing he should stop right there, but he couldn't contain his curiosity. "Please, Father. Tell me about the work you want me to do."

"In a minute, my son. First, there are a few bits of information I want to give you." Tsuji-san pulled a thin file out of the bag he had at the side of the table. "Remember, we're looking for two swords. As we learned this afternoon from Professor Kutani, the trail has grown cold. I have not come up with much, but I want you to use whatever information there is."

"Of course, Father," Sawada said trying to be patient.

Tsuji-san opened the file and showed the first paper. "I just received this letter from Tsunami Genjiro who heads the Art Swords Appreciation Society. I had him look at your rubbing of the Muramasa *tanto*. He determined that it is the dagger taken from the Omon Shrine at Takasaka."

"Now," Tsuji-san said leaning forward to take a soybean, "I've asked Tsunami-san to look farther into the dagger, but his authentication is as good as a guarantee. It means we can move ahead. We want that dagger."

Turning back to his file, Tsuji-san continued in a more tentative tone. "This item may mean nothing, but I want to you look it over." As Tsuji-san pushed another paper across the table to Sawada, he saw that it was a sheaf of papers written in English.

"I got it from Counselor Odagiri who has commissioned us to find the swords. It seems that the abbot of the Omon Shrine recorded the names of the American soldiers who took the swords we're looking for. The Counselor used his political connections to get people at the American Embassy to look into those names. This is a copy of the report they provided."

Sawada started to read the letter, but Tsuji-san stopped him. "Don't read it now," he said waving his hand gently over the paper. "Save it for the plane. In any case, the Counselor assured me that it contains no useful information. I believe him because I'm sure his people did what they could with it. Had they come up with anything he would not have asked for our help."

Sawada nodded his understanding of Tsuji-san's point.

"But look it over. Maybe you'll see something Odagiri missed."

The waitress arrived as Sawada was taking the papers. She knelt by the side of table and smiled as she offered to fill the beer glasses. When she had, she asked, "Would our guests like to begin dinner?"

Tsuji-san said that they would and when she left them to begin the service, he leaned forward on one elbow. "My son, the Takasaka swords are important to our organization. I want them, but I called you back to Japan because we have some other matters to discuss as well."

"Of course, Father," Sawada said and he leaned forward and looked attentively at his *Oyabun*. He was relieved the conversation was finally moving on to the subject that interested him more.

"You've done excellent work with the sword return program," Tsuji-san began. "Certainly, it has been very profitable, but some changes are going to have to be made."

"I'm ready to make any adjustments you want, Father."

"Relax, my son," Tsuji-san said stopping to hold one of the beer bottles out to Sawada. When he had topped up his glass and let Sawada fill his, he continued. "You have been steady and productive, my son, but changes outside of your operation mean that we have to change your responsibilities."

Sawada nodded and sipped his beer.

"To begin with, I want you to become more involved in the financial aspects of our American activities." Tsuji-san paused to take a couple of soy beans. He offered the basket to Sawada.

"Over the years, I tried to isolate you from those matters," Tsuji-san began. "You've had plenty to do and I felt it was best to keep you clear of anything that could give you a police record." Tsuji-san averted his eyes as he said this and reached for a couple more soybeans. Sawada wondered if those were the only reasons he had been excluded from the banking transactions.

"As things have developed, we now need a skilled senior person to take over handling of our American money," Tsuji-san continued.

"I'd be very interested in doing that sort of work, Father."

"Good. For a long while our transactions with America were very small. We had only to pay for some services and a little merchandise and we could do that through regular accounts. For nearly forty years, all of those arrangements were handled by a woman who left Japan when she married a GI."

Tsuji-san passed Sawada a piece of paper. "This is her name and address. I knew her as Takahashi Michiko. She worked in one of our bars out by Tachikawa in the years just after the Korean War. She married a GI and moved to America just when we needed a contact in the New York area. It was very convenient and she could do the work we needed."

Sawada read the address: Mrs. Michiko Carbone, 139 Pikehurst Road, Port Ryan, New Jersey.

"Her responsibilities grew as your operation expanded and we took on some other activities, but she was able to coordinate transfers into accounts in America, the Cayman Islands, and Europe. Several times she also carried cash payments for us. When the sword return operation began, I asked her to arrange your cash payments."

"I've wondered how all of that was handled."

"Perhaps I should have told you," Tsuji-san paused again to sip his beer. "Michiko-san has developed some serious health problems," he said when he continued.

"I see," said Sawada.

"She has been diagnosed with breast cancer," Tsuji-san explained, "and has asked to be replaced. We have discussed this matter, and she is expecting a visit from you sometime soon. Please work that into your schedule."

"Certainly, Father," said Sawada. "I'll have some time by the middle of next week."

"When you meet, Michiko-san will give you all of the details and you will have to decide how to replace her. Certainly you won't have to do the day-to-day work she has done, but I want you to take over the operation. I think you will find it will have to be expanded. In any case, select someone to handle the affairs and make them your *kobun*."

"Of course, Father," Sawada said with a slight bow. He had no obvious candidate in mind, but he realized this was how he would begin to build his *gumi*. "Is this woman familiar with my operation?"

"In general. She coordinated your cash transfers from our friends in the Torelli family. They handled the deliveries and I have always assumed all of that has gone quite smoothly."

"Flawlessly, Father. Did she also manage the return payments?"

"She kept the records, but most of the money is simply transferred from Tokyo into American accounts. Usually, they're recorded as payments for some kinds of service. I understand that one of the Torelli front companies actually got an award from the American government for helping with the American trade deficit."

Tsuji-san smirked as he reported this. "We also make some payments to accounts in Switzerland or the Caymans."

"What do we pay for the cash, Father?"

"It has varied over the years. The rate also depends on whether we are paying in yen or dollars. Currently, I think we transfer seventy-five cents for each dollar of cash."

Sawada nodded. "That's not bad," he said. "Would you mind if I tried to arrange a better rate?"

"Not at all, my son. I'm giving you the responsibility for the matter. I only hope you'll recall that the Kawabayashi Brotherhood has had a long relationship with the Torelli family. I inherited it from my *Oyabun* and I pass it on to you. Please remember our debt of loyalty."

"Of course, Father." Sawada bowed reflexively.

"That brings up another matter, my son," Tsuji-san said as the waitress brought in the plates for the first course of the meal. "I assume that all of my brothers and sons will take care of themselves. I don't expect to get every yen they make. Let me ask, then, have you been able to realize a personal profit on the sword return operation? Have you been able to find some margin you have not reported to me?"

Tsuji-san's voice betrayed no anger, but Sawada was surprised by the question and by the *Oyabun's* directness.

"Oh no, Father. I can't account for every yen, but I have been honest." He was telling the truth and his voice conveyed his sincerity.

"That's what I decided when I looked into your accounts. In fact, my son, I don't know how you do it. You appear to have almost no overhead."

Sawada beamed. "Well, Father, it's hard to explain, but you must recall that much of the material I buy is worthless in this country so I sell it right in America. The profit from those sales contributes to the operation."

"What kinds of things do you sell?" asked Tsuji-san. He seemed truly curious.

"There are many things I buy that I cannot ship back to Tokyo. I sell them in America. I sell most of the German military things, for example, in America. From time to time I also acquire guns. Of course, I have to sell those in America."

"What an amazing system," Tsuji-san said shaking his head. "And you just sell such things?"

"Yes. If I don't sell them, I use them to reward my pickers," Sawada explained.

"Ahh yes, you told me about *pikaahs*," Tsuji-san nodded. "I admire the way you have been able to deal with such a complex system. To speak frankly, my son, I'm not sure I have rewarded you adequately."

Tsuji-san took a piece of paper from his bag and placed it on the table facing Sawada. "I have taken the liberty of placing you at the head of company that has been created with some of the funds generated by the sword return operation and some of our other overseas activities. I called it the Heisei Development Corporation. It has a nice ring, don't you think?"

Sawada was amazed. "It's outstanding, Father."

"A couple of American law firms have recently opened offices in Tokyo and I've been working with one of them. It wasn't especially cheap, but it's been very easy. I've paid them with some of our overseas accounts and they have been very pleased to do whatever I asked. They respect us."

When Sawada shook his head in amazement, Tsuji-san smiled broadly. "They treat us far better than the local lawyers ever have and as long as it's overseas, the Japanese authorities don't seem to care either." Both men marveled at the situation.

"Apparently, you've got to sign some papers, but they say you're all set up to do legal business in New York and Los Angeles. At this point, the company has 1.3 million dollars in its accounts, but that's just to get things started. With the way the exchange rates have been going, it hasn't seemed wise to have too much of our money in dollars."

The opportunity Tsuji-san was offering was very generous, but his expectations were very unclear. Sawada suddenly feared that the *Oyabun's* expectation might be unrealistic.

"I certainly agree, Father. With the dollar so low, I have been trying to buy whatever I can in America, but the supply of good swords in America is drying up. I'm afraid the sword return operation may have run its course."

"I think you're right, son. But that makes this an even better time to get into some other areas."

"I see your point, Father," Sawada acknowledged with a nod, "but I have not had time to explore other activities. Swords have presented us with a special opportunity. I wonder if we will ever be able to find an opportunity nearly as good."

"And again, you're right, son. Swords were a special opportunity and you helped the Brotherhood make the most of it. Now it's time to move on."

Suddenly Sawada realized that Tsuji-san was not giving him an open-ended commission. He had a plan. "Tell me about the opportunities you see in America, Father."

Tsuji-san took a piece of the *sashimi* that had been brought in as the talked. "Mmm, the *maguro* is delicious. Try it." He helped himself to a second piece of tuna before putting his *hashi* down and continuing.

"As you know, my son, the Kawabayashi Brotherhood exists to serve Japanese society. We solve problems others either can't or don't wish to. We provide services our neighbors need and in return we are provided with a share of what society has to offer. It's that simple, my son, that simple." He paused to sample some of the other *sashimi*.

"All of us know there are people who misunderstand us," he continued. "They say we are bad people who should be eliminated. You read that sort of thing in the newspapers all the time."

Sawada nodded to indicate he understood the problem.

"At the same time we never have to look for work! People in all parts of the country and all levels of society need our services. They come to us! And our rates must be reasonable because people pay them."

"And you think our services are needed in America, Father?"

"They're needed all over the world, my son," Tsuji-san said with a broad sweep of his arm. "As Japanese firms have expanded their activities and built factories in foreign countries, they've encountered problems they're not used to solving -- plant security, labor unrest, bill collection, delivery scheduling. At home, these are problems they have been able to assign to us. I want you to bring the services of our Brotherhood to Japanese firms and others in America."

"You're right, Father. America presents the Brotherhood with great opportunities." Sawada found himself full of ideas as he recalled the minor irritations of life in America, the inefficiencies he had to put up with and the petty offenses he had endured.

"In fact, Son, we have already been offered some commissions."

"What sorts of commissions, Father?"

"They seem fairly straightforward," Tsuji-san said with a shrug. "The Teragawa Plastics company, for example, contacted me two weeks ago. They're part of the Imperial Electric *keiretsu* and they wanted to talk about a problem they're having at a plant they opened a couple of years ago in some small American town. Their trash hauler is giving bad service, charging unreasonable rates, *and* demanding bribes. They need the situation smoothed out and who can blame them?"

"That sort of thing should be manageable," said Sawada.

"Of course it should," agreed Tsuji-san. "It's merely a matter of establishing an organization. In another case, I was approached by the Japanese Chamber of Commerce in place called St. Louis."

"I've been there many time."

"There are nearly two thousand Japanese working there," Tsuji-san continued after nodding to note Sawada's familiarity with the place. "Those people need appropriate restaurants and entertainment facilities. Obviously, they can't organize those things themselves, but they thought we might be able to assist them. Clearly we should be able to provide this service to our fellow Japanese. That's what why the Brotherhood exists."

"I'm very excited, Father. I can't wait to get started with this new assignment."

"Well, good, my son. I'm sure you will do fine, but don't move too fast. This must be a long term operation. Spend the money you must and use every available legal cover. Begin building a *gumi* as soon as you can. After you have met with Michiko-san, I'll arrange some contacts. You should also begin to draw together individuals you can trust. You're going to have to cut back on your sword return activities."

"I can do that, Father."

"Perhaps you can move some of your *pikaahs* into that work."

"I'll look into it," Sawada said and the waitress arrived with the main dish, a pair of boiled lobsters that had been split down the middle. The four sides had been arranged in reverse order with the exposed portions loosened and garnished with steamed mushrooms marinated in *sake*. When this was set on the table it commanded Sawada's attention. As the woman arranged small plates yellow melon and white radish pickles, Sawada became very hungry. He remembered that he had not eaten since breakfast and hadn't seen a meal like this in years.

"We've discussed enough business for now, my son. Please help me enjoy this meal."

The men ate slowly and carefully avoided any discussion of work. As they were finishing their bowls of steaming white rice, a woman's voice on the outside of the paper screen, said, "Please excuse me. A guest has arrived." The screen then slid open and Hatamura entered the room.

"Hatamura-kun! Thank you for joining us. Your Brother and I have just been enjoying a fine meal and a pleasant conversation."

Hatamura sat down on a flat pillow the waitress brought for him. He lit up a cigarette and said, "I hoped you'd be finished with your meal and your business by now. Brother Sawada's flight is at five this morning so we'll have to leave for Narita no later than one. I want to show him some of Tokyo in the time we have left."

"What a good idea," Tsuji-san said. "You've had no fun on this trip, Sawada-kun. Take some time to relax."

"Exactly!" agreed Hatamura. "We'll get you to the plane on time and there are a few new bars and clubs I need to inspect. If there's time, I may even have to visit a new disco that is operating in Roppongi."

Sawada smiled his willingness to take part in the adventures.

"It's called the Starlight," Hatamura said. "And it's become famous because office girls from lots of these stuffy businesses go down there to dance and hang around in sexy clothes. I understand the place is really hot."

10 | Sato Yoshimasa

In which recovery of a treasure begins--with disappointing results.

Minneapolis - present day
Sato Yoshimasa - A tour guide at **Ninja Village**.

On the fourth night of his first major assignment, Sato Yoshimasa was alone and miserable in a dark hotel room. Looking back over the events of the recent days or ahead to the challenges before him, he could see only failure. Vital pieces of his equipment had been lost and he was mystified by his surroundings. His attempts to begin the operation had been embarrassing failures. He had told himself and his employer that his bodily control was so extensive that traveling halfway around the world would require no adjustment, but he felt miserable. He was sleepy whenever he was awake and awake whenever he tried to sleep. His bowels were loose and rumbled constantly. He was always flushed and sweaty and sure he had a fever. Had he been at home, he would have visited his doctor days ago.

Now, to make matters worse, Sato found himself making excuses. Sitting idly in his hotel room he had begun to explain to himself why the Japanese art of *ninjitsu* was not appropriate to America. He thought his arguments were good ones, but realized they were only rationalizations for failure, and he was disgusted with his willingness to accept defeat. An honorable suicide would be preferable to a facile admission of failure.

Had it come to that? Was suicide his only option? Sato shook his head, but had to admit he had never felt so incompetent as he had these past days. He did not want to go home in disgrace. He wanted to succeed. He wanted to be a ninja. Did he have any options? Was there any hope?

Struggling to save the assignment and possibly his life, Sato moved to the center of his hotel room and assumed the lotus position. He worked to gain control. If he could clear his mind of worry and doubts, could he find something that would give him hope? If he retraced the events of the past days, could he think of anything that had not gone wrong?

Sato's first mistake had been letting this assignment begin too quickly. He had been completely surprised by Tsuji-san's call and far too hasty in accepting the commission he offered. A real ninja would have had enough faith in his abilities to have anticipated the assignment and demanded adequate conditions. A real ninja would have known what those conditions should have been!

Sato attributed his quick response to an earnest desire to become a practicing ninja. His action was naive, but his motivation was pure. Sato had agreed to undertake recovery of a *tanto* in the possession of an American before he knew anything about the conditions or details of the task. Although he had been too eager, Sato would have to find strength in his foolishness. It would simply have to be another part of his challenge.

Sato had never felt so entirely and miserably alone as he had these past days. Aside from a few brief exchanges, he had spoken with no one for nearly a week. There was no one to confide in and no one who could help him. As he considered his situation and wished for some help, Sato forced himself to find a positive side to his misery. Given all the other disasters that had befallen him, he could at least take pride in the fact that he had so far escaped detection.

Before leaving Japan, Sato had worried that traveling under his own name would be a risk, but that fear was proving groundless. Sato had never really operated anywhere, let alone in a foreign country, so he had never acquired any travel documents aside from the passport he had obtained for a college-sponsored tour of Hawaii and the few tours he had guided to California.

He was not entirely sure how he would have gone about getting another passport or creating a new identity, and Tsuji-san had wanted him to begin immediately, so he had undertaken this operation with his old passport and a tourist visa. Using himself as a "cover" seemed to be working. No one questioned his motives and he felt no limits on his movements. No one seemed to suspect he was anything other than the tourist he claimed to be.

As soon as he left his apartment, Sato began using evasion techniques to ensure no one was observing his actions. He had studied the techniques of backtracking and sudden changes in direction, had practiced them in his everyday travels, but he had never before had the opportunity to apply the techniques on an actual operation. His evasive actions produced some stares, but no evidence that anyone was following him. Sato tried to convince himself he could count that as positive, but still he was swept by discomfort. The truth was, he suspected bitterly, that no one cared about him. No one took him seriously even when he had been exposed as a ninja.

Exposure had come in the Chicago airport when a customs inspector had discovered his *shuriken* throwing stars. It had been the first of many disasters, but Sato could not tell which bothered him more, the loss of his arsenal or the mortifying way it had been taken from him.

The central partition of his suitcase had seemed a suitable hiding place for his throwing stars. Sato had heard that Japanese passengers were rarely searched thoroughly and after he had slipped the stars between the sides of the partitions they were not visible. The inspector felt the extra weight and then found an open seam. In a moment, he shook all six stars out of their hiding place, and confiscated them.

When the first of the stars was removed, Sato knew the operation was unraveling. He shifted nervously on his feet and wondered if he should try to escape or simply kill himself right there. The inspector ignored him until the last star was exposed. When he was sure the partition was empty, the man simply turned to Sato and said, "Is this all?"

Deciding that he would run toward the doors if the inspector tried to grab him, Sato replied in English. "Yes, that's all." He spoke as clearly as he could.

The inspector continued and repeated himself when he saw Sato's puzzled expression. Sato could tell he was speaking slowly, but he simply could not follow the man's words. The inspector beckoned to an Asian woman standing a few counters away.

She walked casually toward the pair and exchanged a few words with the inspector before she addressed Sato in Japanese with a heavy Okinawan accent.

"There is a Chicago ordinance against martial arts weapons," she continued. "We can't let you bring these in," she said holding up one of the *shuriken*.

Sato was relieved to hear the Japanese, but he did not initially understand what was going on. Blankly, he asked, "Martial arts weapons?"

The woman was used to explaining things to visiting Japanese, so she spoke in clear, slow terms. Tossing the star she had been holding on to the pile of the others, she said, "You can't bring these into Chicago."

Sato nodded his head to indicate he had heard.

"Lots of Japanese think they will be nice gifts for their American friends," the woman continued.

"Gifts?" Sato said blankly.

"We see them all the time," she said, "but we can't let them in. You'll have to leave them here."

"I understand," Sato said, realizing no one attached any particular importance to his weapons. "I will give my host's children other presents."

"Fine. Please have a pleasant stay in America," the woman said with a smile and bow. She said something in English to the inspector before leaving with the throwing stars.

Sato watched the inspector finish his work. He did a thorough job, but showed no interest in anything he saw.

Sato had hidden his reddish-black *shunobi-shozoku* clothing by folding it inside a tweed suit. Simply bringing the outfit had been a risk, but Sato decided to take it along because he couldn't conceive of operating without the clothing that symbolized his art. When the inspector felt the extra bulk within the suit and opened it, Sato again prepared for trouble. Any Japanese policeman would have recognized the outfit as the special clothing of a ninja, but the American simply refolded the suit and wadded it back where it had been. Even when the inspector came across the lock picks Sato had hidden in his toiletries case, he paid them no attention. He seemed to care nothing about Sato or the important things he was carrying; he simply stamped Sato's passport and motioned him through the doors at the side of the room.

Sato made his connecting flight to Minneapolis in a cloud induced by jet-lag and the loss of his *shuriken*, then took a cab to the hotel where his travel agent had made reservations. He found his room huge and somewhat too warm, but before he could begin to take in his surroundings, he had to lie down to rest and fell into a deep sleep. When he woke it was dark, but checking his watch, he saw it was only 9:30 PM.

Since he was fully awake and eager to begin his assignment, Sato went to the front desk and requested a map of the city. He was surprised the desk clerk did not have one handy since local maps are always available to guests at Japanese hotels. The large city atlas Sato had finally bought at the lobby gift shop seemed intimidatingly complex, but with the bellman's help, Sato learned the city was laid out in a systematic way that made navigation relatively easy.

Sato stifled the urge to take a taxi to the home of the man who held the dagger he was to retrieve. Instead he spent his first night in America reviewing his instructions and information. He reread the description of the dagger that was his objective. It was just over twenty-five centimeters long and mounted in a *shira-saya* and it was contained in a wooden box. All of that was straightforward.

The information Sato had about the man who held the dagger was, however, very sketchy. Eric Mallow, Number 413, Nokomis Condominium, Nokomis Parkway West. It took nearly an hour for Sato to locate this on the city map. Once he had, he studied the neighborhood, memorizing the names of the nearby streets and visualizing escape routes and traffic flow patterns in the vicinity. There was a large lake nearby; if the park surrounding the lake was wooded and wild as lakes in this area were said to be, it might offer an easy escape route. Sato, who had done both hiking and mountain climbing in Japan, looked forward to exploring the area.

After studying the map, Sato turned his attention back to the information he had on Eric Mallow. The copied business card gave only his name and address. He had been told that Mallow was about 35 years old, but he had no photograph or other description. Identifying Mallow would be one of Sato's first challenges. To begin the process, Sato began to practice the man's name, "Eric Mallow, Eric Mallow, Eric Mallow." Sato tried to be precise, but he had difficulty with the odd sounds so the named turned into "*Eriku Maroh*" which had an even more mesmerizing effects. As he repeated the name, it became a *mantra*--a chant that cleared his mind and focused his attention.

Recalling his disappointments, Sato once again found himself repeating the name, "*Eriku Maroh, Eriku Maroh, Eriku Maroh.*"

When he first practiced this name three days earlier, Sato had been willing to view this person as an objective, maybe even as a challenge. Now repeating the ugly sound made Sato realize that without ever having met the man, he had grown to hate him. "*Eriku Maroh, Eriku Maroh, Eriku Maroh.*" It had become an ugly sound. "*Eriku Maroh*" was Sato's problem and his tormentor. Because of "*Eriku Maroh*" his life was in disarray. Sato knew killing "*Eriku Maroh*" would be easy.

Looking back, Sato decided that aside from his embarrassing start, his first full day in America had not really gone badly. The day began just before noon when a chambermaid opened Sato's door expecting to find nothing more than a messy room. Instead, she startled the would-be ninja awake from a deep sleep. Sato jumped to a an offensive stance at the side of his bed and the maid screamed and slammed the door. As his mind cleared, Sato felt foolish standing there in his underwear, but compared to the disasters of the days that followed, letting a harmless intruder enter his room no longer seemed very serious.

Sato used the first day inspecting the building he would have to penetrate, but simply getting to his target had been very frustrating. He took cab from the hotel, but the driver could not - or perhaps would not - understand the address Sato memorized the night before. He repeated it several times before simply showing the copy of Mallow's card. Then the man said, "Oh sure, the Nokomis Condos," and drove off confidently.

Sato tried to relate sights along the way to the maps he had studied the night before. Everything struck him as strange-- the trucks were huge, the streets wide, and the fast-moving traffic was remarkable. Sato was surprised when the driver suddenly pulled to a stop in front of a large brick building and said, "Here we are."

Sato did not wish to be seen so closely associated with the building he was expecting to enter by stealth or force, so he tried to tell the driver to let him out in the middle of the next block. Again the man was unable to understand. Sato repeated the instruction slowly several times to no avail. In frustration he finally said, "Go there," and pointed a distance ahead. The driver shrugged insolently but did as he was ordered.

The difficulties with the driver left Sato angry and unsettled, but he forced himself to look nonchalant as he got out of the cab. He began his observations by walking casually toward the condominium building the driver had shown him. It stood on the corner of two large streets and was surrounded by a paved parking lot. There was no easy place to stop near the building so Sato walked around the entire block. The street in front of the building was fairly busy, but on the street behind the condominium Sato found a quiet residential area of handsome homes surrounded by well-maintained lawns. The size and spaciousness of these homes was so impressive Sato found it hard to concentrate on the building he was supposed to be studying. He did not linger because he did not want to appear suspicious, but he saw that the condominium was separated from the houses by a wooden fence about two meters high. Vaulting over just this kind of obstacle was one of the ninja skills he regularly demonstrated at the Ninja Village. It did not strike him as a formidable obstacle.

When he finished strolling around the block, Sato retired to a coffee shop across the street. He took a seat in the window and, over several cups of coffee and couple of gooey donuts the waitress had recommended, spent the next two and a half hours looking at the building.

He watched people and cars enter and leave. The postman spent nearly twenty minutes distributing letters to boxes in the lobby. An older woman with golden hair walked around the building picking up litter. Five other older women and two gray-haired men entered the building, but none looked young enough to be Eric Mallow.

Sato made a mental plan of the building. There were five floors and, based on the distribution of windows, Sato decided each floor had five units along each side of a central hall. Finding Mallow's apartment would be easy.

On that first day, Sato felt getting into building might not be too difficult. The front door was glass and located alongside a large clear window. These made it easy to see inside the lobby. The outer door appeared to be open all the time, but Sato could see inner door required a key. He also saw that cars could drive into a basement parking area that had an overhead door drivers raised with another key.

When he left the coffee shop, Sato was rattled by caffeine, but pleased with what he had learned. At that point he had been sure approaching the building would not be hard. The fence between the parking areas and houses would be no problem and he was confident his skill with locks would allow him into the building. The only problem he anticipated would be getting across the parking area. The space afforded no easy hiding places, but he had been optimistic. He was sure he could solve that problem. The optimism he had felt on that first day made his subsequent frustrations more extreme and added to his misery.

When he left the coffee shop, Sato had looked for a taxi to take back to his hotel. He wanted to make notes and think about what he had seen. In Japan there are always cabs available, but as Sato waited on what seemed like a busy corner some blocks away from the condominium, he discovered there are very few cabs in America. Those he saw either had riders or would not stop for him.

After waiting more than fifteen minutes, he began to walk back to his hotel. His work with the city maps had made it easy for him to navigate in the strange surroundings. The trip also gave him an opportunity gather his thoughts.

As he walked, Sato thought more about how he could approach and enter the condominium. He recalled a standard part of the tours he gave at **Ninja Village**. Time and again he explained that though ninja could not really make themselves invisible, they were expert at making themselves hard to see. This meant using features of the terrain to hide their actions and adopting disguises to hide their identity. Walking along the busy street that would bring him to his hotel, he turned these ideas in his mind. As Sato recalled his experiences and searched for some ray of hope, he recalled the disguise he had hit upon as he walked home.

An old ninja axiom Sato had repeated time and again to his tour groups was, "To look like everyone else is to be invisible." Applying that principle in this city of white people had seemed impossible until, as he walked, Sato noticed a fair number of Orientals. Most were Vietnamese, but he noticed that many of the young men wore their hair in distinctive styles. He also studied their clothing and shoes and saw that many of the young men wore colorful satin jackets. As he passed a small clothing store with a sign in Vietnamese, Sato realized he had found a disguise. He purchased two satin jackets and convinced himself they would let him operate near the condominium without looking out of place or attracting attention. Clearly, he could count his disguises as a big success. He smiled as he recalled it.

No matter how well the first day had gone there was no getting around the fact that the second day had been a disaster. Thinking about it was like touching a sore, but to clear his mind Sato forced himself to review the events of the day.

First, there had been the car. His problems with taxis convinced Sato a rented car would offer a better means of transportation. Renting the vehicle had been easy since the rental counter in the hotel lobby accepted his international driver's license without question. Problems began when he pulled out of the hotel parking ramp and went the wrong way on a one-way street. A policeman stopped him immediately and gave him the first of two tickets he received that day. A female police officer gave him the another when he turned into an oncoming lane of traffic while he was exploring the neighborhood around the condominium. He simply could not get comfortable driving down the right side of the street from the left side of the car.

And then, Sato cut a corner while leaving a parking area in the grassy park around the lake near the condominium, ran into a low post and put a huge ugly crease along the side of the car. He did not know how he was supposed to respond to the tickets and had no idea how to handle the damage to the rented car. Recalling the problems with the car made Sato feel very incompetent, and they hadn't even been the worst part of the day.

Sato had parked the car some blocks from the condominium so that he could begin exploring the building he would have to penetrate. What a fiasco that had been.

Wearing one of his satin jackets so he would look like one of the young Vietnamese fellows he had seen the day before, Sato walked toward the building. Entering the lobby had been no problem. He simply walked through the front door when no one was around to see him. Inside the lobby, however, he had discovered that the inner door posed a more serious problem than he had anticipated. He could find no keyhole. Instead, the door seemed to be controlled by a complex electronic lock that he did not understand. In Japan, virtually all houses and apartments are closed with very simple locks. Learning to pick these had been so easy, Sato never gave any thought to learning about more complex systems. He did not know where to begin on this lock. He considered the possibility of simply forcing the door, but that looked like a difficult prospect since it was made of thick, tempered glass backed by steel mesh. The glass outer door also meant that the entire lobby could be seen from the street.

Hoping the rear door or the parking garage would offer easier access, Sato left the lobby and took the sidewalk around to the parking lot. He walked nonchalantly until he got to the driveway. There he looked around to make sure no one was watching and walked to the side of the building. Once there, he proceeded along the wall to the door to the parking garage. Anyone in the lot could have seen him, but there was no one about so Sato had moved easily. The parking garage was closed by a heavy overhead door with no exterior handle. Instead, it was controlled by a key-operated switch on a post that drivers could reach without leaving their cars. Sato decided this door, too, would be very hard to breech and went on to the rear door of the building. A wave of embarrassment swept over him has he remembered what happened next. What a debacle.

There had been no one in view as he moved along the building wall toward the rear door. And he had not forgotten that a ninja must remain constantly vigilant. He was sure he had remained alert. Still, there was no getting around the embarrassing truth. He had let his guard down.

Sato found that the rear door was controlled by the same kind of electronic system he had found in the lobby. He looked at the hinges and lightly shook the sturdy doorknob. As he wondered how he might be able to release the lock, a golden-haired woman stepped out from behind the corner of the building. She shrieked something at him and may have had some kind of stick in her hand. Sato had no idea what she said and he did not even look directly at her because he been taken by total surprise. In a panic he had run toward the street without looking back.

Sato was sure he would never endure anything worse than his second day in America. It had been terrible and recalling it had been painful. He would never forget the shame he felt, but at least he had endured and made himself return to his task. His third day had had its own misadventures, but as he recalled them, he felt they may have seemed worse than they really were.

Simply to get out of the hotel, Sato began by taking the car out of the parking garage. He drove around the city for more than two hours until he became comfortable behind the wheel. Once or twice he caught himself driving on the wrong side of the road or beginning to turn into oncoming traffic, but there had been no more tickets. He even stopped to buy gasoline and slowly became more familiar with streets and neighborhoods around the condominium.

Sato drove around the lake near the condominium building several times. It was surrounded by a grassy park was much less wild than he had thought it might be, but there were many large trees and shrubs planted irregularly all around the lake. Moving across the grassy areas that separated these would be difficult in daylight, but at night Sato felt the area would provide many hiding places. This was the kind of area a ninja could use to good advantage. It would be an excellent refuge either before or after his entry into Eric Mallow's apartment.

Sato parked the car in one of the several turnouts and strolled along the paved sidewalk that ringed the lake. It was a pleasant area, unlike anything he had ever seen in Japan, where open expanses with few people and no buildings are very rare. He would have to return after dark to fully appreciate the area, but it promised to be very useful.

As he returned to his car, Sato walked near a pavilion at the lake's edge. A middle-aged man seated on a bench near the building, smiled pleasantly at him and said "Hi" as Sato passed by. When Sato returned his greeting, the man had invited him to join him on the bench. Seeing no harm, Sato sat down and began a pleasant conversation. The man was dressed in a brown tweed sport coat. He wore a bow tie, a plaid muffler, and a flat cloth cap that struck Sato as stylish. He asked Sato his name and where he was from. Sato was wearing his satin jacket and trying to look Vietnamese, but told the man he was a Japanese tourist.

The man was very impressed. He said, "Really!" and asked Sato if he was enjoying his trip and how he liked American food. He spoke slowly with a pleasant soft voice that Sato found very easy to understand. The pleasantries he exchanged with the man made Sato realize that he had spoken with no one for a couple of days and had grown lonely. Sato remembered to remain on guard, but he let himself enjoy the human contact he had been missing. The man told Sato his name was Victor and they had both laughed as Sato had tried to pronounce it correctly.

During the conversation, the man gradually moved toward Sato until they were nearly touching and he was resting his arm of the back of the bench. Sato thought nothing of this until he put his hand on Sato's thigh and rubbed it gently.

"Yoshimasa, I like you," he said looking into Sato's eyes. "Would you like to go to my apartment?"

As the man's interests became apparent, Sato was swept by a wave of embarrassed realization. He pushed his hand away from his leg and stood up. He was less upset with the man's suggestion than he was with himself. Yet another situation had caught him entirely by surprise. He walked away utterly embarrassed and quite oblivious to the harsh comments the man shouted at him.

The day Sato had just completed as he was making this assessment was so fresh in his memory that recalling its events was not hard at all. It had, however, been another day of embarrassing failure. The best he could say was that he had made it back to his hotel room without detection and only very minor wounds.

Sato had begun his fourth day with a reasonable goal. As he recalled that much, Sato let himself take some pride in the fact that he had picked himself up after the frustrations of the previous days. He had not given up. But he could take little satisfaction in his persistence. It was getting nowhere and leading only to frustration and embarrassment.

Sato had decided that this was the day to explore the area behind the condominium. He hoped the backyards of the houses abutting the condominium parking lot would provide easier access than the front approach he had tried two days previously. He shuddered as he thought of the failure he had just survived.

His sleep schedule still did not match the local time so he had not left the hotel until after noon. When he did, he drove to the neighborhood of the condominium and parked on a quiet side street a couple of blocks from his target. Remembering that much, Sato realized that driving had become quite comfortable. He also realized that he had forgotten about the traffic tickets and the ugly scar along the side of his rented car. There seemed to be a great many damaged vehicles in America so his car attracted no attention. He had driven past the car rental office and even they had not asked about the damage. Deciding to ignore the damage made it easier to also ignore the traffic tickets.

After leaving his car on a side street, Sato walked casually along the street behind the condominium. While driving through the area he identified a house that was directly across from the condominium rear door. It had no lights on inside and the day's mail was still in the mailbox so Sato assumed no one was home. Best of all, in addition to a fence that went around the entire backyard, the backyard was surrounded on three sides by a high hedge. Sato could use this kind of cover to advantage as he tried to get closer to the condominium. All of that analysis had been flawless and he had walked to the front of the house and on toward the rear fence without attracting any attention. Problems began only after he vaulted the fence into the rear yard and crouched on the inside to survey the next part of his route.

His sudden arrival startled a large dog sleeping in the doorway of a doghouse built against the back fence. The dog woke with a start and immediately set up a prolonged bay. It scanned the yard until it located Sato then charged him barking angrily.

Sato remained in his crouched position as the dog raced toward him. He had not consciously decided to remain still, but had been frozen by surprise and terror. The strategy worked, however, because the dog stopped about three feet from Sato's face. It continued to bark loudly and snarled threateningly, but seemed mystified by the crouching figure that had landed in its yard. It snapped and pawed the earth and viscous saliva dripped from its bared fangs. It bounced nervously right in front of Sato, but came no closer.

Dogs are not common in Japan and Sato had never had anything to do with one as large and fierce as the creature now snarling in his face. At first he was terrified, but the dog's initial hesitation gave him hope and after a few moments, he noticed that the dog began to soften its attack. Its barking changed to a lower pitch and it took occasional rests. It began to move from side to side and eventually paced back and forth in front of Sato. Once it even broke the rhythm of its attack to step toward the grassy center of yard where it urinated and scratched the grass with its back legs.

As his fear subsided, Sato was able to observe the dog in detail. What a truly disgusting beast it was. It panted uncontrollably and its breath smelled terrible. It had a dirty red bandanna tied around its neck and a pair of hard, round testicles prominently displayed below its stubby tail and puckered rectum. Looking beyond the dog, Sato saw the yard was littered with well-gnawed bones and hard black turds. He wondered how Americans could stand to have such vile creatures around their homes and he was swept by a strong desire to be back in Japan.

Remaining motionless for long periods of time was an important part of a ninja's ability to remain unseen and a skill Sato had practiced often. Unfortunately, when he vaulted the fence he had landed imperfectly and now his left foot was in a very uncomfortable position. After only a few minutes his leg began to cramp and his foot throbbed. Every time he tried to adjust his position, however, the dog renewed its attack. With his back to the fence, Sato saw no easy escape. He was trapped. Had he even one *shuriken*, he could have buried it deep in the dog's skull. He would have done so gladly, but he was entirely unarmed and helpless. His leg began to throb.

In frustration and anger Sato grimaced and said, "*shiku-sho*". As soon as the word was out of Sato mouth, the dog stopped barking and cocked its head.

"Do you speak Japanese, you vile devil?" Sato asked and the dog looked even more intently. After a moment he growled tentatively and Sato spoke again.

"You are a worthless frog," he said softly in Japanese. "I'd like to feed you to the fish." The dog backed off slightly and sat on its haunches. As it did, Sato began to raise slowly.

"Yes, you are vile scum," Sato said using very harsh words, but a soft voice and polite word forms. "I will be leaving you shortly and I want you to be quiet. Do you understand?. Of course you do, you worthless pile of fish guts."

The dog watched Sato intently and began to growl deeply only when he was nearly fully upright. By that time, Sato could reach the top of the fence and he turned to pull himself out of the dog's domain. His legs were numb and could contribute little to his efforts so his vault was not smooth or fast and as soon as he made his move the dog lunged after him. On its first jump, the dog bit Sato's left ankle. On the second try, it snagged his pants leg and nearly pulled him back. Luckily, however, the garment gave way before that could happen and Sato fell to the ground on the other side of the fence with nothing more than wobbly legs and badly torn pants.

The dog raged as Sato had hurried away. He was very self-conscious about his torn clothing, but he worked hard to attract no attention as he walked back to the car. Along the way he passed an older woman and some young school children, but he made it back to the hotel without incident. When he arrived in his room he was very tired and had let himself take a nap although the rest brought no relief. He woke in the deep misery that began these torturous recollections of the past four days.

His mission was clearly a failure. Everything he tried had failed and there was no hope of success. Perhaps his skills were not appropriate to America. Perhaps he possessed no skills. Whatever the case, there was no point in continuing. The mission was a failure.

Acknowledging that much helped Sato sort out his emotions and lay out a course of action. He was deeply embarrassed and very frustrated. And he was even more angry at "Eric Mallow." He was the person ultimately responsible for Sato's failure, but in acknowledging this, Sato realized he could live with this failure. He need not kill himself. He could return to Japan.

Tsuji-san had given him only an advance on his expenses. Sato could repay that and he still had his job at Ninja Village. He could go back to it even if the experience of the past four days had demonstrated that he was not a real ninja. He had told no one about the real nature of his trip to America so he would not have to tell Ozawa-sensei about his failure. It could be his secret.

Sato resolved to leave America the next day. His ticket was open and he would accept any seat JAL could supply. He felt better than he had in days. He was rested and satisfied with his decision. He felt more energy than he had since arriving in America. He was free and liberated by his decision but the thought of spending his last night in his hotel room was very unsatisfying. As he thought about alternative activities, Sato recalled that he had never let himself explore the park around the lake by the condominium after dark. A visit to that area would let him use some of the energy and vitality he now felt.

Sato would never have to use the lakeside park as a refuge, but he looked forward to exploring it as a relaxing diversion. Driving through the city had become easy and he circled the entire lake before he left the car. He parked in a turnout some distance from the condominium because he wanted to explore the park itself. He had abandoned his assignment and did not want to think about his original challenge. The parking area he selected was lit with electric lights and empty of other cars when Sato arrived. He took this as a good sign, indicating that there would be few other people in the park so that he could explore freely and without interruption. The walkway around the lake was also illuminated, but Sato was pleased to see that grassy areas away from the turnouts and the walkways were quite dark.

As Sato left his car, he had only very general objectives. He wanted to explore the park, but more than that, stealth in the dark was a central skill of *ninjitsu* so that Sato looked forward to using skills he had studied for years. He had wanted to wear his dark *shunobe-shozoku*, which is the appropriate attire for a ninja, but grudgingly decided to stay with his American disguise and worn the darker of his satin jackets. He had, however, let himself wear his comfortable *tabi*, the split-toed shoes preferred by traditional Japanese workmen.

Sato parked his car near the edge of the parking area so he could easily slip into a clump of bushes at the side of the pavement. Stepping out of the car, he crept to the shadowed side of the bushes and moved easily into the darkness. Crouching at the base of a large tree, he remained motionless while his eyes became adjusted to the darkness. This did not take long since the park was far from pitch blackness, but as Sato began to pick out details of trees and bushes, he was sure his night vision had been enhanced by the mixture of powdered deer horns and ginseng his master, Ozawa-sensei, had prescribed.

To convince himself that the discomfort he experienced while crouching in front of the stinking dog was only due to his unfortunate landing, Sato remained in a squatting position even after his eyes became accustomed to the darkness. He remained motionless for more than fifteen minutes without a hint of leg pain. As he waited, he recalled the dog and the frustration he had suffered as it offended him with smell and spit. The desire for revenge is not a positive feeling. It has no place in a ninja's life, but Sato longed to be able to punish the awful beast.

When he had convinced himself he retained the skill of motionlessness, Sato began the next phase of his exploration by jumping straight upward. He was certain he could never have sprung from a crouching posture all the way over the fence he had vaulted to meet the dog. Still, the leap he made as he left the tree let him feel certain that if his leg not been cramped, he could have sprung near enough to the fence top to finish the vault before the dog could have reacted.

From the tree, Sato ran at full speed across the dark grass. As he sprinted he practiced quick turns and rolled and tumbled in evasive movements. The exercise and freedom were exhilarating and he thought about running around the entire lake. He easily could have, but decided instead to become familiar with the terrain closest to the condominium. This was near the intersection of a couple of streets and rather well lit. Still, Sato was able to identify a shadowy course from a parking turn out to the corner across from the condominium. He navigated it twice and was sure that he had done so invisibly.

As Sato returned to his parked car he felt very good. He had forgotten about his misadventures with the dog and was feeling more skilled and competent than he had in days. As he walked toward his car, he looked forward to getting back to a bath and a good night's sleep. With his relaxation he had let his guard down and was well into the lighted parking area before he saw a group of four young black men standing on the dark side of his car. They saw him immediately and ran around the car to confront him. One shouted something Sato did not understand although he thought it included the word "gook."

Sato stood motionless for a moment hoping the strategy he had used with the dog would work again. It did not. The men immediately began to rush toward him. In the moment he hesitated, the two on the margins spread out to cut off Sato's sides. More ominously, one of the men pulled a pistol from under his jacket. Sato turned and ran toward the darkness he had just been exploring.

Sato could hear the black men running behind him and had to work very hard to stay ahead of them. They shouted harshly, but aside from a couple words, Sato could not tell what they were saying. He simply ran as hard as he could. To avoid making himself an easy target, he used the quick turns and other erratic moves he had just been practicing. He made sure he was never silhouetted in the light and tried to stay in the shadows and darkness. His attackers were very athletic and stayed close behind him. Because they covered a broad front, they limited his mobility and forced him in the direction of the next lighted turn out.

As he neared that parking area, Sato heard one of the men behind him breathlessly shout something that included the word "shoot." As the significance of that word registered, he sidestepped and heard a shot. Sato had never heard an actual gun off before, and he was not sure where the bullet had been aimed, but he was sure he had not been hit. He raced ahead with a burst of energy.

As he entered the parking area, Sato ran between two parked cars and darted across the pavement. When he was near the center of the asphalt, a police car drove into the turn out with its red lights flashing. By the time it came to a stop, it was between Sato and the black men Sato looked over his shoulder to see two police officers get out of the car. One had a pistol drawn and the other had a short shotgun which he turned in Sato's direction, but Sato ran into the darkness and hidden at the base of a large tree.

From his resting place Sato looked back at the parking area. The police officers were crouched near their car. He could see no trace of the black men, but heard them shouting. They appeared to have turned their attention to the police and the policeman who had been pointing his gun in Sato's direction turned his attention toward the other side of the turnout. Sato wished he could understand the harsh words that were being shouted back and forth between the two sides.

He began to hear several sirens in the distance just before he saw two flashes of light and heard two barked reports from the darkness on the opposite side of the turnout. From their crouching positions on his side of their car, the policemen returned the fire, shooting into the darkness. The first of several additional police cars arrived as the shots were still being fired. The newly arrived car parked so its headlights were pointed toward the black men and Sato got a glimpse of a figure darting away from the light.

Additional cars began to arrive and one of the officers pointed in Sato's direction. He realized he could watch no longer and began to run away from the lighted area. Almost immediately powerful lights were turned toward him and he had to move smartly to remain unseen.

After running several hundred meters, Sato stopped at the base of another tree to catch his breath and consider his situation. He was free but separated from his car. He could see a variety of moving lights in that area which he took to be evidence that the police were searching for the black men. Sato didn't think he had done anything wrong, but he knew he could not explain what he had been doing in the park. He would have to avoid contact with the police. As he was considering his situation, a police car began to drive across the grass in his direction. It drove back and forth on the grass oblivious to the road and other small obstacles and used its spotlight to scan the area Sato had crossed.

Sato had to move fast. He was sure he could not outrun the car and could not guess where it would go so he turned to the tree that was hiding him and began to scramble upward. If he had brought *te-kagi*, the steel climbing claws he used to demonstrate tree climbing to the visitors of **Ninja Village**, this would have been easy. Using only his bare hands the task was formidable. The rough bark offered few surfaces to grasp and tore his palms. His rubber-soled split-toed *chika-tabi*, however, let him make the most of surface and he was able to scramble to the lowest level of branches. Once he could pull himself upward, he climbed higher. When the police car passed below him, it did not shine its light upward and he escaped detection.

The police car made several passes near Sato's hiding place, and a couple of the officers even walked by with flashlights and drawn pistols. Sato remained motionless in the branches and again was not detected. The police appeared to be most interested in searching in the direction of the black men. And well they should, thought Sato. They had been the ones who started the gunfight! Sato was suddenly struck by his situation. He had been attacked by four armed men. They had chased him and shot at him, but he had evaded them *and* a large number of police. He had been successful. He was being a ninja.

11 | Dawn Watanabe

In which the nature of a lost treasure is revealed but not believed.

Minneapolis - some weeks after the Des Moines show
Dawn Watanabe, children's book editor and aerobics instructor
Eric Mallow, Dawn's friend

"Dr. Mallow's office. This is Pam. How may I help you?"

The receptionist's voice was efficient and cool and for just a moment, Dawn felt a twinge of intimidation. "Pam, this is Dawn Watanabe," she said trying to sound relaxed and friendly. "I don't suppose Eric's standing right there with a minute to spare?" Dawn truly wasn't jealous of Pam or the other women who worked in Eric's office, but she felt herself trying to make her voice just a bit softer than the receptionist's.

"Gee, no, he isn't, Dawn," said Pam. "He's in with a patient. Do you want me to have him call you?"

"Yeah, will you have him give me a buzz? I think I've come across something he'll find interesting."

"Fine. I'll make sure he gets the message," Pam said with precision that struck Dawn as somewhat cooler than necessary.

The day was busy and it was well into the afternoon before Eric could get back to Dawn. When he did, it was good to hear her voice on the other end of the line.

"Hi, this is Dawn Watanabe."

"Hi'ya, tiger," Eric said merrily.

"There you are," Dawn said. "I was afraid you'd forgotten all about me."

"Now, how could I do that?" Eric said soothingly. "It's just been a hectic morning."

"Something special?"

"Nah, just drillin' and fillin', but we've been super busy."

"How was this weekend's show?"

"I had a good time. There wasn't a lot of stuff, and prices were pretty high, but I found a couple of things I'm happy with." Eric waited to see if Dawn would say anything. When she didn't, he continued. "I drove up with Dave Stalgaard and on the way home he wanted to check out some stuff in St. Cloud, so we didn't get back 'til after eleven. I thought it was too late to give you a call."

"You don't have to check in with me," Dawn said. "If you want to spend your weekends with a bunch of right-wing gun nuts at the Fargo Gun Show, that's perfectly all right."

Eric simply chuckled at her sarcasm. He had long along given up trying to defend his interest to Dawn and he knew she was only teasing. She had no interest in guns or the other things Eric collected and she truly did not like many of the people Eric met in the course of his collecting, but she admired the sincerity of his interest and the satisfaction the hobby provided.

"Dave Stalgaard is the guy who's helping you with those Japanese swords, right?" Dawn asked.

"Yeah, that's the guy," said Eric.

"Well, I'm here to tell you that he's not the only one who's helping you with them."

"What do you mean?" asked Eric.

"I've got something on them too. And I bet you'll think its neat."

"Pam said you'd found something for me," Eric said with obvious curiosity. "What do you have?"

"The name of the guy who supposedly made that dagger was Muramasa, right?"

"Yep, Muramasa," repeated Eric, pronouncing the name more precisely than Dawn. "Don't tell me you found another one of his swords."

"I wouldn't know how to identify one of his swords, but," she said teasing him with a slight pause, "I think I came across a story about him."

Eric could tell from Dawn's tone that she thought the discovery was important. She also seemed pleased to be able to offer Eric something relevant to his collecting. He wasn't sure how significant Dawn's story could be, but he was pleased at her interest in his hobby. "And you think it's neat?"

"It is!" Dawn continued, happy to be able to tell him about her find. "I found it in a volume of young peoples' stories that was published in England in 1882. It's called 'The Wicked Blade of Muramasa'."

"That's the name of the book?" Eric said, still trying to understand why Dawn thought her discovery was important.

"No, no. The book's called *Young People's Stories of Old Japan* and there's just one story about the sword maker, but it's just creepy as shit. You'll probably love it," Dawn said playfully.

"Neat," said Eric. His enthusiasm continued to be mildly forced, but he was enjoying how obviously pleased Dawn was in telling him about her find. "You going to read it to me this evening, maybe over a bottle of wine? In fact, why don't you come over after work? I'll make dinner. Pasta maybe?"

"Gee, that sounds great, Eric, but I've got my aerobics classes tonight."

"You're still gonna have to eat," Eric said. "And I want to see you. Come over after your last class and we'll make an evening of it. We'll end with your bedtime story."

Eric hung up with a smile and headed back to work.

Shortly after eight, having worked out and led a pair of aerobics classes, Dawn arrived at Eric's condo. She was freshly showered and very hungry. Eric greeted her with a glass of Australian shiraz and a large plate of freshly cut vegetables. Over salad and pasta primavera, the pair spent half an hour in conversation. Dawn shared some juicy bits of office gossip and described a job offer one of her co-workers was considering. She also merrily told Eric of the problems she had had trying to configure her new computer. She described spending an entire afternoon on an 800 line talking to "one dork after another." She also made Eric tell her about the gun show he had attended the previous weekend, but he couldn't make his adventures as interesting and fun as hers, so for most of the evening Dawn did the talking.

After dinner, while Eric loaded the dishwasher and cleaned the kitchen, Dawn began to steer the conversation in the direction of the story she wanted to show Eric. "So, what's happening with these fancy Japanese swords you brought home from Iowa?" she asked from the door of Eric's kitchen.

"Not too much," he said. "This fellow, Dave Stalgaard, who's handling the deal for me, has been doing a lot of research and figures he's got the long one pretty well pegged. It belonged to a famous guy in the 1300s. He says it's worth a lot of dough." He paused to flip the switch of the garbage disposal. When he flipped it back off, and its noisy whir ended, he continued.

"The other one, the dagger signed by this Muramasa guy, is more of a problem. Dave says it's a real good blade, but so far he hasn't found anything very specific on it."

"The story I found is about a swordsmith named Muramasa," said Dawn. "Was that a common name or something?"

"I don't think so," said Eric as he wiped off the counter top. "But Dave said Muramasa was pretty famous, so he's probably the guy in the story."

"I'm not sure that's good news," said Dawn. "The story makes Muramasa sound pretty creepy."

"Creepy! I thought you said it was a kid's story."

"It is, but Victorian authors had some pretty weird ideas about what was appropriate for children."

"Do you think it's appropriate for me?" asked Eric.

"Oh, I don't think it'll give you bad dreams. You may even find it kind of interesting."

"Great," said Eric, picking up a pot of coffee and two cups. "Let's go downstairs and you can read it to me."

"You want to do it down in the arsenal, huh?"

"Yeah, it's comfortable down there and that's were I've got the swords."

"Taking me down to the gun room to show me swords! How Freudian!" Dawn giggled as she followed Eric down the stairway.

"You don't have to worry about it. I'm not into symbolism," said Eric as he switched on the light.

"I'm not worried about it, Eric," Dawn deadpanned. "I just don't want you to dismiss the obvious phallic symbolism out of hand."

Eric chuckled. "You're terrible," he said shaking his head and smiling broadly.

"I'm glad you noticed," Dawn said as she sat down on the couch. Then in a more serious tone she asked, "Where did these swords come from? I mean, do you know how they got to America?"

"They were brought back after the war by this woman's husband," said Eric as he sat down in an easy chair.

"Where'd he get them?"

"Not sure," shrugged Eric. "GIs were really into souvenirs and it sounds like Japan was wide open, so they could have been picked up anywhere." After a pause, he added, "I got a photo album with the swords. I've never really looked at it, but I'll bet it's got some information about where the guy was and what he was doing. Let's take a look."

Dawn wanted to get to the story she had found, but she said, "Sure," and Eric got up to get the album. He set it down on the coffee table and sat beside Dawn.

The album had a thickly padded cover. The pages were black construction paper. Aside from several blank pages at the end of the album, most had four black and white snapshots mounted in corner brackets with captions written in white pencil. A couple pages contained other souvenirs. A set of staff sergeant's stripes was pasted on one page. Another had the menu from the 1945 Christmas at Camp Hata along with a snapshot of a group of men in class A uniforms seated at a formal dinner.

After flipping through a couple of pages, Eric said, "Wait a minute. Let's go through this systematically." He opened the album to the first page where there was a neatly lettered title, "Staff Sergeant Lee James, 57877342, U. S. Army, 1942-46."

"That's got to be the guy who muled the swords back to this country. I got them from his widow, Viola James," Eric said and he turned the page.

The next several pages held pictures of Japanese people and places. Several of these looked potentially interesting, but they were all small and poorly composed and the captions written below them were cryptic at best. One picture of a group of young women holding small wooden barrels was labeled, "The honey bucket brigade." Another, showing a couple of smiling boys, was marked, "Too young to be Kamikazes." A picture of a woman with a nursing baby was labeled, "The only Jap who's not hungry."

When Dawn saw the last of these she said, "Look's like he was a real sensitive traveler." Then she added with a trace of bitterness, "When he was taking these, my folks were just getting out of Manzanar."

Eric was aware that both of Dawn's parents' families had been interned during the war, but they had never talked about the experience and he wasn't ready to start then. "Yeah, these aren't very informative are they?" he simply said.

Toward the end of the album was a page labeled, "Assigned to Civil Affairs at Camp Hata." The pictures that followed were better labeled. One of the first pictures was labeled, "My Buddies, Arlon and Hervey." When Dawn saw the picture she said, "That guy's Japanese!" Looking at the next picture, labeled "The Three of Us," she added, "There he is again."

"This guy must be Sergeant James," said Eric pointing to the third GI in the photo.

"And the Japanese guy must have been one of the Nisei language specialists who served in Japan after the War," added Dawn. She was now more interested in the album and leaned forward so she could examine the photos in detail.

When Eric turned the next page, Dawn said, "Look at that! There are your swords." The page contained a number of pictures of the three GIs in various poses with a large collection of swords. The page was captioned, "After Getting Back from Takasaka." Each of the individual photos was also labeled.

"There's the long sword right there," said Eric as he pointed to a photo of Sergeant James smiling into the camera as he proudly held the tachi. "Me with the sword I won," Eric read.

Looking at the next picture, Eric excitedly said, "And there's the dagger!" This picture showed the other two GIs getting ready to flip a coin. The caption read, "Flipping a coin for the dagger."

"That's the box the dagger came in!" said Eric pointing at a wooden box at their feet.

In the next photo, the two GIs identified in the 'buddies' photo were again posed together. The Nisei sergeant was smiling weakly into the camera as he held what looked liked a mounted dagger. The other GI was making a menacing face as he held an exposed blade in his right hand. Eric could see the plain wood scabbard was in his left hand and the wooden box had been moved beside his foot.

"Holy shit," he added excitedly. "And this is when the dagger and the fittings got separated."

"What do you mean?" asked Dawn.

"Mrs. James had the dagger in a box," Eric explained. "That box right there," he said stabbing the picture with his finger. "When I got it, the blade was in that box and stored in plain wooden mountings. The fancy mounts that should also have been in the box were missing." Eric was clearly very excited. "The top of the box says the mounts were supposed to be very good, like solid gold! And now I see the reason they're missing is because these silly bastards just flipped a coin for them!" Eric was tapping the photo with his finger as he repeated, "Holy shit."

"You think they flipped coins for the swords?" Dawn asked still trying to get Eric to explain things completely.

"Sure! That's exactly what happened," Eric said as if no other interpretation were possible. "This picture shows James with the long sword. See, it says right there, 'The sword I won'," Eric said reading the caption below the picture of James and the tachi.

"That's what it says, all right," agreed Dawn.

"And in this picture, the other two guys are cutting up what was left of the jackpot." Eric said, forging the next link in a logical chain. "They only had the sword and the dagger, but the dagger came in two parts, so they must have flipped the second coin to see who got the blade and who got the mounts." Eric was now entirely convinced.

"This guy got the blade," he said tapping the image of the GI grimacing at the camera. "And that guy got the mounts," he continued pointing at the Nisei GI. "This explains a lot."

"Maybe it does, Eric, but it seems to leave a lot unanswered," countered Dawn.

"Like what?" asked Eric eager to have Dawn help him make the next set of connections.

"Well, for starters, it would be nice to know who these other two guys were."

"That's easy," Eric said turning back to the captioned picture on previous page. "They're his buddies, 'Arlon and Hervey.'"

"Which one's which?"

"Haven't figured that out yet," Eric said with a playful wave of his hand. "We'll have to work on it."

"Oh, we will, huh?" teased Dawn.

"Yep, but it's merely a problem." As Eric spoke, he turned the next page of the album to find a sheet of folded notepaper. With Dawn looking on, he opened it to see a neatly written note, "Arlon Matsuda, 1512 Lancaster, Milwaukee, Wisc. Let's stay in contact."

"I told you it'd be easy," Eric said as he looked up with a broad smile. "Arlon Matsuda of Milwaukee, Wisconsin got the mounts. Now all I have to do is find him."

"A Nisei Language Specialist named Arlon Matsuda ought to be easy to find," said Dawn. "I'll ask Mother. She may have run across his name in the Asian Pacific Citizen or through the Japanese American League."

"Great!" said Eric with genuine emotion. "Have her do some digging. If we can find Arlon, we might be able to come up with the mounts for the dagger and, let me tell you, that would make Dave very happy."

"You know, there's another problem, Eric," Dawn said.

"What's that?"

"If you're right, and this other guy, Hervey, won the dagger and the box, how come it ended up with Mrs. James in Iowa?"

"That's a good question," Eric said nodding his head. "And I don't have an answer, but it doesn't really matter. Maybe Hervey sold it to James. Maybe he gave it to him. Who knows, maybe he died and left it to him. All that really matters is that James ended up with it."

"I hope no one ever accused you of being a romantic," Dawn said leaning back from the coffee table and the photo album.

Eric also leaned back into his seat. "What do you mean? I can be very romantic. It's just that all this seems pretty straightforward. These guys picked these swords up, did some mixing and matching, and fifty years later, here they are."

"That's exactly my point, Eric. What if there's more to it than that?"

"What more could there be?" asked Eric with another shrug.

"This story I've been trying to tell you about makes it sound like there might be a hell of a lot more," said Dawn.

"I'm all ears," said Eric leaning back and putting his feet up on the coffee table. "Tell me about this story. Make me a romantic."

"It's about time! I've been trying to tell you about it all night long."

"Where'd you get it?" asked Eric.

"I told you. I came across it last weekend in a book of young peoples' stories I bought in Boston a couple of years ago. You know, I kind of collect old children's' literature."

Eric knew that Dawn had a large library of children's books. They had even gone to used book stores together. Still, he had never heard her describe her library as a collection and had never thought of Dawn as a "collector." Her statement struck him as a revelation about a person he thought he knew well. It was a revelation he liked.

Dawn sensed his reaction. "Well, I don't collect like you do," she said defensively, "but I've been buying old kids' books for years."

"I know," said Eric. "I just never thought of your books as a collection."

"What did you think they were? A way to cover broken plaster on my walls?" Dawn asked with real irritation. "Just because somebody doesn't make collecting the center of her life doesn't mean she doesn't collect."

"I know," agreed Eric. "It's just that I never realized you were a collector." He smiled, "I think it's neat. You just keep getting better and better."

Dawn smiled as she continued. "I hadn't looked at this book in a long time," she said reaching into her gym bag to get the book. It was quarto size and bound in a textured fabric. The title was stamped in gold letters that were written in a mock Oriental style.

"Over the weekend I was thumbing through it and my eye caught on the name Muramasa," Dawn continued. "I must have read the story, but I'd forgotten all about it. When I looked closer and realized the story was about a swordsmith, I was sure it had to be about the guy who made your sword."

"Muramasa made the dagger," Eric corrected. "That one isn't mine. It still belongs to Mrs. James down in Iowa. I'm selling it for her."

"Well, that's probably just as well because the story makes this guy sound spooky as hell."

"Who wrote the book?" asked Eric.

"An Englishman," she said as she flipped back to the title page and read, "Algernon Black-Buxton, Lord Reedslan. I've never run across his name before, so this may be the only kids' book he ever wrote. He explains these are stories he recorded while traveling in Japan. It was published in 1882 so he must have been there fairly early."

"That name seems real familiar," said Eric as he took the book. "I think he may have been an early gun collector. Yeah, that's it," he recalled with a smile. "I've read some things he wrote on English flintlocks. I had no idea he was interested in Japan." Eric flipped through the pages with increased interest.

"I think there was a lot of interest in Japan around the turn of the century because I've seen lots of books on Japan from that time," said Dawn.

As she was speaking, Eric stopped at a dramatic color plate of a crouching figure swinging a hammer above a red hot dagger blade. The figure's face was contorted in a wild grimace and a shadowy fox-faced creature hovered over one shoulder. A horned skeleton was at the other. "Don't tell me this is Muramasa," Eric said as he held the picture out for Dawn to see.

"You found it," she said taking the book back and turning to the next page where the story began. "The Wicked Blade of Muramasa," she read. "You want to hear it?"

"I'd love to," said Eric.

The Wicked Blade of Muramasa

Until the present generation, the leaders of all Japan were drawn from a special class known as the samurai. Although this class has recently given up its monopoly on power, virtually all of the country's modern leaders are the sons of the samurai. They carry the princely mien of their fathers' class and keep alive much of its refined culture and courtly tradition. Thus, knowledge of the country's knightly caste is essential for understanding the character of our newly emerged neighbor in the East.

Among all the anecdotes I recorded while traveling in the Land of the Rising Sun, none, I think, more clearly illustrates the virtues of the samurai than a story told to me by Marquis Genshichiro Kutani while I visited his family estate at the castle of Furukawa. This is the story I relate to my readers in this chapter.

Before doing that, however, I must first explain that I initially met Sir Kutani in the course of official duties in Tokyo. In all of those meetings, the young nobleman was a thoroughly modern citizen of the world. His command of English was near complete and he demonstrated deep understanding of the need for military and industrial modernization. On several occasions, when our work was finished, Sir Kutani hosted me at places of either entertainment or historical significance. He also graciously invited me to pass time at Furukawa where, he assured me, I would see a side of old Japan that had been lost in the cosmopolitan capital. As my duties were coming to an end and I was free to plan a trip into the Japanese hinterland, I recalled Sir Kutani's kind offer. I arranged to visit Furukawa while I traveled along the Tokkaido, the ancient roadway that for centuries connected the eastern and western ends of old Nippon. I traveled much of this ancient road on foot, just as did the courtiers and commoners of old. Only occasionally did I avail myself of a jinrikusha, one of the lightly built two wheel gigs drawn by bandy-legged human pullers who can trot for hours without apparent need for rest.

The castle of Furukawa is an impressive sight indeed. A graceful structure, it stands in the centre of a fertile agricultural plain. After four full days of constant travel, I arrived at the castle near exhaustion. Sir Kutani greeted me most graciously at the wide moat that protects his family estate. Whenever we had met in Tokyo, the young noble wore Western clothing of the most current cut, but here, standing on the massive narrow gate to his ancient home, he greeted me in richly brocaded kimono, with crisply presented hakama, and a vest-like haori that bore for all to see his family crest. He bowed deeply as I approached and I truly felt as if I had been transported back in time to a Japan that is now forever lost and gone.

With my host's generous hospitality, I passed five pleasant days at Furukawa, recovering from the rigors of travel and savoring the richness of Old Japan. With Lord Kutani as my guide, I explored several of the samurai arts. I practiced traditional Japanese archery, or kyudo. I drank tea from rustic bowls of great antiquity and incredible value and saw dramatic demonstrations of the warriorly arts of fencing and horsemanship. The noble, who as my friend I was now honored to call Genshichiro, also showed me many of his family's great treasures. Deep in ancient storehouses, we examined beautiful scrolls, fine pottery, and wonderfully complex armors worn by the warriors who founded the Kutani family nearly four centuries ago.

Among all the treasures I saw at Furukawa, none were greater than the Kutani family katana, the fine old swords carried by the valiant warriors who established the family's right to the lands they, until recently, commanded. Sir Kutani showed me the flawlessly polished surfaces of blades that that were old enough to have served at Hastings but still keen enough to kill in a single stroke. He showed me how to handle these blades with the respect and care that are their due, and how to see within them the beauty that marks them at once as objects of art as well as fearsome weapons. Indeed, it was at Furukawa that I came to realize that the sword is the soul of the samurai.

Samurai were men of action, trained to rapid response and given to decisive acts. No value was dearer to their hearts than loyalty to superior and to cause. Out of loyalty they would gladly die or kill. Holding the weight of their awesome weapons in my hand, I could sense why they were ferocious fighters, capable of taking the life of an enemy or giving themselves in a cause they had accepted.

When I showed special interest in the samurai, Sir Kutani did me the honor of letting me examine some of the many ancient texts held by his family. I could not, of course, decipher these documents, which were written in the Chinese style characters of old, but my friend explained their content and thrilled me with the deeds and events they recorded. Among the stories he related to me, based on these ancient texts, was the tale of the wicked blade of Muramasa.

The events of this story took place during a time the Japanese know as the Kokoku Era. Westerners reckon these years as 1340 - 1346 AD. The central figure of the story is a swordsmith named Muramasa. Like others of his profession, Muramasa was a craftsman and not a samurai. In Japan, however, the craft of swordmaking was a special one, more like a religious calling than a career. It is work requiring extreme skill, and Japanese swordsmiths approached their work with sincerity and dedication that paralleled the values of the samurai. They labored like common blacksmiths, developing great strength through Vulcan's work, they lived among the common masses, having no special social standing. Still, theirs was a career with special honor and responsibility. None appeared to understand this more than Muramasa.

Muramasa was born in a village called Yasuda where his father practiced the swordsmith's craft. The ringing of his father's hammer as it struck the anvil face was the first sound the child heard and without conscious thought, he accepted the swordsmith's life as his own. As luck would have, however, while he was still of tender age, his father died and Muramasa was left without a teacher. An orphan's prospects are rarely good and an ordinary lad might have abandoned his goal or transferred his allegiance to some other convenient smith who would pass along whatever skills he might command.

Muramasa took neither of those easy options. He was set on continuing and, indeed, enhancing his family's tradition by studying with the most famous swordsmith in Japan. That man was Munemasa, an artist now remembered as the greatest swordsmith who has ever practiced in Japan.

At the time when young Muramasa settled on his course of action, Munemasa worked at a forge he had established at a place called Osone in the rugged mountain vastness to south of the Imperial capital of Kyoto. This spot was carefully chosen because, in its isolation, it afforded few diversions and ample protection. Munemasa had reason to desire both these qualities.

Munemasa initially learned and practiced his skill at an Imperial forge in Kyoto, patronized by the Emperor Go-Tembo. Occasionally, the Emperor would take time from his official schedule to visit the forge where Munemasa worked. He praised the swords Munemasa made and supported him most generously. This was not hard since Munemasa made blades of great beauty and amazing strength. Munemasa earned a great reputation and as a loyal retainer he attributed his success to the generous support he had received from his Emperor.

Munemasa immersed himself in his craft and paid no attention to politics or other everyday matters. He did not know that strife and conflict swirled through the capital. Go-Tembo was an honest leader who sought to make the throne strong by decreasing the power of country warriors who contributed little to the well being of the people. For that reason, dark forces sought to drive him from the throne. The leader of those who opposed him was an ambitious country warrior named Genko Natsushima. His goal was to reduce the Emperor to a puppet who would command no real force and make no real decisions. Drawing on the troops under his own command and crafty alliances with other rural leaders, Natsushima assembled a force that drove the Emperor Go-Tembo out of the capital. But the dethroned emperor refused to relinquish his position. Instead, fleeing from Kyoto, he established a court in exile some distance to the south of the capital and drew around him a small but dedicated band of loyal supporters.

The emperor's actions took Munemasa by surprise, but as soon as the swordsmith heard of his patron's departure he recalled his debt of loyalty. He immediately abandoned the capital along with the emperor's other supporters and followed his patron into exile. That is how he came to establish the forge at Osone, which is where the orphaned Muramasa found him.

The Osone forge became a center of arms production for the Imperial forces. The small group of smiths who joined Munemasa worked to make blades that would let their side prevail and their emperor return to his rightful post. Fueled by the purest of intentions, the swordsmiths of Osone worked with intensity and purity and great skill. How could their blades be anything by splendid? It was at this forge that Munemasa reached the pinnacle of the swordsmith's skill. It was to this forge the young boy Muramasa came to study the swordsmith's art and it was in this community of devotion and industry that the orphaned lad came of age.

When Muramasa arrived at Osone he was barely in his teens, but the dedication he demonstrated in coming to the remote outpost and the earnestness of his request for instruction convinced Munemasa that he would be a worthy apprentice. For nearly ten years he labored with Munemasa. He began his service with chores like drawing his master's bath and sweeping up his workshop, then progressed to cutting charcoal and swinging the long-handled maul. Munemasa recognized in the boy a star pupil. He taught him to listen to the ring of the steel as it was struck and to judge from the sound the quality of a billet. The master showed the boy the secrets of using the color of heated metal to judge a fire's temperature. In time, the boy developed into a man and came to command the skills of sword making. For reasons we will soon review, modern judges rank Muramasa below the level of skill attained by Munemasa. Still, there is no question that he learned skills that let him create blades of great beauty and strength.

Unfortunately, the support of excellent swordsmiths was not enough to preserve Go-Tembo. Led by a noble warrior named Hidetaka Ashiya, the Imperial forces resisted the forces arrayed against Go-Tembo for several years. The Imperial forces made their small size a virtue by fighting a war of skirmish and mobility. Unconstrained by bases that required defense, Imperial troops moved more freely than their stronger foes. They fought valiantly time and again and won many victories. In the end, however, the greater size of the Natsushima forces wore them down. The tiny force that survived until 1337 was finally destroyed at the fateful Battle of Sumitani.

With the jewel of his forces destroyed, Emperor Go-Tembo's position was weakened, but even then, he steadfastly maintained his position. With time, however, his friends were reduced in number and power so that Natsushima was able to undertake a direct campaign against the exiled court at Ozone. As his forces drew near, the Emperor Go-Tembo made the hardest decision a sovereign can. Rather than see more of his loyal supporters slaughtered, the noble leader took the personally repellent step of abdication. He abandoned his claim to power, acknowledged the authority of the usurper on the throne in Kyoto, and retired himself to a monastery where he would live out his life in quiet contemplation.

As he had followed his patron into exile, Munemasa now felt compelled to follow Go-Tembo into retirement. He felt his debt of loyalty as deeply as ever. It would allow him to take no other action. Certainly, the senior smith would not risk making arms that might be used by the warriors who had driven his emperor from power. He also was by now of an age that made retirement appropriate.

Still, the decision to end his career was not an easy one for Munemasa. First, he felt his student Muramasa had not yet learned all he could. With more time, the master was sure he could help the apprentice achieve a level of excellence that exceeded the skills even he himself then commanded. But more importantly, Munemasa had no heir. To assure his family name would continue, he planned to wed Muramasa to a niece and adopt him as his son and heir. He had taken the first step in that strategy by seeing to the marriage of Muramasa one of his female kin. Formal adoption that would finish the plan was blocked by Go-Tembo's precipitous action. Thus, instead of ensuring the survival of his family, Munemasa did no more than ensure the continuation of Muramasa's father's line. The master smith himself would die without issue, a fate worse than death for the sons of Nippon. Munemasa explained all of these things to his apprentice and then closed his forge and retired to a monastery.

For the second time in his life, Muramasa was cut loose. The young smith would have been proud to be his master's heir, and he wanted to spend more years in Munemasa's tutelage, but none of that was to be. Bringing with him little more than his clothes and his young wife, Muramasa left Osone for his family home in Yasuda. There he found his father's forge in poor condition, but by dint of labor pure, he made it a serviceable workshop where he was able to resume sword making. He used all of the skills Munemasa had imparted and worked to refine them as best he could so that his blades began to win the respect by those who saw them. In time, the girl who should have borne the grandsons of Munemasa gave birth to a fine young boy whom all could expect to take up Muramasa's family name and the calling he had inherited from so many quarters. Indeed, all seemed well for the young swordsmith and so it should have been if only the political intrigues that unseated both the emperor and his master had been at an end.

As so often happens to those who villainously attack established authority, the forces that drove Go-Tembo from the throne fell to squabbling soon after their victory was secure. Genko Natsushima found himself threatened by fighters who had previously been his friends and fighting continued throughout the land.

Eventually, for a brief period, Natsushima wrested power enough to take up residence in the capital. He chose that moment to take his own retirement and pass the leadership of his family's affairs to his son, Koka. History remembers Koka barely at all because he was a rustic who held sway for the briefest of times. Like his father, Koka aspired to power and prestige, but he was born to the rough life of the countryside and lacked finesse. He was quite incapable of refinement and unfit for polite leadership. Lacking real quality, he thought assembling crude symbols of office and victory would make others see him as a force deserving respect. It was his desire for the trappings of power that brought him directly into Muramasa's life.

As a very public symbol of his family's victory, Koka decided he must have a sword by Munemasa who had been, after all, arms maker to his family's famous enemy. He dispatched his agents to find the master swordsmith and compel him to create a blade the

Natsushima heir could wear. When his men returned to him they reported that Munemasa could not fulfill his demand because he died shortly after departing Osone.

Now, Koka was not a man to suffer frustration easily. Moreover, he had become absolutely convinced that he not only wanted a sword from the forge of Munemasa, but, indeed, that he needed one to prove himself and his family. In a deep rage, he demanded his agents find a substitute. Fearing for their own lives, the agents learned that Muramasa was considered the best of active smiths who had worked at the Munemasa forge at Osone. Reporting this to Koka, the petty tyrant demanded that they bring him a blade of Muramasa's creation.

Thus, without announcement but a clear mission and a menacing escort of heavily armed fighters, Koka's agents arrived one day at Yasuda. They appeared at the door of Muramasa's home forge and made their demand. He was ordered to begin work immediately on a blade that would be Koka's personal sword.

Muramasa demurred. The conflict between the Natsushimas and the Emperor Go-Tembo was not his, but he knew that his teacher Munemasa had made his loyalty to the dethroned emperor a central pivot of his life. As his master's student, Muramasa had inherited that debt of loyalty and did not wish to abuse it by working for the emperor's enemies.

The young smith explained that he could not comply with the agents' request because, he said in total truth, he had neither the raw iron nor charcoal he would need to make a full-sized sword. He bowed low as he said these things and tried to sound respectful yet firm.

The agents would accept no excuse for they knew their master's ire. They did not rage, however, and they did not threaten. They simply broke into Muramasa's small home and found his wife and young son cowering near the kitchen fire. Seizing the boy who was no more than three years of age, they brought him to where guards were holding Muramasa. At the entrance to the workshop, the chief agent held the crying lad up to his father and explained that if Muramasa did not produce a blade in five day's time, the child would be put to death. To speed the process, he also said that with each passing day a finger would be cut from the lad's tiny hand. To make his point, he immediately chopped the little finger from the boy's right hand.

Muramasa gasped in anguish. He did not wish to aid the

enemies of his friends and well he knew that loyalty sometimes demands the sacrifice of life. Still, he had a father's love for his son who with time should have been the heir of his beloved teachers, Munemasa. He could not let him be put to death and so in agony he agreed to create the blade of Koka's demand.

The chief agent commended his decision, and agreed that if steel were in short supply, a dagger would suffice if it were a good one. He would accept no delays, however, and took the infant as a hostage. Each passing day would see one of the poor lad's fingers lost, he reminded, and if Muramasa could not produce a blade in five day's time, he would never see the lad alive again.

The young father was in deep distress. Even with well-arranged supplies, it takes a skilled smith ten days of undivided attention to make a dagger in the Japanese manner. A long sword takes three times as long at least. Muramasa's task was daunting but deep feelings for his son guided him to begin the work before him.

As he considered his challenge, Muramasa decided he needed guidance from a source beyond himself. He retired to his village's shrine of Shinto to seek advice and implore the assistance of the gods of his country. His village shrine was one sacred to the Fox, a creature the sons of Japan revere for its special power and propensity for perverse intrusion into human affairs.

As Muramasa was lying prostrate in front of the Fox God's shrine, he explained his dilemma and begged for assistance. He presented his predicament with a father's anguished heart, but felt no immediate response until he rose to leave. When he looked up he saw a clear vision of the Fox God. The swordsmith made a start, but the spirit calmed him with a gesture of his paw-like hand. "Be at rest Swordsmith Muramasa. I know you to be a good man of pure heart and I have heard your plea. Return to your forge and let me help you make a blade that will destroy your enemies as it saves the life of your son." And with that, the vision of the Spirit disappeared.

Muramasa did not understand what had happened, but he rushed back to his workplace trusting only that his predicament would somehow be resolved.

Arriving at the gate of his home, the swordsmith found the village charcoal burner waiting for him. The soot-blackened dealer in fuel announced that he had brought a load of the highest quality oak charcoal because he thought it might be useful. Muramasa thanked him most profusely as he accepted the straw-bound bales the old man offered.

Inside the yard, sitting at the very door of the forge itself, another neighbor waited. When Muramasa drew near, that man rose and said he had that morning found in the ruins of a long fallen temple, some pounds of rusty nails. He offered these as potentially useful material and left before the swordsmith could offer more than hurried thanks.

With the fuel and materials he would need for his required task, Muramasa set right to work. He stoked his forge to special heat and reduced the nails to well-formed fragments which he sorted by size and quality. Then, in a shower of fiery sparks, he fused those fragments into solid billets. He stopped for neither food nor rest and rejected all sustenance his wife brought to him. He worked with such fiery intensity that his own energy seemed to contribute to the heat within his forge. As he worked, Muramasa could feel the spirit of the Fox God standing by his shoulder. He could feel his help as he swung the heavy hammer. He could sense his advice when he judged the temperature of his billets or decided how many times to draw them out.

When the billets were pure, Muramasa had to file them to shape so they would weld together well. As he did, the sound of the file seems to have a message. He listened as he passed the file over the work and the words formed clear. Muramasa heard the file saying, "Son Killer!" These horrid words sent a shiver up his spine, but he could not stop his work.

In the dark of night after hours of labor, Muramasa fused the billets into a solid bar that would become the finished blade. As he began that task, he again felt the Fox God at his side and heard whispered instructions in his ear. With encouragement he could not understand, Muramasa recalled the fact that his master would never have a son of his own name. He recalled the threat that then existed to his own dear boy and he found himself repeating the words, 'Son Killer' each time he struck the red hot steel. "Son Killer, Son Killer, Son Killer!" And so, as he worked, his hatred was welded into the steel of the blade he wrought.

By morning's light, he saw that he had formed a blade of highest quality although it was one, he knew, infused with evil and hated. He did not stop to consider the wicked work he had done, however, because as he saw the light of dawn he also knew that his son was about to lose another finger. He pushed ahead with the task of tempering the blade.

There is no more delicate step in swordmaking than the

treatment that makes the body of the sword resilient as the edge is brought to glass hardness. To do this work, Muramasa filled the quenching trough with water from the well at the Fox God's Shrine. He darkened his work area to block out the light of day and built a fire of special intensity. Caking the raw blade with a mixture that would hold the heat in a special way, the swordsmith passed the blade above the white hot forge.

As Muramasa played the blade between the flames, he looked up to see that he had again been joined by the Fox God. Speaking in a soft voice, the Fox said, "Trust me friend, Swordsmith, for I have a brought one who understands fire."

Looking toward the spirit, Muramasa saw at the side of the Fox the fearful figure of a ghost. It had a skull-like face with eyes aflame and horns upon its pate. As he saw this terrible visage he felt an icy breeze sweep the workplace that only seconds before had been of blazing with heat. The swordsmith's sweat turned cold on his brow. In fear and fatigue, poor Muramasa shuddered, but the Fox bade him continue with his work.

Finding strength he did not know he had, the swordsmith worked on, passing the blade back and forth within the fire. When the blade approached the critical heat, the ghost suddenly shrieked, "NOW!" and Muramasa plunged the red hot blade into the trough of water.

Going from red heat to water cool, the blade cried with stress and made an awful hiss. As if the trough had been living flesh, when Muramasa pierced it with the fearful blade, the water turned blood red!

Taking the blade from the water, Muramasa looked for the Fox God and the ghost but found they were gone. He was suddenly alone and in his solitude certain of only one thing and that was that he wanted to be free of the wretched object he had been forced to make.

He pushed back the shutters of his workshop and set about he final task of polishing the now nearly finished blade. Again he worked with focus and total dedication so that by the fall of night, he had the flawless shining blade ready to bring to Koka's men. He hurriedly carved the characters of his name on the tang of the blade to witness his responsibility for the monster he had wrought. With that finishing touch completed, he rushed to where the warriors were camped to rescue his hostaged son.

Koka's men had not expected him for days and they were truly surprised by the swordsmith's quick return. As he entered their camp, Muramasa held up the dagger he had made and demanded to have his son. The chief agent rejected that demand until he had inspected the blade that was offered. Taking it from the swordsmith, he examined it with the judgmental eye of a man whose life had more than once depended on the quality of the sword he carried. He knew his commander would accept nothing less than an excellent blade and so he expected to be critical. Still, as his eyes played across the shining surface Muramasa presented, he could find no fault.

"You did fine work, Swordsmith," he said as he turned the blade in the light. "My master will accept this and I have no desire to linger longer in these parts. Bring the boy," he ordered.

When the infant appeared his face was stained by tears and both of his tiny hands were bound. As he was handed to Muramasa, the boys eyes dried and Koka's agent said, "I was no more than good to the promised threat I made. The lad's alive and, if eight fingers are enough to make a sword, he can expect to take up his family's calling."

With that the warriors departed Yasuda and Muramasa rushed himself and his son back to their family hearth hoping only that he and his son could overcome the damage that Koka had imparted to their bodies and their souls.

When the sun rose the very next day Muramasa again presented himself at his village Shrine. There he sincerely thanked the Fox God for the strength he had imparted and for the safe return of his son. The young swordsmith was also so bold as to implore the friendly Fox for yet another favor. With deepest emotion, Muramasa begged that he should never again have any contact with either Koka or any of the Natsushima family.

Muramasa lived out his life in Yasuda making blades as was his lot in life. He remained a loyal supporter of the Fox God, never forgetting to leave small gifts at his Shrine or take part in the seasonal festivals that happened there. His son grew up without his little fingers, but he did take up the swordsmith's calling and maintained his family's reputation reasonably well.

Muramasa never again saw the Fox God, but the kindly spirit honored the second request the swordsmith made of him. Neither Koka nor any of the other Natsushimas ever had any further contact with Muramasa or his family. Indeed, within a week after Koka began to wear his new dagger, his oldest son and heir was killed in battle. In another week his second son and only other heir was similarly dispatched. In less than a year, the forces of the Natsushima family were in total disarray and Koka himself was dead.

Who can doubt it was because of the wicked blade of Muramasa?

"Spooooky," said Eric with a shiver when Dawn closed the book. "You say that's a kid's story?"

"Well, young people's'" said Dawn. "Those Victorians had pretty high standards for what teenagers ought to read."

"High standards, my ass," said Eric. "That stuff is just dense and when you can figure out what it's all about, it's scary. Cutting babys' fingers off," he shivered again. "You don't see that sort of thing on Sesame Street."

Dawn smiled her agreement as she put the book down on the coffee table. "They didn't pull any punches, did they?" she agreed. "But I don't think they figured this stuff was especially scary. To Lord Reedslan I'll bet you this was educational realism. He wanted to make all those upper class brats into the stiff-upper-lip types the Empire needed by showing them what the real world was like."

"You literary types amaze," said Eric. "How could anybody see that story as realistic? Ghosts? Spirits? Wicked blades? That's scary, but nobody could believe its real."

"And you science types just amaze me," responded Dawn. "You really don't believe there's anything out there beyond what you understand and can see. Maybe this guy Muramasa really could make daggers that were wicked. You know, negative karma? Unfavorable auras? Inharmonious vibes? Bad juju?"

"Nah, I can't buy it." said Eric. "You can't blame stuff for what people do with it. Stuff's neutral," he added with a note of finality.

The air conditioning unit of Eric's apartment chose that moment to kick in and a cool breeze swept through the room. The draft made Dawn shiver. As she hugged her arms together, she asked, "Why in the world is that thing going on?"

"I don't know," said Eric getting up to adjust the thermostat. "It acts up sometimes. I think it may have something to do with what my neighbors are doing. Some of the old ladies keep their heat turned up so high it messes up the system." He twisted the thermostat control ring back and forth a couple of times before ending the flow of cold air.

While Eric was at the thermostat, Dawn looked down at the coffee table and absently reopened Lee James' photo album. She fanned through the unused pages at the end of the volume until she found a piece of folded newspaper inside the back cover. She was opening it when Eric returned to her side.

"What do you have? asked Eric as he sat down.

"It was in the back of the album," Dawn explained as she began reading the page. "It's from the February 12, 1946 Stars and Stripes, Far East Edition," she read from the masthead.

"Look at that," Eric said, pointing to a story that had been circled near the bottom of the page.

GI Killed in Street Attack

CAMP HATA. A GI attached to Camp Hata in Shizuoka City was attacked and fatally stabbed in a late night altercation in suburban Shizuoka City on Feb., 9. SSgt Hervey Stimpson was pronounced DOA at the Camp Hata Base Hospital where he was returned by MPs who had been alerted by an unidentified Japanese male who informed guards at the Camp Gate that he had seen an American soldier in need of help. Stimpson had been in Japan since Aug 1945. At the time of the attack that took his life, Stimpson held a 12-hour pass. He appeared to have been returning to the Base, but it was not certain where he had been and no witnesses to the attack have come forward or been found.

The Japanese civilian who informed MP's of the incident indicated where Stimpson was lying but said he had not seen the attack and left before he could be interviewed. Operators of bars in the vicinity of the attacked were interviewed. None reported any unusual activity and none said they had seen the attack. Both Military and Civil Police are investigating the incident.

SSgt Stimpson was from East Liverpool O. He enlisted in June 1942. After serving in various bases in the US he took part in the invasion of the Philippines and landed in Japan in Aug 1945 with the 132 Eng Cbt Bn. He was assigned to Civil Affairs in October and was awaiting reassignment at the time of the incident. Capt. Oran Johnson MP, Camp Hata, said robbery has been ruled out as a motive for the attack, but declined to suggest other reasons for the incident.

12 | Jerry Lupinski
In which a profitable new alliance is formed.

JAL Flight 308, Tokyo to Chicago - present day
Jerry Lupinski, American businessman interested in Japan
Ken Sawada, Japanese businessman returning to America with a new assignment

The visit to Tokyo had been brief but so intense that Ken Sawada was looking forward to sleeping through most of the flight back to America. The flight would be a long one since he had to go all the way to Chicago in order to make connections that would get him to Lexington, Kentucky, where he had a round of sword buying ads scheduled to begin on the coming weekend. Ken would have to attend to a sea of details as soon as he arrived, but there was nothing he could do now so he resolved to relax while he could. He gladly accepted the steaming *oshi-bori* the stewardess offered as he took his seat and he felt much better as he wiped his hands and face with the moist towel.

As always, Ken had booked a window seat in the upper, "business class" compartment of the 747. He liked the service in that area because its sixteen seats were usually assigned their own stewardess. It was also far quieter than the rest of the plane because there were no service carts or strollers on their way to the toilets. Ken had discovered this small area of relative comfort in the course of many trips back and forth to America. It was a detail, but Ken felt it reflected the expertise he had developed. It was the sort of thing he wished he could let his colleagues know about.

While he waited for the boarding to be completed, Ken took out the sheaf of papers Tsuiji-san had given him. He decided to look them over at the beginning of the trip to get them out of the way so he could relax through the rest of the flight. He nodded to the well-dressed young American who took the seat next to his, but set right to work on the documents as the plane was pulling away from the jetway. The sheaf was impressively thick but paging through it, Ken

saw that most of the sheets were government forms. He had never
seen this specific form before, but it looked like other official papers
he had handled. He glanced at a couple of the sheets and saw that
most of them were blank except for a name typed on the line at the
top and a line or two of typed information at the bottom. He paged
through the sheaf until he found a longer typed memo that seemed to
be a cover. As the pre-takeoff video began, Ken turned his attention
to this document.

Mar 12, 1990

TO: L. Knox,
   Political Section
   U.S. Embassy
   Tokyo, Japan
FROM: J. Ortiz, for
   John R. Grabhaus, Chief Record Reconstruction
Branch
   National Military Personnel Records Center
   9700 Page Boulevard
   St. Louis, Missouri 63123

Re: Requested Search of Military Personnel Records

Your request for records investigation of US Army
personnel was forwarded through official channels to
this facility on a "high priority" basis from the
Department of State, Washington, D. C. The request
was processed in cycle with others of the same priority.
   As specified in the documents received with the
request, in conjunction with investigation of the loss of
Japanese cultural patrimony, we were directed to
determine the likely identity of three individuals, two
Caucasian and one Japanese-American, who served with
the US Army of Occupation in Japan during the period
of late 1945. In addition to renderings in Japanese which
are beyond the capabilities of this facility, the names
presented for investigation were as follows:
   JYAIMUZU RII, Sgt. Caucasian
   SUJIMUPUSON HAABI, Ssgt. Caucasian
   MATSUDA AARON, Ssgt. Japanese-American

Investigations into this matter were limited by incomplete records. Military records most likely to bear on this investigation would have been in the area that suffered heavy damage in a fire that occurred on July 12, 1973. Investigations, therefore, drew on available alternative record sources. The results of the research into the possible identity of these individuals are contained in the attached STATEMENTS OF SERVICE (NA FORM 13041(9-85). I take the liberty of summarizing those results below.

JYAIMUZU RII, Sgt.

Available records indicate that no person with a name of this spelling served in US Army during WWII. Assuming the forwarded name reflects a Japanese rendering of an American name, searches were done for the names JAMES REE and JAMES LEE

A Lt. named James REE was killed in combat in Italy in Sept. 1944.

Records indicate that 212 individuals named JAMES LEE served in the US Army in the period of 1941-1945. Of this total, three Caucasian non-commissioned officers are known to have served in Japanese Army of Occupation. These are:

LEE, James D. 13765209, Attached Hg Co 32nd Div. Aug 45 - May 46, Discharged May 17, 1946 in the rank of Corporal. No record of veteran's contact.

LEE, James C. 82105663, Flight Engineer, 134th Observation Wing, 8th AF UAAF, Sept 45-June 46. Transferred USAF, June 1946. Discharged May16, 1963 in the rank of Msgt. Widows benefits paid until Aug 1988 to Ethel Lee, Port Everglades, Fla.

LEE, James NMI, 72090572,129th Inf Reg. 33rd Div, Jan 1944-Dec. 1945, Discharged Dec. 3, 1945 in the rank of SSgt. No record of veteran's contact.

SUJIMUPUSON HAABI, Ssgt.

Available records indicate that no person with a name of this spelling served in US Army during WWII. Assuming the forwarded name reflected a Japanese rendering of an American name, searched were done for

Caucasian Non-commissioned officers with variants of the surnames HARVEY, HERBY, or HOBBY, and first initial S or Z. Among a total of 117 names obtained in this way, the following five individuals served with the Japanese Army of Occupation.

HARVEY, Sherman P. 58925547, 305th Inf Rgt 77th Div, May 1943-May 1946, Discharged May 12, 1946 in the rank of TSsgt. No record of veteran's contact.

HARVEY, Stephen K. 49026640, C Co 365th FldArt Btl, May 1942-Jan 1946, Discharged in the rank of Ssgt Jan 28, 1946. No record of veteran's contact.

HOBBE, Sulamon J. 69815530, 98th Counter Intelligence CorpsDet 98thDiv, Jan 1944-April 1945, Discharged in the rank of Sgt Mar 2, 1946. GI Bill benefits paid in New Haven, Conn. between Aug 1947 and June 1951.

HERVE, Spencer J. 8832508, D Co 163 Inft Reg, 41st Div, May 1943-Dec 1945, Discharged in the rank of Sgt Jan 1946, Prior active service and decorations as noted. Re-enlisted June 12, 1950 with the rank of 2nd Lt. Discharged as Col. Aug. 29, 1969.

"Would you like something to drink?" The stewardess spoke with a pleasant tone, but Ken had been trying hard to find meaning in the document he had been reading so that her words made him look up with a start. "I'm sorry," she said soothingly when he did. "Something to drink?" she repeated.

"Ahh, yes. Please bring me a Wild Turkey and water." She nodded and Ken went back to the memo.

HARBY, Sullivan C. 74902155, 19th SpOp Btl 32nd Div Nov 1943-Mar 1946, Discharged 1946 in the rank of Tsgt. GI Bill benefits awarded between Mar 1947 and Aug 1952 in Milwaukee, WI. Admitted to Pehawka Veteran's Hospital Aug 1989. Veteran's insurance death benefits allocated, June 1991, beneficiary not noted.

If other renderings of the name "SUJIMUPUSON HAABI" are possible or appropriate, we will, of course, research them upon your direction.

MATSUDA AARON, Ssgt

Available records indicate that no person with a name of this spelling served in US Army during WWII. Assuming the forwarded name reflected a Japanese rendering of an American first name, a search was carried out for a Japanese-American non-commissioned officer with surname MATSUDA and first name Al(l)an, or Arlon. That search produced one potential candidate.

MATSUDA, Arlon, K. 285661048, enlisted as a language specialist May 12, 1942, assigned to Ft. Snelling Language Training Center as a Pvt and PFC Aug 5, 1942 to Sept 2, 1943. Crpl and TSgt Intell Sect. WESPAC HQ, Oct 1943 to Aug. 1945, SSgt 2nd Civ Aff Brgd, Aug, 1945 to Jan 1946, Discharged in the rank of Ssgt, Feb 1946. GI Bill benefits paid to the University of Iowa between Ap 1946 and June 1948 and to Northwestern Optometry College, Nov 1948 to June 1950. Veteran's insurance records administratively terminated June 22, 1950. No further record of veteran's contact.

When Ken's eyes reached the end of the memo he shook his head reflexively. He had understood most of the words he had read, but the document remained a mystery. Tsuji-san had suggested it might help him find the swords that had been taken from Takasaka, but Ken saw no usable information. He looked at a couple of the forms attached to the memo and saw that each of them had information on one of the individuals mentioned. There were a few bits of information not been repeated in the memo, but none of it seemed at all significant. Even if the men who had stolen the Takasaka swords were among the names listed in the memo, Ken had no idea how he might find them today. America is a huge country and this was very old information. Ken shook his head again as he decided he would simply have to tell Tsuji-san this was a dead end.

"That look's like an important project you're working on."

Ken looked up to see the young man seated next to him smiling. "Yes," he replied as he jogged the papers he had read into a neat stack. "It is research."

"I'm sorry to interrupt," the young man continued with a slight bow. He swept a business card out of his shirt pocket and offered it to Ken. "Please let me introduce myself. I'm Jerry Lupinski with Thompson-Gere Public Relations in Chicago. Please accept my *meishi*."

Ken took the business card and politely spent a moment reading it. "Public Relations, I see. Thank you." He smiled pleasantly and bowed to his neighbor. "I am Sawada Kenji, please call me Ken." Lupinski bowed somewhat lower and said, "*Hajimemashita, Doozo Yoroshiku, Rupinsuki-desu.*"

"Ah, you speak Japanese," said Ken.

"*Sukoshi dake*," Lupinski smiled with another bow. "*Mada, heta desu.*"

Ken could guessed from Lupinski's accent that he was unlikely to be able to carry on a serious conversation in Japanese so he continued in English. "No! Your Japanese is very good. You studied in school?" he asked with a smile.

"*Hai, soo desu*," Lupinski continued. "*Chicago Daigaku de, watakushi wa, Nihongo o benkyo shitamashita.*"

"I see," said Ken. "Chicago University, that's very famous."

"I was a journalism major," Jerry said, finally surrendering to English. "But I took a whole year of Japanese and now that's coming in handy. My firm is trying to expand our activities in Japan. I've spent the past week calling on firms in and around Tokyo."

"I see."

The young man continued. "Yes, Thompson-Gere believes that many Japanese firms operating in America are under-served in the area of public relations. We want to make sure that they understand how we can help."

"What is public relations?" Ken asked with a tone that could have reflected a sincere interest although he wasn't sure he cared all that much.

"Thompson-Gere is a full service firm so we can help with any kinds of contacts or presentations." The young man spoke with smooth sincerity. He was a good looking fellow, dressed in a well-tailored blue suit and a boiled white shirt. Ken liked the fact that he was wearing suspenders. "Mainly, we do press relations and focus groups that help firms aim their products and campaigns. But we can handle product evaluations, institutional coordination, executive recruitment, and liaisons with state and local governmental agencies. That sort of thing."

"I see," said Ken. "Very interesting."

"Thank you." Lupinski spoke slowly and clearly and Ken found him easy to understand. "We feel that many Japanese firms currently operating in America are very poorly served in the public relations area. You may know that the Japanese Office of Foreign Affairs has recently recommended that Japanese firms pay special attention to their image and presentation. Thompson-Gere is eager to help in those areas."

"That is interesting to me," said Ken leaning forward slightly.

"Are you a businessman?" the young man asked pleasantly.

"Yes," said Ken. "For several years I have lived in the States. Mainly I have been in sales and acquisition."

"That sounds very interesting," Lupinski said, excited that Ken was listening. The time he had just spent in Tokyo had been very frustrating and totally unproductive. Most of calls he made were to firms he knew to be active in the US. Some of the conversations had been pleasant enough, but none of the men he met even acknowledged their firms' American presence. He had handed out a great many business cards, but made no firm contacts. Wouldn't it be ironic if his best lead should come on the flight home? "You know your English is really terrific," he added. "Very colloquial."

"Thank you," Ken nodded with a smile. That was a cheap compliment, but Ken was impressed. The kid looked good. He spoke with a soft tone that was easy to follow. And best of all, he seemed very willing.

"My firm will be expanding in the next few years. We are forming a development corporation. We call it the Heisei Development Corporation." Ken pulled his business card holder out if his shirt pocket. "It won't ever be really big, but we plan to do various kinds of business. I'm sorry I don't have those cards yet, but this one has my name." Ken held out one of the generic cards he used from time to time. It mentioned nothing about swords, but was printed on very rich paper. It showed only Ken's name and a post office box number in Portland.

"Thank you very much," Lupinski said enthusiastically as he took the card.

13 | Lotte Swanson

In which recently discovered treasures are suddenly placed in danger of being lost.

Minneapolis - present day

Lotte Swanson, Eric Mallow's neighbor and president of the Nokomis Condominium Association

Eric Mallow, gun collector who finds himself learning about Japanese swords

"Ric, this is Dave Stalgaard. How's it going?"

"Great, Dave. How about you?" Eric Mallow said into the phone.

"I finally found something out about the *tanto* and I wanted to fill you in. I'm not calling too late, am I?"

"No, it's not too late," Eric said. "You're a real bird dog on this, Dave." Eric made an effort to sound positive. He liked Dave and enjoyed his company, but he had become very tired of the swords he had brought back from Des Moines.

Eric had been especially irritated by series of calls he had received from Ken Sawada. In the first of these, Sawada had increased his initial offer of five thousand to twenty-five thousand. When Eric rejected that offer, he went up to fifty and then, in a subsequent phone call, to a hundred thousand. As his offers increased, Sawada became more demanding and Eric had to make his rejections more emphatic. When Eric declined the last offer, Sawada demanded that he name a price that would be acceptable. Before hanging up, Eric told Sawada not to call again.

"It been real frustrating," Dave continued. "I haven't come up with any specific information on the *tanto*. Remember it wasn't on that list of lost National Treasure swords we looked at."

"Yeah, I remember that's what you said." On one of his visits, Dave had brought a Japanese publication to Eric's condominium to point out a listing that he said was certainly Eric's long sword. He had also run his finger up and down the list as he had explained that there were no listings like the boxed dagger. As usual, Eric had been impressed that Dave seemed honest and expert as he had explained all of this, but the Japanese text remained a total mystery.

"Since I was coming up with screw-all, I decided to get some help. Last night I called Hagi-san at the Sword Museum in Tokyo," Dave explained.

"They've got a whole museum for swords?" Eric asked.

"Oh yeah. It's a real big place," Dave said. "Hagi-san is a vice-director and a nice guy. I run most of my polishing through the Museum and he's also helped me get a bunch of blades certified."

"It's amazing the way you people repolish your swords," Eric said. "If I refinished one of my Mausers or shined up a nice old flintlock it would destroy them."

"It's a different tradition, Ric. Japanese blades have got to be brightly polished so that you can see all of their construction details. From across the room they're all supposed to look like Buick bumpers, but up close on a well-polished blade you can tell how the smith worked the steel and tempered the edge."

"It wouldn't do to have them buffed up over here." Eric asked.

"It sure wouldn't," Dave said earnestly. "A bad polish can ruin a blade and a good one can make a good sword great."

"And if I had to make a guess, I'd bet that a polish is not cheap?"

Dave knew that Eric was teasing him, so he replied very earnestly. "Of course not. Everything about swords has got to cost a lot. A good polish can easily run $300 an inch these days."

"Are you kidding?" Eric asked incredulously.

"Not a bit," said Dave. "There are a couple of polishers who have been designated Living National Treasures and they get more than that. Swords are a rich man's thing in Japan, Ric. One of the things that really pisses the Japanese off is that so many American sword collectors are real low rent types."

"Like you, for example?"

"Exactly," said Dave.

"Japanese sword collecting is way too complex for me, Dave. I think I'll stay with simple things like Broomhandle Mausers," Eric said shaking his head. "So, tell me what you found out about the dagger."

"Oh yeah, that's why I called. The date on the box says the *tanto* was designated an Important Cultural Property in 1938, but the records on that sort of thing just aren't available in this country."

"I'd imagine those are some pretty obscure records, even in Japan."

"The Japanese are very good about such things. I'm sure they're available. The tough part is finding the guy who knows where to look."

"And you figured your pal at the sword museum would be the guy."

"Yup, and it turns out I was right," said Dave. "As soon as I got hold of Hagi-san and told him I was looking for information on a Muramasa *tanto* that had been designated a Cultural Asset in the thirteenth year of the Showa period, you'll never guess what he said."

"No, I never would, Dave," said Eric flatly. "What'd he say?"

"He said, 'Ahh, you're looking for that *tanto*, too.'"

"So, he knew about the dagger?" asked Eric.

"He did," said Dave. "*And*, it turns out a couple of other people have asked him about it recently."

"No kidding," said Eric. "Can we assume that one of those others is my friend Ken Sawada?"

"To the serious players in Tokyo, I think Ken's just another American picker," Dave said. "And Hagi-san didn't mention a name. He just said a dealer in Tokyo had asked about the dagger a couple of weeks ago. The guy who actually contacted Hagi-san was probably one of the dealers Ken buys for."

"Whoever made the contact, Sawada had to be involved," said Eric recalling the irritation of the calls he had received. "A couple of weeks ago is just about the time he started calling me again."

"I'll bet you're right," Dave agreed. "There's no question that somebody's interested in the blade. Hagi-san also said he got a call from a member of the Diet. Now that could be cool because it may mean the government is looking for the *tanto*."

"And that would be good?" asked Eric.

"It's good for people to be interested in the dagger, and the Japanese government has deep pockets." said Dave.

"What it probably means is that from now on Ken Sawada won't be the only Japanese hassling me." Eric was not looking forward to more problems with the dagger.

"Don't worry, Ric," said Dave. "You'll be able to handle things."

"I'm glad to hear that," said Eric sounding less than convinced. "Tell me what else your man in Tokyo told you."

"Well, to begin with, Hagi-san confirmed our suspicion that the *tanto* was taken from the same shrine as the Munemasa *tachi*."

"Did you tell him about the long sword?" asked Eric.

"No. I didn't mention it at all," said Dave. "I figured we'd leave that until later. Hagi-san brought up the other sword and made a point of saying that the two blades weren't actually a pair even though they were stored and stolen together."

"Dave, tell me something. If the swords were stolen, doesn't that mean I have to give them back?"

"No, it doesn't, Ric, although it's a question a bunch of us have wondered about. Japanese law is real clear on that issue. The deal is, their statute of limitations has run out, so regardless of how they were acquired, swords in this country now belong to whoever's got them."

"So if they get to be too much of a hassle, I can't just give them back?" asked Eric.

"Well, Hagi-san could probably find somebody who'd take them, Ric, but I don't think it will come to that," Dave chuckled. "You'll survive this experience and make some money."

"Did your pal in Tokyo tell you that too?"

"No. As a matter of fact, Hagi-san told me he figures the *tanto* is a piece of shit."

"He used those words?" said Eric.

"Not exactly," Dave said lightly, "but they sum up his sentiment. He figured that if the blade had been any good at all, it would've been made a National Treasure along with the *tachi*. Since it didn't, he assumes there's something wrong with it. As far as he's concerned, it's got to be a piece of shit."

"But you said it was pretty good," said Eric.

"It's terrific," said Dave. "You and I know that because we've seen it. But Hagi-san hasn't seen it and the story he's giving everybody in Tokyo is that it's a piece of shit."

"So the question becomes, why does Ken Sawada want to pay a hundred grand for it?"

"That's the questions that came to my mind," said Dave. "There must be something more we don't know about. I asked Hagi-san if he had any other information on the *tanto* and he told me he'd done some looking, but hadn't come up with anything because the records used to document the blade in 1938 had all been burned up with some castle that got firebombed during the war."

"Wow," said Eric. "This deal never gets simpler."

"I hear you, Ric, but we're making progress. I'm still having a good time with the *tanto* and I'm still sure I can put together as good a deal as Sawada will. If you want to deal with Ken, though, you should feel free to," Dave said earnestly.

"Hey, remember the dagger is still Mrs. James's," cautioned Eric. "It's up to her. I called her last week to fill her in. I didn't tell her exactly what kind of money you've been talking about, but she seems to be in no special hurry. She might want to be involved in the transaction, though. When it goes down, I might just pull out of the whole deal and let you or whoever handle it with her."

"However you want to do it, Ric."

"To tell the truth, Dave, I'm real uncomfortable with the swords. I just don't like having them around. I don't even want to make any money. I'd just like to wrap the deal up soon."

"I understand completely, Ric, but give me another week or so to make sure I can't find out just a little bit more. If we haven't got anything by then, I'll put it on the market."

Eric wanted to ask Dave how he planned to market the swords, but the phone call was interrupted by a distinctive tap on his door.

"There's somebody at my door, Dave. I'll talk with you later, okay?"

"Sure, Ric. We'll be in contact," Dave said and Eric hung up.

Eric knew that the knock on his door had to be Lotte Swanson's. Mrs. Swanson was President of the Nokomis Condominium Association and the only of Eric's neighbors who regularly visited him. She always knocked on his door with a series of regular sharp taps that seemed to match her personality.

Lotte had been President of the Association for as long as any of the residents could remember. Many of her neighbors, especially the single women, found her imperious and even arrogant, but she kept her position of leadership because she worked hard for the building and because no one was eager to challenge her for a post she obviously wanted.

She and her husband moved into the condominium shortly before he retired from a post as an engineer in an electronics firm. Rudy Swanson was an easy-going fellow who liked to read and hang around the apartment his wife kept spotlessly clean. The girl he had brought home as a German war bride in 1947 was anything but easygoing. She oversaw the Nokomis Condominium like a Prussian Graf overseeing a personal fiefdom.

Without being overtly intrusive, she kept track of the personal lives of all of the Nokomis residents. At any given moment she knew who was at home and who was away. She knew who was ill and who was buying new furniture or redecorating. She also knew a great deal about of the resident's personal lives. No one ever saw her looking through the garbage, but she knew everyone's preferences in food and drink. The fact that the Nokomis building was a solid concrete structure did not prevent Lotte from keeping track of even more intimate details. In one conversation with Eric, Lotte had mentioned that she knew the exact evening one young couple had conceived the child that meant they would have to leave the condominium (which had a strict "no children" covenant).

Like most of his neighbors, Eric was more than willing to put up with Lotte's assertive oversight because she also did an excellent job of managing the maintenance and operation of the building. She chaired the quarterly association meetings like a Field Marshall. She accounted for every penny in the association's maintenance fund and made absolutely sure that work she contracted was performed to the highest standard. When the new roof was being installed two years previously, Lotte had climbed up to make sure that the full layer of tar was being applied.

Eric knew she patrolled the building and the perimeter of the adjoining parking lots far better than a watchdog. She walked all the halls and the parking area several times every day, picking up litter and looking for breaches of security. She made a point of knowing which doors were squeaky and which locks stuck. She immediately recognized people who were strange to the building and called the police for anyone she thought looked suspicious. The security lights she had installed around the building made it quite possible to read a newspaper in the parking areas at midnight.

"Hallo, Dr. Mallow. I hope it is not too late for a short visit. I saw your light was still on," Lotte said with a smile and a coquettish cock of her head as Eric opened his door. Her hair had turned white, but she wore it in a current style and kept it tinted a very slightly golden color that--with her still trim figure--made it clear she had been a classic German beauty in her youth.

"Good evening, Mrs. Swanson. How are you?" Eric said with a wide smile of genuine fondness.

"I am fine, thank you, but Rudy has no pep. I tell him he should get out and walk with me, but it does no good." She shook her head slightly before she continued. "There are a couple of things about which we should speak. I hope it is not too late." Nearly fifty years in America had not entirely erased Lotte's German accent.

"Not at all. Please come in. I was just doing some paperwork downstairs. I've got a pot of coffee down there. Would you like a cup?" Eric said as he beckoned her in.

"That would be nice," she said. "I won't stay long, though. I think one of the lights in the parking lot has gone out and I want to leave a message with the maintenance company."

Eric picked up an extra coffee cup as he passed by his kitchen and led Lotte in to the lower portion of his condo. Lotte was familiar with Eric's room's, but as she walked down to Eric's gun room, she looked automatically at the alterations he had made to the basic apartment. She had not initially approved of the modifications Eric proposed, but he had been careful to ask her advice on all of the changes and had kept her informed of the money he was spending.

"Doctor, there are two matters," Lotte began as she sat down on one of the leather easy chairs. "First, I am sending a card to Mrs. Abbott on the second floor. She is in hospital for gall bladder surgery. Please sign the card." She held the card and a pen to Eric as he poured the coffee.

"This is very nice of you, Lotte. Thank you for taking care of it," Eric said as he signed.

"The building fund pays for the cards," Lotte explained. "Mrs. Abbott eats too much fat and that is why she has gall bladder problems, but she is too old to change."

Eric couldn't help smiling.

"The second matter I must discuss with you, doctor, involves the new security system we had installed last month," Lotte continued. "How do you like the new system? Is it working all right for you?"

"Yes it is. Lotte. I like it," Eric said agreeably. "The plastic cards are real slick. They're easier to use than keys and they're real smooth. I think you selected a good system."

"Thank you. I wanted the best so I slightly overspent the amount we had approved. We needed a somewhat better system than I had described at our meeting. I think you will agree that it is excellent." From Lotte's tone, Eric understood that she was building an argument and that it was not open to debate. "I need the approval of the association for an extra $1487.00. We have the money."

"You think the extra expenditure was necessary?" Eric could not help testing her.

"Absolutely," Lotte said firmly. "The neighborhood is changing. Just the other day I caught one of those Oriental kids looking at the back door. I was in the storage area so he hadn't seen me. When I shouted at him, he ran off, but the police tell me there are more and more of these Vietnamese gangs forming. And there are the Blacks and the rest."

"If you think the better system was a good idea, Lotte, I'll support it." Eric knew Lotte was uncomfortable with minorities, but he had never argued with her. It was a battle he knew he'd never win.

"Thank you. I will record your support. The system we install, with the plastic cards, was one Rudy found. He did some research and found these locks made by a German company. They absolutely cannot be picked." She held out a colored brochure for Eric to inspect.

Eric had been using the new system for a just over a week and liked it. The key cards were working fine. "I like the system, Lotte and I have no problem with the extra money. I appreciate your work on this matter. Mark me down as a 'yes.'"

"You are one of the last ones I needed to talk with," Lotte said closing the brochure. Clearly, she had ordered the new locks without consulting her neighbors. Eric knew this would have some of the members up in arms, but he was not disposed to object. Instead, he simply made a mental note to avoid the next meeting of the condominium association.

With the necessary business completed, Lotte looked around the gun room and asked, "How is your gun collecting going?"

Lotte had visited Eric's gun room and inspected the construction of his gun safe so she was very aware of his hobby and she was also rather interested in the guns themselves. Once when Eric had asked her help with the translation of a German technical manual, Lotte pointed to a picture of a P38, the standard officer's sidearm of the German army during World War II, and said, "That is the pistol I used to shoot." When Eric looked surprised, she explained that as a colonel's daughter, she had been a Leader of the Hitler Youth. One of her responsibilities had been teaching marksmanship and shooting range safety. To see what her reaction would be, Eric got out a P38 he happened to have at that time. Lotte beamed when she saw it and said, "Yeah, yeah. That is the one I shot."

She had taken it from Eric and, handling the gun with skill and assurance, pulled the bolt open to make sure it was unloaded. When she was sure it was safe, she squared her shoulders, grasped the pistol in both hands and pointed it one of the pictures on Eric's wall. Eric had been impressed.

"Oh, it's going along well," Eric said pleasantly. "I've found some interesting things."

"Have you still got the Kaiser's pistol?" Lotte asked pleasantly.

"I sure do. In fact, I just had a case made for it." Eric went to a sideboard where the gun was on display in a handsome maple case and brought it to the coffee table. As he set it down in front of Lotte, he showed her how the case had a hinged cover that swung down to close it and present a brass handle to make it portable.

"This is very handsome," said Lotte. She worked the cover a couple of times and then looked down at the gun. "You know, the Kaiser really was an exceptional person. He was a strong leader and a good man. You are fortunate to have something of his. My father always said that if the Kaiser had been allowed to stay, he could have done all of the good things the Nazis did and none of the bad."

As if to change the subject, Lotte looked at the box containing the Japanese dagger which was also sitting on the coffee table. "Is this a Chinese gun?" she asked looking over the characters on the lid.

"No, it's a Japanese dagger."

"Ahh, Japanese, like Miss Watanabe." Lotte smiled. "Are you collecting Japanese things now?"

"No, I just happened across a couple of Japanese swords," Eric said taking the lid off the box so Lotte could look inside. He lifted the dagger out of the case and began to pull it out as Dave had taught him to do. He carefully slid it free of the storage case so that Lotte could examine the polished surface. Just as he was going to tell her not to touch the blade, however, an alarm sounded in the hallway and both of them looked up in mild surprise.

"What's that?" asked Eric.

"It is the smoke detector," said Lotte looking toward the door to the hallway. "And it isn't supposed to go off. Something is the matter." She rose and walked to the door.

"Just a minute, Lotte," Eric said following her. "That door's got a double bolt on it."

Lotte stepped aside to Eric let open the door. As soon as he swung it aside, both of them stepped into the hallway to find it dark and filling with acrid smoke.

"There is a fire," said Lotte as she turned to Eric. "You call the fire department and I will go to help the old ladies," she continued with a firm voice. "The fire cannot be serious, but I do not think we should leave the Kaiser's gun here. I will take it with me while you close these doors and the ones up stairs. Please move along."

Eric had no desire to trust the prize piece of his collection in a burning building so he stepped back to his gun room to retrieve the cased pistol. "I'll take it, Lotte. You go ahead."

"Very well. I will see you outside," Lotte said as she walked back toward the door. Once in the hall, Eric heard her announce in a large voice, "Leave the building, Everyone must leave the building."

As Eric walked to his gun room telephone, he recalled that the builder who had installed his gun safe had assure him it was fireproof, but he had never expected to put it to any kind of a test. He kept the Kaiser's Mauser under his arm as he dialed 911 and gave the operator the information she needed. When he hung up he looked briefly around the room, but decided there was nothing more to do.

By the time he got to the hallway the smoke was quite thick, but all of his neighbors appeared to have been awakened. Most of them appeared to have already left the building and Eric could hear sirens as he began to head for the exit.

14 | Osatsu Juken

In which recovery of a treasure moves ahead - with deadly result.

Minneapolis - present day
Osatsu Juken, professional name of Sato Yoshimasa, a modern ninja, focused, prepared, and about to carry out an assignment

The rental car attendant stepped back into the work area of his office, set his clipboard down on the counter and said, "Mr. Sato, there is some serious damage along the side of the vehicle, but you elected to take the extended coverage so it will all be covered. No problem." He smiled pleasantly.

"No problem?" Sato Yoshimasa asked tentatively unsure he'd heard correctly.

"No problem," the man smiled with a wave of his hand. "The insurance will cover the cost and I can take care of it from here."

"Good," nodded Sato. "I will need another car," he continued trying to be as clear and articulate as possible.

"Well, all right," the attendant said with only a trace of hesitancy in his voice. His job was to rent cars. If the company was willing to let these foreigners have them, he wouldn't stand in their way. "What kind of car would you like this time?"

"A small one. Maybe a dark one, black or blue, maybe." As he finished his reply, Sato realized that he had understood the question immediately and spoken without hesitation. The attendant also seemed to have understood since he went right to work scanning a list of cars. Sato took all of this as further evidence that he had overcome the failures of the past days. Surviving the gun battle the previous evening had clearly and unquestionably changed his life. For the first time since he had come to America he felt rested, relaxed and competent.

"Well, let's see. It's Saturday, so we've got quite a few cars," said the attendant as he ran his finger across an array of paper receipts on his desk. "How about a dark blue Mazda 626? That's a sporty little car."

Sato had only understood the words 'blue Mazda', but he responded immediately. "That's good."

The attendant began the paperwork and Sato got out his credit card. As he set it on the counter and saw his name written in English he realized that for the public aspects of his stay in America, he would have to remain Sato Yoshimasa. On a deeper level, however, he knew that the previous night had changed his life. It had freed him to operate as Osatsu Juken, last student of the last active ninja, Ozawa Seiken.

"And you'll be taking the extended coverage again?" asked the attendant as he filled out the rental form. Sato recognized this as a question, but hadn't understood what had been asked. He simply returned the young man's smile and confidently said, "Yes." The attendant checked a box on the form and went on about his business.

Sato had spent nearly an hour in the tree he had climbed to avoid the police. From a comfortable perch in the shadowed branches he had watched the police as they searched the area around the traffic turn-out where the gunshots had been fired. The police hadn't done a very thorough job. They concentrated in the area around the turn-out where the shots had been fired. Sato was not even sure they got as far away as the parking area where he had left his car. When the last police car drove away, Sato waited a bit longer to be sure the park was completely empty. When he was sure no one was left, he slid down the trunk and took a dark route to where he had left his car. Without incident, he had returned to his hotel and, for the first time since he had come to America, slept soundly through the night.

In the morning, he woke refreshed and far more assured than he had been since he had accepted Tsuji-san's commission. As he showered and started the day, he realized that he still had no clear plan for recovering the *tanto* held by 'Eriku Maroh', but he was full of confidence. He resolved to be decisive and calculating, to move with assurance, and to deal positively with the problems of his commission. Those were qualities of a ninja.

Sato's first decision of the day had been to deal with his damaged rental car. The deep scrape along the side of the car had weighed on his mind for days so that taking care of it would have to improve his spirits and free him to focus on the more serious challenges. He had worried that reporting the damage would be traumatic and costly, but, as he learned while he waited while the young man filled out the necessary forms for his next car, it turned out to be trivially simple. As the attendant had said, it was, "No problem."

When he got the keys to his new rental car and he was free to go, Sato set out for the next activity he had planned for the day. He drove directly to the area of Eric Mallow's condominium. Among all the problems before him, gaining access to that building and to Mallow's rooms were Sato's major challenges. Since he was not sure how he would deal with those tasks, he wanted to consider them and gather more information. He could think of no better place than the bakery and coffee shop he had visited on his first full day in America. He recalled that the shop had afforded a clear view of the condominium and the time he had spent there had been among the most pleasant interludes of this American adventure.

He parked some distance from the shop and walked to it as he had that first day. He took the same window seat and the same waitress served him.

"Hi," she said as she brought a glass coffee pot to his table by the window. "You came back to visit us again," she continued pleasantly as she filled the coffee cup at Sato's seat.

"Thank you," Sato replied with a smile. On his first visit, Sato had paid the waitress very little attention since he had been more interested in the condominium building. Now, however, as he looked at the girl, he was deeply struck by her beauty. Her features were perhaps rather large, but she had a wonderfully light complexion, flowing yellow hair, and extremely large breasts. Indeed, it was all Sato could do to keep from staring at her.

"You were in the other day," the girl said after she had filled his cup.

"Yes, I am tourist. I like Minneapolis a great deal," Sato smiled.

"That's nice. Where are you from?" she asked cocking her head.

"I am from Japan. Please call me Yoshi."

"Well, Yoshi, my name is Gail," young woman smiled. "Would you like anything to go with the coffee?"

Sato had not enjoyed the donuts he had had on his first visit, but he was hungry because he had skipped breakfast in order to get right on to problem of his rental car. He said, "Ahh, yes. I would like a sweet. What would you suggest?" This was a line he recalled from a tourist's guide book he had studied when he had been in the travel business.

"How about a nice danish? You had donuts last time you were here," she said.

Again, Sato had not understood the question so he simply smiled and said "Ah, good."

When the waitress returned with a large frosted roll, Sato smiled and said, "Ahh, that looks very delicious." It was easy for Sato to be positive. He felt alive and well and, for reasons he could not explain, he was even recalling bits of polite dialogue he had learned in various English classes. After the several lonely days he had passed, he was enjoying conversations and human contact. He felt glib and maybe even charming.

"Are you interested in buildings?" asked the waitress.

"Ahh, yes, I like buildings," responded Sato as if he were taking part in a language lab drill.

"When you were in the other day, you seemed real interested in the condo. You looked it over real careful," Gail said pointing across the street to the Nokomis Condominium.

The waitress had spoken very clearly and Sato had followed enough of her question to find it discomforting. When he had been in the shop earlier, he had tried to hide his interest in the building. He had pointedly not stared at it and made only a few notes on the building's layout. Obviously, however, the girl had been paying more attention to him than he had realized.

"Yes. I like that kind of building. I am a builder," Sato said with what he hoped would be a sincere nod of the head.

"Oh, I see," said Gail. "That explains it."

"I build apartment buildings," Sato added confidently.

"Oh, I see," said the waitress. "You should go over an take a look at the inside. They're having an open house in one of the units this afternoon."

Sato had understood enough of this statement to find it very interesting, but he needed clarification. He looked blankly at the girl and said, "Please repeat."

Gail bent down to point out the window at a sign in front of the building. "See that sign by the front door?"

"Yes, I see," said Sato.

"It says there'll be an open house Saturday afternoon from two to four. You can go in and have a look."

"Go in and have a look?" repeated Sato.

"Sure. One of the units is for sale so they're showing it."

"Oh," said Sato as the situation became clear. "I would like to see it. I will go there this afternoon from two to four."

"Good," smiled the waitress. "You can come in here for a cup of coffee when you're done."

Gail walked away to go on to her other customers and Sato noticed how her white uniform swelled over the curves of her figure. She was truly a voluptuously interesting woman and for a brief moment Sato had to wonder what it would be like to have sex with a woman of that size and shape. As soon as it was formed, however, he forced the thought out of his mind. Erotic urges were absolutely inappropriate for a ninja on assignment.

As Sato sipped his coffee and ate the sweet roll Gail had recommended several people entered and left the shop. He paid them no particular attention and instead tried to think of things he could do to fill the time until the open house would let him see the inside of the condominium building. Clearly, he would need information from that visit to plan his attack so there was no point in making specific preparations until it had been completed. He wished there was some specific action he could take to fill the time, but there was nothing more he needed to do.

He was satisfied that he was moving unobtrusively through the area around the building. Except for this morning, he had worn one or another of his satin jackets whenever he had visited this neighborhood and no one had ever paid him any particular attention. Clearly his disguise had been a very good idea.

Beyond that, Sato was sure of his understanding of the area around the condominium building. By walking or driving virtually all of the streets near the condominium he had assessed the problems of approaching the building. He knew all of the ways of getting to and from the area of the building and identified a couple of places where he could safely leave his car during the attack.

All that remained was to determine some way of actually entering the building. Seeing the inside of the building during the open house would give him information he would need to plan that part of his attack. There was little he could do until the open house. He would have to relax and be patient. Perhaps he would do some sightseeing in other parts of the city.

Resolved to relax until he had to be back for the open house, Sato put the last bit of the sweet roll into his mouth and looked up to catch Gail's eye for the check. As he did, he saw a sandy-haired man enter the shop and walk toward the bakery sales counter.

"Hi'ya, Gail," said the man. "How are you this morning?"

"Hi, Dr. Mallow," Gail smiled as she walked to meet the man at the counter. When she got behind the counter she took a large white pastry box from a shelf and said, "I've got your order right here."

Sato's mouth fell open as he realized that Gail had called this man `Dr. Mallow.' This was `Eriku Maroh', the man who was the source of Sato's troubles!

Gail pulled the receipt free from the top of the box and said, "That's two dozen mixed, right Dr. Mallow?" As the girl spoke, Sato thought she smiled more broadly at the man than she had at him. He also wondered what Mallow intended to do with two dozen of the greasy donuts.

"That's right," Maroh replied with a smile that nearly turned Sato's stomach.

"Have you got a meeting today, doctor?" the waitress asked as she rang the sale up on the cash register.

"I sure do," Maroh said. "There's a tenants' meeting at the office this noon and you guys make such great donuts, I'm always the one who gets to bring the treats."

"Lucky you, doctor," Gail said. Sato did not follow all of this dialogue, but he watched Gail cock her head slightly and give Mallow a playful wink. "That'll be $8.38."

Sato watched Mallow give her a bill and she said, "Out of ten." When Gail counted the change into the Mallow's hand Sato was repelled that the pair were having even that much contact. He wondered if Mallow had explored Gail's voluptuous curves.

After he watched Mallow leave, Sato paid his bill and left the coffee shop himself. Gail was as friendly when he left as when he had entered and, although he tingled with emotion as he left, Sato had maintained a pleasant appearance. Seeing Mallow had been a stroke of luck. Sato now knew the face of his enemy. Still, the man's Caucasian good looks and the comfort with which he had moved and interacted with Gail had been deeply disturbing. Sato truly hated that person. He was ready to get on with his assignment if only because it would let him deal with Mallow.

Sato was unsure of how to fill the hours until the open house would let him explore the inside of the condominium building. He was vaguely aware of some tourist attractions in and around Minneapolis, but he had no desire to either see them or visit new parts of the city. He was comfortable driving in the areas he had so far explored and certainly did not wish to run the risk of encountering new problems that might be met in other neighborhoods. Thus, he began by driving along a winding boulevard he had come to know quite well. He followed it to a very pleasant road that wound along the wooded bank of a large river. This road in turn led him to a commercial neighborhood on the edge of the downtown. The area seemed safe and potentially diverting so he parked his car in a ramp and got out to look around.

His only goal was to fill the time until the open house so he walked slowly along a street lined with small shops that offered a variety of goods in their front windows. Along the way he wandered into a couple of the stores and was impressed that the goods offered were extremely inexpensive. He was impressed that one bookstore he visited had not one Japanese publication. In another store he found a handsome pair of shoes that seemed incredibly cheap. He decided not to buy them, however, since bargain shopping seemed inappropriate for a ninja on assignment.

As Sato continued on this way, the shop windows began to take on a sameness that made them boring. Many of the objects they presented were unfamiliar enough to be hard to consider in detail. As he was beginning to acknowledge his boredom, Sato stopped long enough in front of one cluttered window to realize that it was a novelty shop. He lingered just a moment longer to take in the masks, magic tricks, funny hats, and colorful trinkets it offered. Sato scanned across this trash with no more than mild interest until he saw something that literally took his breath away. There, next to a couple of fake dog turds and in front of a sign saying "Asian Throwing Stars" were several small piles of blued steel *shuriken*!

When Sato left the store, he carried twenty of the disks. This was far more than he could use in a single attack, but the sudden ability to rearm had made him greedy. The shopkeeper had let him look at all of styles he was offering and watched with disinterest as Sato weighed them in his hand and flicked his wrist as he held them to judge their balance. The disks came from Hong Kong and were not as well made as the weapons taken from him at the Chicago airport. Still, Sato was sure he could make them work and the weight of the weapons in his pocket made him feel secure and confident.

Sato headed straight back to his car, stopping along the way only long enough to buy a small file at a hardware store he had passed earlier. He took his new arsenal to a grassy picnic area he had seen along the river parkway. Midday had turned pleasantly warm and sunny so there were a few people enjoying an outdoor lunch when he arrived. A few others were walking by on a path that meandered by the area, but Sato had no trouble finding an isolated table. Sitting in a position that would hide his work but let him see anyone who might approach, Sato set about "tuning up" his newly purchased *shuriken*.

He began by inspecting each of the disks more closely than he had in the store. They still met with his approval, although he could see now that they had been stamped out of blued steel and that their edges and points were not well-finished. Even well-made Japanese *shuriken* had to be balanced and sharpened, though, and when he ran his new file across the edge of one of the eight-pointed stars, he could feel it cut smooth and fast. Putting the weapons in fighting order would not be difficult and Sato was pleased to have a specific task to keep him busy until the open house. He looked forward to letting the routine of a familiar task free his mind and focus his attention.

Sato had bought both four and eight-pointed stars since he had not yet decided which weapons he would need for his attack. With their extra weight and better balance, eight-pointed stars were accurate and easier to throw. They were not appropriate for a lethal attack, however, because their closely spaced points could not penetrate a target deeply. Well-sharpened four-pointed stars, on the other hand, could easily tear through three or even four inches of flesh.

He started his work with one of the eight-pointed stars. Working in a clockwise direction Sato gave each of the points five strokes with the file. He turned the disk over and repeated the process before switching to do the counterclockwise sides of the points. When all four sides of each point had been done, Sato checked the balance of the disk by spinning it on his index finger. When it passed that test, he gave the disk a quick back hand flick into the air above the picnic table. He imparted enough back spin to make the disk whirl above the table. In his demonstrations at Ninja Village, he would catch the whirling *shuriken* in the air. This time, however, he let the newly sharpened disk fall into the top of the picnic table. It struck with a thud and stuck deeply into the surface.

After all of the eight-pointed stars were sharpened, Sato turned to the four-pointed pieces. As he worked with these he realized the disks were, indeed, well-designed. Their points were slightly thickened so that they could take a very keen edge. He was absolutely sure these would be wonderful weapons and he looked forward to using them.

It was nearly two when Sato finished sharpening the last of his *shuriken*. He looked at his watch and realized that he could now go on to the open house. There was no urgency, however, and as he stretched his shoulders and rolled his head, he realized the intensity with which he had worked. He needed to loosen up, to relax, and he also truly wanted to test his weapons.

The people who had been in the picnic area when he had arrived had all left and there were only the occasional walker on the path. Sato thought it would be safe to give his new arsenal a workout. He walked into the wooded portion of the river bank until he could no longer be seen from the parkway. With four crisp sweeps of his right hand he threw four disks into a tree he had picked at random. When the last of them hit home, he turned and sent two more eight-pointed disks into another tree. As the last of them hit, he rolled away from that target and took a group of four-pointed disks from his pocket. Running toward another tree, he threw a pair of disks with two sharp moves. Both struck the tree, but only one stuck so Sato whirled, faced the tree with set feet, and cast the remaining disks. Both of them hit true and stuck deeply.

Holding his pose as he would in a real attack, Sato looked around. There were other trees and still more *shuriken*, but he decided the exercise was over. It had been a success. Sato stood up and shook some more cricks out of his neck and shoulders. Returning the disks he was holding to his pocket, he massaged his fingers and cracked his knuckles. He felt wonderful.

When he retrieved the disks, Sato found that all of them had stood up well and hit their target with force. Even the four-pointed disk that had not stayed in its target, had sliced away a large section of bark. In a man, it would have opened an ugly wound. After hitting the tree, however, that disk had spun off into the brush that covered the ground and Sato could not find it. He searched for a short while, but decided to abandon it. With 19 well-honed *shuriken* he felt well enough armed to move ahead with his attack.

Sato's visit to the condominium building went incredibly well. A sign in the lobby told him to press a button on a console near the inner door. He responded to the crackly, "May I help you?" that came over the intercom by simply saying, "Open House" into the speaker by the door. The intercom voice had replied, "Please come to room 318," and a buzzer announced that the inner door, the one that had stopped him earlier, was now open.

To look over the building, Sato took the stairs to the third floor. He also walked the length of the second floor which let him see that his reconstruction of the building had been entirely accurate. Each floor had 16 units, arranged eight to a side facing a central hallway. Each floor was similarly numbered so that finding Eric Mallow's unit, number 413, would be no problem at all.

On the way to the third floor Sato also saw that the individual apartment doors were closed with standard key locks but that each door also had some kind of an electronic combination lock. The keyed locks weren't a serious challenge. Sato was sure they could be opened with the picks he had brought from Japan. The numbered push button system, on the other hand, looked more problematical. He had never seen anything like it and decided he would have to study it further before beginning his attack.

The real estate agent showing the unit met Sato at the door of unit 318. A neatly dressed middle aged woman, she smiled broadly and extended Sato her hand as he entered the room. Once inside the apartment, the agent showed Sato the spacious rooms and encouraged him to look closely at all of the features. As they progressed through the apartment, the agent asked Sato his name and wondered if he was interested in the unit himself or someone else. Sato had expected this kind of inquiry and had a story ready. He said he was a Japanese businessman looking for a residence for an employee his firm would be sending to Minneapolis. This answer satisfied the agent and she eagerly answered all his questions.

Sato was polite and attentive. He looked at the features the agent pointed out, noted the room sizes and the kinds of appliances supplied with the kitchen. He also made a point of asking about the building's security system. The agent assured him that it was a secure, peaceful space. She told him that most of the residents were older people who were asleep by 10:00 PM. She also explained how residents could enter the front door of the building with a magnetic card and that the garage door could be raised by punching in a five digit number into the push buttons on the control post outside the door. When Sato was unable to follow her description, she brought him down to the basement and demonstrated the security system. As she did, Sato saw that the numbers 5, 3, 31, 6, 9 would open the door. On the way back to the display rooms, the agent showed Sato the garbage bins on the ground floor level and explained that garbage was emptied on Mondays and Thursdays.

Returning from the basement, Sato asked nonchalantly about the numbered push buttons on each door. With earnest expertise, the woman explained that each unit had it own security alarm that could be deactivated by punching in a three number sequence before turning the key. Each residence had its own combination, she explained.

By the time they had returned to room 318, a plan had begun to form in Sato's mind. There was little more to be gained on this reconnaissance so he began to excuse himself by asking the agent the price of the unit being offered for sale. He listened politely to what she had to say and told her that he would have to check with his office in Tokyo before making any commitments. This seemed to satisfy her and she let him be on his way.

From the condominium Sato drove directly to the picnic area where he had sharpened his *shuriken*. As he had expected, by this time in the late afternoon, the area was nearly deserted. There were no people at any of the tables and only a few walkers and bicyclists moving by the area. It would be a perfect place for Sato to refine the plan that had formed in his mind. He perched himself on the side of one of the picnic tables, looking away from anyone who might pass by. He kicked off his shoes, assumed the lotus position, and locked his fingers in a posture that would help him concentrate.

When Sato left the picnic area, the sun was down and his attack was planned in meticulous detail. He had a clear course of action that was elegantly simple but fully practical. He had considered the implications and probable outcomes of each step of the plan. He had assessed the risks and alternatives and now he was absolutely sure his strategy would succeed. He was eager to set it in motion.

In his hotel room, while he waited for the night sky to darken, Sato called the 800 number of Japan Air Lines and reserved seats on a flight to Tokyo. The arrangements he was able to make exactly meshed with the schedule he had visualized. With all of his other successes he had experienced in the past day, however, this did not strike him as surprising. On the contrary, it seemed like nothing more than evidence of the unassailability he felt.

Next, he called the front desk to announce his departure. He asked that his bill be tallied and waiting. He gave the same request to the car rental agency. He wanted to leave this country calmly and unobtrusively with the dagger and no problems.

With these details attended to, Sato took his *shunobi-zoku* out of his suit case. Sato loved these clothes because they were the uniform of the *ninja*. He regretted not having been able to wear them so far on this operation, but he was sure now that at least the comfortable britches and secure split-toed *chika-tabi* were appropriate for the coming attack. He put them, the darker of his satin jackets, and a small tool kit in a paper sack that fit unobtrusively under his arm.

When he walked through the hotel lobby on his way out, Sato made a point of greeting the desk clerk, a young Hispanic woman. "Good evening!" he said cheerily. "I'll be a little late tonight."

She returned his smile and said, "Have a nice evening," and Sato had to suppress a sly smirk. Clearly, the girl suspected nothing out of the ordinary.

Next, on the way to the picnic area where he would complete his preparations, Sato stopped at a brightly lit MacDonald's restaurant. When he pulled into the parking area, he could see that other cars were driving up to a service window. Since he was not sure how that system might operate, however, he parked and walked into the service area to buy a single hamburger. The rich aromas in the dining area made him realize that he had eaten nothing since the sweet roll he had had at the coffee shop in the morning. All of his energies were now focused on his mission, however, and he had no desire to eat.

As he had expected, the picnic area was a perfect place to make his final arrangements. It was totally deserted when he pulled in and he was able to park so that the driver's side of his car was completely hidden from public view. He slipped into the trees and quickly donned the dark clothing that would make him invisible in shadows and darkened areas. The smell of his *shunobi-zoku as* he pulled it on gave him great satisfaction and he could feel the muscles in his legs and feet respond to the snug, split-toed *chika-tabi*. Certainly they would let him move silently across any kind of obstacle. To complete his outfit, Sato put on the darker of his two satin jackets. This disguise had let him move unobserved through the city so far and he counted on it to let him get to and from his objective one last time. He placed his lock picks in his breast pocket along with a disposable cigarette lighter.

Back at the car, Sato made arrangements that would let him get back into his street clothes even while he was driving. To do this he arranged his trousers on the floor below the driver's seat. He had purposely selected baggy pants that would slip over his dark britches. Then he draped his shirt, inside-out, over the back of the seat.

With these preparations, Sato was ready to proceed. He was more than ready, but he made himself wait by recalling the emphasis his teacher, Ozawa-sensei, had always placed on mental preparation. Ozawa-sensei taught that every mission must begin with a period of concentration and mental exercise. Sato was sure of his plan and every part of his body was set to begin, but with a deep breath, he made himself go back to the darkened area at the side of the picnic ground. There he assumed the lotus position and made himself finish his preparations.

Concentration is a skill and Sato knew how to focus his attention. He cleared his mind without even a deep breath and systematically worked his fingers through a well-studied series of postures he knew would aid his mental exercise. He started with the postures of symmetry that knitted his folded hands into a series of arrangements in which the left and right hands mirrored one another. These were postures that would balance Sato himself. They would help him explore himself and his preparations. As he moved through them, Sato felt no uncertainty, but he had to fight his impatience. He worked to make his motions automatic and to feel the mystical powers the postures could free within himself.

Next, he began the asymmetrical postures. This series of six deeply secret grasps brought his hands through contortions that Ozawa-sensei said would let him project his concentration outward to feel the thoughts of others. At the third posture of asymmetry, with his hands tightly grasped and his right thumb splayed away toward his solar plexus as his left index finger pointed in the exactly opposite direction, Sato worked to know what Eric Mallow was doing at this moment. He let the power of the posture force his mind outward and waited for some reaction.

There was none.

Sato held the posture until his fingers throbbed, but nothing came to him. There was nothing. Mallow suspected nothing. The way was clear. Sato could come to no other conclusion. The fifth and sixth postures also produced no hint of a reaction, no trace of power or preparation save his own. It was time to move.

During his explorations of the neighborhood around the condominium, Sato had found a spot on a side street, far from a street light, where a large hedge came almost to the curb. When he arrived back at this spot, it was as dark and as lonely as he had expected and a perfect place to leave his car. No one saw him as he stood in the darkness and put four of his eight-pointed *shuriken* into the left pocket. He put four of the well-honed four-pointed stars in his right pocket and tucked another one into the back of his pants. He patted his breast pocket to be sure he had his lock picks. Then, with his preparations completed, he stood up, straightened his satin jacket on his shoulders, and walked confidently toward the street behind Mallow's condominium.

As he knew it would be, the street was lonely and quite dark. Several houses had porch lights on, but the main light came from the street lamps at the corners and they left many shadowed areas. There was no one else out walking at this time of the evening, but it was not so late that a stroller would attract attention. Sato effected a nonchalant gait. He tried to look as if he were out for a late evening stroll and kept up that pretense until he got in front of the house directly behind the condominium building. When he reached it he couldn't help recalling with disgust and rage the smelly dog that had embarrassed him here.

Sato darted onto the lawn and ran into the dark shadows where the bushy hedge met with the fence that separated the front and back yards. In the moment it took him to regain his bearings, Sato smelled the stench of the filthy dog and knew he was at the right place. He took another moment to scan the back of the house and saw that it was entirely dark. There had been no lights apparent in the front and now he assumed the house was either empty or that the occupants were asleep. His attack was proceeding smoothly and exactly as he had planned.

Looking between the fence boards, Sato saw that a few slivers of light leaked through the rear hedge from the condominium parking lot. One of them cut across the dog to show that it was rolled like a dark ball in the doorway of the doghouse. Sato took the MacDonald's hamburger from his jacket pocket and quietly removed its paper wrapper. The aroma again made Sato aware of his hunger and for a moment he toyed with the idea of eating a part of the hamburger himself. He rejected that impulse with the expectation of getting a far greater satisfaction from the greasy morsel.

Speaking in a soft conversational voice through a slot in the fence, Sato said, *"Oi! Wan-chan."*

The dog raised its head and looked curiously around.

"Kochi, kochi, wan-chan!" Sato continued. When it looked in his direction, Sato asked, *"Sukoshi, tabemasenka?"*

As if it had understood this question, the dog rose to its feet. When it did, Sato threw the hamburger over the fence in a high arc that put it a few feet in front of the doghouse. The beast saw the burger land and approached it tentatively. After a single investigatory sniff, it set about consuming the windfall. Sato's actions were as decisive as the dog's but much faster.

As soon as the dog turned its attention to the food, Sato jumped up and vaulted over the fence. He landed quietly on his toes and took three quick steps toward the doghouse. The dog continued chomping but looked up to see what else had fallen into its yard. As it did, Sato swept his right hand across the back of his pants. In a single smooth movement he grabbed the four- pointed *shuriken* he had tucked in his belt and hurled it toward the dog's face.

The animal comprehended none of this and probably didn't even know something hit it in the forehead. It stopped moving its jaw, but it did not change its stance or its satisfied expression as the *shuriken* tore into its head.

The disk performed wonderfully. The first point reached nearly two inches into the central suture of the dog's skull. Sato had thrown it with such force and imparted so much spin that it moved onward through the dog's brain, stopping only when it reached the mass of wrinkled hide at the base of the dog's head. It was surely dead by then, but it stood motionless for a moment before quietly slumping straight forward, gagging out the uneaten remnants of its hamburger.

Sato stepped into the shadows between the doghouse and the hedge without looking at the dog's body. The attack was only beginning and he wanted to move ahead while things were going smoothly. Still, as he felt his way through the hedge, he realized that killing had been easy. He had never before thrown a *shuriken* at living flesh, but it had not been especially difficult. Indeed, Sato had to acknowledge that he was experiencing feelings of retribution and power and that he was enjoying those feelings.

The condominium parking lot was illuminated by a pair of lights mounted on poles about thirty feet high. As he crouched between the hedge and one of parked cars, Sato could see that only one of the lamps was aimed at the garage door. If it were darkened, he would be able to approach that side of the building in nearly complete darkness.

He moved down the hedge toward that lamp and used the space between a pair of parked cars to move toward the center of the lot. The cars provided cover as long as he was crouched down and they gave him an angle on the lamp he had to extinguish.

Lying on the paved surface between the cars, Sato looked around to make sure no one else was present. He saw no one and there were no indications anyone was likely to be watching. Most of the parking places were filled and only one of the rear-facing units of the condominium still had lights on. The agent had said that most residents of the building were asleep by ten and it was approaching eleven. The risk of discovery, therefore, could not be great.

Sato slipped an eight-pointed star from the right pocket of his jacket. He set it in his hand, moved to a crouching position, took a deep breath, and stood quickly upright. With his full strength, he sent the disk whirling toward the lamp. As soon as it was on its way, Sato crouched back down between the cars. He watched the *shuriken* spin toward the lamp and fall short by perhaps a foot.

Long throws into a bright light are difficult so Sato did not despair. Instead, he scrambled back to the hedge and moved a few cars closer to his target. From there it was an easy throw. His second disk was true, and appeared to hit the lamp but it failed to extinguish the light. Sato felt a pang of disappointment but did not allow himself time to worry. Instead, he moved one pair of cars closer and squinted toward the lamp. Looking straight into the light, he could see his second *shuriken* lodged in the reflecting shield just to the side of the bulb. His target was smaller than he had realized and as he set for a third throw, he was glad he had decided to carry the extra weapons.

The third throw was harder than any he had ever demonstrated at **Ninja Village**. Since he was now in a part of the lot that was in the direct glare of the light, he had to make it from a crouching position. He also had to send the *shuriken* nearly straight upward. The throw had not felt good as he made it and in the bright light of his target he lost sight of the disk as soon as it was out of his hand. He realized it had succeeded only when the he heard a light tinkle of glass and the light blanked out above his head.

The sudden darkness was comforting but Sato did not stop to enjoy it. He whirled around immediately so that he could face the condominium building and be ready for any reactions to the change in lighting. His eyes adjusted to the darkness as he waited for something to happen, but there was nothing. No one came. No lights went on in the building.

After waiting long enough to be certain of this conclusion, Sato proceeded with his attack. He ran to the control panel on the post outside the garage door and punched in the combination of numbers he had seen the real estate agent use to open the door: 5, 3, 31, 6, 9. It seemed too easy, but as soon as the last button was pushed, the overhead door began to move up. Sato darted toward the door as soon as it began to move and rolled into the garage when the bottom of the door was less than two feet above the threshold. Once inside, he hurried to get between two parked cars and scanned the room to make sure he was alone and unobserved. Of course he was.

Nearly every parking space was filled and there were no signs of life in the garage. It was darker than it had been earlier in the day and the only sound came from the overhead door as it slowly finished its trip to the top of the doorway. Aside from that, all of what he saw was exactly as he expected. Still, he felt neither relief nor satisfaction. The sequence of successes he was having couldn't be coincidence. It had to reflect a foolproof plan and flawless execution.

Sato moved carefully along the length of the garage. He was sure there was no one present, but he crouched behind parked cars and darted between the cement pillars out of habit. When he got to the door at the far end of the building, he slipped into the hallway and up the half flight of stairs to where the real estate agent had shown him several bins of garbage waiting to be picked up. Sato hadn't examined the bins when the agent had shown him through the building, but now he lifted their lids and looked in the open one directly under the garbage shoot. Sato selected one closest to the stairs which was wadded full of dry paper and white foam packing pellets. Holding the lid open, he used his lighter to ignite a small fire. When the flames were well-started, Sato let the cover drop and pulled the bin toward the center of the hallway. As smoke began billowing out of the bin, Sato opened the door to the stairs so that draft from the upper floors could draw the smoke into the staircase.

Sato stepped through the smoke and ran up the stairs to the fourth floor where he planned to wait behind the hallway door until the fire alarm sounded. He expected all of the residents, Eric

Mallow included, to leave the building. Between their departure and the arrival of the fire department, his intention was to pick his way into Mallow's apartment, find and retrieve the dagger, and withdraw in the confusion sure to follow. This plan still seemed as elegantly simple as when he had made it and with the successes he had experienced so far, Sato was sure it would unfold smoothly.

To make his hiding space larger, Sato pulled a chair from beside the elevator to just in front of the hallway door. As he was doing that, he flicked a light switch he had not noticed during his earlier visit. This was an impulsive act and as he did it he worried it may have been unwise. The happy result was, however, that the hall lights went out. Now he would be very hard to see as he crouched behind the door. He was in that position when the loud buzz of the fire alarm began to sound.

The very first door to open was the one Sato calculated to be Eric Mallow's, but the first person out of it was an older blonde woman. Mallow followed her into the hall but then went back into his apartment. Sato found this puzzling and wondered if it meant he would have to fight his way into Mallow's room. If it came to that, he would be ready. He might even welcome the chance to harm Mallow, but it was far too early to make his move. He drew back as the blonde woman walked toward his hiding place. She was shouting to the other residents and pounding on their doors as she came down the hall and did not to even look in Sato's direction as she walked by on her way to the third floor.

Other doors began to open and the residents of the other apartments appeared in the hall. There was mild confusion as they looked around and spoke to one another. Generally, though, the people moved toward the exits as Sato had expected they would. After most of the other rooms had been abandoned, Eric Mallow finally stepped out of the door.

Sato smiled in satisfaction when he saw Mallow pull the door shut and shake the knob. As he began walking down the hall toward the stairs, Sato saw Mallow was carrying a box under his left arm. This was a disconcerting development since it had never occurred to Sato that Mallow might take the *tanto* with him when he left his apartment. His mind raced to recall the details he had been given about the *tanto*. He had been told the blade was mounted in plain wood *shira-saya* and it might be stored in a *kiri* wood box.

Among all the facts he learned for this assignment, he could not remember if he had been given other details of its shape, size, or construction. In frustration and uncertainty, Sato strained to remember what he had been told about the box. More importantly, he tried to think of some way of handling the situation that confronted him now. He had no weapons ready for use and from his crouched position behind the door and the chair, any sort of an attack would be very difficult. In uncertainty, Sato watched Mallow walk by his hiding place and down the stairway.

Sato knew he had made a serious mistake. The box Mallow carried was exactly the size and shape of a *tanto-bako*. In the darkness of the hallway, Sato had not seen the details of its construction, but he thought it looked like it was plain wood. As Sato thought about the situation an even more obvious question crossed his mind. What else would Mallow bring with him out of a burning building *but* the Muramasa *tanto*? It was all too obvious and Sato couldn't believe his stupidity. Mallow had clearly gone back into his room to pick up the *tanto* and now he had brought it out of the building. Sato had been stupid not to have thought of this possibility. He had been stupid not to have a *shuriken* ready to throw. And he had been stupid not to have attacked Mallow when he had the chance.

Only quick action could save the operation. With the *tanto* gone there was no point in staying in the building. Although he did not have a clear plan, Sato stepped out from behind the door and followed Mallow and the others who had gone down the stairway. As he walked, he zipped up his jacket and fluffed up his hair hoping those actions would somehow make him look less like a ninja on assignment.

In fact, leaving the building turned out to be easy since the first of three fire trucks pulled into the parking lot just as Sato got to the lobby. There was a crowd of people on the sidewalks in front of the building but all attention was diverted and Sato was able to simply walk out of the lobby and into the darkness.

Darkness is a ninja's closest ally. It provides cover when there is nothing else and can be an impenetrable defense. Sato recalled these principles when a rank of large floodlights on the second fire truck was switched on to illuminate the front and sides of the condominium building. By drawing attention to the firemen as they began their work, the lights defined the area behind the crowd as dark and hostile. Standing at the back of the crowd, Sato looked around to see pockets of darkness and shadows to cover his actions and provide avenues of escape.

As Sato watched, the scene took on order. Tenants and a few passers-by organized themselves into a regular ring around the front of the building as the firemen unfurled their hoses and unpacked the other equipment they would need. One of them dragged the flaming garbage bin into the parking lot where others immediately doused it with a heavy spray that sent sodden bits of garbage across a wide area. Other firemen entered the back of the building to wet down the area of scorching that had appeared around the garbage bin Sato had set on fire. Another pair set a large fan in front of the lobby door to draw the smoky air out of the condominium. Others walked in and around the building looking for more fires. When it became obvious the fire was a small one, the crowd began to relax. Sato watched people move around, greeting one another and exchanging short conversations. Sato had no trouble finding Mallow in this activity. He was standing near the driveway into the parking lot with the wooden box under one arm.

To get a clearer view and a better position, Sato crossed the street toward the bakery, walked through the darkness to the other side of the crowd, and recrossed the street. This put him just a short distance behind Mallow. Unlike most of the others, *Maroh* did not move around within the crowd. He stayed near the edge of the parking and watched the firemen working at the rear of the building. Many of the older residents of the condominium came over to speak with him and ask him about what was going on. The older blonde woman Sato had seen leaving Mallow's apartment was especially active. She moved through the entire crowd and made several trips to where Mallow was standing.

As Sato watched Mallow, it became obvious that the box he carried had to contain the Muramasa *tanto*. Mallow handled the box easily as if it contained something as light as a single *tanto*, but it had to be valuable since he never set it down and never let anyone else hold it. The box had to be Sato's objective and as the firemen finished their work, Sato realized he would have to act quickly or retire and develop another attack strategy. Could he ever get as close to Mallow as he was right now? Would it ever again be possible to breach the building after this unsuccessful attack? Would Sato ever be more invisible than he was standing at the edge of this crowd? Would he ever be more ready to act than he was at this instant? The answers to all of these questions were obvious and Sato knew what he had to do.

Glancing over his shoulder to be sure his escape route into the darkness was clear, Sato slipped the last of his eight-pointed *shuriken* out of his jacket pocket. He also got a four-point star ready to throw. He could have managed three of the disks, but this pair would be adequate since he expected to make only a single throw. With the eight-pointed *shuriken* set in his right palm, he walked into the light until he was about twenty feet behind Mallow. From that distance he could deliver a blow that could be lethal and would at least disorient Mallow long enough to let Sato race in to recover the *tanto*. He felt exposed standing on the well-lit sidewalk, but Mallow and the rest of the crowd were more interested in the activities of the firemen. Sato was aware of no one looking in his direction but as he drew his arm back to make his throw, someone shouted loudly.

Sato hadn't understood what had been said, and wasn't even sure it involved him. As he sent the *shuriken* on its way however, he saw the blonde woman running in his direction.

Mallow became aware of the commotion just as Sato did and turned to see what was happening. As he turned, the disk Sato had sent squarely toward the back of Mallow's head flew by his ear. He may have felt the breeze as it passed by, but he obviously hadn't understood its significance. He looked blankly from the blonde woman toward Sato just as the second disk was sent on its way. Instinctively, Mallow swung the box he was carrying up to shield himself from whatever it was that was headed in his direction.

Sato's second throw was not one of his best. It had been hurried and his concentration had been broken. Still, it was delivered with such force that when it spun into the side of Mallow's box, it moved across the back of his hand. As it tore up his forearm, Mallow gasped in pain and let the box drop. It spilled open at his feet and exposed a pistol. In the same instant, Mallow fell backward onto the paved surface next to it.

None of this was what Sato had expected and for an instant he stood motionless trying to take in the situation. Sato expected the box to contain the *tanto* he had been sent to recover and he wondered why Mallow had been carrying a pistol with the dagger. As an automatic precaution, he took another four-pointed *shuriken* from his left pocket and moved toward the box shattered beside Mallow.

The blonde woman moved in the same direction, but she showed no hesitation whatsoever. She yelled loudly as she ran to Mallow's side so that others in the crowd and even a couple of the firemen looked in her direction. When she arrived at the box the blonde woman acted with no trace of fear or uncertainty. She pushed the smashed remains of the box aside and confidently pulled the pistol free.

As she did this, Sato could see that there was no dagger in the box. It contained nothing but the gun. He took a couple of tentative steps backward as he realized this mistake. As he did, he saw the woman snap a wire from the top of the gun, flick a lever on its side and smoothly pull back its hammer. Above all of the other noise, Sato heard a distinct click as she did this. Then, he saw her point the gun in his direction.

Sato now understood he had made a serious miscalculation. He should not have followed Mallow. He should not have abandoned his plan and now he certainly should retreat as quickly as possible. He knew he was in trouble but the old woman pointing an old gun in his direction did not seem to be the most serious of his problems. He recognized the gun as an old Mauser automatic. His family treasured a picture of his grandfather holding a similar weapon taken from a dead Chinese soldier.

To divert the old woman and create confusion to cover this withdrawal, Sato decided to throw his four-pointed *shuriken* in her direction. He didn't actually intend this to be a serious attack. His throw was nothing more than a diversion, a delay, a reflex. Still, as he raised his arm, Sato saw the woman point the gun straight at his head. He watched her grip tighten and saw her pull the trigger. Sato was sure she had missed as soon as he saw a burst of light at the end of the barrel, but when his arm could not complete the throw he had begun, he thought something must be wrong. When he felt a sharp pain tear up his arm he knew he was in trouble. When he felt warm moisture run down across his armpit and onto his side he knew he would have to get into the darkness immediately.

15 | Hagi Akira

In which, with relief but some complexities, treasures find homes.

Minneapolis - present day
Eric Mallow, dentist with an uncertain career future.
Dawn Watanabe, Eric's friend.
Dave Stalgaard, art dealer.
Hagi Akira, Curator at the Museum of Japanese Swords, Tokyo.

After dropping Eric at the front door of his condominium and parking her car, it took Dawn a moment to put some things into a bag and lock the doors so she had expected to meet Eric at his apartment. When she got to the building lobby, though, he was sitting on the bench beside the security door.

"What's the matter, Eric? Why didn't you go on up?" she asked hoping there was no problem.

"I didn't go up because I couldn't get the fucking security card out of my fucking wallet and through the fucking slot." Eric looked pale, tired, and unhappy. Over his shoulders and on his left arm he wore a tweed sport coat. His right arm was outside the jacket because his hand and forearm were wrapped in a bulky cast that kept his wrist flexed backward in an obviously uncomfortable angle.

Dawn sympathized with his frustration and hoped to be supportive. "Oh, we should have thought of that. Let me get it for you. Where's the card?" she asked.

"It's in my wallet in my hip pocket," Eric said with tired exasperation. "I can't even reach into my own hip pocket!"

"Oh, Ric. It'll be okay," Dawn said soothingly as she reached around to get his wallet. "Is this it?" she asked.

"Yeah, that's it. Thanks," he said. "Sorry I snapped."

Eric had been in the hospital for the eight days since he had been attacked on the night of the fire. At first his injuries had not seemed bad, but by the time he was brought to the emergency room, it was obvious the damage was serious. The knife-bladed disk the Asian kid had thrown at him had severed his little finger and opened the length of his forearm, cutting several tendons, and severing some nerves. Attempts to reattach the finger had failed and an infection settled in to extend his hospital stay. The tendon repairs had all been successful and the nerves had all been spliced back together so the doctors assured Eric the healing was proceeding smoothly. Since tendons heal slowly, however, his hand would have to be immobilized in a cast for at least another two weeks. It would take twice that long for the nerves to regenerate enough to return feeling to his fingers. As if all of that weren't enough, when he had fallen backwards after being struck by the disk, Eric landed hard on his left elbow and bruised his left ulnar nerve. The doctors were optimistic that feeling and control would return to his left hand within a week or ten days. For now, though, the fingers of Eric's left hand were numb.

As Dawn looked for the magnetic card in Eric's wallet, Lotte Swanson appeared inside the security door. She was smiling gaily as she opened the door.

"Hello, Dr. Mallow! It is so good to see you." Lotte said with her mellow German accent. "I heard the car door and I knew it was you. Welcome home. Welcome home. Welcome home! Miss Watanabe, thank you for bringing the doctor back."

Eric returned Lotte's smile and felt his spirits rise as he did. "Thanks, Lotte. It's good to be here." He bent forward to pick up the bag Dawn had brought from the car.

"Let me take that," Lotte said lifting the bag out of Eric's left hand. "Then we can go on up to your apartment. On the way, I will show you the work we have been doing. I don't think you will see any sign of the fire." Leading the way to the elevator, she continued speaking to Eric over her shoulder. "It was a mess and of course the smell was terrible, but there was no serious damage and it was time to repaint the halls. I think it looks pretty good. Don't you?" Lotte asked stopping in front of the elevator.

"It looks great, Lotte," agreed Eric and smiled at Dawn who was standing behind Lotte rolling her eyes and shaking her head.

"Yeah, yeah. The painters were here until yesterday so it still smells like paint, but that is a clean smell and it will go away. Here is the car, please go in," Lotte said, again making a point of holding the elevator door for Eric. As soon as he was in, she followed and then, possibly as an afterthought, turned to hold the door for Dawn.

"There was no structural damage. I checked into that right away," Lotte continued after punching the fifth floor button. "Walter has a friend who is a structural engineer. He came to look and he said the building is fine."

"Have you heard anything about how the fire got started?" asked Eric.

"I think that is still a problem. The fire inspector asked me about it several times," said Lotte. "But no one seems to know for sure. He told me maybe a slow fire got started in one of the garbage cans because somebody threw away something that was smoldering, but that has never happened before. I think somebody started it." she said assuredly. "I can't say for sure, but I think it had to be that Oriental kid who attacked us. Here we are," she said when the elevator stopped. "Shall we go down to your room?"

"Have the police told you anything about the fire or the attack?"

"Right at the time, of course, I spoke with the officers. And some police came by the next day. Also a fire inspector. Since then, however, I have spoken only with the regular officers. They don't know what happened."

"That's sure how it seems," said Eric. "A couple of detectives came by the hospital the day after I was admitted. They asked me if I knew the kid who attacked me. I had to tell them I'd never seen him before and that pretty much ended their investigation," he added.

"The newspaper made it sound like it was gang related," said Dawn. "You think it was more than that?"

"I wish I knew. One of the detectives did say he thought the whole thing was about gang territories," Eric admitted.

"I think that's it," said Lotte as they got to Eric's door. "I told the police I have seen some of these Oriental kids looking around the building. They said maybe this building has become a 'boundary marker' between their territories."

"There was that shoot-out down by the lake a night or two before your fire," added Dawn as Eric tried to get his key out. "Can I help you with that Eric?" she asked when she saw he was having trouble.

"Yeah, will you? My key ring is in the pocket, but I can't reach it with the cast."

When Dawn pulled the keys out, Lotte took them from her and said, "I'll open the door for you. Your security number is 7-6-5 isn't it?" Without waiting for an answer, Lotte punched the numbers into the alarm block and turned the key to open the door. Swinging it open for Eric she said, "We aired the rooms out for you and Mrs. Johnson baked some cookies. I put some flowers out as well." She was clearly happy to have Eric back and proud of the work she had done to prepare for his return.

"It looks great, Lotte," Eric said as he entered his apartment. The curtains were pushed back and at least a couple of windows were open so the space was fresh and airy.

"If there is nothing more you need, I'll let you go now," said Lotte with a slight shrug that was almost a curtsey.

"Oh, no, Lotte. Please come in for a while," Eric said. "I'd like to talk some more about the attack."

"Good, good. That will be nice," Lotte said and followed Eric into his apartment.

Eric looked around approvingly. "It feels good to be home. Thanks for opening things up for me." Turning to Lotte he paused briefly before continuing. "The police said they released the Kaiser's pistol to you. Where did you put it?"

"It is downstairs in the gun room. They gave it to me in a plastic bag, but I took it out and made sure it was clean."

Eric blanched. "You cleaned it?" he asked with a worried expression.

"You don't need to worry," Lotte said with pursed lips and a shake of her head. "I know how to care for firearms. I had Walter bring me down to a gun shop on Lake Street and we bought some *gewehrol*. I don't know what you call it in English. I put it in the gun."

Eric couldn't muster the energy it would have taken to express the concern he felt, but Lotte read the worry on his face. "Don't you worry, Dr. Mallow. Please come downstairs. I'll show you," she said heading toward the gun room. Eric followed her until, at the top of the stairs, Lotte turned back to Dawn and said with a smile, "Miss Watanabe, why don't you bring Mrs. Johnson's cookies?"

When Lotte turned to continue on her way, Eric saw Dawn's pained expression. He gave her a shrug of tired acquiescence. She responded by giving him a private look of irritation and the finger

She did, however, pick up the tray of cookies and followed the others down the stairway.

As the group got to the gun room, the lobby buzzer sounded. "That's probably Dave Stalgaard," said Eric walking to the intercom by the gun room door. "I asked him to come over." He used his left hand to push the speaker button. "Is that you, Dave?" he asked the microphone in a slightly louder than conversational voice.

"It sure is, Ric," the grid above the button crackled back.

"Great. We're down in the gun room, but it'll be easier to let you in on the fifth floor. Come on up." Eric pushed the button so Dave could enter the building.

Dawn was sure Lotte would ask her to get the door, so she said, "I'll go up and let him in."

"Thanks," said Eric with a wink. As Dawn left, he looked around for the Kaiser's pistol.

"The gun is there," said Lotte, pointing toward a table at the back of the room.

Eric could see that someone, presumably Lotte, had reassembled the wooden display box on the table. It was badly fragmented and when he lifted the top, one side fell away. He carefully removed the other sides to expose the pistol, sitting just as it was supposed to on the felt-lined base. Picking it up, Eric saw there was a scuff across the right side of the gun from the grip to the receiver, but no other damage. The engraved inscription on the left side of the frame was still perfectly intact. Eric could also see that Lotte had done no more than lubricate the gun. She hadn't scrubbed it with abrasives and it didn't even appear that she had taken it apart.

"Thanks for taking care of the pistol, Lotte. It looks like you did a great job." Eric's thanks were sincere. He felt a responsibility for his things and hated the idea he had allowed something as important and interesting as the Kaiser's pistol to be damaged.

"Thank you," Lotte said crisply. It irritated her that Eric had doubted her ability to care for the gun. "There are a few other things I need to show you. First," she said picking up a piece of fine silver cable, "this is the wire that sealed the gun. I had to pull it off in order to shoot the kid who attacked you."

"Do you think you hit him?" asked Eric.

"Of course I hit him," Lotte said as if there were no other possibility. "I missed his head. That's why he got away, but I got him here in the arm," she said pointing to her forearm. "Or maybe down here," she said moving her finger closer to her elbow. "It was someplace there, I know."

"The police told me they checked all the hospitals and emergency room, but no gunshot wounds were reported." Eric accepted the wire and Lotte went on.

"This is the medallion that was on the wire. That is the Hohenzollern family crest so that is a very important piece."

Eric could think of nothing to say.

Next Lotte passed Eric a small plastic 'evidence bag' containing a pair of metal discs with pointed metal projections. "These are the disks the kid threw at you," she said as Eric took the bag. "The police released them to me."

"Great," said Eric and looked through the wall of the bag.

"And this is the *patronenhulse*," Lotte continued holding up a brass cartridge case. "I think in English you call it the cartridge."

"Case, the cartridge case," Eric corrected. "The cartridge is the whole thing. The case is the part that's left after it's been fired and this one's been fired." He took the case and examined its head stamp. "The Kaiser's last bullet," he said with a sigh.

"Nearly a hundred years old and still good, " Lotte marveled without noticing Eric's expression. "I found it in the grass the day after the fire. I didn't tell the police I had it, but I thought you might like it."

"I'm glad to have it. Thanks," said Eric.

"Finally," said Lotte as they heard Dawn letting Dave in on the upper floor, "These are some nice clean copies of the paper with the picture and article."

"Oh, good," said Eric. "I was hoping you'd get some for me. I saw the article in the hospital, but the nurses took the paper away before I could get it cut out. It's a terrific picture." And indeed it was. The photographer had arrived after Eric had been brought to the hospital. By that time the police had taken temporary charge of the pistol, but Lotte had retrieved it long enough to pose for a picture that had appeared on the front page of the next day's paper. Holding the pistol up for inspection, Lotte had smiled winningly into the camera. The story that accompanied the picture explained how Lotte had used the antique gun to drive off a young Asian gang member who had mysteriously attacked a resident of the burning condominium building. Eric's name was mentioned along with Lotte's. In addition to telling about her exploits, Lotte had described the gun's historic significance so the headline read, "Historic Gun Drives Off Attacker." The story and picture had picked up by the wire services and had appeared in several other newspapers.

"Maybe I can frame the paper and keep it with the pistol," Eric said thinking out loud as he reread the article. "It kind of explains what happened to the gun."

"Oh I think so," agreed Lotte. "It is a part of the gun's history," she added, as if it never occurred to her that her use of the pistol was less important than the Kaiser's or that using it, even to drive off an attacker, might have diminished its value.

"I've got some friends who do high quality framing," said Dave who arrived in the gun room to catch the end of the conversation. "They could set it up with a nice frame and UV glass so the page would be a nice compliment to the gun."

Eric and Lotte turned to greet Dave who was wearing a large off-white cowboy hat with a horsehair band, faded jeans with a concho belt, and a colorful Seminole jacket of intricately pieced bits of cloth. Lotte considered this outfit, along with Dave's ponytail, and the forward manner he used to assess her picture, and set her face in a look of icy neutrality.

"Lotte, I don't know if you've met Dave Stalgaard," said Eric. "Dave is working with me on those Japanese swords." Then turning to Dave he said, "This is Lotte Swanson, the president of our building association."

"I have seen you here before," said Lotte.

"And I recognize you from the picture in the paper, Mrs. Swanson," said Dave holding out his hand. "That was a real quick reaction and some pretty good shooting," he added with a smile and a charming twinkle in his eye.

Dave's response softened Lotte. She acknowledged his compliment with a nod and a grin as she shook his hand.

"And you must have met Dawn upstairs," Eric continued.

"Yeah, I introduced myself," said Dawn. "Eric, Dave mentioned that the mailman was in the lobby when he was at the door and he was having trouble because your mailbox is full. If you'll show me where your key is, I'll go down and get the stuff for you."

"Yeah, yeah," said Lotte. "They won't let me pick up anybody's mail so your box is full."

"Sorting through a bunch of mail is just what I'm up for this afternoon. If you'll get it that would be great, Dawn. The key is right up by the kitchen sink," said Eric pointing up the stairs.

"I'll be right back," said Dawn and ran up the stairs.

"And I will go now, too," Lotte said looking at Dave. "I know you must be tired and we shouldn't take too much of your time, doctor." She hesitated for just a moment to see if Eric would ask her to stay. When he didn't, she turned to follow Dawn. "Thanks again for all your help, Lotte," said Eric as she left. "It feels good to be home."

Turning to Dave, Eric pointed toward an easy chair and said, "Sit down, Dave." Taking one of the seats himself and putting his feet up on the coffee table, Eric continued, "I appreciate your coming over. I've got to get my life back together and I want to start by getting rid of the swords. Have you been able to make any progress?"

"In fact, I have, Ric. If you're still serious about this, I think we're about ready to roll."

"I haven't changed my mind, Dave. Those swords have been nothing but trouble from the word go. I want to dump 'em." Eric smiled as he said this, but he spoke with firm certainty. "Like I told you in the hospital, I'm sorry if I'm cutting you out of the deal, but I definitely want to get out from under them."

"Okay, I'm glad to be able to help," said Dave leaning forward in his seat. "We've got to talk about the two blades separately," he continued. "Let's start with the *tanto*."

"Okay."

"Right after you and I talked in the hospital, I tried to call Ken Sawada," said Dave. "It looks like something's changed in Ken's operation. I called both of the numbers he uses in his ads. One of them was disconnected. I left two messages on the answering machine of the other number. He only called me back after the second one when I mentioned that I was calling about your Muramasa *tanto*."

"He was real hot for the dagger just a couple of weeks ago," said Eric.

"Well, that was then," said Dave. "Now he seems very lukewarm. I told him I was calling for you because you were in the hospital and I told him that you were ready to part with the *tanto*. When I asked if he was still interested, you know what he said?" Dave paused for effect. "He said he'd have to get back to me!"

"I wonder what happened. He was ready to fly out with cash in hand," said Eric.

"He wasn't entirely disinterested," said Dave, "but in that first conversation, he was very cool. I wasn't even sure he was still interested in buying it. Whatever the problem was, though, it didn't take long for him to make up his mind. He called me back the very next day--that was three days ago--and told me that he was largely out of the sword business."

"You're kidding!" said Eric.

"That's what he said," shrugged Dave. "It amazed me too because I always figured that swords were what Ken was doing in this country and that when he had bought the last blade, he'd be on the boat back home."

"So he doesn't want to buy the dagger?" asked Eric.

"No, *he* doesn't," said Dave. "But he told me he had arranged for another guy to buy it. He gave me that guy's name and a telephone number in Tokyo and asked me to give him a call."

"Amazing," said Eric. "When he was talking with me, he made it sound like he wouldn't settle for anything less than personally owning that dagger. I wonder what changed his mind."

"Who knows?" said Dave. "Maybe he found out something we don't know about it. Whatever it is, he told me he didn't want anything more to do with the deal and that I should work directly with this dude in Tokyo."

"Amazing!" said Eric shaking his head. "Did you give the guy in Tokyo a call?"

"That very evening, so I'd catch him during working hours," said Dave. "The guy's name is Odagiri Satoshi--Mr. Odagiri. Ken must have told him I'd be calling because I think he was waiting for the call. He knew my name and he was not at all surprised when I mentioned the Muramasa tanto."

"Did you speak English?"

"I tried," said Dave, "but we were getting nowhere so I switched to Japanese and we got along pretty well. My Japanese isn't great, but I don't think there were any communication problems.

"How'd the deal go down?" asked Eric.

"Real smooth. I told him I represent the owner of the dagger. I said we were prepared to guarantee its authenticity and that I was authorized to offer it for sale."

"Okay," said Eric, indicating he was following the story and that everything was accurate so far.

"Odagiri immediately asked, 'How much?'"

"And you said?" asked Eric in curious anticipation.

"I decided to ask for $200,000."

"Gulp," said Eric. "What did Mr. Odagiri say?"

"Without missing a beat, he asked if that price included my commission."

"Wow!" Eric grimaced in mock pain. "I'd love to play poker with this guy."

"He wasn't being very cagey," smiled Dave. "I took his question to mean that he hadn't shit his pants or had a heart attack. So I said 'no,' and told him he'd have to come up with another fifteen percent on top for me to close the deal."

"Under the circumstances, that seems positively conservative," said Eric. "Why didn't you ask for twenty?"

"I should have," shrugged Dave, "cause he immediately said, 'Good.'"

"So the deal's done? Just like that?" asked Eric.

"Just like that. We didn't talk anymore about price, only details of the transactions. I explained to Odagiri that the owner of the dagger is a little old lady who lives in a small town in Iowa. He didn't seem to care where that was, he just told me to fax him her name and address so he could arrange payment. I gave Mrs. Johnson a call to fill her in so she knows what's going on"

"Is she satisfied?" asked Eric.

"Oh, absolutely! My call was like a visit from Ed McMahan. She kept asking if I was serious. I think I finally convinced her, but you should give her a call."

"I will," agreed Eric. "Did you remember I promised a finder's fee to her next door neighbor, the fellow who got me together with Mrs. Johnson? We have to cut him in somehow."

"Dealing with you honest guys can get awful complicated, Ric," said Dave with a semi-serious wince. "But I think we've even got that angle covered. As soon as Mrs. Johnson got convinced the deal was for real, she said, 'Oh I'll just split the money with Lloyd. He set it up.' That's the guy you're talking about isn't it?"

"Yup. Lloyd Peterson. That's the guy," nodded Eric. "So all that remains is to arrange the actual transfer?"

"And that appears to be all taken care of, too," Dave continued. "The second time I talked to Odagiri, it came out that he wants to pick the dagger up himself so he can personally bring it back to Japan. I get the impression he's a high profile type of guy, but if he's spending 230 K, he can be. I told him I'd arrange for him to pick the *tanto* up in Iowa. He liked that and wanted to know if he could fly right to Adel. I told him that wouldn't work, but that he could go to Des Moines and rent a car. That satisfied him. His next question was if there might be a newspaper in the area that could send a photographer. Apparently he wants to make a media event out of the deal. I saw no problem, although I told him it would be impolite to make the transaction price public. I think we can trust him to be discreet. So," Dave said with a pause, "he's flying to Des Moines next Thursday to give Mrs. Johnson the money and pick up the *tanto*."

"The whole deal is about worked out," said Eric happily. "We just have to decide how to get the dagger back down to Mrs. Johnson."

"If it's all the same to you, Ric, I'll take care of that. If I'm there when the transfer takes place, Mr. Odagiri can just put the commission right in my hand."

"You think he'll pay you in cash?"

"That's how I told him I wanted it," said Dave. "I'm not expecting to have any kids so I don't need to put a lot of money in the bank and I'll be able to recycle the cash without involving the IRS."

Eric certainly did not want to get involved in Dave's finances so he took this as the moment to move onto another matter. "Okay, the dagger's taken care of. What about the long sword? Have you been able to make any progress on that?"

"Yeah, I have," said Dave, once again moving to the edge of his chair and leaning toward Eric. He looked to the side for a moment and stroked his chin before continuing. "Now, Ric, you're sure you want to go ahead with this."

"Absolutely."

"You understand the *tachi* is worth a lot of money. We're talking about a quarter of a million bucks, here."

"I understand, Dave, and I don't want to argue about it," Eric said firmly.

"Okay," said Dave. "But, the sword is yours, right? You bought it fair and square."

"Absolutely. I didn't know beans about what I was getting, but I paid a thousand bucks and Mrs. James agreed to the deal. I've asked her about it and she is still entirely comfortable with the whole deal."

"I understand, Ric," Dave said soothingly. "And I think you've been treating her real fair. I just got to tell you there's no need for you to worry about making a profit on this deal."

"Dave, I really don't want to argue about this. I don't want to make any money on the deal. I just want to get rid of the sword."

"Got'cha," said Dave with another small wave of his hand. "I'm really not trying to hassle you, Ric, but the Japanese got lots of money. They want the sword back and they can afford to pay for it. There's no reason you have to give it away. There's nothing un-American about a profit."

"Dave, I want to give the sword back," Eric said firmly.

"All right! I just wanted to make sure you were serious and clear about this." Dave leaned back in his chair. "After you and I talked, I called my pal, Hagi-san, at the Sword Museum in Tokyo. Actually, I had to make a couple of calls to get hold of him. My phone bill this month is going to be massive."

Eric started to say something, but Dave waved it off. "Don't worry. I can cover it. Anyway, I finally got hold of Hagi-san the day before yesterday and explained that I was calling for you--I mentioned your name and everything. I told him you had asked me to arrange the donation of the Hidetaka Munemasa to the Sword Museum.

Eric nodded to indicate his agreement and approval.

"His reaction was kind of surprising," said Dave.

"Didn't he just say 'yes,'" asked Eric. "I mean I want to give him the sword, no strings."

"In Japan there are always strings, Ric, so you have to expect he'd be careful. Still, after I had explained things to him and it was his turn to say something, he didn't say anything. I could hear that he was on the line and I think I even heard him sucking on his teeth which is something a lot of Japanese do when they're thinking. Finally, he said, 'Have you mentioned this sword to anyone else?'"

"Not the first question that pops into my mind when someone offers me a gift," said Eric.

"Me neither," agreed Dave. "I told him you and I are the only people who know anything about the sword. He liked that response but asked a couple of question about you. He wanted to know if you were a good person. He asked what you did for a living. He asked where and how you got the sword. I told him you bought it from the widow of a GI and assured him that you had perfectly legal title. He also asked what you wanted out of the deal. I told him nothing."

"Wow," said Eric, "giving away a National Treasure seems pretty tough."

"Hagi-san definitely wasn't jumping at the offer," agreed Dave. "After we covered the 'no strings clause' one more time, Hagi-san wanted to know if the sword had been together with the Muramasa *tanto*."

Dave shifted in his chair before continuing. "I didn't see any disadvantage in telling the truth, so I told him they had been together. There was another pause while Hagi-san framed the next question. Eventually, he said, 'No one else knows about the *tachi*?' I assured him nobody knew about it. He still asked if the parties dealing on the *tanto* knew about the *tachi*."

"So he has to be aware that Ken Sawada has been looking for the dagger," observed Eric.

"If not Ken, at least somebody," agreed Dave. "I told him the person buying the dagger did not know about the sword. I didn't mention any names and he didn't either, but I think I finally convinced him he had the inside track on the sword."

"Didn't he want to know anything about the sword itself?" asked Eric.

"Not much," said Dave. "He asked if I was sure it was legit. I said it was and he took my word for it. I also told I had sent him a full-length rubbing of the blade, but he hadn't gotten it when we were talking. It should be there by now."

"He didn't ask about condition or the mounts or anything?"

"Nope, but none of that would matter because they'd expect to repolish and remount it anyway."

"So, with all of that cleared up, I assume he told you he'd take the sword," said Eric.

"Nope, he didn't. After all of that, what he said was that the Sword Museum doesn't maintain its own collection so they couldn't accept the Munemasa blade."

"Holy cow," said Eric in exasperation. "If they couldn't accept it, why did he ask all the questions?"

"I'm not sure. Maybe he was simply interested, but he may have been thinking about arranging a deal for somebody else," explained Dave. "He said he'd like me to call him again the next day so we could talk some more about the sword."

"He wanted to *you* call *him*?" asked Eric. "We're trying to give him a quarter of a million bucks worth of Japanese cultural patrimony and the son-of-a-bitch wants you to call him back?"

Dave chuckled. "Yeah. I was kind of impressed by that, too, but what could I say? Before we hung up, Hagi-san asked me twice not to tell anybody about either the sword or our conversation. He clearly wants to keep this deal secret."

"That makes a lot of sense. We certainly wouldn't want anybody to know that Hagi-san is an indecisive jerk."

"Give him a break, Ric," said Dave. "The deal might be more complicated from his end than it is from ours. Besides, the Japanese don't shoot from the hip very often."

"So, where do we stand?"

"Last night I called him back just like he asked," Dave continued. "He thanked me for calling and started the conversation by asking if I'd spoken with anybody about the sword. I told him I hadn't and that seemed cool. Then he said that although the Sword Museum couldn't accept the sword, he thought it could be donated to a place like the National Museum where he said they would probably accept the sword."

"They probably would, huh?" asked Eric. "Where's the National Museum?"

"It's in a big park in downtown Tokyo, Ueno Park," said Dave. "It's a good museum and in a kind of neat part of town so it would be a great home for your sword."

"Great. If that's where the sword belongs it's fine with me," said Eric, relieved the affair was coming to an end. "Will Mr. Hagi give us a hand in arranging the donation or are we on our own?"

"He will," nodded Dave. "In fact, he volunteered to help with the arrangements."

"I'm glad that Mr. Hagi also sees his way clear to giving us a hand in the matter. What do we do next?"

"Hagi-san would like you to call him."

"Are you kidding me? Dave, this is crazy. I'm trying to give *him* the sword and he can't even do me the courtesy of calling me?" Eric was frustrated and amazed. "Is he being chicken-shit, or is he that poor?"

"I don't know what the deal is, but it can't be poverty. The Museum could certainly afford the call," said Dave. "Hagi-san must feel he's got to be very discreet on this one."

"So what do you think I ought to do?"

"Oh, give him a call," Dave replied immediately.

"Why should I keep going to him, Dave?" asked Eric. "Is he showing me any respect at all on this?"

"I think so, Ric. If he weren't interested, we wouldn't have gotten this far. If nothing else, I'd appreciate it if you'd call him just to make sure he knows I wasn't bullshitting him. Tonight would be a good time to get him. Here's his number," Dave said passing Eric a sheet of paper with a neatly printed telephone number and address. As Eric accepted it with his left hand Dawn returned to the room and dropped an armful of mail on the coffee table.

"Am I going to be able to talk with him?" asked Eric. "My Japanese isn't very good, you know."

"No problem. Hagi-san speaks good English so you won't have any trouble talking," said Dave. Looking over at the mail Dawn had begun to sort into piles he added, "Looks like a lot of people have been writing to you, Ric."

"All I see are magazines," said Dawn. "Look at this stuff, *Shooting Times, Gun Report, Shotgun News, Man At Arms.* Eric, it's amazing your mailman hasn't got powder burns."

"Aren't they great?" smiled Eric as he reached for the pile Dawn had made. "Look at all the reading I've got to do to catch up on what I've missed. I can hardly wait." Eric leaned forward to pick the magazines up, but he found the pile hard to manage. They dropped back on the table.

"Can I help?" asked Dawn.

"No, I can get it," said Eric managing to get the top magazine moved to his lap. "A guy could sure get very tired of not being able to use his hands."

"Yeah, that's tough, Ric. How long are you going to have the splint on?" asked Dave.

"It'll be another two weeks," answered Eric. "And a couple of weeks after that before I get full feeling back."

"Boy, that's tough, Ric," Dave repeated. "Have you shut your practice down or what?"

"We canceled a couple of days' worth of appointments, but I couldn't abandon the practice so I've got a couple of people filling in for me. We'll have to see how it works out."

"The free time will let you jet over to Tokyo to bring the sword to the National Museum," grinned Dave.

"What a good idea," said Dawn. "You've been working pretty hard. A vacation would be good for you."

"I'm afraid this may be more like early retirement," said Eric.

There was an uneasy silence since none of the three knew what to say.

"Your hand will be all right, Eric," Dawn said soothingly. "And you've still got the Kaiser's gun," she continued. "The police didn't confiscate it."

Eric looked at her with a rueful smile. He was sure she was trying to be sympathetic and he appreciated her concern. "Yeah, you're right. I've still got the gun and it's still neat, but Dawn, you've got to know that when Lotte broke that seal and pulled the trigger, it lost a lot of value."

"Ahh, you can relax about that, Ric," said Dave.

"What do you mean?" asked Eric.

"I don't think the value of the gun has been hurt all that much," said Dave leaning back in his chair. "To begin with, you weren't going to sell it right away, were you?"

"No! It's the best Broomhandle in the country as far as I'm concerned."

"Exactly," said Dave.

"But it's not like it was," countered Eric.

"You've still got all the parts of a very interesting grouping," said Dave with a shrug. "If you put them together right, it's a very neat package, very collectible. A loaded gun that waited like a century to run off a gang member. That's the kind of thing that would really appeal to some collectors."

"Maybe you're right," agreed Eric.

"In fact, you know what you ought to do," Dave said with building enthusiasm as an idea crystallized in his mind, "is get the NRA to feature it as one of their 'Armed Citizen' stories in the *Riflemen*. Shit, they'll love it, a little old lady runs off an Oriental attacker with a sexy gun." He smacked his lips. "It absolutely proves the Brady Bill is bullshit."

Both Dawn and Eric laughed at Dave's sarcasm.

"I'm serious, Ric," Dave said earnestly. "The story's a natural. If you make it a part of the package, it'll only add to the gun's historical significance. You might even get a lot of press out of it, too. Every neat Mauser in America will be headed in your direction."

Eric nodded. "That wouldn't be all bad."

"Furthermore, Ric," Dave continued, "it seems to me that whatever that gun cost you might have been a bargain."

"Why's that?"

"Who's going to sweat collectors' value when somebody's throwing *shuriken* at you? If that kid had hit you with another of those things he could've done some serious damage."

Eric chuckled ruefully. "As opposed to simply cutting off a finger and threatening my livelihood? You sure know how to raise a guy's spirits."

"I'm not trying to be cold here, Ric," Dave said seriously, "but I think the gun saved your life."

"Could those stars really be lethal?" asked Dawn.

"The book on them is that they're supposed to maim rather than kill, but who wants to explore the envelope on something like that?"

"What did you call them?" asked Eric.

"They're called *shuriken*. I've never really had much to do with them because they weren't serious weapons in Japan."

"They were only designed to maim," said Dawn.

"What I mean is, they weren't weapons the samurai used," Dave clarified. "Supposedly, they were developed in the nineteenth century by the ninja along with techniques like needle spitting and sneezing powder guns. I have a hard time taking that kind of stuff seriously. It all strikes me as comic book hype."

"Mutant turtles," said Eric.

"Exactly," said Dave. "I think a lot of these low end karate and kung-fu types are into that stuff now. And if some sociopath wants to work hard enough, I'm sure they can make the *shuriken* quite lethal. The kid who attacked you probably worked hard to perfect his skill."

"You know they killed a dog right behind us here?" Eric said pointing over his shoulder toward the house behind the condominium.

Dave shook his head. "You could have been next, Ric," he said.

There was a brief pause which Dawn broke. "That's a pleasant thought."

"But you weren't," Dave said rising to leave. "And in a little while you'll be as good as new."

"Thanks for your optimism," said Eric.

"Remember, you've got that conversation with Hagi-san to look forward to. You will give him a call this evening, right?"

"I'll do it for you, Dave," Eric smiled and Dave left.

"Good Morning." Eric answered the phone along side his bed on the first ring because, although he had tried to sleep in, he was looking for something to do.

"Good morning, Ric. How're you feeling?"

"Fine, Dave," Eric said recognizing the voice on the phone. "I think I've even got some feeling back in my left hand."

"That's super," said Dave. "I hope I'm not calling too early."

"Not a problem. What's up?" asked Eric.

"I wanted to see how the call to Hagi-san went. You did give him a call?"

"I sure did, but I can't really tell you how it went."

"Why's that?" asked Dave.

"Well, the call went through fine and Hagi-san got on the line right away. And just like you said, his English was great so we communicated all right. Everything was real positive, but I'm still not sure where the deal stands."

"What happened?" asked Dave.

"Hagi must have been expecting my call, because he recognized my name. He called me 'Mr. Maroh.'" Eric added as an aside. "He mentioned he'd talked with you, but he didn't say anything about the sword until I mentioned it. Then he said he was studying the rubbing you sent to him."

"Good. I'm glad it arrived."

"Hagi said the sword was 'very good.' He said it a couple of times, actually, but that was all and he sure didn't ask for it or anything. Finally I said I wanted to give it back. To be entirely clear, I said I wanted to donate it to a museum. He said it was a good idea."

"I can hear him saying that," said Dave.

"But he still wouldn't take the lead, so I told him that you had suggested that it should go to the National Museum. Then he said it would be okay to do that.

"It must be cool then," said Dave.

"Yeah, but then he told me to write him a letter saying I wanted to donate it to the National Museum. He was specific. He told me I could send him the letter, but said I should mention the National Museum by name and I should *not* mention anything about the conversation we were having."

"He sure isn't interested in getting out ahead of you on this is he?"

"Why is that, Dave? Why won't he just line this up? Am I missing something on this?"

"I've been wondering about that, myself, Ric. Hagi-san is not a bullshitter and he's never given me the run around before so I think there has to be something special about this deal or this sword. When I first asked him about the *tanto*, he said something about a politician being interested in these swords."

"I remember you saying something about that," said Eric.

"Well I'm wondering if Hagi-san might be caught in the middle of something on this one. He clearly wants the Munemasa *tachi* to go to the National Museum, but maybe there's somebody who wants it to go somewhere else. If he's in a jam, he might be trying to make it look like you're the one insisting the sword has got to go to the National Museum. If it's your call, if you're the one who is making the stipulations, his hands are clean."

"Would he be that manipulative? I mean, isn't that pretty devious?" said Eric.

"I don't think so. What the hell, Hagi-san isn't making you do anything you don't want to. In fact, he's helping you quite a bit. He's just making it look like you're doing all the work."

"That's one way of looking at it, I suppose," said Eric.

"And you've got to remember, Ric, Japanese tend to take the long view in their social relationships. This is an in and out operation for you, but after you've gone back to the Midwestern gun shows Hagi-san's going have to live with the situation. If this deal pisses off a politician, it could have long term repercussions for the Sword Museum."

"And he doesn't need to take care of me." said Eric.

"No, no," corrected Dave. "He's got to take care of you because you're with me on this one. He and I go back far enough that we can count on him to take care of me and my friends. It's just that on this one, it looks like he's got to take care of some other people, too. Americans get real uncomfortable when they aren't number one, but Japanese society makes people learn to fit in, to take turns, and to share."

"So what am I sharing on this?" asked Eric.

"I don't know. Maybe even Hagi-san doesn't know, but there must be something else involved and some others who have to be taken care of. You'll just have to act Japanese on this one."

"How's that?"

"Well," Dave said. "You just have to assume that if you do your part, good things will happen for you and everybody else."

"So I should write the letter and wait for good things to happen?"

"That's what I'd do."

"Maybe you're making me a Japanese on this, Dave, but that's what I decided to do. I called my office first thing this morning and dictated the letter. Pam, my receptionist, is expecting to hear from you with Mr. Hagi's address. I've got nothing else to do until my hands get better so I figured what the hell."

"That's the attitude, Ric. I'll give your office a call right now. I think things should develop pretty fast from here on out."

"That's probably Dave right now," said Eric when the front door buzzer sounded. He wiped his hands on a towel and walked to the panel by the front door of his apartment. "Is that you Dave?" he said into the microphone.

"It sure is, Ric," Dave's voice crackled back.

"Great! We want to hear all about your trip. Come on up," Eric said using his left hand to press the button that would open the lobby door.

"Now we can go ahead with dinner," Eric said turning back to Dawn. "The table looks great. I appreciate your help."

"Dinner smells good," Dawn replied. "What are we having?"

"I made a little gumbo, spinach salad, and a baked custard dessert."

"You know, Eric, you're a very good cook. You'd make a great husband for a dynamic young professional woman."

"Oh, I think you're right," Eric agreed with mock seriousness, "but I've always been more attracted to the sex kitten type." He picked up a wineglass with his left hand and held it out toward Dawn. "Pour me a glass of that merlot, will you?"

"Sure," said Dawn reaching for one of the wine bottles on the sideboard. "So is gumbo something you learned from Grandma Mallow?"

"Nope," Eric said returning to the kitchen. "I was really bummed out right after I got out of the hospital and didn't feel like doing much but watch television. That probably only made me more depressed, but one day, it was right after Dave picked up the dagger to bring it down to Iowa, I watched this old guy's cooking show. He was making gumbo and it sounded real good so I decided to give it a try."

"I'm real glad you're feeling better," Dawn said softly, pouring the wine.

"Me too," Eric said peeking into the oven to check the progress of the custard. "I feel great. The subs are keeping things together at the office so it looks like the business won't fall apart. The physical therapist says my hands are doing real well, so what the heck. Things could be a lot worse." After adjusting the oven heat downward, Eric walked to the front door. "I'll have to keep the cast on the right hand for a while, but the left is doing just fine. See," he said using his left hand to turn the knob and open the door just as Dave was about to knock. "Come on in, Dave." he smiled.

"That's what I call perfect timing," said Dave as he entered the room. "Hi Dawn," he added when he got inside.

Eric took Dave's jacket. The cast on his right hand clearly limited his movement, but he seemed to enjoy showing that he was able to put the jacket into the closet. When he was finished, he gestured Dave to a seat. "Before you tell us all about the trip to Iowa, can I get you some wine? I've got some merlot and a chablis open and I'll get something else if you'd like."

"I'll have a glass of the red, Ric," Dave said pointing to the merlot.

"It looks like you survived the trip," said Dawn as Eric poured the wine. Dave took the glass and said, "Yeah, I blew a tire out on the way down, but other than that it was okay."

"Tell us all about it," said Eric sitting down. "I want to hear everything. You met Mr. Odagiri in Des Moines?"

"Yup. Odagiri-san and his guys got in the night before I arrived so I met them at their hotel."

"Who'd he bring along?" asked Eric.

"There were four of them. Beside the main man there was a Japanese assistant. I think he was there to deal with luggage and stuff. Then there was an American college kid who had been on some kind of an English teaching fellowship. He was supposed to handle the translations, but his Japanese wasn't very good."

"Odagiri doesn't speak English?" asked Eric with mild surprise.

"It didn't look like it," said Dave. "We did all our talking in Japanese. I didn't even try English, but really, Odagiri-san didn't have to do too much talking. He pretty much stayed above the whole scene."

"Did you have to do the dealings?" asked Eric.

"No. I really didn't have very much to do," explained Dave, "because the third hanger-on was a PR guy. He handled most of the arrangements. Basically, I just had to give the *tanto* to Mrs. James."

"Odagiri brought a public relations agent?" asked Dawn.

"Yeah, I was pretty surprised about that, too," said Dave. "It was a guy named Jerry Lupinski from Chicago. He spoke a little Japanese and was real pleasant."

"Does Odagiri have this guy on retainer or was this a one shot deal?" asked Eric.

"I wondered about that too," said Dave. "Apparently, Jerry's firm recently got an account with another Japanese company, some kind of a development corporation, and they somehow lined this deal up. Jerry wasn't sure if he'd be doing anything more for Odagiri-san, but he was sure seemed willing."

"So, did you go out to Mrs. James'?" asked Eric trying to get back to the thread of the story.

"No. The whole deal came down at Airport Holiday Inn. Odagiri-san and his guys flew into Des Moines on Wednesday evening and spent the night there. I showed about noon Thursday, right on schedule, and Mrs. James got there about two in the afternoon. Your pal Lloyd Peterson drove her down," Dave added nodding to Eric, "so I met him. They both send their regards."

"And that was it?" asked Eric. "The transfer took place right there at the motel?"

"Yeah," said Dave. "Mrs. James and Lloyd came up to Odagiri's room where we all shook hands and said hello. We only schmoozed for a couple of minutes, though. Odagiri-san and the assistant looked at the box the *tanto* was in and scoped out the dagger. I think they were only making sure it was there because they didn't seemed particularly interested in the blade itself. After they checked it out, I passed it back to Mrs. J. and we all went down to a meeting room the PR guy had lined up. There were a couple of reporters and photographers waiting because Jerry had gotten a press release out. He took charge of the deal. He thanked them for coming and introduced Mrs. James and Odagiri-san. Then he stepped aside and the two of them stood up and made the switch. Mrs. J gave Odagiri-san the dag and he gave her a check for two hundred grand and the photographers took some pictures."

"Slam-bam, thank you ma'am," said Eric, leaning forward to pour Dave some more wine.

"Thanks," said Dave holding out his glass. "The reporters asked a few questions. That's enough, thanks, Ric," he said when the glass was filled. "But the press release must have covered what they needed. The whole deal took like ten minutes."

"How anti-climactic," said Dawn.

"I guess," agreed Eric. "After all the intrigue and adventure, I thought it would be a bigger deal." He paused before adding, "You got paid all right?"

"I sure did. After the reporters left, we all shook hands with Mrs. James and Lloyd and they split. I think they were expecting a little bigger deal, too, but there wasn't much more to do."

"Maybe I'll give them a call," said Eric.

"I'm sure they'd both like that," said Dave. "After they were gone, the assistant asked me to return to Odagiri-san's room. When we got up there, he gave me my commission."

"Cash?" asked Eric.

"Yep. US funds in a brown envelope. The interesting thing was that I saw Jerry pass that same envelope to the assistant earlier in the day. He must have brought it to Des Moines."

"What do you think that means?" asked Eric.

"It means Odagiri paid me out of funds he had in this country and his PR guy handled the matter. I don't see it as a problem."

Eric had not explained Dave's commission to Dawn and he saw no reason to do so now. He simply said, "I suppose not."

Dawn could tell there were things being left unsaid. She didn't want to pry but she didn't want the men to think she was unaware. "What good's a PR guy if he can't be the bag man?" she asked.

Dave looked at her and paused briefly to consider her question. Then he nodded and said, "Exactly."

"Well, with all that cleared up and the dagger out of my life, I think it's time for dinner," Eric said cheerily. "Dave would you light the candles and Dawn, maybe you'd give me a hand with a couple of plates."

"Sure thing," said Dawn as she and Dave rose.

Dinner was a great success. The gumbo was delicious and the conversation continued non-stop. Dave described a nice library of railroad books he had found in a country antique shop on the way home form Des Moines. That let Dawn mention her interests in antique children's books. Dave encouraged her to talk about her collection and helped her describe both her interests and collecting. He seemed genuinely interested and asked where she had found her best pieces. It turned out that he was familiar with some of her favorite bookstores.

When the main course was done, Eric began to clear the plates. Both Dawn and Dave rose to help him, but he said, "No, no, sit down. I've got to at least try to use my hands." As he began to assemble the plates, he said, "Dawn, you haven't told Dave about your discovery."

"Oh, no. I haven't," she said recalling that there had been something she had wanted to tell Dave. "I think I've found Arlon Matsuda," she said happily. "He was the GI we found in the photo album."

"Yeah, I know. Ric showed me the album," said Dave. "Matsuda was the Nisei guy who ended up with the *tanto* fittings, right?"

"That's the one," said Dawn. "Although if I'm right, I think he's dead," she added with her eyebrows raised in a pained expression.

"Tell me about it," Dave said leaning back in his chair.

"Well," she said placing her napkin on the table where her plate had been, "right after Eric and I looked at the album, I asked Mom if she knew anybody named Arlon Matsuda. She knew lots of Matsudas, but nobody named Arlon. I must have got her looking though, because last week she called to tell me about a memorial note in the Pacific Citizen."

"That's the Japanese-American newspaper," said Dave.

"That's right," nodded Dawn. "My folks have subscribed forever and it really does keep them in touch with a lot of people."

"I've seen it," said Dave. "There are a lot of Nisei sword collectors out in California."

"I'm sure," agreed Dawn as she got up to get a slip of paper from her purse. "I've got a copy of the note right here." She read it to Dave. "'The Mazda Family notes the Anniversary of the Death of Arlon Mazda, Soldier, Optometrist, Citizen, Father, Friend. We Miss you, Dad. And the names at the bottom are Emiko Mazda and Cheryl Mazda-Lenowski.'"

"You think it's the same guy?" asked Dave as Dawn passed him the clipping.

"It sure sounds like it could be. 'Soldier' means he was in the Army. And a lot of families Americanized their names after the war. That could explain how Matsuda became Mazda."

"You could be right," agreed Dave as he looked over the text of the notice.

"And he'd be about the right age," said Eric as he returned to the table with the custard.

"It sure sounds interesting. Do you mind if I check it out?" Dave asked Dawn.

"Not at all," said Dawn. "That's why I brought it."

Conversation stopped when Eric set the dessert on the table and poured brandy over it.

"That looks delicious, Ric. Did you make it?"

"I sure did," he said setting the brandy aflame. "We thought you could probably get the Mazda family addresses from either the newspaper or the JCL," he continued as the fire burned itself out

"I was just thinking that myself," said Dave.

"Do you suppose there's any possibility they still have the mounts for the dagger?" asked Dawn.

"It's a long shot, but I've found stuff on leads that were weaker than this," Dave said before taking a taste of the custard. "This is great, Ric."

. "Isn't he a good cook?" said Dawn. "In fact, we were talking about that when you arrived, Dave."

Dave looked from Dawn to Eric and saw they were sharing a smile. To break the silence he cleared his throat and said, "In fact, I've got to tell you two about a call I got from Hagi-san."

"He called you?" asked Eric. "That's a switch."

"I was pretty surprised, too," said Dave.

"I don't suppose he wanted to talk about my sword?"

"Well, he said he was calling to tell me that a sword I've got over being polished is ready to be sent home. That only took a total of two sentences though, and he's never bothered to call about any of the other swords I've sent to him before, so I'm pretty sure it was a dodge. As soon as it was out of the way he asked about you."

"What'd he want to know, why I'd want to give away a National Treasure?" Eric asked playfully.

"Maybe that's what he wanted to know, come to think about it," Dave said with a nod. "He just asked how well I knew you. I told him that you've got a good reputation and a good business. He said, 'Ahh, good, good.'"

"I'm glad I passed that test."

"Then he wanted to know if you were married," Dave continued. "I told him 'no,' so then he wanted to know if I thought you'd be willing to come to Japan to return the Munemasa *tachi*."

"Amazing!" said Eric. "My offer hasn't even been acknowledged and he's trying to see if I'll deliver it. 'Swords R Us, We Deliver.'"

"Give him a break, Ric. He doesn't want to invite you if you can't make the trip," said Dave.

"It also has to mean they're going to accept the donation," said Dawn.

"Exactly," agreed Dave. "If he's as far as wondering if you can travel, it must mean the deal's going to go through."

"So what did you tell him?" asked Eric. "Am I going to go to Japan?"

"I told him that I figured you would be able to make the trip. I didn't go into detail, but I said that right at the moment you'd probably be able to put some flexibility in your schedule."

Eric held up the cast on his right hand and said, "You're trying to say I've got time on my hands right now."

Dave chuckled. "I didn't put it in such artful terms, but I told him you were mobile. Then he wanted to know if you'd be traveling alone."

"Another amazing question," said Eric. "Was he asking if you'd be going a long?"

"I don't think so," Dave said shaking his head. "He could have asked me straight out if I wanted to make the trip."

"So what'd you tell him?" asked Eric.

"I said that you had a lady friend named Dawn Watanabe and that she'd probably be making the trip with you."

"You didn't!" said Dawn.

"I did," Dave shrugged. "I didn't think I was boxing you into anything. You could back out if you want to. But what the heck, you'll have a great time."

Eric clearly liked the idea of Dawn accompanying him to Japan. "So what did Hagi say?"

"He obviously recognized Watanabe as a Japanese name," Dave said turning to Dawn, "so he asked me if you were Japanese. I said Japanese-American."

"And that was all right?" asked Dawn.

"Oh, for sure. He said, 'Ahh, Japanese-American,' and then he repeated your name Japanese style, 'Watanabe Dawn, Ahh. Very interesting.'"

"So, you want to go to Japan?" Eric asked Dawn.

"Sure, why not," she replied lightly. "When do we leave?"

"Looks like the trip's on, Dave," said Eric. "Did Hagi tell you what I should do next?" Before Dave could reply, however, Eric held his hand up and said, "Let me guess. He wants me to give him a call."

"You got it," Dave said with a grin. "He finished the conversation by asking me to have you call him." As he spoke he looked at his watch. "You know, he's probably in his office right now. Why not give him a call?"

"Do it, Eric," said Dawn. "I want to know if this is going to happen."

"It's the wine that's making me do this," Eric said as he got up to go to the phone on his desk. He found Hagi's number in his rolodex and punched the numbers as Dave and Dawn joined him. "It's ringing," he said switching his phone to 'speaker' so they could listen to the conversation.

"*Moshi, moshi. Token Hakureki, degozaimazu,*" said a high pitched feminine voice.

Eric replied in firm, slow English. "This is Eric Mallow calling for Mr. Hagi."

"*Hai. Sho-sho machi kudasai,*" replied the voice as connection went to soft music. Eric smiled at the others as he waited for something to happen.

After only a few seconds, Hagi's voice came on the line. "Mr. Marrow, thank you for calling me once again. I received your letter," he said.

"Very good," said Eric. "As I explained in the letter, I would like to give the sword to the Japanese National Museum." He spoke in the same firm tones he had used initially.

"Very good," Hagi said again. "If you want to do that, I will be able to help you. I showed your letter to the National Museum. They will be happy to accept the sword." Dave gave Eric a wink and a thumbs up sign when Hagi said this.

"Fine," said Eric.

"It would be best if you could bring the sword to this country," Hagi continued.

"I'd be willing to do that," said Eric as Dawn nodded her encouragement.

"Please?" asked Hagi as if he had not completely understood. "You will bring the sword to Japan?"

Dawn nodded her head and whispered, "Tell him yes."

"Yes. I will bring the sword to Japan," said Eric.

"Ahh, very good," said Hagi. "That is very good. You will have to make your own travel arrangements, but maybe some people will try to help."

Eric would have liked to know what Mr. Hagi meant that, but when he looked at Dave for advice he got only a smiling shrug in response.

Hagi-san continued without pause. "Could you please come to Tokyo in two weeks?"

Eric blanched and said, "Well," as he looked at his friends for advice. Dave softly said, "Go for it," and Dawn tapped herself on the chest and whispered, "Don't forget me."

"Yes, I could travel at that time," Eric heard himself saying. "I will be traveling with a friend, Miss Dawn Watanabe," he added.

"Ah yes. Miss Watanabe. That will be good. Maybe you should plan to be in Japan for 10 days."

"Okay," said Eric.

"I think you should call Japan Air Lines, maybe. They will help you." Hagi's tone was businesslike but tentative and Eric was struck by the uncertainty of his words. He turned to the others. Dawn shrugged and Dave whispered, "Don't worry."

Before Eric could ask for clarification, Hagi continued. "Please apply for a tourist visa. Miss Watanabe too."

Dawn gave a double thumbs up and whispered, "Yes!"

"I think the Museum will send you a letter today," said Hagi.

Eric found this as unclear as Hagi's other comments, but Hagi continued without a break.

"Maybe you should call Japan Airlines tomorrow."

"Tomorrow?" asked Eric.

"Yes, call them tomorrow," Hagi repeated.

"Okay," Eric said to indicate that he had understood what Hagi had said.

"Well, good," said Hagi positively. "I think it is all arranged. If you come to Tokyo in two weeks, you will bring the Munemasa sword. I will look forward to meeting you then." The tone of this statement made it clear that Hagi felt the end of the conversation had been reached. Eric could not give form to the uncertainties he still felt so he simply said, "All right. I'll be in contact."

"Good bye," said Hagi. "Thank you very much," and the line went dead.

"Sounds like the trip's on," said Dave as Eric hung up the phone.

"Sure does," agreed Dawn.

Eric awoke the next morning feeling vaguely light-headed and uncomfortable. At first he thought this was because he had poured himself an especially large glass of wine right after getting off the phone with Hagi-san. As he brewed a pot of coffee and prepared his breakfast however, he realized he did not have a hangover. His discomfort was caused by the uncertainty he felt about the trip he had agreed to make to Japan. It wasn't simply a matter of expense, although he had no clear idea of how much it would cost. What was unsettling was the uncertainty he felt about the arrangements he would have to make. At one point, as he waited for the coffee to brew, the hassles of arranging a ten day trip in Japan seemed so serious that he considered simply calling Hagi and telling him that the sword would be arriving in the mail. As he spread a dab of raspberry jam on a toasted bagel, however, he decided the problems couldn't be insurmountable. Dawn obviously wanted to make the trip, he rationalized, and he had nothing else to do while he waited for his hand to heal. Besides, how hard could it be to arrange a trip to Japan? The place to begin, Eric told himself as he wiped the kitchen counter, was with an airplane ticket.

After he poured a second cup of coffee, Eric looked up the Japan Airlines' telephone number. That was the carrier Hagi-san had suggested so it would be a good place to start. As he punched the number into his phone, however, Eric resolved not to buy a ticket until he had done some comparison shopping.

A female voice answered and listened as Eric introduced himself and explained that he was calling to inquire about connections between Minneapolis and Tokyo. The voice asked when he would be traveling and Eric explained when he had agreed to go. There was a pause while Eric heard the soft tap of fingers working on a keyboard.

After a pause, the voice said, "Here it is. Dr. Mallow, right?"

"Yes," said Eric tentatively because he hadn't said anything about being a doctor.

"The reservation looks like it's entirely in order," the voice continued. "You and," here the voice paused there for a moment, "Miss Watanabe are confirmed in First Class on flight 309 out of Chicago on the twelfth." Again, the voice paused. "In fact, it looks like you've got Kiku class seats, which I'm sure you're going to find very nice."

"And let's see," the voice continued tentatively. "Here's your connecting flight on Northwest Flight 536 from Minneapolis. That's also First Class," the voice read. "And your return is a mirror image of outbound trip, leaving Tokyo on evening of the 25th and that includes a limousine pick up from your hotel. It looks like you'll be staying at the Imperial, right?"

"I have no idea," said Eric incredulously.

"That's what it says," said the voice flatly. "And the payment," there was another pause, "has already been received, but I'll just check this note." There was yet another paused "Okay," the voice continued after only a moment. "It says that if these arrangements aren't convenient we can change them any way you want. It looks the trip is all set up," the voice said pleasantly.

Afterward
Three Phone Conversations and an After Dinner Chat

1. Dave Stalgaard to Cheryl Mazda-Lenowski

"Cheryl Mazda-Lenowski?"

"This is Cheryl."

"Mrs. Mazda-Lenowski," Dave began with a businesslike tone, "My name is Dave Stalgaard. I'm calling from Minneapolis because I'm doing some research I think may involve your father. Is this a convenient time?"

"Well, yeah. This isn't a bad time," Cheryl said with more than a hint of hesitance in her voice.

"Thanks," said Dave. "I'm trying to locate a Japanese Specialist who served with the US Army in Japan after World War II. His name was Arlon Matsuda."

"Oh, that was Dad," Cheryl said immediately and firmly. "He served through the whole war and was sent to Japan after it was over."

"Great," said Dave excitedly. "I wasn't sure because of the way you spell your name now."

"Yeah," Cheryl said. "Dad tried to Americanize it when he set up his optometry practice so I grew up as a Mazda, but his family name was Matsuda until 1950." As an afterthought she added. "You know Dad died just over a year ago."

"Yes, I do," Dave said sympathetically. "In fact, a friend who knew I was trying to find your dad suggested I give you a call after she saw the anniversary notice you placed in the Pacific Citizen."

"I see," said Cheryl. "It's nice to know somebody saw it."

"I was looking for your father because I'm an art dealer," Dave continued hoping to move the conversation along. "One of my specialties is Japanese swords. I've been trying to run down a couple of swords that were lost right after the war."

"I don't think there's anything I can help you with," Cheryl said with a tone that sounded sure but not disinterested in the problem Dave was presenting. "I know Dad got into some interesting places while he was in Japan, so I suppose anything could have happened. But I've never seen any swords in his stuff."

Dave didn't say anything because it sounded like Cheryl had more to say. After only a brief pause, she continued.

"When Mom moved into her condo last spring, we went all though Dad's stuff and I brought most of it out here. I'm sure there were no swords at all." She had a very thoughtful tone. "No, I can't think of anything like that."

"What I'm actually looking for," Dave said, "is a set of mounts for a dagger. There's no blade, or maybe the fittings are on, like, a wooden blade, but the mounts themselves are still valuable."

"Well, yeah," Cheryl said with a note of recognition. "There is a kind of a wooden knife up there that was in some of Dad's stuff. It's kind of, I don't know, brass or something, I guess. It's in a silk bag, but I always thought it was a souvenir or something."

2. Eric Mallow to Dave Stalgaard

"Dave, this is Eric Mallow. If you're there, pick up the phone," Eric said knowing that Dave always screened his calls

"And I'll get back to you just as," the recorded voice continued until Dave came on the line. "Hey Ric. You're back!" The recording continued so he said, "Just a minute here. Wait a minute 'til the machine plays itself out." Both Eric and Dave paused until the answering machine gave its beep. "There. Now we can talk. You're home safe and sound, I hope. How was the trip?"

"Fabulous," said Eric. "We had a great time. The transfer went off without a hitch so the sword's now the property of the Japanese National Museum and they're happy about it. Hagi-san was fabulous. He's really a nice guy, just like you said. He and everybody else treated us like royalty. It was great. We took a bunch of pictures that I want to show you as soon as they get developed."

"I want to see 'em and hear all about the trip," Dave said. "I'm glad it went well."

"It was great. We were, like, celebrities the whole time. We got our picture in the papers and we were on the nightly news. Returning the sword was a big deal, front page news."

"Excellent," said Dave. "I'm looking forward to hearing all about it. I also want to know what you heard about my friend Odagiri-san, the dude who bought the *tanto*."

"We didn't get together with him," Eric said apologetically. "I mentioned I'd like to meet him, but it never developed and I didn't push it because I don't know him or anything. I hope that wasn't a problem for you."

"It's not a problem for me," Dave said. "But you know he's had his name in the news for the past couple of days. It sounds like he's gotten himself in a bunch of trouble and I though you might have heard something."

"Is that your guy? The politician who just got indicted for bribery? Oh wow. I had no idea he was the buyer. The papers were all full of it while we are over there, but I never figured out all the players. I hope it's not a problem for you."

"I can't see how. My dealings with him are done and by this time Mrs. James has already cashed her check."

"I read about it in the papers, but I'm not sure what he did. Sounds like he is in deep shit."

"Every couple of years it seems like a Japanese politician is caught with his hand in the cookie jar. This year it was Odagiri-san's turn. I'm more interested in how things went for you. With the yen so high, I was afraid that life in Japan would be just impossible."

"It might be if you're spending dollars, but we never had to pay for a thing. The whole thing was seamless. Everywhere we went the arrangements were made, tables were waiting, or people were pleasant. It was like we were guests so all we had to do was go with the flow. We never even got to see a bill. I couldn't spend money even when I tried." Eric was bubbling over. "In fact, just about the only thing I bought the whole trip was the gift I brought home for you."

"All right!" said Dave.

"We had a couple of free days and Hagi-san asked me if there was anything I wanted to see in particular. I didn't know what else to say, so I said I wanted to see a *shuriken* demonstration."

"The throwing stars?" asked Dave for clarification.

"Yeah," said Eric. "I mean, what the hell, I'm still curious about how my hand got all chewed up and I thought Hagi-san must know somebody who could show me how they work."

"Makes sense to me," agreed Dave.

"I thought it would be an easy one. But, just like you said, none of the sword guys knew anything about *shuriken*. Apparently Hagi-san took the problem to the Museum Director and he arranged for one of his curators take us down to a placed called 'Ninja Village' where they do all the Ninja stuff."

"Sounds like a tourist trap."

Eric chuckled. "Well, it was a little cheesy."

"But you got to see the real things in action?"

"No! We didn't," said Eric. "We took the tour and saw a couple of people jump around and disappear into secret passages, but we couldn't see any throwing stars. Apparently their main *shuriken* guy screwed up his throwing arm so he isn't demonstrating them anymore. Instead, we watched him spit needles."

"Bummer!" said Dave. "Not nearly as exciting as throwing stars"

"I guess not," Eric agreed. "But they were selling the stars in the gift shop, so I bought you a couple of real Ninja Village *shuriken*. I want to add them to the Stalgaard collection of Japanese weapons."

3. Ralph Williams to Eric Mallow

"Dr. Mallow, the call you were expecting has just come in." Pam said as Eric walked toward his office.

"Thanks, Pam. I'll take it at my desk. My schedule's clear for the next half hour, right?"

"It sure is," said Pam with a smile. "We had a cancellation and we kept it clear just for this call."

Picking up the receiver Eric said, "Hi, this is Eric Mallow."

"Dr. Mallow, this is Ralph Williams. I'm following up on the letter I sent you last week. I'm general counsel of the Kanda Dental Supply, North America. As I outlined in my letter, you have been nominated to serve on the KDS Board of Directors. I wanted this opportunity to explain the offer and the requirements and to answer any questions you might have."

"I had my attorney look over the papers you sent, Mr. Williams."

"Good. I hope everything checked out."

"It did. She said everything looked fine. In fact, she said the offer was attractive, and she advised me to go ahead."

"Wonderful," said the lawyer. "As I explained, KDS is a Japanese firm that has formed a North American branch to facilitate its expansion into the American, Canadian, and Mexican markets. The initial capitalization has been pegged at twenty eight million and, although this is not the time to go into detail, I can also tell you there are a couple of additional mergers in process that will make the company even larger."

"That all sounds very interesting," said Eric. So far he had committed to nothing and the conversation was costing him no more than a missed appointment. He had many questions, but he saw no reason to be anything but positive.

"At the moment, KDS is assembling the legally required four member board. We can expect to have three meetings annually and in addition to stock options, the board stipend is being set at eighty-five thousand." Williams paused to see if Eric had any questions.

"I understand," said Eric.

"You were recommended for the Board by Dr. Saiji Kanda who heads KDS-Japan."

"I remember Dr. Kanda," said Eric with genuine surprise. "He's on Japanese Sword Museum Board and he took us to lunch when we were in Tokyo last month. He said he was a dentist, but it never occurred to me he was anything more than that."

"He owns the company and you must have made a good impression."

4. Dawn and Eric

"Eric, that was fabulous," Dawn said folding her napkin and setting it alongside her plate. "There's no way around it. I'm marrying a great cook."

"You're marrying a happy cook," Eric said with a warm smile. "I'm glad you liked it. I worried it might be a little spicy. You're feeling all right?"

"Oh, yeah," Dawn said with a sweep of her hand. "I just had a bit of an upset stomach. It's not a problem."

"I was thinking about having just a bit of brandy. Would you like some?"

"No, I'm fine," Dawn shook her head and smiled lovingly.

"Are you becoming a teetotaler, Dawn? No wine with dinner and now not even a taste of good brandy?"

"No," Dawn shook her head. "I just don't think I'll have anything."

"Well, okay. Maybe some coffee. Shall we sit down in the living room?" Eric went to the kitchen for the coffee and a pair of cups. When he returned, Dawn was seated cozily on the living room couch. She took the cup Eric offered her and didn't speak until she had taken a sip.

"Eric, I want to start looking for a place to live."

Eric was surprised both by the statement and by the seriousness of Dawn's tone. "You mean for after we're married?" he asked uncertainly.

"Yeah. I think we should get a place real soon."

"Ah, well, of course, Dawn." The pair had discussed moving into a house, but Eric was surprised Dawn was bringing the issue up again now and with such seriousness. "We can start looking right away, but I sort expected we could start out here in the condo until we found the right place."

"That's not going to work, Eric," Dawn said firmly. She didn't sound angry or upset, but her voice was certain.

"You've always kind of liked the condo," Eric said.

"I still do, but it isn't going to work out for us to stay here."

"Why not, Dawn?" Eric truly had no idea what Dawn saw as the problem.

"I don't think your neighbors are going to change the no children policy. And, Eric, it looks like that's going to count us out."

Author's Notes

This is a work of fiction that explores topics, characters, and situations I have discovered in the course of my career as an archaeologist in Japan and collector of Japanese swords. Nothing in this story should be taken as fact, but if the topics addressed prove interesting, their realities can be investigated in a larger number of books.

Warriors of early Japan who are wonderfully presented in Helen Craig McCullough's rendering of the *Heike Monogatari* and *Yoshitsune; A Fifteenth-century Japanese Chronicle*. Her translation of Hiroshi Kojima's *Taiheiki*, is another great read. Anyone who might want to appreciate the richness of early Imperial Japan and the conflict that Hidetaka would have felt as he wandered outside the capital should read McCullough's *Genji & Heike: Selections From The tale of Genji and The Tale of the Heike*. Ivan Morris' *The Nobility of Failure: Tragic Heroes in the History of Japan* may help explain Hidetaka's actions and motivations.

Men like Maeda Nobuhide were called samurai, but they operated with different powers and approach from those of Hidetaka. Their difference is well presented in Harold Bolitho's *Treasures Among Men: the Fudai Daimyo in Tokugawa Japan*.

Most Japanese will find the treatment of the men I call the Kawabayashi Brotherhood far too positive since real gangsters use force to exploit others. *Paternalism in the Japanese Economy; Anthropological Studies of Oyabun-Kobun Patterns* by John W. Bennett and Iwao Ishino shows, however, that their actions have fit into the web of traditional Japanese society. Walter L. Ames' anthropological treatment of Japanese the police system, *Police and Community in Japan*, presents a readable treatment of the other side of this relationship.

The complex relationship between the Japanese underworld and the American authorities of the Occupation period is only now becoming clear. Again, the relationships were too complex to be simply treated, but *Tokyo Underworld: The Fast Times and Hard Life of an American Gangster in Japan* by Robert Whiting describes the conditions that caused thousand of treasures, including innumerable swords, to leave Japan after the Pacific War. The sensitive observations of anthropologists and historian assembled by

Otis Cary in *War-wasted Asia: letters, 1945-46* present problems facing Japan at that time in human terms.

Anthropologist Thomas P. Rohlen's studies of basic Japanese institutions that may amplify situations present in National Treasure. I especially recommend *For harmony and strength: Japanese White-collar Organization in Anthropological Perspective* and *Japan's High Schools*.

Nineteenth century European and American travelers were fascinated by Japan and left charming accounts of the country and its culture. Edward Morse's *Japan Day by Day* is my favorite because it shows how an archaeologist can blend focused research with broad curiosity. Likewise, Algernon Mitford's recollections in *Tales of Old Japan* can be read again and again.

Japanese swords truly are the most complex weapons of the traditional world. Their art, history, and craft have been explored in literally thousands of publications. I warn readers that exploration of this literature may lead to a lifelong commitment. Kazan Sato's *Token: The Japanese Sword* and Leon Kapp's *The Craft of the Japanese Sword* are good places to start although they hardly exhaust all that needs to be said of the treasure swords of Japan.

I would not have written this story if Andy Quirt had not sat next to me in Japanese 101, if Takahashi Nobufusa had not showered me with sparks, if Clarence Siman had not shown me that collecting is an adventure, and if Chosuke Serizawa had not made it clear that traditional and modern Japan are one.

Quick Order Form

Postal orders:

 RKLOG Press
5878 S. Dry Creek Court
Littleton, CO 80121-1709

Name: _____

Address: _____

City: _____ State: _____ Zip: _____

Telephone: _____

e-mail: _____

_____ National Treasure at $19.95 each $ _____

_____ Spirit Bird Journey at $15.95 each $ _____

Plus shipping ($4.00 for first book,
$2.00 for each additional book) $ _____

TOTAL $ _____

*Make check or money order payable to **RKLOG Press***